Read what people are saying about

JASMINE CRESSWELL

"Ms. Cresswell once again demonstrates her flair for international intrigue. Her storytelling takes you to a world you can only read about."
—*Romantic Times* "Top Pick" on *The Conspiracy*

"Cresswell's superb story matches her best work, stretching nerves to the breaking point."
—*Publishers Weekly* on *The Disappearance*

"Ms. Cresswell masterfully creates a full, rich story with characters who will touch your heart. She drops clues skillfully, unwinding the tale piece by piece in such a way as to capture readers from the very first."
—*Romantic Times* on *The Refuge*

"Cresswell's woman-in-jeopardy plots are tightly woven with no loose ends."
—*Publishers Weekly*

"Fast-paced and exciting, the events twist in and around the romance as characters are pushed to their limits...."
—*Rendezvous* on *The Conspiracy*

"Seat-of-the-pants tension and a surprising last-minute twist make this fast-paced story another winner."
—*Publishers Weekly* on *The Daughter*

Also by JASMINE CRESSWELL

DEAD RINGER
THE THIRD WIFE
THE CONSPIRACY
THE REFUGE
THE INHERITANCE
THE DISAPPEARANCE
THE DAUGHTER
SECRET SINS
NO SIN TOO GREAT
DESIRES & DECEPTIONS

Watch for JASMINE CRESSWELL's thrilling follow-up to DECOY

FULL PURSUIT

Coming November 2004 from MIRA Books

JASMINE CRESSWELL

DECOY

ISBN 0-7783-2012-X

DECOY

Visit us at www.mirabooks.com

Printed in U.S.A.

For Sarah Siobhan,
with fondest love and best wishes
for a wonderful few years in Kansas City.

One

Off the coast of the Yucatán Peninsula
April 18, 2002

Rosalind Carruthers Beecham, known to the tabloid press on both sides of the Atlantic as Lady Roz, greeted the arrival of her fiftieth birthday with all the enthusiasm of a lifelong vegetarian offered a platter of rare prime rib. The fact that she spent the day as a guest on board the oceangoing yacht of Johnston Yates, a former vice president of the United States, eased her pain only slightly.

Johnston Yates was rich, and a powerful man as former vice presidents go, but the knowledge that Johnny's wife was also on board destroyed most of Roz's pleasure in her minor social triumph. The presence of the fat and dowdy Cynthia reminded Roz that being beautiful, aristocratic and beloved of the paparazzi wasn't all it was cracked up to be even when you were young, much less when you were about to become old.

It was a mystery to her how Johnny, still lean and handsome at sixty-eight, could tolerate having a frump like Cynthia for a wife. Somebody, for God's sake, really needed to take the woman aside and tell her that one simply did not wear polyester in polite company. Yet butterball, pug-faced Cynthia had been married to the former vice president for thirty-three years, whereas Roz had barely managed to hang on to Wallis Beecham for seven.

Not that she had ever regretted her divorce from the wealthy but boring Wallis Beecham, at least until recently. In her opinion, fidelity was vastly overrated as a lifestyle choice, and alimony had always struck her as a much better companion than a demanding husband. Now, too late, Roz recognized that remaining single had been a stupidly shortsighted decision, despite the multiple aggravations of living with a husband underfoot. Christ, what had she been doing to protect her future while her thirties slipped into her forties and flew past into her fifties? Why the hell hadn't she realized that she needed to get married again?

Her ex-husband's attitude had recently become a source of real worry for Roz. Ever since he'd found out about her misguided little fling, Wallis had refused to be blackmailed and her financial situation was spiraling downward into a state too grim to think about. Life without copious amounts of money was simply too horrible to contemplate, and how else was she supposed to support herself if Wallis continued to be stubborn? She was really going to have to do some more digging about the Bonita partnership, whatever the devil that was. She'd only had to mention the words tonight at dinner and half the men at the table had immediately looked cross-eyed with panic.

It wasn't that she liked threatening people, but these days being the daughter of a British earl didn't mean that a woman had a decent income beyond what she could earn herself. She'd have made a really good eighteenth-century aristocrat, Roz thought with a flash of morbid humor: highly decorative and utterly useless. Pity she'd been born two hundred years too late to maximize her assets.

She shivered as she wove her way to her stateroom, although the tropical night remained warm despite the rising wind. She would just ignore the fact that she was fifty, she decided. Why not? Ignoring inconvenient facts was one of the things she did best.

She flopped onto the bed, nursing a glass of champagne on her taut, tanned belly. Unexpectedly, she was pierced by a sudden sharp regret that she'd chosen to spend her birthday with Johnston Yates and his tedious right-wing friends, especially since the business deal that had brought her here had ended in a total debacle. Men were such a bloody nuisance, she reflected with a flare of resentment. Who would ever have expected Johnny to be so hard-nosed?

Even more unexpectedly, Roz realized that she missed Melody, her daughter. Melody had suggested that the two of them should spend the day together, then share an intimate dinner at La Rive Gauche, a fashionable new restaurant overlooking the river Thames at Henley. Roz had refused, claiming it was much too cold and dreary to fly back to London at this time of year.

The rotten weather hadn't been her real reason for refusing, of course, even though she loathed gray skies and drizzle. Perhaps because fifty was a benchmark that demanded at least token self-examination, Roz admitted what she'd spent most of the past two decades denying: that she was jealous of her daughter's beauty, intimidated by her intelligence, resentful of her youth and even more resentful of her effortless ability to attract the opposite sex. Whereas Roz had worked her ass off to attain her title of sex goddess, Melody had won it with no effort at all.

No wonder she'd been such a lousy mother, Roz thought. It was hard to be nurturing and supportive when your child had been balancing your checkbook for you since the time she was ten, and capturing the attention of every man on the goddamn planet since she was seventeen and first graced the cover of *Sports Illustrated*'s annual swimsuit edition.

What the hell. Melody was a grown woman now and it was way too late for Roz to wallow in regrets about her maternal instincts, or lack thereof. Craning her neck to swallow the final few sips of her drink, she noticed that a crewman had placed a small slice of leftover birthday cake on the coffee table, next to a candle set into a pink spun-sugar rose, along with a silver fork, a linen napkin and a bottle of white wine, chilling in an ice bucket.

Roz wrinkled her nose, letting her gaze glide over the cake and unlit candle, not in the least grateful for the crewman's thoughtfulness. Bloody hell, it seemed she couldn't get away from reminders of the fact that she was fifty. Menopausal. Over the hill. *Old.* No wonder she was going to spend the night alone. What man wanted to have sex with a hag?

Roz set down her empty glass and glared toward the table. After years of stringent dieting, she was immune to hunger and the cake didn't tempt her in the slightest. But the wine beckoned. With a shrug, she gave in to the lure and crossed the room to inspect the label. They'd sent up a rather nice bottle of Chassagne-Montrachet. If she couldn't celebrate her birthday with a virile lover, she might as well drown her sorrows in a glass of wine.

"Happy birthday to you, Lady Roz," she muttered as she expertly uncorked the bottle. "Here's hoping you don't screw up the rest of your life as badly as you did the first half century." She sat down on the sofa, brooding her way through a full glass.

That final drink might have been a mistake, she decided a few minutes later. A storm had been predicted before morning and the wind had started to blow with real force. Despite state-of-the-art stabilizers, the yacht had begun to roll, and Roz's stomach rolled right along with each new wave.

All she needed was to end her birthday puking her guts out, she reflected wryly. Her seasickness must be another wretched consequence of turning fifty. Usually she had a cast-iron stomach and could ride out storms that sent other people moaning and groaning in search of their beds.

Roz dragged herself to her feet, alarmed to discover that her legs had developed a tendency to give way at the knees. She had intended to return to her bed, but the air in the cabin suddenly felt stale and hard to breathe, so she lurched out into the corridor, heading toward the deck. Strong gusts of wind snatched at her hair and buffeted her face, making it hard to walk. Or was it just that her legs felt too weak to support her? She gulped fresh air into her lungs, but they seemed to be malfunctioning and were refusing to absorb oxygen. The harder she breathed, the more she had the horrible sensation of suffocating. Christ, this wasn't just seasickness: she was really ill!

Roz leaned over the rail, retching painfully. Her legs buckled beneath her and in a moment of stark disbelief she recognized that she was losing control of her basic bodily functions. She heard a sound and realized that somebody had followed her up onto the deck. She finally understood the uneasy pricking at the back of her neck: she had been watched for the past several minutes, ever since she left her cabin.

"Help," she croaked, too ill even to be embarrassed by the smell of vomit and urine that clung to her. "I need help."

The howl of the wind was her only answer. Maybe she was hallucinating, imagining lurking observers who weren't really there. Between the rain and the darkness she could barely see a yard in front of her nose.

Roz clung to the safety rail as she sank onto the wooden planks of the deck, but she lacked the power to haul herself away from the dangerous edge. She knew a crewman would be keeping watch at the helm of the boat even though everyone else was sleeping. Maybe that was the presence she had sensed? But the night watchman was so far away. The fifty feet that separated her from the helm might as well have been fifty miles for all the hope she had of crawling there.

She tried to scream and attract the attention of the crewman, or anyone else who might be awake, but her vocal cords were as dysfunctional as the rest of her body. What in hell had happened to her? One minute she'd been fine—a little tipsy, perhaps, but not even drunk. Then she'd opened the new bottle of wine and before she could finish a single glass she'd begun to feel ill.

Shivers racked Roz's body and her limbs felt as heavy as her mind. She kept slipping in and out of awareness, but she was functional enough to realize she might die unless help came soon...that a sharp roll of the yacht could easily send her body slithering overboard. How in the world had she become so ill, so fast?

The wine was drugged.

The knowledge came to her in a flash of lucidity that contrasted with the increasing fuzziness of her hold on reality. She had noticed nothing wrong when she opened the bottle, so how had the poison been injected into the bottle? Roz tried to think, but she couldn't keep focused on the problem long enough to come up with an answer.

Not only was she going to die, her death throes were being watched by her murderer.

The thought formed with stark clarity between convulsive waves of pain. The realization that her murderer was lurking in the shadows burned her ass. But even rage was impossible to hang on to for more than a second or two. Roz's anger blurred into another bout of retching. This time she tasted blood.

"Johnny, are you there?"

The wind soughed in response. She should have known better than to try to blackmail Johnny, she thought, eyes closing. He'd been ruthless about beating out the competition and getting elected as vice president of the United States. She should have remembered that under Johnny's old-boy Southern charm lurked the instincts of a piranha on steroids.

Her body convulsed once more, drenching her in ice-cold sweat. Or maybe that was seawater splashing over her. Roz's left leg squeezed up against the safety plate that stretched upward for nine inches from the edge of the deck. Right now that nine-inch barrier was all that protected her from plunging off the yacht and into the ocean. She recognized her danger, but she'd lost the power to move herself out of harm's way.

Another sharp roll of the yacht and she could be gone…into the black, churning sea. A single push, and it would be all over.

Terror changed to acceptance. What a pity that she was never going to discover how to grow old gracefully. Turning fifty had been a rotten experience, but she would have enjoyed the chance to discover what it was like to turn fifty-one.

She wished Melody were here. Melody was strong. Melody would have kept her safe. With an irony her daughter would have appreciated, the incurably self-centered Lady Rosalind Carruthers Beecham finally gave her neglected offspring a piece of advice that came from the heart.

I did love you, Melody, even though I was such a rotten mother. Try not to fuck everything up the way I did.

It was her last coherent thought. A gentle push from her killer was all it took to send her sliding into the violent embrace of the stormy Atlantic Ocean. For Lady Roz, old age was never going to be a problem.

Two

Malmesbury, England
April 28, 2002

The April sun shed warmth and clear light over thatched roofs and daffodils dancing in the window boxes that lined the cobbled streets of the picturesque town of Malmesbury. A soft breeze carried the smell of fertile earth and leaves unfurling on apple trees into the heart of the market square. To complete the idyllic setting, the grass surrounding the famous abbey was the intense springtime green celebrated by generations of poets, providing a startlingly lovely background for the soaring stone buttresses of the abbey itself.

The beauties of nature and architecture were entirely wasted on the jostling crowd of spectators, photographers, journalists and TV crews gathered inside the rope barricades that marked off the entrance to the eleven-hundred-year-old church. The spectators had made the ninety-mile trek out of London to ogle the glittering assortment of mourners scheduled to attend the memorial service for Lady Rosalind Carruthers Beecham, and they weren't about to get distracted by mundane details like sunshine and flowers.

Celebrity spotters had already been rewarded by a steady stream of rich and famous mourners arriving at the abbey. Wallis Beecham, former husband to Lady Roz, had been among the first arrivals. A silver Rolls-Royce had drawn up to the curb and an ordinary-looking man of average height and build got out, his expression somber. He wasn't handsome, but his multimillion-dollar commercial empire endowed him with an aura of power and confidence that drew the eye and held it. Wallis Beecham had shunned the media even during the exuberance of the nineties, and few people in the crowd had seen him in person before. Dozens of cameras flashed, capturing his brisk progress to the abbey doors, the smell of serious money trailing in his wake.

The Earl and Countess of Ridgefield, Lady Roz's parents, arrived seconds after Wallis Beecham. The couple had met on the battlefields of World War II, where she had been working alongside the French Resistance and he had been a pilot downed behind enemy lines. Despite their adventurous backgrounds, they were even more reserved than most English people of their class and generation, and nothing about their appearance hinted at the gallantry and daring of their pasts.

Managing to ignore the spectators with such completeness that even the most hardened paparazzi felt invisible, the earl and countess walked into the abbey accompanied by their two sons, their daughters-in-law and four of their five grandchildren.

Only Melody Beecham, daughter of Lady Roz and Wallis Beecham, was missing from the quartet of

Ridgefield cousins accompanying the earl and countess. Speculation immediately began as to why Melody hadn't joined her grandparents. Was there a family feud in the making? Or was Melody simply living up to her notorious reputation for being late on any and every occasion?

The earl and countess were followed by a steady stream of the famous and near-famous, including a contingent of mourners from the United States. The American ambassador arrived in his official limo with Johnston Yates, former vice president. In contrast to most former VPs, Yates was still a major player among Washington insiders, a real power broker in the Republican party. Johnston's plump, good-natured wife, Cynthia, tagged at his side, solid and reassuring. Polls showed that among spouses of former presidents and vice presidents, only Barbara Bush was more popular with American women than Cynthia Yates.

Next came Lawrence Springer, another millionaire businessman, sharing a limo with the chairman of America's largest bank. The next limo delivered Senator Lewis Cranford of Kentucky, his wife and two teenage daughters. Springer, the bank chairman and the Cranfords had all been guests on board the Yates yacht when Lady Roz disappeared, so their attendance was obligatory, especially since there were still a few cable TV outlets encouraging conspiracy theorists to spout warnings about Lady Roz having been eliminated because she knew too much about Senator Cranford's dealings with the Russian Mafia.

The Mexican authorities had already exonerated the Yateses and all their guests for any blame in Lady Roz's death. Piecing together the events of the night, the authorities concluded that she had chosen to go up on deck in the middle of a storm, even though rough weather had been forecast and the guests had been warned to stay in their cabins. Worse, she hadn't been wearing a life jacket—a major flouting of the rules. In view of the nearly empty bottle of wine in her stateroom, alcohol had clearly played a significant role in clouding her judgment. So it was hardly surprising that she'd been swept overboard, her body disappearing into the churning ocean waves before anyone could attempt to save her.

Lady Roz had been such a splendid source of entertaining gossip when she was alive that the public on both sides of the Atlantic was sorry to see her go. Unwilling to lose one of their prime assets without squeezing out every last column inch of scandal, most tabloids refused to accept the authorities' simple explanation for her death and substituted more exciting theories of their own.

Suicide was one possibility, of course, although the other guests on board the yacht swore that Lady Roz had been in excellent spirits when she left them for the night, and the crew confirmed that she had seemed perfectly happy. Besides, suicide was almost as boring as an accident, so the media didn't have much interest in pursuing that angle.

Since nobody had actually seen Lady Roz fall into the ocean, a few enterprising tabloids decided to run with the story that she was still alive. Sure enough, two American tourists in Cancún reported seeing Lady Roz swim ashore at dawn the morning after she went missing. True, they were smoking reefers and probably couldn't have told a dolphin from a clump of seaweed from Lady Roz, but the unreliability of the witnesses was considered irrelevant by all the tabloids and most of their readers.

The Mexican authorities pointed out that the tourists could have seen Lady Roz only if she'd swum a hundred miles in less than six hours, an impossible feat of athleticism for anyone. Conspiracy theorists were undaunted. Maybe a speedboat had dropped her just offshore. They saw no reason to believe a bunch of Mexicans when there were "eyewitness reports" to prove that officialdom had lied.

The possibility that Lady Roz was still alive rapidly gained popular appeal, and theories as to why she might have faked her own death became wilder as the days passed. A couple of TV talk shows had even suggested that Lady Roz would most likely turn up at her own funeral, a possibility that added an element of ghoulish fascination to today's memorial service.

Unlike tabloid reporters who could earn big bucks by spinning stories based on nothing more than their lurid imaginations, the photographers had to earn their money by taking pictures of real people. Consequently, the photographers had already switched their attention from Lady Roz to Melody Beecham. Fortunately, this wasn't a hardship. Melody had been discovered by a modeling agency while still at boarding school, and for a few years her face, not to mention her body, had glowed on the covers of glossy magazines all over the world.

Then, at the ripe old age of twenty-one, Melody had announced that she was retiring. To the astonishment of everyone, she gave up her wildly successful modeling career to study art history at London University's King's College. She'd followed this up by taking graduate courses at the University of Florence.

By all the rules, Melody ought to have become yesterday's news the moment she started college, since former models usually enjoyed a shelf life of about five minutes. She turned out to be the exception that proved the rule. The daughter of two rich and famous parents, she'd grown up rubbing shoulders with the powerful and well-connected on both sides of the Atlantic. Even as a college student she still got invited to all the important parties, galas and charitable events. She wasn't a social butterfly like her mother, but she attended enough charity functions to provide plenty of glamorous photo ops, in New York as well as in London.

Above all, she had an unerring sense of style and looked fabulous in photographs. She also had the advantage of being twenty-eight and never married, rather than fifty and divorced like her mother, so her love life made for fascinating copy.

The tabloids didn't even have to invent some of the gossip about her sex life. She'd had real, honest-to-God love affairs with a Swedish prince and an Italian opera singer, as well as a passionate liaison with one of America's most famous Olympic athletes, making it almost believable when the tabloids took care of slow news days by linking her name with celebrities ranging from Prince William of Windsor to George Clooney.

Ralph Fiennes was currently the media pick for her love interest, and she'd actually been photographed at a nightclub in Ralph's company on one occasion, which gave a veneer of reality to the rumor that they were dating. Hopes ran high among the paparazzi that Ralph might escort her today, which would make for a truly great shot.

Right now, however, the memorial service was five minutes away from its scheduled start and the most urgent need was simply for Melody to put in an appearance so that she could be photographed looking tragic. Or inappropriately dressed. Or escorted by somebody famous. Anything, in fact, that could be manipulated to bolster her status as a celebrity whose image sold magazines.

Finally a silver Jaguar XK convertible drew up to the curb and a collective sigh escaped from the crowd as Melody Beecham was observed leaning across to kiss the driver's cheek before stepping out from the passenger's side of the car. Hatless, dressed in a simple black suit with a skirt short enough to display her trademark long legs to full advantage, she ignored the explosive flash and click of cameras as she walked down the path to the abbey. She kept her gaze fixed ahead, ignoring the strands of blond hair blowing into her face. The Jaguar drove off, allowing the crowd enough of a glimpse of the middle-aged driver to ascertain—regretfully—that although rather handsome he wasn't anybody famous.

Grief-stricken and tragically alone, the photographers decided, mentally captioning their pictures, and ignoring the fact that Melody's father, grandparents and cousins were all waiting inside the church, so it was stretching the truth more than somewhat to describe her as being alone. They started to pack up their equipment, only a handful of die-hard celebrity watchers remaining to wait out the memorial service and catch a second glimpse of the attendees. Even in honor of Lady Roz, there was a limit as to how long the paparazzi were willing to hang about in a small country town where the last important event had taken place right around 900 A.D.

Melody was shaking with the effort of remaining composed by the time she made it inside the soaring nave of the abbey. The air, chilled by the ancient stones, smelled of dust and eternity—the sort of place Roz had spent most of her life avoiding. Fortunately the pew in which Wallis Beecham was seated was already full, so Melody was able to slip into a seat next to Edward, her favorite cousin. Melody tried to love her father, but they had very little in common, and coping with him right at this moment loomed as a more demanding task than she could manage.

Edward gave her hand a quick, welcoming squeeze. "Glad you made it, Mel. Where's Jasper?"

She drew in a deep breath, not sure if she could keep her voice steady. "Off parking the car somewhere. He isn't into funerals. He said he's happy to make himself useful by acting as my chauffeur."

Edward pulled a face. "He flew a long way just to play chauffeur. But he seems a nice enough chap."

There was a definite question in Edward's voice, which almost made Melody smile. Almost. "Jasper's wonderful," she said. "I'm incredibly lucky to have him as a friend."

"That's all he is? Just a friend? You seem to have been hanging out with him forever."

She gave a tiny smile. "That's because he's a friend, and I try to keep those. It's lovers that I trade in before they can get boring."

The bishop came out of the vestry, cutting off their conversation, and the service began. Melody soon discovered that she couldn't listen if she wanted to maintain her composure. She wasn't sure why she was so grief-stricken by her mother's death. Roz had always been a haphazard parent and Melody had pretty much been fending for herself since she was seven and her father filed for divorce, sending his ex-wife and daughter back to England so that he could marry his pregnant mistress.

In the past five years Melody probably hadn't seen her mother more than a dozen times. They called each other quite often, but their last phone conversation had followed the usual frustrating pattern. Roz had listed all the glamorous parties she'd attended and the famous people who'd paid her compliments, while Melody had attempted, with significant lack of success, to bring her mother up-to-date on the renovations to the mews house where she was about to open an art gallery, supposedly as a joint venture with Lady Roz.

It had been a toss-up which of the two found the other's choice of topics more irritating, Melody reflected wryly.

Perhaps she felt such a huge sense of loss because Roz's death had been a bolt from the blue. There was so much about her mother that Melody didn't understand, and now never would. She'd lost her last chance to put their relationship onto a better footing, and that knowledge left her with mixed-up feelings of frustration and regret that kept toppling over into anger. Roz had been only fifty, dammit, and bursting with health. It wasn't fair that she should be dead. Surely a little more care on somebody's part could have prevented the accident? Roz was thoughtless, yes, but she rarely drank to excess, and going up on the deck of a yacht in a major storm wasn't just careless, it was flat-out reckless. Melody had never considered her mother a reckless woman. Why had Roz drunk so much wine? Why had she been on deck? Melody always tried to be honest with herself, but she shied away from admitting that suicide was the most rational explanation for what had occurred.

However much she tried to rationalize her grief away, Melody felt bereft. She was a little girl again, left in her dormitory at boarding school and aching for one more absentminded hug, one more careless kiss, before her mother turned and walked out the door.

Now it was too late for all those hugs that had never happened. Tears suddenly clogged Melody's throat. She swallowed, pushing away the urge to bawl her head off. This was not the moment for maudlin childhood memories unless she wanted to break down, which she definitely didn't plan to do. Not in front of her grandparents, who were struggling with their own grief, and certainly not in front of the other five hundred or so mourners. Having been in the limelight for so long, Melody had perfected the art of never saying or doing anything in public that she didn't want to see playing that night on the evening news. She couldn't prevent the media dogging her heels, but she'd learned long ago how to avoid serving up her inner life for them to feast on.

She made it through her grandfather's eulogy by dint of staring at the stained-glass windows and trying to decide if they were originals or nineteenth-century replacements. Stained glass wasn't her area of specialty, but she concluded the windows were probably nineteenth-century replacements, since the glass was too even to be genuine tenth century.

The stained glass was beautiful, but not enough to prevent thoughts of her mother creeping back. Melody had never really thought much about the process of dying, but she'd always assumed that she wouldn't care what happened to the bodies of the people she loved. Even if her mother had been laid to rest in the family crypt, she was quite sure she wouldn't have paid frequent visits to the tomb, bringing flowers and chatting with whatever ghostly remnant of her mother might linger. Now, though, she felt a piercing sense of loss that her mother's body had no real resting place. Much as she tried not to dwell on the image, Melody kept picturing her mother's corpse, chewed on by sharks, the bones drifting aimlessly around the world, scattered by random currents.

Melody blinked hard, staring blindly at the order of service card in her hand. She was going to howl like an abandoned wolf cub if she didn't snap out of this gloomy mood pretty damn quick. With profound thankfulness she realized the bishop was saying the final prayer.

"The Lord lift up the light of his countenance upon us, and give us peace, now and forevermore. Amen."

Melody hoped that eternal peace was what her mother wanted. Knowing Roz, she wouldn't have bet on it.

Three

After the memorial service, members of Lady Roz's family gathered with many of her closest friends at High Ridgefield, the country estate of Melody's grandparents. The mourners drank the earl's excellent sherry, nibbled hors d'oeuvres, admired the spectacular array of spring flowers coming into bloom in the expansive gardens and told each other polite lies about how much Lady Roz would be missed.

Jasper Fowles kept close to Melody's side, hoping to provide a buffer zone while she built a protective layer over her raw emotions. Unfortunately, there was nothing much he could do to shield her from Wallis Beecham's booming heartiness. After all, the guy was her father, even if he didn't seem to have any idea how to offer her comfort.

The moment Wallis walked into the drawing room, he made a beeline for Melody, enveloping her in a big hug. "Well now, how's my little girl doing at this sad time? You look pretty as a picture, as always."

"I'm doing okay, thanks." Melody kissed her father's cheek, but Jasper could see that she derived no real solace from her father's embrace. She stepped back and put her hand on the sleeve of Jasper's jacket, drawing him forward. "Dad, this is my good friend Jasper Fowles. He was also one of my mother's closest friends, and we've known each other forever. Have the two of you met before?"

"I don't believe I've had the pleasure," Wallis said, pumping Jasper's hand. "And which side of the pond do you hail from, Jasper?"

"From New York. I live right in midtown Manhattan. On Park Avenue, in fact."

"Great location, but you're a braver man than me." Wallis reached out to snag a glass of sherry from the tray carried by a passing waiter. "I was born and raised in Tennessee, and I guess there's still a lot of the hillbilly in me. Frankly, all that noise and congestion in Manhattan scares the bejesus out of me. I like to wake up to the sound of cocks crowing, not the sound of fire engines blaring their horns."

Wallis Beecham's folksy, down-home manner grated, since Jasper knew the man was not only a multimillionaire, but also a graduate of the Harvard Business School, and had the reputation of being more ruthless than tyrannosaurus rex when it came to ripping apart his prey. Still, for Melody's sake, Jasper was willing to be friendly.

"You get used to the noise after a while," he said, glossing over the fact that Wallis spent most of his working life in Chicago, which could hardly be considered a prime example of peaceful, small-town America. And a city where he sure as hell didn't wake up to the sound of cocks crowing in the barnyard. "It's a pleasure to meet you, Wallis, even though it's a sad occasion. Melody's spoken of you often."

"Has she, now?" Wallis gave a beaming smile,

wrapping his arm around Melody's shoulders. "Well, it's real good to hear that my little girl keeps me in mind when I'm not around. We don't see each other nearly as often as we should."

"How true. It's been nearly three years since our last face-to-face meeting." Melody's voice was so bland that it was just possible to believe that there was no sting hidden in her words.

Wallis didn't even blink. "I sure do regret that it's been so long," he said, his voice every bit as bland as hers. "But now is the perfect moment to make up for past mistakes. You shouldn't be alone, honey, not right now when you're missing your mother. You should come and spend a few weeks with your stepmother and me. We'd love to have you. Your brother would like to see you, too. Chris has changed his mind about going to law school and he's working with me."

Melody's gaze froze for a split second when Wallis mentioned her brother, but she thanked him for the invitation as if she meant it. "I don't know how soon I can take you up on the offer, Dad. My new gallery's scheduled to open in two weeks, and there's still a lot of work to finish up if I'm going to be ready. Perhaps you and Sondra could fly over for the grand opening?"

"I wish we could, honey, but it's a crazy time for us right now. Sondra is chairing the committee for the annual benefit of the Chicago Symphony and I'm buying another company...."

She gave him a wry smile. "You're always buying another company."

Wallis chuckled. "Not really. It only seems that way." He folded Melody's hand within his clasp.

"Now that I'm looking at you closer, you seem more than a tad down in the dumps, honey."

She avoided his gaze. "I...miss my mother."

Jasper knew even that small admission of vulnerability had cost Melody quite a lot. Wallis appeared supremely unaware that he'd been offered a genuine—and rare—confidence. He gave his daughter's hand another pat, but Jasper sensed impatience rather than affection. "Try not to take your mother's death so much to heart, honey. You need to remember that Roz lived a full life and she would have preferred to go this way. She wasn't a woman who would have enjoyed growing old."

Melody hesitated for a moment before replying. "I just wish she hadn't died alone, you know?" There was a catch in her voice that Jasper found heartbreaking, in part because she tried so hard to conceal it. "Mother wasn't good at being alone."

"No, she wasn't," Wallis acknowledged. "Roz always liked company. But the authorities say the end must have been real quick, honey. She most likely never had any idea she was dying."

It would have to be damned hard to drown without knowing what was happening, Jasper reflected acidly. The water choking off the breath in your lungs would probably be your first clue that all was not entirely as it should be. Besides, Melody was smart enough to realize that neither the "authorities" nor Wallis were in any position to make pronouncements about the final minutes, or even hours, of her mother's life. Roz had last been seen alive shortly after midnight, and her disappearance wasn't discovered until dawn, when Eleanor Cranford, wife of Senator Cranford, got up to use the bathroom and saw the door to Roz's stateroom standing ajar. The light was on, the bed clearly hadn't been slept in and Roz was nowhere to be found.

In other words, the precise circumstances leading up to Roz's disappearance remained a mystery. In fact, Jasper was pretty sure the Mexican police were being so vague in their pronouncements because they believed Roz had committed suicide and wanted to save her family the pain of having that possibility officially explored. He wondered if Melody had already worked that wrinkle out for herself. Probably. She was way too smart not to have connected the missing dots.

Wallis had finished his sherry and was clearly becoming bored. Five minutes of conversation with the daughter he hadn't seen in three years appeared to be his limit. His gaze veered around the room and came to rest on a tall, silver-haired man. "Ah, there's Nathaniel Sherwin—"

"Nathaniel is my mother's solicitor," Melody murmured to Jasper.

"I need to have a word with him," Wallis said. "I'll see you in a little while, honey. In fact, why don't we have dinner together tonight?"

"I'd like that."

"Great. We're on, then. Jasper, good to have met you. Join us for dinner tonight if you're at a loose end, why don't you?" He walked off, smiling and shaking people's hands as he crossed the room, like a politician working the crowd.

Jasper wondered how somebody whose words and gestures were so warm could leave him feeling so cold. However, that was a puzzle he would have to work on later, since he could see that Melody hovered on the brink of emotional meltdown and was in no state to be polite to a slew of friends and relations, most of whom were trying too hard to say the right thing. It was painful even for him to listen. For Melody, it had to be excruciating. He led her from the drawing room before anybody else could buttonhole her to offer stumbling condolences.

Jasper had first met Melody when she was ten years old and he was in his mid-thirties. Roz had attempted to seduce him after a party at his penthouse, and instead of simply rejecting her advances with one of the clever lies he'd used successfully with dozens of other women, he'd astonished himself by admitting he was gay.

Roz had taken the admission—and his rejection—in graceful stride. It was one of her most surprising attributes that she had the power to elicit intimate confidences from people who were normally reticent about their personal lives. It was one of her greatest charms that she then kept the secrets she elicited to herself.

For whatever obscure reason, Roz had decided that a gay man who concealed his sexual orientation was exactly what she needed as an occasional escort and provider of free lodging when she was in New York. Jasper had been more than willing to participate in the illusion she deftly created about the two of them. Being photographed with Lady Roz hanging on his arm was a good way to keep the truth about his sexuality hidden from his parents, and he was always willing to sacrifice his integrity on that particular altar.

His unexpected love for Melody had been a delightful bonus to a cynical deal. His relationship with

Roz remained superficial and frothy, rarely requiring any effort on his part. His relationship with Melody was of another order entirely, the deepest and most intimate in his life. After eighteen years of watching out for her, he considered her the daughter he would never have.

And, God knew, Melody certainly needed him. Beneath her cool, sophisticated exterior the poor kid was so goddamned loving that she'd even managed to care about Roz, despite twenty-eight years of blatant maternal neglect. She was shattered by her mother's death, but as far as Jasper could see, there was nobody in her family capable of stepping in and offering comfort. Wallis Beecham sure didn't strike him as a candidate for warm and fuzzy provider of sanctuary. Once, when he knew Wallis was in Manhattan, he'd suggested to Melody that the three of them should have dinner together. Wallis had claimed prior engagements five nights in a row until Jasper finally got the message that Wallis was never going to make time for dinner with his daughter.

Jasper wished that Melody would allow herself the luxury of crying, but there was almost no chance of that. Like her grandparents, she worked hard at repressing her feelings, another legacy of life as the only daughter of Lady Roz. Jasper remained a devoted admirer of Lady Roz's elegance and her charismatic charm, but he often thought that she had been about as well suited to motherhood as Tinker Bell.

Fortunately, Jasper soon found the perfect way to keep Melody distracted. She offered to show him her grandparents' art collection, and their tour of the house provided him with all the fodder he needed to keep up a stream of frivolous commentary that occupied just enough of Melody's attention to prevent her exploding.

He was genuinely torn between despair and wild merriment at the sight of walls hung randomly with priceless works of art and the nineteenth-century equivalent of glitter paint on black velvet. Hideous Victorian oils of sweating horses and slaughtered animals were displayed haphazardly alongside exquisite eighteenth-century watercolors. Melody even took him to see a Turner landscape, which was buried at the end of a dark corridor, flanked by two vaguely obscene paintings of dead grouse.

At least the Turner wasn't being damaged by excessive exposure to sunlight, Jasper thought wryly.

"You don't need to search for stock in order to open your gallery," he said to Melody, turning to gaze in awe at a Gainsborough portrait of one of her ancestors. The woman, bedecked in gray satin and pearls, had eyes of the exact same blue as Melody's, a rare shade somewhere between cobalt and violet. "You can just buy up the wall hangings from a few of your grandparents' spare bedrooms and announce the grand opening. Not to mention the splash you could make with that entirely fabulous Grinling Gibbons carved fireplace in the drawing room."

"I wish." She managed a smile. "Unfortunately, there's not a chance that my grandparents would let me buy any of their paintings."

"Why not?" Jasper was genuinely curious. "They clearly don't give a damn about this stuff. They can't, or it would be displayed properly. Or at least adequately."

"It's better cared for than you might imagine.

They've had expert advice on temperature, light and humidity control,'' Melody said.

Jasper acknowledged that the paintings looked to be in decent physical shape. ''So why don't they hang the Turner and the Gainsborough where everyone can see them?''

Melody smiled at the note of bewilderment in his voice. ''Because they have no interest in displaying the paintings as if they were on sale in a gallery. They want the pictures to hang just where various generations of the family chose to put them, so that this house looks like a home, not a museum. They care about the pictures, though. Quite a lot, in fact. My grandmother comes to look at this Turner every morning when she gets up.''

''I'll take your word for it.'' Jasper straightened an oddly charming painting of mallards swimming on a pond surrounded by autumn foliage. He grimaced when his fingers came away coated in dust. ''Although if your grandparents care about their art collection, I'd hate to see how they treat the parts of their inheritance they *don't* care about.''

She grinned. ''I'll take you up to the attics sometime—''

''Don't.'' He didn't have to pretend horror. ''My heart probably couldn't stand the shock.''

''Seriously, my grandparents are realists. They know that if they want to keep High Ridgefield in the family, along with its contents, then they have to do a better job with family finances than the previous few generations. That's why they put in nine-hour days, seven days a week, making sure the farm and the estate are profitable. I guess from their perspective, dusting off the family portraits always takes second place to making sure the farming operations are running smoothly. Mad cow disease almost wiped them out when their prize herd had to be destroyed, and they're still recovering."

The earl came up at that moment and invited them to join him in the library for the reading of Roz's will, which saved Jasper from finding something intelligent to say about farming, a subject about which he was delighted to know nothing. He accompanied Melody into the library at her request, but having escorted her to a chair next to her cousins in the center of the room, he retreated to an inconspicuous corner near the door where he could be a spectator rather than a participant in the proceedings.

The scene unfolding in front of him could have been lifted straight out of an Agatha Christie murder mystery, and although the quaintness of the situation ought to have appealed to his mordant sense of humor, Jasper found himself strangely worried. He tried to pinpoint the source of his worry and decided there was something about the solicitor's body language that was setting off his internal alarm signals.

Nathaniel Sherwin was slender and mild-mannered, but he managed to command the attention of the family members gathered in the library without once raising his rather soft voice. He put on a pair of reading glasses, opened a leather portfolio and removed a sheaf of typewritten pages. At the rustle of the papers, everyone turned toward him. He cleared his throat just once and the room fell instantly silent.

"The last will and testament of Lady Rosalind Carruthers is a straightforward document," he said, having offered his condolences to the family. "Lady Rosalind first came to us for legal assistance on the occasion of her divorce from Mr. Wallis Beecham—'' The solicitor nodded in acknowledgment toward Melody's father and Wallis nodded back.

''At that time, my firm recommended that Lady Rosalind should draw up a will so that her wishes in regard to the custody, education and care of her daughter would be spelled out in detail. Nine years ago, at which time Melody Beecham was both legally an adult and also self-supporting financially, we began to urge Lady Rosalind to draw up another will that took account of her changed circumstances. Lady Rosalind took our advice and signed a new and much simplified will five years ago. Unless anyone here is aware of a more recent document, that five-year-old will is the document I am about to read to you.''

The solicitor waited for a moment, but nobody suggested there might be a later version of Lady Roz's will, and he proceeded to read two pages of legalese designed to demonstrate that Lady Rosalind had been in full possession of her mental faculties when she signed the will, and appointed her brothers as joint executors. He cleared his throat a second time, signaling that he was about to proceed to the meat of the document.

'''I hereby instruct that my nieces and nephews, the offspring of my two brothers, James and Thomas, each be given the sum of two thousand pounds so that they can enjoy a holiday at my expense, thus reminding themselves that life is short and the blessings of hard work are exaggerated. I further instruct that my sisters-in-law, Chloe Carruthers and Philippa Carruthers, each be allowed to choose a piece of jewelry from my collection to keep for themselves. I hope they will wear whatever item they select with pleasure and remember me fondly. We have absolutely nothing in common beyond the fact that they married my brothers, but they have always been kind to me and I wish them well.'"

So far, there was nothing to explain the prickles running down his spine, Jasper decided. The bequests were exactly what might be expected, right down to the way Roz had managed to inject her own personality into the normally dry, legal language of a will.

The solicitor turned to a new page of Lady Rosalind's will and continued reading. "'The residue of my estate, consisting of such cars as may be in my possession at the time of my death; the furniture and furnishings of my home in Chipping Weston, Gloucestershire; the monies and financial instruments held in my account with Barclays Bank, 423 High Street, Rodborne, Gloucestershire; and other monies and financial instruments held in my account with the First Bank of Chappaqua, 357 Oak Street, Chappaqua, New York; along with the jewelry collection held in my safety deposit box at the aforementioned bank in Rodborne, I leave in its entirety to my beloved daughter, Melody Rosalind Beecham. I hereby acknowledge that my home in Chipping Weston, Gloucestershire, is the property of my former husband, Wallis Beecham, and that the house and grounds form no part of my estate.'"

Jasper expelled a soft breath, which was inaudible because of the subdued rustle of astonishment rippling through the room. While she was alive, Roz had never once hinted that the lovely eighteenth-century manor house she called home did not, in fact, belong to her. Was that why he'd read tension in

Nathaniel Sherwin's body language? Jasper wondered. Did the lawyer dislike breaking the news to Melody that her inheritance was going to be a lot less substantial than she had expected? Jasper was fairly sure that Melody had no idea her mother's home had been provided courtesy of Wallis Beecham. Roz had apparently been as good at keeping her own secrets as she was at keeping those of other people.

The solicitor took off his reading glasses and pinched the bridge of his nose. "There is one additional paragraph that Lady Rosalind insisted upon including in her will. I suggested to my client that even if she chose to include this paragraph, she might prefer for the contents to be conveyed privately to the two parties involved. However, Lady Rosalind was insistent that the information should be made public, and she specifically instructed me to read this final paragraph along with the rest of the will. Accordingly, I am following her instructions." Nathaniel Sherwin put his glasses back on, distaste thinning his lips. "The paragraph reads as follows. The language, as you might guess, is entirely Lady Rosalind's.

"'One of the more delightful aspects of being dead is that one is beyond the reach of human retribution. As for heavenly retribution, God undoubtedly gave up on me long ago, so I may as well take my pleasures where I can find them. Ever since the birth of my daughter, Melody Rosalind, prudence has required me to remain silent as to her true parentage. Now that I am dead, there is no longer any reason for prudence. Accordingly, I give my daughter this final and precious gift, namely the knowledge that Wallis Beecham, one of America's most dangerous and unpleasant hypocrites, is not her father. Enjoy your freedom, Melody. You have earned it.'"

Four

The solicitor's words beat against Melody's ears and reverberated deep inside, making her stomach ache. She instinctively dropped her gaze, staring at her hands so that her hair tumbled forward and hid the heat that flared in her cheeks. She felt the solicitor's gaze resting on her bent head, and wished she could look up to meet his eyes, but the power of physical movement seemed beyond her.

Melody couldn't remember another occasion in her life when she had so little idea what to do or say. Her thoughts raced in circles, trying to pin down what she was feeling. After a moment she realized that her emotions had spilled so far into overload that she actually felt nothing at all. She'd just been robbed of her father days after she'd lost her mother, and she was numb.

The room fell oppressively silent in the wake of Roz's bombshell. Nobody spoke. Nobody coughed or wriggled. It seemed as if nobody even breathed, so acute was the pall of embarrassment shrouding the room.

Way to go, Roz, Melody thought, a hint of anger extricating itself from the tangled skein of her emotions. *Did you really need to lob that grenade at me right now? Was it that important for you to get back at my father?*

Except that Wallis Beecham wasn't her father. Or maybe he was. There were plenty of reasons Roz might be a less than reliable witness. Through a haze of misery, Melody recognized that her mother was quite capable of lying if it suited her purpose, even if that purpose had been nothing more profound than a burst of spite.

Unfortunately, she couldn't ignore her mother's revelation forever, so Melody forced herself to look toward Wallis. Her ex-father and fellow victim. Seeing his stocky and familiar figure, she was seized by a profound yearning. Wallis hadn't exactly been the father of her dreams, but right now she desperately wanted him to assure her that Roz was lying and that she was still his daughter. Not as well loved as Christopher, his son, but loved at least a little. For a woman heading toward thirty, it was surprising to discover how badly she didn't want to be an orphan.

At some level Melody must have been expecting Wallis to reject her silent plea, because relief swept over her when he met her gaze and immediately came over to where she was sitting. Resting one hand on her shoulder, he squeezed gently.

"Don't look so devastated, honey." He spoke quietly, but in the silence of the room everyone could hear what he said. "You can't let Roz's unpleasant little games get to you. We all know what she was like."

Aware of their audience, even if it was made up of close friends and members of her family, Melody fought to keep her voice steady. "You think my mother might have been lying?"

"Of course I do, honey." His tone of voice suggested that Wallis wondered why she bothered to ask the question. "When have you ever known Roz to demonstrate more than a passing interest in telling the truth?"

Melody gave a tight smile. "I would have thought death might have a sobering effect even on my mother."

"Nothing could make Roz behave when she got the bit between her teeth." Wallis gave Melody's shoulder another squeeze. "Besides, when you get right down to it, what she said isn't all that important, is it?"

"Not important that you're not my father?" Melody blinked. "I'm not sure I understand...."

"Even if Roz told the literal truth, she was only talking about genes and the mechanics of things, and what do they matter? Not much, in my book. You've been my daughter for twenty-eight years, coming up for twenty-nine in another few weeks. Nothing that Roz wrote into her will can change that. I'm your dad, honey, just like I've always been."

A relieved murmur of agreement came from the family members assembled in the room, and Wallis acknowledged their approval with a brief nod of his head toward the earl and countess. Then he shot an inquiring glance at the solicitor. "Apart from anything else, my paternity is a legal fact, isn't it? I believe the law considers me to be Melody's father regardless of what Roz claimed in her attempt at mischief making. Am I correct, Mr. Sherwin?"

"You are indeed correct, sir. On both sides of the Atlantic, I believe. Until very recently there was no scientific way to prove who had fathered a child, so the law assumed that any child born during the course of a marriage was the offspring of the woman's husband. Our legal systems both here and in the States are only now struggling to accommodate the changed realities brought about by procedures such as surrogate parenthood, sperm and egg donation, and DNA testing. But for the moment the situation remains as you suggested, Mr. Beecham. Regardless of Lady Rosalind's statement, and regardless of any...um...extramarital activity, the law considers you to be Melody's father."

"As I do myself," Wallis said, and gave Melody a warm smile. "For once the law and I are in complete agreement, which sure makes a nice change."

The earl rose to his feet, his expression bleak despite Wallis's determined effort to put a cheerful face on disaster. Melody felt another flash of anger toward Roz. Her grandparents had loved their only daughter, despite the fact that they had never understood her. As for Roz, she'd always seemed to reciprocate their affection in her own careless way. And yet Roz's need to inflict a final wound on her ex-husband had apparently been so overwhelming that she didn't care if she devastated the earl and countess, not to mention Melody, as long as she hurt Wallis in the process.

Why had Roz felt such intense anger, such hatred? Another mystery to add to the many that her mother would now never answer, Melody reflected ruefully.

Her grandfather spoke with a quiet dignity that Melody wished Roz could have emulated, at least when writing her will. "I imagine this would be a good moment to leave Wallis and Melody alone for a little while," he said. "If the rest of you would care to join me in the drawing room, I believe the staff are planning to serve tea.''

The assembled guests surged to their feet, eager to escape the confines of the library, which was much too full of tension for comfort. They practically galloped from the room in the wake of the earl and countess. Apart from Nathaniel Sherwin, Jasper was the only person who didn't leave. He came and stood at Melody's side, giving her hand a quick, reassuring squeeze.

''Do you want me to stay with you?'' he asked, his gaze fixed so intently on Melody that Wallis Beecham and the solicitor both seemed to fade into the background.

Melody shook her head, not quite able to smile. ''Thanks, Jasper, but my fath…'' She stumbled to an awkward halt. ''My grandfather was right. Wallis and I need to talk.''

''I'll be waiting in the drawing room when you're ready.'' Jasper gave her hand another tight squeeze, nodded to both Wallis and the solicitor and walked quietly from the library.

Nathaniel Sherwin waited until the door had closed behind Jasper, then apologized to Wallis and Melody.

''Forgive the intrusion into your privacy, but I'd like to take this opportunity to express my sincere regrets to both of you. I failed in my professional responsibilities and the two of you are suffering as a result. I can only assure you that I did everything in my power to prevent Lady Rosalind delivering this information in this particular way. However, she was adamant and I couldn't persuade her to change her mind.''

''Melody and I have coped with Roz for years,'' Wallis said, sounding more indulgent than angry. ''You've no need to explain to either of us how impossible it was to convince her to behave reasonably.''

Melody managed to nod. ''That's true, Mr. Sherwin. I know how...forceful...my mother could be on occasion.''

''I appreciate your understanding. You're both being very gracious in the face of unpleasantness that wasn't necessary.'' The solicitor reached into his portfolio and removed another set of papers. Something about his expression warned Melody that there was more bad news to come.

''There is one further matter that I'd like to clarify,'' he said. ''It concerns the veracity of Lady Rosalind's assertions about the paternity of her daughter.''

With his burst of long words he sounded much more pompous than before, and his gaze flicked between Wallis and Melody without managing to settle. Nerves, Melody thought. The poor guy really dislikes what he's doing right now.

''You think we should run a paternity test to make sure Roz told the truth?'' Wallis asked. He nodded, responding to his own question. ''Yes, I'm in favor of that. I was going to suggest the same thing to Melody myself. Just so that we can be sure of our facts, regardless of whether we choose to ignore them.''

''In normal circumstances—'' The solicitor broke off, realizing that his choice of phrase was hardly appropriate, since very little about the current situation could be considered normal. He cleared his throat and tried again. ''In fact, the appropriate DNA tests have already been done.''

''What?'' Melody exclaimed. ''How is that possible?''

''Lady Rosalind made the arrangements—''

''She would have needed blood samples,'' Wallis said. ''I didn't give her one, for sure. How about you, Melody?''

She shook her head. ''No.''

The solicitor referred to the documents in his hand, but Melody realized he was using the papers as a prop, not as a genuine source of information. When he finally looked up, he spoke in a rush. ''It seems that Lady Rosalind took steps to obtain the necessary samples from both of you....''

''She sure as hell didn't have my permission to obtain such a sample,'' Wallis said.

''Nor mine,'' Melody agreed. A little knot of grief tied itself in the pit of her stomach, caused as much by her mother's deception as by the loss of Wallis as her biological father. A loss that she assumed was certain, given the way the lawyer was behaving.

Nathaniel Sherwin flushed an agitated pink. ''If Lady Rosalind had informed me of what she was doing, I would have explained that her actions were completely unethical, not to mention illegal. However, she was quite well aware of how I would react, and so she didn't inform me. It was only after her death that I opened a letter she had left for me, as per her instructions, and discovered that it contained a comprehensive report from a genetic testing laboratory.''

Wallis spoke with icy control, as if he was afraid to raise his voice for fear of totally losing his temper.

"I still want to know how my ex-wife obtained a sample of my DNA. How do we know that it's my blood that the lab examined? Roz could have taken a blood sample from virtually any man on the planet and submitted it to the lab, pretending it was mine."

"That's true. However, Lady Rosalind was at pains to authenticate the sources of the samples she submitted to the lab. Her letter informed me that she obtained a sample from you, Mr. Beecham, when you cut your hand on a glass during a meeting that took place between the two of you in March of 1999 at your offices in Chicago. March 2, to be precise. She claims that she provided you with first a tissue and then a Band-Aid to staunch the blood. She kept the tissue and used it to submit to the lab. Do you recall such a meeting with Lady Rosalind?"

Wallis looked straight ahead, avoiding the lawyer's gaze as well as Melody's. "Yes," he said, memories of the meeting seeming to make him uncomfortable. "That was the last time I ever saw Roz in person and I do remember cutting my…thumb."

"How did she get a sample from me?" Melody asked. "I certainly don't remember cutting myself on any occasion when Roz was around."

"Your mother didn't need blood for testing purposes," the solicitor explained. "Saliva works equally well, or skin tissue. In your case, Lady Rosalind apparently removed strands of hair from your hairbrush, and the lab then extracted DNA from the follicles. You and Mr. Beecham could repeat the tests, of course, but the laboratory your mother used is entirely reputable."

Nathaniel Sherwin coughed into his hand, then brought himself to the point. "I'm sorry to inform you that their report confirms that Mr. Beecham is not Melody's biological father. As the lab phrases it, 'The male subject A is excluded as a possible father to the female subject B.'"

Melody sought for something to say. Absolutely nothing suitable sprang to mind. Even Wallis Beecham appeared at a loss for words.

The lawyer pushed two sets of papers across the desk, fanning them out toward Melody and Wallis. "I have copies of the lab report here for both of you to examine at your leisure, along with Lady Rosalind's detailed explanations of precisely how she obtained the necessary samples for the lab. I think you may safely conclude that there is no biological relationship between the two of you, but I repeat that—in law—nothing has changed. Mr. Beecham remains your father, Melody."

He picked up his portfolio, tucked it under his arm and nodded toward both of them, obviously doing his best to lower the emotional temperature by behaving with determined professionalism. "As your grandfather said earlier, I believe this would be a good moment for me to leave you alone for a little while. I'm sure there are some things you need to say to each other."

"Yes, we do need to talk." Melody held out her hand. "Thank you for trying to make a difficult situation as easy as possible, Mr. Sherwin."

The solicitor shook her hand. "I sincerely wish I could have done more. My secretary will be in touch next week to set up an appointment with you and your uncles so that we can start carrying out the other instructions contained in your mother's will."

He extended his hand toward Wallis. "Mr. Beecham, if I can be of assistance to you in any way, my office phone number is on the card attached to the documents I've just given you. Once again, I apologize for the fact that I was not able to convince Lady Rosalind to behave more reasonably. Good day to you both."

"Wait!" Melody said. "Don't go, Mr. Sherwin. There's something else...."

The lawyer stopped and turned to face her. "Yes? How can I help you?"

Melody was furious with her mother for putting her in this situation, furious with herself for needing to ask the question now, when Wallis was still in the room, but the need to know overrode all other considerations. "Did...my mother leave any messages or envelopes for me to open now that she's dead?"

The solicitor knew exactly what was on her mind, of course, and he sent her a look of mingled sympathy and frustration. "No, I'm very sorry, but she didn't."

"And she never told you who my father really is?"

Nathaniel Sherwin shook his head. "I'm so sorry, Melody. When we wrote the final paragraph of Lady Rosalind's will, I did point out several times that you would want to know who your biological father is. My strong advice was that your mother should remain silent, but that if she insisted on making this information public, then you had the right to know who your father was. Or is. She insisted that the name of the man in question couldn't be revealed."

Wallis gave a bark of angry laughter. "I'll just bet his name couldn't be revealed. How could she pick among so many possible candidates? I'd say that Roz had the morals of an alley cat, but I don't want to insult the cat.''

The solicitor looked appalled, and Wallis appeared to realize belatedly that this was not an appropriate way to talk in front of Melody, whatever he thought about her mother. Clamping his lips together, he ducked his head toward her in silent apology, but he was clearly seething with silent rage.

''I'm sorry,'' Nathaniel Sherwin said again, not specifying which of many sins he was apologizing for, his own or those of other people. He recognized that Roz's underhand DNA testing had been one betrayal too many. Learning about the secret lab tests had ripped away the veneer of courtesy that had brought Wallis and Melody safely through the reading of the will. Eddies of raw, unfiltered emotion now swirled around the room, waiting to coalesce into something rancid.

Unable to hide his relief that he was not responsible for directing the flow of those emotional currents, the solicitor repeated his goodbyes and very nearly ran from the library.

Melody stood by the desk long after the solicitor had left the room, chiefly because she wasn't altogether sure if she could make it across the floor without tripping. Her body seemed to have switched itself back into paralysis mode and for a few seconds she couldn't remember how to breathe. Then her lungs sucked in a huge gulp of air and she was physically functional once again, although her brain remained devoid of higher function and her emotions still whirled with all the focus of a helicopter in free fall.

Wallis seemed to have no more idea what to say than she did, although the fact that he remained in the library suggested he shared her need to establish some guidelines for the new relationship Roz had thrust on the pair of them. Since she couldn't find any words to make sense out of her confusion, Melody simply watched as Wallis moved to the window and opened the casement, letting in a waft of blossom-scented air. He studied a pair of swans gliding across the ornamental pond, his face betraying none of his thoughts.

The silence was becoming so heavy that it pressed down on the top of Melody's head, crushing her. She had to speak. Anything was better than this oppressive weight of nonspeaking. "Maybe we should join the others," she said. "We can give ourselves a couple of hours to assimilate what Mum said and wait a while to—"

"We will not wait." Wallis swung around, words spilling out of him in a furious torrent. "Your bitch of a mother made a fool out of me for the best part of thirty years. You're sure as hell not going to do the same. This is the last time I ever plan to speak to you, so let me be quite clear about what you can expect from me in the future." He jabbed his finger in the air for emphasis. "Nothing. That's what you can expect from me. Absolutely nothing. Do you understand me?"

Melody knew she ought to have been prepared for his sudden descent into rage. She'd been aware for years that Wallis's cozy charm was a facade that hid ruthless self-interest. But she was caught off guard, and the rejection intensified the unbearable sense of loss she already felt.

As always when she was hurting, Melody took refuge behind a barricade of ice-cold calm. "I understand you very well,'' she said. She was wearing two-inch heels, which made her taller than Wallis. She looked down into his eyes and spoke with the faint mockery she normally reserved for annoying journalists. If she concentrated on appearing in control, she could tolerate the pain that threatened to rip her apart.

''You never did give me anything except money, Wallis. And fortunately I don't need that.''

He examined her with visible loathing. ''You're so goddamn sure of yourself, aren't you? I can practically see the damn tiara on your head when you speak, just like your mother. The aristocrat dealing with the annoying peasant.''

''I have no control over my ancestry. I didn't pick my grandparents any more than I picked my father.''

He waved aside her comment with an impatient gesture, ignoring the sharp edge. ''You're too damn quick to dismiss the importance of my money. That's real easy for you to do when you've been sponging off my hard work for years—''

That hurt. ''I haven't taken a cent of your money since the day I left school. I've earned every penny I've spent for the past ten years.''

''Hah! Think again.'' Wallis sputtered as he spoke, anger forcing his words out in staccato bursts. ''The mews house where you're planning to open your new gallery belongs to me. And as of today you're no longer a welcome tenant.''

Melody hoped she didn't flinch, but the news that Wallis Beecham owned the property she had just finished renovating was a blow she hadn't expected. Another fine example of Roz concealing the truth, Melody thought bitterly. Roz had said the house belonged to a friend who was willing to charge them a low rent in exchange for Melody paying up front for the necessary modifications and refurbishment. Some friend.

"I have a three-year lease on that property with an option to renew for another ten years," Melody said. "Your name doesn't appear anywhere on the lease."

Wallis snapped his fingers. "I used the name of one of my subsidiary companies."

"Even so, the lease presumably remains valid. What grounds do you have for canceling it?" She had been working flat-out toward opening this gallery for the past year. For seven years, if you added in the time spent in college and graduate school. Melody couldn't bear to hear that Wallis had the power to snatch her dream away, squandering the last of the money she'd saved from her career as a model.

He gave a derisive snort. "What grounds do I have for backing out? Get real. I employ an army of corporate attorneys who earn their high salaries by making sure that I can tear up a contract whenever the mood so takes me. Trust me on this, Melody. Wherever you open your new gallery, I can assure you it isn't going to be in any piece of property owned by me."

She shrugged, her indifference not entirely feigned. In the final analysis, she realized that she didn't care very much what he did about the lease. There would be no pleasure in making a success of her gallery if success left her beholden to Wallis. And she certainly wasn't going to humiliate herself by requesting a refund of all the money she'd spent redecorating and outfitting the gallery to her specifications. She'd go back to modeling before she'd ask him for any financial favors—and she'd thought until this moment that nothing would ever be sufficient to drive her back to that dreary career.

"When you first heard that you weren't my biological father, you claimed it didn't make any difference." Melody wouldn't have made the comment if she'd been fully in command of her tongue.

"There were people in the room, listening." He stopped abruptly and she doubted he'd have been so honest if he, too, hadn't been shaken out of his usual control.

"I see." And she did. Wallis was smart enough that he wasn't going to risk his image as a folksy, honest and good-natured businessman by letting loose with a string of vituperation in front of an audience. But now they were alone, he could afford to express his true feelings.

She couldn't think of anything more that needed to be said. Wallis had pretty much said it all. She turned to go without attempting to extend the conversation, which seemed to irritate him.

"We haven't finished," he said. "Wait!"

She continued to walk away.

"I said wait, goddammit."

"And I'm ignoring you."

He ran across the room to fling himself in front of the door, panting more from the effort of controlling his rage than from the exertion of running to catch up with her. "Do you believe I'm stupid?"

She considered for a moment. "Not exactly," she said, finding unexpected release in telling the truth. "You're nowhere near as smart as you think you are. You're too self-centered and grasping in your relationships. On the whole, though, you have a decent IQ."

He shoved his hands into the pockets of his two-thousand-dollar suit. Probably to prevent himself from throttling her, Melody reflected wryly. He must be mad as hell that he'd opened himself up to her scathing assessment.

Having been burned once, Wallis was savvy enough not to ask any more rhetorical questions. "I know Roz must have told you the truth years ago," he said. "Admit it. You knew you weren't my daughter. How you must have enjoyed laughing to yourself all these years behind my back! Well, now you're going to pay for all the fun you've had at my expense. Believe me, I'm going to find ways to make you pay."

She had just enough sympathy left inside her to tell him the truth. "I had no idea you weren't my father, Wallis. My mother's revelation was as much of a surprise to me as it apparently was to you."

He was so far from believing her that he didn't even bother to argue. He stepped aside, unblocking the door so that she could leave the room. "You're right—we have nothing more to say to each other. I don't want to see you ever again." His mouth twisted into a sneer. "I have no use for my ex-wife's bastards. Within the next hour I will be issuing instructions that you are not to be admitted to my home or to my place of business. You will not contact my wife, and you will not speak to Christopher. Is that clear?"

The knowledge that she would never again have to cope with Wallis's son—that Christopher wasn't her younger brother or in any way related to her by blood—was the one narrow beam of sunshine in the day's miserable events.

"Your instructions are crystal clear," Melody said. "And so are mine. Please leave my grandparents' home at once."

She walked out into the hallway without looking back. She'd pick up the pieces of her shattered life later, when she was alone. She had lots of experience in coping alone. In that, Wallis had taught her well.

Five

Manhattan
September 2003

Jasper had inherited 50 percent of the Van der Meer Gallery on Madison Avenue a decade ago when his father died. His mother, Prudence Fowles, retained ownership of the remaining 50 percent and exerted her ownership rights just often enough to keep Jasper hovering permanently on the verge of nervous apoplexy. The official cause of Hubert Fowles's death had been heart failure, but unkind friends suggested the poor guy had simply died from the sheer exhaustion of being married to Prudence.

Any visit to the gallery by his mother left Jasper frazzled with frustration and wrung out from the effort of not committing matricide. This morning was no exception. Prudence breezed in, false eyelashes long enough to compete with Carol Channing, dressed in a designer orange wool suit that clashed spectacularly with her newly dyed auburn hair. She whizzed through the gallery offering outrageous comments on Jasper's recent acquisitions that were remarkable equally for their profound ignorance of the art world and the panache with which she delivered them.

After she left—*I'm having lunch with Rudi, darlings. Too delicious*—Jasper sank into the reproduction Louis XV chair in his office and collapsed facedown on his desk.

Trying not to laugh, Melody perched on the corner of the desk and spoke to the top of her boss's head, noting with affection the tiny bald spot Jasper usually was at pains to keep hidden. He was in such great physical shape that she sometimes forgot he was already well into his fifties.

She rested her hand on his shoulder, massaging gently. "Prudence adores you, you know."

"I'm aware." Jasper sighed and lifted his head. "One of these days that's not going to stop me calling a friend with connections and ordering a hit. I'll regret it later, but by then she'll be gone."

Melody grinned. "You don't have friends with connections."

"Well, I'm thinking of getting some very soon. In fact, I plan to work on it this afternoon." He wrote "Find Hit Man" on his calendar and underlined it with a flourish.

"Since you're obviously going to be very busy for the next few hours, do you want me to take care of your appointment with Lawrence Springer? His assistant called early this morning to confirm a 2:00 p.m. appointment." Melody managed to keep her voice casual, despite the fact that she'd been working for six weeks to persuade Springer to pay a visit to the gallery. And not because she was especially eager to sell him a painting, or one of their new shipment of Victorian marble busts.

Jasper constantly surprised Melody by the seemingly effortless way in which he remembered details without ever getting bogged down in them. "You sent him the sales brochures for the Maurice Prendergast oil and the watercolor by William Merritt Chase when I was in Paris, didn't you?"

Melody nodded. "I heard his brand-new wife likes the American Impressionists, so he seemed a likely candidate to be interested in them. They're taking longer to sell than I would have expected." Which was all true, as far as it went.

"You're more than welcome to handle the meeting," Jasper said. "Especially since you initiated the contact. I'm not sure that I could survive dealing with my mother and Lawrence Springer in the same day."

"Thank you, but what's so tough about handling Springer?" *Other than the fact that he's a corrupt son of a bitch with close ties to Wallis Beecham.* Melody kept the pitch of her voice businesslike. "His file shows he's been a regular customer of the gallery for the past six years."

Jasper looked gloomy. "The last time he came in here, he bought a hundred thousand dollars' worth of Italian sculptures for his guest cottages in the Hamptons."

"That's *good* news, Jasper. I know you'd really prefer to keep everything on display as if we were a museum, but selling our stock is what keeps the accountants happy."

He gave a huff of pretended indignation. "Contrary to office gossip, I'm not opposed to making sales to the right people. I love doing it, in fact."

Melody raised an eyebrow. "Lawrence Springer, multimillionaire, champion of industry, patron of several of New York's most fashionable charities, isn't a *right person?*"

Jasper scowled. "He has no appreciation for the beauty of what he's buying. He only cares about what it cost and the profit he might make on resale. Besides, when he bought those Italian marbles three years ago, his telecom company had just gone bust and the employees had been informed the pension fund was empty and their stock holdings were worthless. The contrast between Springer's financial situation and theirs didn't sit well with me."

Melody gave him a quick hug. "You know what your problem is, Jasper? You're a softie. Beneath that sophisticated Manhattan exterior beats a heart with all the toughness of a warm marshmallow."

"Takes one to know one," he said, smiling.

Jasper was both intelligent and sensitive, so Melody was always jarred by reminders that he had no inkling how profoundly Roz's death and Wallis Beecham's rejection had affected her. If she had ever been softhearted, she no longer was. Somewhere between stonehearted and totally devoid of any heart at all might best describe her current emotional state, she reflected with rueful honesty.

She had been working for Jasper since her plans to open her own gallery in London had gone belly-up, a direct consequence of Wallis's first ripping up her lease and then preventing her finding alternative financing by circulating rumors in banking circles that she was a major credit risk with no head for business—a feckless wanna-be who had already been bailed out of serious money problems by him on multiple occasions. With the savings from her modeling career consumed by renovations for a gallery she could no longer open, and with her mother's legacy amounting to a few thousand dollars' worth of jewelry and furniture, Melody had gratefully accepted Jasper's offer of a job.

She had been living in Jasper's Park Avenue apartment for fifteen months now, and enjoyed sharing some aspects of his social life. Both of them were more amused than upset by the rumors that suggested Melody had inherited the role of Jasper's mistress from Roz, Jasper because he still nurtured the faint hope that his mother didn't know he was gay, Melody because she'd learned years ago that a screen of nonsensical gossip was the easiest way to hide the reality of her life.

She shared more of her true thoughts and feelings with Jasper than with anyone else. Which, perhaps, wasn't saying much. Still, if Jasper failed to notice the changes that had taken place in her since Roz's death, then her facade of brittle sophistication must be pretty convincing.

Melody slid off the desk, subduing a twinge of guilt. Her affection for Jasper was deep, so there was no reason for her to feel dishonest because she kept secrets from him. Just as he chose not to discuss issues of his sexuality with her, she chose not to discuss issues that she had with Wallis Beecham and his brutal rejection. They both had nights when they left the penthouse without saying where they were going. If Jasper assumed she was spending the night with a lover, then he was only making the same mistaken assumption as a lot of other people, who all believed her love life was a rich feast of sexual encounters.

If only they knew how long it had been since she

had last shared her bed with anyone other than the Bart Simpson doll she'd been given years ago by one of her cousins, Melody reflected with wry amusement. She was pretty damn close to a born-again virgin if ever there was one.

"I'll take care of Mr. Springer, then," she said. "Although you owe me big time for the favor, you know."

"Nonsense." Jasper's eyes gleamed with silent laughter. "You love selling mediocre American Impressionists to millionaires with no taste. I'm doing you the favor."

Jasper didn't realize how accurate his statement was. Melody's heart beat a little faster, as it always did when she contemplated advancing the project that had virtually consumed her life for the past sixteen months. Lawrence Springer was one of Wallis Beecham's partners in the Bonita Project, and her current obsession was gaining access to Springer's home filing system.

The Bonita Project was a partnership incorporated in Rhode Island, with a small corporate headquarters in New Jersey and a research facility located in rural Arkansas, in a town known chiefly for its neighboring chicken factories. The locals believed the research facility was investigating ways to vaccinate against a flu virus that could spread from chickens to humans and therefore required the slaughter of entire flocks if it was ever detected in one of the factory farms that were the staple of the American poultry industry and the spine of economic activity in Arkansas.

Melody had paid a visit to the research facility and was damn sure that the Bonita Project had little or nothing to do with chicken flu. But so far—despite lots of digging—she hadn't been able to penetrate the complex layers of corporate padding to find out what project was really buried inside. However, after months of investigation, she was confident that if she wanted to cause Wallis Beecham the same sort of financial setback and public disgrace that he'd caused her, then the Bonita Project was her most likely ticket to success.

"You're looking suddenly ferocious," Jasper said. "It's positively intimidating, sweetie. What's up?"

"Nothing much." She smoothed her brow and shot him a quick smile. "I must be hungry. I'd better eat before Mr. Springer gets here or I'm likely to snap his head off." She tugged at the hem of her tailored charcoal-gray skirt until it reached midthigh, then walked through the elegant main gallery to the catering kitchen in search of food—and an escape route from Jasper's too-observant eyes.

An hour and a half later Lawrence Springer was the owner of two new paintings and the Van der Meer Gallery was richer by several thousand dollars. Melody hoped Mrs. Springer would like her gift. Given the amount of time Lawrence Springer had spent ogling her legs, not to mention attempting to squeeze her ass, Melody wouldn't have taken any bets on how long the new Mrs. Springer was going to be able to indulge her fancy for American Impressionists. Ol' Larry didn't seem very securely attached to his new bride, despite the fact that he'd just dropped eighty thousand bucks on a birthday gift.

"Claire is going to be thirty tomorrow and she's feeling depressed," Springer said, signing his check with a gold Mont Blanc pen that had his initials engraved on the side.

"I'm sure the paintings will cheer her up," Melody said, managing to keep all trace of irony out of her voice. "They're a lovely and thoughtful gift." And probably expensive enough to buy ol' Larry some really hot sex from a grateful Claire.

Springer tucked his pen back into the inside pocket of his jacket. "Can you get them delivered to me tonight so that I can surprise her first thing in the morning? I'll pay whatever it costs to get them there."

This was a better opening than Melody had hoped for in her most optimistic fantasies. The paintings weren't very large, and she'd been afraid Springer would volunteer to take them with him.

"Where would you like to have the paintings delivered, Mr. Springer?"

"To my house in Chappaqua," Springer said. "Hill View Lane. I'm sure you already have the address in your records."

"Yes, we do." Melody had no trouble giving him a happy smile. The house in Chappaqua was not only Springer's legal residence, but also the place where he spent most time and therefore, she hoped, the most likely repository for papers about the Bonita partnership. Melody had already searched his offices in Lower Manhattan and turned up nothing in regard to the project, so the house on Hill View Lane seemed to be the place where she had the best chance of finding something useful. She sure as hell hoped so, since she'd already searched both of Senator Cranford's homes without turning up more than scraps of information, and that left only the former vice president, Johnston Yates, before she was left with nowhere to turn but Wallis Beecham himself. Still, for now she was going to work on the optimistic assumption that searching Springer's house would provide invaluable leads.

"It would be my pleasure to arrange for the delivery of your paintings this evening, Mr. Springer. I can have them crated by our staff here, and they will be fully covered by our insurance until you or your authorized representative accepts delivery at your house."

Springer nodded. "That's settled, then." He put his checkbook back into his briefcase and returned her smile, managing to brush against her hip in the process. "Thanks for your help, Melody. I'm really hoping the paintings will jolt Claire out of her attack of the blues."

They might, Melody thought. On the other hand, Claire might be regretting her marriage to a man who apparently had no idea what was meant by the concept of marital fidelity. She moved out of reach of Springer's roving hands, suppressing a strong urge to kick him in the balls.

"I just had an inspired idea," she said, as if she hadn't been planning this from the moment she sent Springer the brochures.

"Yes?" He sounded grumpy, perhaps because he considered that he'd just dropped enough money at the gallery to entitle him to a few sexual favors from the hired help.

"Instead of having the paintings delivered by carrier, why don't I come myself first thing tomorrow morning? That way I could help Mrs. Springer decide where she would like to hang the paintings.

Since I'll be on the spot, so to speak, I could even take care of hanging them for her if she would like that. I'll bring my measuring tapes, a level and the appropriate wall hooks."

"Hmm..." Springer stroked his chin. "That might work—"

"What time would you like me to arrive?" Melody didn't want Springer to have time to decide that he'd prefer delivery by carrier. Offering to help Claire Springer hang the pictures provided her with a unique chance not only to get inside the house but also to wander from room to room at her leisure. If she could locate the internal security controls, for example, that would be a major plus. She'd nearly been caught at the Cranfords' home when they'd arrived home unexpectedly and—okay, she'd admit it—she was a little nervous about this second excursion into the realm of home invasion. Her burglary skills were pretty good, but she suspected that Springer's security systems would be efficient enough to intimidate her.

"How about eight o'clock?" Springer suggested. "Claire always gets up to have coffee with me before I leave for the office. But please make sure you're not late. I want to give her the paintings first thing."

Melody flashed him the bright smile of an eager sales assistant with nothing on her mind beyond pleasing the customer. "I'll be there without fail. I'm really excited to see Mrs. Springer's reaction to her lovely gift."

Melody arrived at the Springers' Chappaqua estate twenty minutes early, as she had planned. She parked the gallery's delivery van by the service entrance and took a few seconds to orient herself before getting out and leaning against the hood. The air was crisp with the promise of fall, and invigorating enough to give her a moment of unalloyed pleasure, untainted by thoughts of why she was really here. She breathed deeply, filling her lungs, then looked carefully around the yard. There was nobody in sight, not even an early-morning jogger. A couple of squirrels scurried between a magnificent oak and an even more magnificent maple. This was the sort of neighborhood in which a visitor or a parked car was going to stand out like a sore thumb, she concluded. She'd have to work on finding somewhere inconspicuous to park her car before she came back for her planned breaking and entering.

Fortunately, the Springer mansion wasn't located in a gated community, and there was no camera-based security system to be negotiated at the property line. However, the house itself was posted with warning signs from one of the best commercial home protection companies. Thank goodness she wouldn't need to guess the details of the system, Melody reflected. Under the pretext of assuring the safety of the new paintings, she could ask Claire exactly what sort of antitheft protocols had been installed. Once she had those specific details, it shouldn't be too difficult to find a way to break in to the house.

Her in-depth study of security techniques was turning out to be one of the most useful aspects of the professional training as an art curator that she'd received in Florence. Since coming to the States, Jasper had encouraged her to keep up-to-date on all the latest in theft prevention technology, and—fortunately—most of her instructors were delighted to discuss with her possible ways to circumvent their systems.

Melody rang the bell to the service entrance, and was answered by the housekeeper, a friendly woman who spoke English with only a trace of a Spanish accent. The housekeeper informed Springer that the paintings had arrived, then led Melody to the utility room, where she helped unwrap the pictures. Setting them on the table to triple-check that they'd survived transportation unscathed, Melody was struck by how pretty the colors of both the paintings were in the clear morning light. The landscapes might lack originality of concept, she decided, but they were charming for all that and would fit well into Lawrence's imitation French château.

Esperanza, the housekeeper, returned to say that Lawrence was ready for them to carry the paintings into the garden room, where he and his wife were eating breakfast. Claire appeared thrilled with her birthday gift and thanked her husband with a passionate, openmouthed kiss, along with many happy giggles of gratitude and suggestive little wriggles of her body promising future delights. Lawrence in turn seemed pleased that his wife was duly appreciative of his stupendous generosity, and both of them agreed that it would be a great idea for Melody to spend a couple of hours helping Claire decide where the pictures should be hung.

Lawrence left for his Wall Street office and Claire's bubbling little-girl enthusiasm vanished along with her husband. She tossed her linen napkin down on top of her uneaten muffin and ran a visibly assessing eye over Melody.

Perhaps she was afraid of facing a rival for her

husband's affections, Melody thought ruefully. What a pity she couldn't come right out and tell Claire the truth—that she wouldn't start an affair with Lawrence unless her life depended on it, and even then it would be a close call.

"I'll walk you through the main living areas of the house," Claire said finally, her tone of voice mildly hostile. "That way you'll have an overall idea of what wall space is available for the new paintings."

"Excellent suggestion," Melody said, and spent the next fifteen minutes trying to convince Claire that she had no designs either on Lawrence's body or his millions. It was amazingly difficult to do, she realized with silent amusement, when neither of them was prepared to acknowledge the game they were playing.

Even if she didn't have much taste in husbands, Claire had superb taste in decorating her house. She pointed out that the formal living room was already crowded with works of art, and the dining-room walls were covered in burgundy silk, which would overpower the delicate colors of the two paintings.

"If you don't want the pictures in the living room or the dining room, how about hanging the William Merritt Chase watercolor in the alcove at the end of the hallway leading to the master bedroom?" Melody suggested.

Claire shook her head. "There's already a Sevres vase on the console table in the alcove."

"That's true, but the wall itself is actually a little bare. With the special lighting you already have installed, that could be a very appealing spot for a floral study, don't you think?"

Claire considered for a moment. "You're right. That would be a good place for it, since we never put flowers in the vase, of course." She looked at Melody with grudging approval. "You have a good eye. I wouldn't have considered that alcove."

Melody smiled. "I'm glad you approve. So we have one down, and one to go. How about upstairs? Would you consider hanging the Prendergast in one of the guest bedrooms, or would you prefer it somewhere more people would be likely to see it?"

"I'm sure Larry would prefer to have it downstairs." Claire glanced down at the diamond Cartier watch on her wrist, then looked up with a genuinely apologetic smile. "I'm sorry to cut and run, but could you make the decision about the other painting yourself? You're the one with the professional expertise, after all."

"But it's your home, Mrs. Springer, and you'll have to live with the placement, not me."

"I trust your judgment, Melody, and I wouldn't say that to many people. Besides, I simply don't have time for this right now. My personal trainer will be here in ten minutes and then I'm leaving to go into the city." The faintest trace of color ran up into her cheeks. "I'm meeting an old college friend for lunch and I'm feeling pressed for time."

"I understand," Melody said, looking away from Claire's betraying blush, embarrassed by the transparency of her lie. "I have a good sense of what you like now, Mrs. Springer, and I'll be happy to take it from here."

"Thank you. If you need any help, just call Esperanza. She's wonderful."

What a complete farce the Springer marriage was,

Melody thought, watching Claire rush upstairs to get changed for her workout. Lawrence had spent eighty thousand bucks on a birthday gift, and Claire had thanked him with an openmouthed kiss, yet neither one of them had any intention of being faithful to the other. He felt up the hired help, and she slipped off to lunchtime assignations with "old college friends."

Still, Melody didn't have time to waste contemplating the ironies of the Springers' marriage. She needed to seize this gift of freedom from supervision and get busy exploring the layout of Lawrence's study. Could she risk searching a few drawers? Or checking Lawrence's laptop, if he'd left one lying around? Too dangerous, she decided. The laptop, if it contained anything useful, would undoubtedly be password-protected, and the desk drawers might be alarmed. She needed to have a friendly cup of coffee with Esperanza in the kitchen and check out the details of the security system before she started opening drawers. Then she needed to find out when the Springers both planned to be away from home for the night. Maybe Esperanza could help with that, too.

Melody got out her measuring tape, concentrating on the practical details of hanging the William Merritt Chase watercolor in the alcove. It was taking longer than she'd ever imagined to accumulate the information she needed to bring Wallis Beecham down, and she was getting impatient.

It was past time to bring reality to her favorite fantasy: turning on the television news and seeing her erstwhile father being led away in handcuffs.

Six

Nikolai Anwar, chief of operations for Unit One, made his way through the glittering and perfumed throng assembled in the grand ballroom of New York's Plaza hotel. The official purpose of the black tie event was to raise money for the restoration of the governor's mansion, although Nick doubted if many people in this sophisticated Manhattan crowd cared much about the repairs needed on a 150-year-old house located half a day's drive north of the city. These dyed-in-the-wool Manhattan sophisticates were more likely to take a trip to outer Mongolia than venture upstate to Albany.

Bree, a recent recruit to Unit One, walked at Nick's side, her hand tucked through his arm. She was fresh out of nine weeks of basic training, working her first assignment, and was so excited to be taking part in a real, honest-to-God mission that she practically vibrated. A passing waiter offered her his tray of hors d'oeuvres, and she helped herself to a stuffed mushroom cap. Nick foresaw disaster too late to take evasive action. Sure enough, her hand shook and she dropped hot cheese onto the sleeve of his dinner jacket.

Bree blushed bright scarlet, grabbing a paper napkin and dabbing at the mess. "I'm so sorry, sir—"

"Don't worry about it, *Callie*. It's nothing." Nick emphasized her cover name and fended off the dabbing napkin before she could turn a small stain into a giant grease spot. He smothered a sigh. They were supposed to be married, and she'd just called him sir. Added to which, his wig was making his head itch and his eyes ached from wearing tinted contact lenses for too many hours at a stretch. Wearing disguises wasn't usually part of his duties, but he couldn't afford to be recognized tonight.

"Tell me where you think we should go for our next vacation," he suggested, putting his arm around Bree and leading her deeper into the crowd where they were less conspicuous. "I might be able to swing an extra five days off at the end of next month and I feel in the mood for Mexico. How about you, honey?"

"Oh, yes, Mexico would be lovely."

As a conversation stopper, Bree's response was damn near perfect. Nick persevered. "Great. We've picked the country, now we have to choose west coast or east. Would you prefer Cancún or Acapulco? It's up to you, honey."

Bree suddenly overcame her verbal block and began to chatter nonstop about the wonders of Cancún. She'd been informed that her assignment was to create the impression that they were two well-heeled donors accustomed to contributing their time and money to worthy causes. She knew Nick was here to check out a person of interest to Unit One, but she didn't know who that person was. She had also been informed that the mission was strictly observational, but even that reassurance didn't seem enough to prevent her behaving as though any minute bullets were going to start flying.

Thank God they weren't doing anything remotely dangerous, Nick thought wryly, because nobody looking at them closely would believe for a minute that they were married. Bree radiated so much repressed tension that her cute auburn curls were practically bouncing. On a mission where they faced real hazards—let alone real bullets—she'd have sent clanging alarm signals to any target within a ten-foot radius.

Fortunately, this was such a simple assignment that Nick didn't need the cover she was supposed to provide. He'd brought Bree along for her sake, since she couldn't be field-certified without operational experience, and new graduates were always tested first in risk-free environments to limit the chance of unpleasant surprises later on. High scores on simulated practice missions didn't always translate into the ability to function in the field, as Bree's performance tonight proved.

She was a nice kid, Nick decided, responding to her prattle with the ease learned on a hundred past missions where his ability to play a role really mattered. Unfortunately, in the harsh environment of Unit One you needed more than niceness to succeed. He took two flutes of champagne and offered her one of them. She shot him an uncertain glance, clearly remembering the rules about not drinking while on assignment. Pretending not to notice her doubt, he lifted his flute and took a hefty swallow. He could almost see her wondering whether he expected her to follow his example and flout the rules. Luckily for her, she decided to play it safe.

"Thanks, but I'll stick with my ice water," she said, holding up her glass, the gesture awkward. The knowledge that she was acting a part distorted her body language and robbed her of the ability to behave naturally.

She was hopeless, Nick concluded, but she had enthusiasm and dedication, and he had a soft spot for those qualities even when the rest of the package was missing. "Right answer," he said very softly, and she flushed with relief that she hadn't blown it.

Bree made him feel about a hundred years old. And counting. Nick couldn't remember a time in his life when he'd been as naive as she was, even before his parents were assassinated. But perhaps that came from having a father who'd worked for the CIA and a mother who'd spent her youth working for the KGB. They both treated life in the American suburbs as a precarious gift that might be snatched away at any moment. As it had been, within days of his mother's cover being blown.

Flicking a mental switch, Nick steered away from the minefields of the past and refocused his thoughts on the task at hand. Aware that Bree was an only child, he asked if her sister was planning to come to New York this fall. She started to say that she didn't have a sister, then caught herself just in time.

Beyond hopeless, Nick decided. Bree would be given one more chance on an actual field mission, in part because the training she'd already received was so damned expensive, but unless she underwent an amazing transformation, she wasn't going to make the cut as a Unit One field operative.

Bree didn't follow up on his lead about a make-believe sister, which in other situations might have caused problems, but she finally managed to initiate a topic of her own, and was now telling him about the play she'd seen last night at a dinner theater off-off-Broadway. Something dire about the meaning of life as interpreted by a woman who was dying of AIDS.

Nick managed to appear fascinated, an acting feat of impressive proportions. It was time to close in on his quarry, he decided, chiefly because his boredom threshold had been breached ten minutes ago and he wanted to get the hell out of here. Besides, he had another assignment to complete tonight, an assignment that was neither risk free nor trivial and he needed time to focus.

He'd spotted Melody Beecham within seconds of entering the ballroom, although he'd made no effort to move toward her. But with the decision taken to approach her, he wove a seemingly random pattern through the crowds and in less than a minute he was close enough to overhear what she was saying.

She was chatting up Chester Bloom, the governor's chief of staff, and even making the guy laugh, quite an achievement given that Chester was as humorless as he was efficient. Of course, it wasn't difficult for Melody to charm people, Nick reflected. Especially men. Not only was her body the personification of male sexual fantasy, she had a smile that suggested you were the most interesting and desirable man she'd met in this lifetime. Add impeccable social graces to the package and most men parked their brains in their pants and forgot to notice that in addition to being beautiful, Melody was also exceptionally smart and about as pliable as a granite pillar.

Nick, who had taken the trouble to read her university transcripts, didn't make the mistake of underestimating Melody's intelligence. He wasn't taken in by her smile, either. He had the exact male equivalent in his arsenal and he knew just how little it meant except as a weapon to achieve his purposes.

This was the second evening he'd been assigned to observe Melody Beecham. Once again he felt a tightening in the pit of his stomach, a faint prickle of something he identified as irritation as he watched her charming the socks off her quarry. She was totally in control of the conversation with Chester, as she always seemed to be whenever he listened in. Apparently Melody Beecham didn't indulge in idle chitchat. By the time the conversation ended, the hard-nosed chief of staff had melted into warm putty and was promising to speak to the governor about the need to provide more funds for art education in the schools.

Her mission accomplished, Melody moved on. Nick followed at a discreet distance, keeping his arm around Bree's waist. Based on Bree's performance so far, he wouldn't put it past her to get lost if left untethered. He watched as Melody approached the chairman of the Stock Exchange and then the senior managing partner of Smith Kassen Lampton, one of the country's most successful investment groups. In both cases it appeared as if the meetings were accidental. In reality, the encounters were planned by Melody, Nick concluded. During both conversations she managed to slip in casual references to newly acquired paintings in the Van der Meer Gallery that she thought would appeal to the man she was talking to. The sales pitch was so subtle that even Nick wouldn't have realized what she was doing if he hadn't watched the process unfold brilliantly in front of him from start to finish. She was using the fund-raiser to work the crowd in the interests of the Van der Meer Gallery. He'd seen her pay stubs and knew that Jasper Fowles paid her really big bucks. Clearly, she earned them.

He'd seen everything he needed, Nick decided. He was more than ready to make his report to the director. Just as he was about to tell Bree he was ready to leave, Melody Beecham swung around and looked straight at him.

"I don't believe we've met," she said, bypassing the couple he'd carefully left as an intervening shield and confronting him head-on. "Did you want to speak to me?"

Nick was shocked that Melody had noticed him. He was flat-out stunned that she'd betrayed no sign that she was conscious of his presence until it suited her to do so. Even more than he prided himself on the ability to conduct invisible surveillance, he prided himself on his ability to read the most subtle clues in other people's body language. How in hell was it possible that he'd picked up no hint of awareness from Melody Beecham? Still, he was too experienced to be distracted by his own surprise, much less to betray even a glimmer of it.

He produced a smile from his repertoire, perfectly pitched between ingratiating and embarrassed. "Well, shoot, we've been caught out! I apologize for intruding, Ms. Beecham, but I'm such a fan I couldn't help hovering. My name's William Wolfe, and I'm with Jerrard & Colmes, the advertising agency. I'm the account executive for Infinity Cosmetics and I wanted to meet our most famous Infinity

Woman.'' He drew Bree forward, keeping her hand tucked through his arm for reassurance. The poor kid was truly shaking now. ''And this is Callie, my wife.''

''Hello, Ms. Beecham, it's great to meet you,'' Bree said stiffly. At least she'd managed to pick up on Nick's mention of Melody's name, which was one positive point to include in her evaluation.

''How do you do?'' Melody shook Bree's hand, giving her a pleasant smile, then immediately turned her gaze back to Nick. For him, he noticed, she didn't bother with her patented you're-the-only-man-in-the-universe gaze from her amazing violet-blue eyes.

''It's been almost eight years since my contract with Infinity expired,'' she said. ''I'm surprised you remember me, Mr. Wolfe. Eight years is a lifetime in the advertising world.''

''Not for the great campaigns,'' Nick replied easily. ''I've found real inspiration looking through some of the work our agency did when you were the Infinity Woman. Those ads for the 1996 Super Bowl were among the most creatively satisfying sixty-second spots ever produced by our agency.''

Melody's eyes glazed with boredom in response to his gushing, suggesting the information in Unit One's files was correct: she didn't look back on her years as a model with pleasure. The smile she finally directed toward Nick was polite but weary. ''Given your job, Mr. Wolfe, you of all people must know that I had nothing whatever to do with the creativity of those ads. I just turned up and stood around waiting to be photographed.''

He could argue with her about that. Even he knew

that the models who made it to the megastar level achieved by Melody Beecham didn't wait for other people to tell them how to pose. They had an ongoing love affair with the camera, and their passion not only shone through, it shone through with burning individuality. Melody might have followed a script and accepted tight direction when she worked for Infinity, but the appeal of those spectacular TV ads was at least as much hers as the producer's.

However, since his goal was to get out of here and be wiped from her memory, Nick accepted her comment as if he hadn't recognized it for the dismissive ploy that it was. "I'm sure you're being too modest, but I make it a rule never to argue with a lady." He held out his hand. "It's been a real pleasure meeting you, Ms. Beecham. You're even more lovely in real life than you are in your pictures."

She winced at his patronizing language and his clumsy compliment, Nick noticed. Which pleased him more than it should have, since no part of his agenda was advanced by tweaking Melody's sensibilities. His work here was done, and it was time to leave. Repeating his goodbyes, he took a firm grip on Bree's elbow and led her toward the exit.

It was a damn good thing he planned to recommend strongly against recruiting Melody Beecham to Unit One. The gnawing feeling she produced deep in his gut pissed him off big time. Nick wasn't used to feelings he couldn't control, especially in regard to a woman, and he didn't like the unfamiliar sensation one bit.

Nick was seated in a dimly lit corner of the Dublin Tavern in SoHo when Lawrence Springer arrived, shortly after eleven. Springer had donned a curly brown wig for the occasion, added a beard and padded his stomach so that he looked much heavier than he really was. As promised, he had a maroon silk scarf draped around his neck and he carried a copy of the *Wall Street Journal* so that he could be identified.

Nick was quite impressed by the disguise, which wasn't as complete as his own, but pretty effective nevertheless. Springer didn't have the resources to draw on that Nick did and yet Springer's wig didn't look fake, nor did the beard. If Nick hadn't already known precisely who he was dealing with, this meeting would provide few clues to help him find out. For an amateur, Springer had handled this whole negotiation pretty well.

Of course, Springer wasn't exactly an amateur. Nick had tracked him as the money man behind no less than three recent contract murders. The only reason Springer had gone looking for a new hit man was that Springer's previous assassin of choice had been eliminated. By Unit One.

Nick took a final swig of his Coke and watched as Springer glanced around the crowded room in an effort to identify the assassin he'd arranged to meet here. If Springer could pick him out of the crowd, then the guy ought to walk away from the deal right now, Nick thought with silent amusement. An assassin who stood out in a crowd wasn't worth the quarter of a million dollars Springer was willing to pay him.

Nick let Springer sweat for a few seconds, then got up and crossed to the bar. Standing behind

Springer, he spoke into his ear. "Don't look around. Choose a table, and I'll follow you over there."

Springer, of course, immediately looked around, but Nick had anticipated the move and had already melted into the anonymity of the crowd. Not at all pleased to find himself following orders rather than giving them, Springer scowled, but he selected a table by the door as instructed and sat down with his back to the wall, his gaze once again raking the room. He kept a briefcase—presumably holding the fifty-thousand-dollar down payment—clutched on his lap.

More to amuse himself than for any other reason, Nick kept out of sight as he made his way across the room, and was sliding into the bench opposite Springer before the man even realized he was there.

"I'm Harry," Nick said.

Springer glared at him. "You startled me."

Nick looked bored. "Is the money in the briefcase?"

Springer nodded.

"Unlock the briefcase, but don't open it," Nick ordered. "Then swing it around so that it's facing me."

Springer unlocked the briefcase, swiveling it around as instructed, with the key on top.

Nick pocketed the key, then waited to be sure they were unobserved before lifting the lid of the briefcase just far enough to check the contents. Used fifty-dollar bills were laid out in ten neat stacks. The money appeared to be all there, although he hadn't doubted that it would be. Springer was extremely anxious to have Kenneth Chung killed, and a fifty-thousand dollar prepayment was insignificant, given that Chung's death would bring Springer a payoff of more than a quarter of a billion dollars.

"I'm assuming you're too smart to have cheated me on the amount," Nick said, closing the briefcase. "It looks correct."

"Of course it's corr—"

Nick cut in. "Just so we understand each other, if this isn't the full prepayment, the job doesn't get done."

"It's all there," Springer said. "And while we're on the subject of conditions, *I'll* remind *you* that we're working on a tight schedule. I need action within forty-eight hours or less."

"You'll get it." Nick slid a scrap of paper across the table containing a typed e-mail address. "You can contact me here for confirmation that the job has been completed and I'll inform you where and how to make the final payment. The account will only be active for five hours between 1:00 and 6:00 p.m. on Friday, so make sure you don't miss the window or you won't know where to go to deliver the final payment." He spoke with deliberate blandness. "You really don't want to be late in making your final payment."

"I understand," Springer said, seemingly untroubled by Nick's implied threat. "Why do I need confirmation from you that the job's complete? Won't I read about your success in my favorite newspaper?"

"The media might not have time to report within the forty-eight-hour window. The e-mail address is a more accurate and reliable method of confirmation." He paused for emphasis. "As a guarantee that the job's been done, I will provide pictures."

Springer thought about that for a moment, then

nodded. "You don't look or sound the way I imagined."

Nick permitted himself a small, tight smile. "That's a plus in my trade."

Springer stared intently at Nick, as if trying to read in his face whether or not he could be trusted. "You come highly recommended," he said finally. "Are you sure you have everything under control? You know exactly where to find the…subject?"

"Your directions were clear. Everything is under control."

Springer looked as if he wanted to say something more but didn't quite know what. "There's a lot riding on this," he said finally. "You'd better be sure you don't fuck up."

"I never fuck up," Nick said. "That's a promise you can bank on."

Seven

Nick stepped off the elevator that had brought him from the warehouse situated on a busy street in Newark, New Jersey, down to the multilevel, 300,000-square-foot basement that housed Unit One's headquarters. He keyed in the day's entrance code, and as soon as the elevator doors opened he was confronted by Martin McShane, the agency's executive director.

"I need to talk to you!" McShane didn't bother with a greeting. It was barely seven-thirty, but the director was already wired on what was undoubtedly his fourth or fifth espresso of the day and he didn't have time to waste on social niceties. McShane was five feet three inches tall and weighed in at 115 pounds—if he wore his boots when he stepped on the scale. But what the director lacked in pounds and inches he made up for in energy.

"So what happened with Springer last night?" he demanded, propelling Nick into his office like a mouse triumphantly cornering the cat.

Nick put Springer's briefcase on the desk. "We closed the deal. I'm to kill Kenneth Chung within forty-eight hours. Actually it's now within thirty-nine hours."

McShane grunted by way of reaction, then nodded

toward the briefcase. "He brought you the down payment?"

Nick nodded. "Fifty thousand, as promised. I was about to check the money in with Accounting."

"Later." McShane's speech patterns became shorter as his concentration intensified.

"Here's the recording of my conversation with Springer." Nick took the tiny tape from his jacket pocket and pushed it across the desk toward his boss.

"Incriminating?"

"Not incriminating enough for a court case. Springer could be hiring me to find his missing granny or paint his garage for all this says to the contrary."

McShane shrugged. "Doesn't affect our plans. Moments like this, I'm real happy we work off the books and outside of FBI rules."

"You're always happy that we work outside of FBI rules."

McShane gave another grunt. He took the tape and tossed it into his In tray. "I'll listen to that later. Is the extraction team for Kenneth Chung ready to go? If he's supposed to be dead within thirty-nine hours, we need to get him out of Arkansas pretty damn quick."

"I'm finalizing arrangements this morning. We'll leave this afternoon."

"Have you decided on your personnel?"

"Dave would be my first choice, but he's in California working the Glasser case, so I'm taking Sam and Tony. I've scheduled a briefing with the two of them for thirteen hundred. The most complicated part is going to be arranging for a body to be identified as Chung's."

"Your plan for that?"

"We've got a corpse on ice. He was a vagrant, and nobody's been able to make an ID. The vagrant's body is going to be found on federal land, which takes care of the need to deal with local law enforcement. The feds will be provided with information that causes them to identify the body as Chung."

"Hmm. Chung's family?"

"Fortunately, he's a scientific genius who spends virtually his entire waking life in his lab. His wife divorced him ten years ago and there were no kids. His parents are dead. He's widely respected, but his supposed death isn't going to cause anyone extreme grief."

"Time of extraction?" McShane asked.

"The actual extraction will be at nineteen hundred. Chung thinks he's going to a private one-on-one dinner with Springer. We'll be there instead."

"Transportation?"

"We're flying to Arkansas this afternoon, using a Unit One plane. Lewis and Jose will be the pilots," Nick said.

McShane made no comment, which was his equivalent of a ringing endorsement of the plans. "What are you going to tell Chung when you take him?" he queried.

"Nothing," Nick said crisply. "We'll extract him first and make explanations later. Once he's safely on board the plane, I'll let him know that his life is in danger and he's being taken into protection not only for his own safety, but also to insure that the new electric car battery he's developed actually goes into production."

''How will you identify yourself and the other team members to Chung?''

''I decided to stick to the truth,'' Nick said. ''I'll tell him we're from a covert U.S. government agency and that we're going to keep him in a place of safety, with access to all the lab equipment he needs, until we're sure that his technology is sufficiently advanced to be patented, at which time he'll be free to sell his product on the open market. Chung's profile suggests that once he's back in a lab, he'll have zero interest in pressing for more information about the precise agency that put him there. We're talking your stereotypical obsessed scientist here.''

McShane sprang to his feet, energy and disgust radiating from him in equal portions. ''Make sure Chung knows that Lawrence Springer—his hero—is the person who ordered his murder.''

''I intend to. Don't worry. I'll make sure Chung understands that Lawrence Springer and his partners in the Bonita Project sold him out.'' Nick paused. ''And are taking more than a quarter-billion-dollar payoff from a group of Saudi Arabian princes to suppress development of his battery.'' Nick pushed back his chair, preparing to leave. ''Okay, that's about it for my report. I'll get started on the extraction pla—''

''Wait. Did you attend the governor's fund-raiser at the Plaza last night?'' McShane asked.

Nick nodded. ''Yes, and Melody Beecham was there, as anticipated. Bree Bennett isn't going to work out in the field, by the way.''

''Why not?'' McShane scowled and walked across to his espresso machine.

''Basically, she froze from a combination of excitement and nerves. On an assignment where success or failure hinged on her ability to think fast on her feet, she'd have been a disaster."

McShane busied himself with packing coffee into the espresso basket. "Pity. She performed well on basic training. Enthusiastic kid."

"Yeah, she struck me that way, too. I'll give her one more chance on a field mission, but I'm not optimistic. There's another really easy surveillance task coming up this afternoon. If there's no improvement, we'll transfer her to the Bureau. She was a slam-dunk recruit for them and they'll be glad to have her back."

"Security issues all taken care of?"

Nick nodded. "She's safe to release. She only has minimum information about the structure and operations of Unit One. She met Bob Spinard's people and various intelligence analysts, but she has no knowledge of who works for us in the field. Especially any of the agents using their own names and identities."

"Except you, of course." McShane frowned. "The fact that all recruits meet you is going to rise up and bite us on the ass one day, Nick."

Nick didn't deny what he knew was a valid point. "Maybe we should rethink my role as final screen for all new recruits. But in the meantime, whatever problems Bree has, she isn't a security risk."

"Okay, take your word for it. She's gone, then." McShane was protective of his agents from the moment they stepped through the doors on the first day of their training. He was also ruthless in getting rid of anyone who didn't make the grade. Bree was already dismissed from his thoughts.

He watched coal-black coffee hiss into his cup, sniffing appreciatively at the aroma. "And Melody Beecham? What's your assessment of her?"

"I recommend strongly against recruitment," Nick said, once again getting up to leave. "You'll have my written report before I leave on the Kenneth Chung extraction."

"Don't waste paper. Hate goddamn memos. And e-mail is worse. Tell me now."

Nick sat down again. "I agree with your assessment that we could potentially send Melody into situations and settings where right now we can only infiltrate our operatives as service people. Her social connections are top-drawer. She's attractive—"

"Not just attractive," McShane interjected. "Sexiest damn woman I ever laid eyes on."

"You think so?" Nick shrugged. "She strikes me as too self-controlled to be sexy."

"Then take yourself off field assignments, because you must be going blind."

Nick grinned. "If she can inspire you into speaking in whole sentences, Mac, then I'll accept that Melody Beecham is incredibly sexy. She's also intelligent, and she's accustomed to being in the public eye, so she has no trouble concealing what she's really thinking—"

"Those are all excellent reasons to recruit her," McShane pointed out. "When you take into account her connection to Wallis Beecham, it's a no-brainer to go after her. Why are you recommending the reverse?"

"Because in my judgment she would be incapable of working as part of a team. Consequently she would be a danger, especially in the field. On the other hand, if we keep her out of the field and confine her to a desk, then we negate the reasons we recruited her in the first place. Plus—and this is my biggest concern—if Melody Beecham ever decided to disobey orders, I believe she would be capable of concealing her intention until it was too late for us to realize we'd been betrayed."

McShane took a sip of his espresso, wincing pleasurably at the heat. "Takes an exceptional man or woman to conceal their intentions from you."

It pained him to acknowledge it, but Nick told the truth. "I believe Melody Beecham could do it," he said quietly. "Her connection to Wallis Beecham is valuable, but not enough to outweigh the inherent risks. Also, putting aside my objections for a moment, on a practical level, how do we recruit her? I can't imagine any way that she could be persuaded to cooperate with us."

"Blackmail usually works well," McShane said dryly.

"She's hardly the ideal candidate for blackmail," Nick responded with equal dryness. "Coercion tends to work better when you're dealing with recruits looking for a way to slither out of lifetime prison sentences."

"Find a way to exert some pressure," McShane said. "There's always a way."

"Set her up, you mean? Easier said than done. Besides, in my professional judgment, based on a close study of her file and my own observations, she's not the sort of woman who could be blackmailed into loyalty. She's stubborn, and any attempt at blackmail could easily reinforce her decision to oppose us any way she could."

"Once she understood the value of what we do, she might grow to love us," McShane said. "After all, we're very lovable folks down here."

Nick ignored the irony in his boss's voice. "The amount of information we give to operatives is always an issue for us, and we'd be taking a big risk in giving Melody sufficient information for her to be useful. I believe she'd be a constant source of potential danger to Unit One. I repeat my recommendation against recruitment, and I especially recommend against attempting blackmail as a recruitment device."

McShane hesitated, which was out of character. "What's up, Mac?" Nick asked.

"You're going to be overruled," McShane said finally. "The Commander wants her on board."

"The Commander?" Nick was startled. The Commander was a shadowy figure, not identified by any other name, who occupied himself with concerns of overall strategy and almost never got involved in the day-to-day details of running Unit One. "Why is he personally weighing in on the relatively minor matter of whether or not to recruit Melody Beecham?"

"He doesn't consider Wallis Beecham a minor matter—"

"Neither do I. But we can take care of Wallis without involving Melody Beecham."

McShane cocked an eyebrow. "You're a hell of a lot more sure of that than I am. Anyway, the Commander is convinced Melody is our best and fastest way to get to Wallis Beecham. Given that we've been trying to unravel Beecham's criminal enterprises for two years and we're not exactly speeding to success, the Commander's getting impatient to try a new route."

"Then the Commander needs to be a little more patient," Nick said. His respect for the judgment of a man whose input and experience was entirely theoretical was always ambivalent. On the subject of Wallis Beecham they'd already clashed several times.

"Beecham is a brilliant man, with a highly complex network of commercial activities stretching across several continents," Nick added. "It's easy to hide the occasional illegality. In addition, a lot of what he and his partners are doing is unethical, but borderline legal. And when he does something flat-out criminal, he tends to leave the dirty details to surrogates like Springer—"

"I'm aware of the difficulties and so is the Commander. But the need to expose Wallis Beecham for the corrupt man he is becomes more urgent as each month passes and he moves closer to his goal. That's why as soon as you've extracted Kenneth Chung and taken care of Lawrence Springer, you should start working on how we can recruit Melody Beecham."

"Is recruiting Melody Beecham a direct order, sir?"

"Yes. Find whatever you need to use against her and use it. We need her inside Unit One before the end of the month."

Nick shook his head in frustration. "Melody's been facing down the media since she was a three-month-old infant and her mother invited a tabloid reporter to her christening. She's not going to roll over because we take photos of her in bed with her married lover—"

"As you know, she doesn't currently have a lover, married or otherwise. Probably a plus from our point of view."

"Apart from Jasper Fowles, she doesn't have any friends, either. According to the dossier we've compiled, Melody Beecham has more friendly acquaintances than anyone in the world, with the possible exception of Elmo and Big Bird, but there are no intimate relationships in her life on this side of the Atlantic except for Fowles. How the hell do you blackmail somebody who has no intimates and whose entire life has been played out in glossy, four-color spreads?"

"That's what I like most about you, Nick. I know I can always count on you to define the precise problem and then find a way to nail it." McShane started work on yet another cup of espresso, a hint that he wasn't as unconcerned as he appeared. "I'll look forward to hearing your plans for recruiting Melody Beecham as soon as the Springer mission is complete."

"Yes, sir." Nick allowed himself the luxury of sounding as sour as he felt. It was rare for Mac to give him a direct order that ran counter to all of Nick's instincts. His gut told him Melody Beecham was trouble, and he had an extremely reliable gut.

Eight

It was shortly before midnight when Melody got off the subway in Queens and walked to the lockup garage she rented on Starr Avenue. The inconspicuous gray Ford Taurus she'd bought six months ago was housed inside, along with the equipment that she'd acquired during her previous forays into the world of breaking and entering. Those efforts at burglary had provided tantalizing confirmation that the Bonita Project involved Wallis Beecham, Lawrence Springer, Johnston Yates and Senator Lewis Cranford in a secret partnership, but Melody had been unable to penetrate the layers of concealment to discover what enterprise lay at the core of their joint venture. She wished her mother's notebooks had provided more and better clues, but Roz was scatter-brained by nature, and what's more, Melody suspected there had been an element of fear underlying her mother's deliberately cryptic jottings. Roz's request that Melody should use the Bonita Project to "go get Wallis Beecham" hadn't been backed up with enough data to make that possible.

Tonight Melody hoped finally to penetrate the obscurity. The adrenaline rush that came from being committed to action kept her heart thrumming and her senses in overdrive, but her mind was crystal clear and her emotions battened down under tight control.

She went through her mental checklist methodically, determined to avoid screwing up. It wasn't so much that she feared being caught and prosecuted as that she dreaded being prevented from exposing Wallis Beecham for the criminal she knew him to be. The knowledge that tonight she might take a big step forward in her quest to expose her onetime father was a potent high, but she controlled her excitement by channeling it into a fierce determination to succeed.

She was already dressed in the basics of her burglary outfit: a close-fitting black bodysuit teamed with black ski pants and special lightweight running shoes. For warmth once she reached Chappaqua, and to travel here on the subway, she'd concealed the curve-hugging spandex with a baggy flannel plaid shirt, and hidden her hair under a cap emblazoned with the logo of an electrical repair company. Nobody on the subway had paid her any attention, which Melody recognized was less of a tribute to her nondescript outfit than the fact that—since this was New York—she could probably have dyed her hair in scarlet and purple stripes and worn a neon-pink ballet tutu without attracting more than a couple of bored glances. Still, it never hurt to take extra precautions.

She checked to make sure that her latex gloves and black ski mask were in the pouch suspended under the front passenger seat, along with her illegal set of lock picks and the equally illegal, astonishingly expensive device that enabled her to deactivate electronic alarm systems. With the cap and flannel shirt folded on the seat beside her, she carefully reversed out of the garage and onto the street. This would definitely not be a good time to get stopped by a cop for careless driving.

At this hour of the night traffic was as light as it ever got on the routes out of the city, and less than an hour later she reached the Chappaqua automobile repair shop where she planned to leave her Taurus. She'd noticed on a trial run last night that there were several vehicles, presumably waiting for service, parked in the forecourt of this garage, which happened to be located conveniently close to the Springers' house.

She had worried the lot might be empty tonight since the weekend was ahead, but to her relief there were three cars and a couple of pickup trucks lined up outside the service bays. More than enough vehicles to provide the cover she needed for her Taurus.

Once again forcing herself not to rush, Melody checked for any sign of passersby before bending down to retrieve her supply pouch from under the seat. When she was sure there were no insomniac joggers or police squad cars in the vicinity, she buckled the slim pouch around her waist. It was black, like the rest of her outfit, and no thicker than a cummerbund. As soon as she put the flannel shirt back on it was invisible. Even if she was stopped by a cop—extremely unlikely given the cross-country route she planned to take to and from the Springer house—she might be able to talk her way out of trouble without the cop noticing anything sufficiently amiss to prompt him to do a body search. Her upper-crust British accent, which she could put on and take off at will, had a tendency to intimidate many Americans into believing whatever she chose to tell them.

Shirt buttons fastened, Melody shoved her ponytail under her cap and got out of the car, tucking the ignition key into a tiny inner pants pocket that closed with Velcro. Luckily for her, skiers as well as burglars needed somewhere to carry their car keys.

It took her twelve minutes to jog the mile and a half over the rough terrain between the repair shop and Lawrence Springer's house. If absolutely necessary, she could cut that time by more than two minutes on the return journey, and she could sprint a hundred meters in sixteen seconds over any stretches of flat ground. Not that she anticipated having to draw on her speed or her athletic abilities tonight. She would have failed badly in her planning if she needed to run.

Melody had managed to acquire a lot of useful information during the hours she'd spent pretending to select the best locations for hanging Claire's new paintings. She'd made friends with Esperanza, the housekeeper, and learned that Lawrence and Claire would be leaving Chappaqua this evening to attend the opening performance of a musical version of Shakespeare's *Taming of the Shrew*. Better yet, they planned to spend the night in town, at the Hotel Carlisle.

Esperanza wouldn't accompany them, of course, but fortunately she planned to have dinner at her daughter's brand-new apartment in Yonkers and then sleep over. Friday was her regular night off and Mr. Springer had specifically given his permission for her to visit her daughter even though that would mean leaving the Chappaqua house empty for twenty-four hours.

The contents of Lawrence Springer's personal filing system were about to be at her fingertips. Melody found it hard not to gloat at the success of her planning. All in all, she concluded, covering the last few yards of wooded area that separated her from the Springers' backyard, she was never likely to have a better chance than tonight to find out exactly what was going on with the Bonita Project. It was one thing to feel certain that Springer and Wallis Beecham's other partners were using the project as a cover for some illegal enterprise of breathtaking scope. It was another thing entirely to have adequate proof of her suspicions.

Although she usually managed to keep her expectations low in regard to Wallis Beecham, tonight Melody couldn't squash the hope that she might finally get the proof she needed to bring him down. At the very least, she expected to unearth useful clues as to where she should look next for ammunition to build her case.

She stopped at the edge of the woods, hiding in a tangle of undergrowth, the branches of an elm tree increasing the darkness of the area immediately around her. Letting her senses grow accustomed to the night sounds, she examined the rear of the Springer mansion. Then she strained her ears until she could distinguish the rustle of a small animal moving through the bracken from the rustle of wind stirring the dry autumn leaves. At that point she felt sufficiently in tune with her surroundings to be confident that she was the only human being hanging out in this neck of the woods.

She switched her attention to the security features of the house. As she had anticipated, the exterior lights rimming the perimeter of the building were on, making it impossible to cross from the woods to the house without being observed. Always providing, of course, that anyone was looking. Melody was counting on the fact that, since the house was empty and it was two in the morning, nobody would be looking. In addition to the perimeter lighting and the electronic alarm system, the side door and the separate service entrance both had security cameras in place. When she'd checked on Tuesday, the cameras had been operational and both had been capable of filming at night. She assumed they still were functional, but even if she was photographed, the record would show nothing except a shadowy figure wearing a face mask. Her bulky shirt, she hoped, might even disguise the fact that she was female.

Melody stuffed her cap into her shirt pocket and pulled on latex gloves and a thin knitted face mask that she'd made herself. The mask fitted so precisely that she got maximum range of vision and ability to breathe, combined with minimum exposure of her features. All those hours her nanny had spent teaching her to knit had finally come in handy, she reflected wryly.

Once she was confident that the mask covered every strand of her conspicuously blond hair, Melody moved silently around the outer edge of the Springers' backyard until she was directly opposite the side door, which was her chosen point of entry into the house. Then she stood still and just observed. A few dead leaves tumbled across the grass, stirred into an ethereal dance by the night breeze, but that was the only sign of movement she detected. Drawing a succession of deep breaths, she stepped out from the protection of the bushes and sprinted across the fifty yards of manicured lawn that separated her from the house.

No alarms went off. Nobody called out. Safe inside the overhang of the covered side porch, she didn't bother to check if the camera was working. Smashing it might trigger an alarm, a risk she didn't need to take as long as she kept her head low and her face covered. Cupping her electronic code reader in the palm of her hand, Melody quickly placed it over the security keypad and held it there. A red light on the reader blinked and she heard the distinctive electronic hum of the device attempting to override the setting of the electronic switches that controlled the alarm system. But after ninety seconds, instead of a green light flashing to tell her that the system was disarmed, her device continued to hum and whir, as if unable to detect the position of the internal switches it was attempting to neutralize.

Finally, when her stomach had tied itself into a giant knot of anxiety, a yellow light on the code reader blinked, then steadied into a continuous glow. A yellow light meant that her device had concluded the system was not armed and so there was nothing for it to override.

The knot in Melody's stomach pulled tighter. Was her alarm buster working properly? Or was it possible that the Springers had installed a security system that could defeat its capabilities? Or had the housekeeper simply forgotten to set the alarm on this rarely used door?

The last explanation was the one she would prefer, but it was the least likely of the three, Melody suspected. Under the guise of worrying about the safety of Claire's new paintings, she had asked Esperanza a lot of questions about the security system. The housekeeper had insisted that she and her employers were always careful to double-check that the system was properly armed after service crews had come into the house, and whenever any of the residents left. In fact, Esperanza had demonstrated to Melody that it was impossible to exit through any exterior door without a warning light flashing to indicate whether alarms on that and all the other exterior doors were properly activated.

It was possible that Esperanza had canceled the visit to her daughter's new apartment, meaning she was now sleeping upstairs in her bedroom over the garage. But given how adamant the housekeeper had been about the need for protection against thieves and wandering drug addicts, Melody thought it was unlikely Esperanza would have gone to bed without checking to make sure the security system was fully operational.

If her code buster was working correctly, Melody was left with three possible explanations: either there was a problem with the functioning of the Springers' security system or somebody had failed to set the alarm or something was going on that she didn't know about.

It was taking a huge risk to assume that Esperanza or the Springers had screwed up in setting the alarm. It was taking an equally huge risk to assume the system was malfunctioning. The only safe course of action at this point was to assume that something was going on that put her mission at risk. If an unknown factor outside her ability to control had entered into the calculus of risk and benefit, she needed to turn around right now and come back another night.

Except, Melody had no idea when she could return. She'd already used up her best chance to get inside information about the Springers' comings and goings, and that had taken weeks of careful planning to engineer. Springer wasn't going to be buying any more paintings in the next few months, and it wasn't as if she could call Esperanza out of the blue and ask when Lawrence and Claire would next be out of town for the night.

What she needed was more information about the situation inside the house, Melody decided. She pressed her ear against the opaque glass panel set into the door, straining to hear the slightest sound. After a minute or two, she gave up. This wasn't a cheap apartment; it was a well-constructed house with brick facing and top-quality insulation. The fact that she could hear absolutely nothing was no guarantee that there was nothing to hear.

Face it, you need to get the hell out of here before you and disaster meet head-on.

She couldn't stand here debating herself for many more seconds, but Melody wasn't quite ready to call it quits. If she started to pick the lock and the alarm went off, she could assume the cops wouldn't be here for at least nine minutes, which was the security company's guaranteed response time. Nine minutes was almost long enough for her to reach her car, and it was more than long enough for her to have disappeared from the scene of the crime. If the cops were busy checking out the house, how could they track her into the woods? She would be back on the highway before they even confirmed that the call wasn't a false alarm.

What the hell. Live a little and be prepared to run fast. The risk was worth taking.

Melody grabbed the door handle and turned it before she could second-guess herself yet again. The door didn't open, and she expelled a giant breath of relief both because no alarm bells went off and because the door was locked, precisely as it should be. Maybe Esperanza had simply been careless about the security system after all.

Emboldened, Melody switched on the flat pencil light strapped to the back of her wrist and pulled out one of her picks, starting to work gently on the tumblers of the lock under the narrow, high-intensity beam of the flashlight. In contrast to the twenty-first-century code buster she'd used to deactivate the alarm, the lock picks she was using hadn't changed much in the past 150 years.

She was getting pretty damn good at this breaking-and-entering business, Melody decided one minute and ten seconds later when she turned the handle and the door swung inward, its lock sprung. She stepped into the rear service hallway, opening her senses to the environment of the house as she let her body adjust to the pleasurable warmth after the chill of the September night air. A night-lighting system built into the baseboard kept the hallway illuminated just sufficiently to make walking toward the kitchen easy. She breathed the faint smell of lemon-scented cleanser and heard the rumble of the furnace kicking in somewhere in the basement.

So far everything was perfectly normal, she concluded, making her way silently through the kitchen and following another hallway into the main living section of the house. Despite the hiccup with the security system, there was no indication that she needed to cut her losses and sprint for the safety of her car.

That reassuring thought had barely formed when Melody reached the point where the service corridor passed through an arch into the formal atrium in the center of the house. She stopped abruptly, her adrenaline rush changing into a sickly sensation in the pit of her stomach.

Dammit, something wasn't right.

She scanned the atrium, trying to find the trigger that had sent her internal alarms to high alert, but everywhere looked just as she remembered. An elaborately carved front door marked the main entrance to the house, and the keypad next to it indicated the alarm was deactivated. The chandelier, large enough to illuminate Grand Central Station, hung serene and ghostly from the twenty-foot ceiling. Moonlight filtered through the two-story windows on either side of the front door, mingling with the soft glow of the night-lights and burnishing the polished wood floor. The bronze of a nineteenth-century cavalry officer stood on its slender pedestal in the center of the atrium, gleaming with a luminescence that was silvered by the moon. Nothing appeared out of the ordinary in the formal living room. There was no fire in the grate, which was laid with fresh logs, although the faintly acrid odor of burned wood lingered in the air. The dining room was equally nonthreatening, except for the huge Venetian-glass mirror over the sideboard, which reflected her image as an eerie black shadow against a gray background.

What was there in this elegant and peaceful scene to have her so spooked? Apparently something. Melody's skin was pricking and sweat was beginning to gather at the back of her neck beneath the knitted face mask. She strained to hear any sound, however faint, that would indicate she had rational cause to be worried, but she heard nothing beyond the normal creaks of a house at night.

She shook her head, suddenly impatient with herself. Enough already. She'd wasted almost two minutes triple-checking phantoms and it was time to move on. It was one thing to be cautious, another to be paranoid. Right now she wasn't demonstrating caution—she was blowing a unique opportunity to acquire information she badly needed to pursue her case against Wallis Beecham.

The library opened directly off the atrium to the left of the front door and she could see the oak paneling and shelves of leather-bound books through the double doors. She knew from her picture-hanging trip on Tuesday that Lawrence Springer's study was situated directly behind the library, accessible only by first passing through the library.

Her heart beating fast and hard, Melody crossed the atrium and stepped into the library. Once again she met with no surprises. The handsome fireplace was cold, the oversize leather chairs empty. What in hell had she expected? Lawrence Springer reading a magazine in the corner armchair, waiting to pounce on her?

She reached behind her head and patted the base of her face mask, so that the thin knitted wool absorbed the sweat that had begun to collect at the back of her neck. Between the latex gloves, the padded shirt and the mask, she was much too hot, which must be why she was sweating, something she rarely did unless she was exercising really hard. There were no internal security cameras in the house, and as soon as she reached the safety of Springer's study she would take off her face mask and cool down. Maybe the mere fact of being too hot was causing her uneasy feeling that something was seriously wrong.

Her rubber-soled shoes made no sound as she crossed to the pocket doors that separated Springer's study from the library. They were closed, but not locked. She pushed the left-hand door open, wincing when it grated on its metal runner, even though there was nobody to hear. Unlike the rest of the house, the study was pitch-black. Obviously the night-lighting system didn't extend into Springer's inner sanctum, and the heavy velvet drapes on the windows must be drawn so that no moonlight was getting in.

Melody switched on her flashlight so that she wouldn't be walking into darkness. The beam illuminated Lawrence Springer's desk and the English hunting scene by Alfred Munnings that hung behind it. She had a strong suspicion she would find a wall safe behind the Munnings, although she had no real hope that she'd be able to crack it in the time available to her. Pity. Springer's safe would probably provide a wealth of goodies for her Wallis Beecham investigation.

Satisfied that once again there were no surprises waiting ahead of her, she crossed to the desk and sat down in Springer's thickly cushioned leather chair, ripping off her face mask with a sigh of relief. Grateful for the sudden coolness, she lifted her ponytail, flipping it a couple of times to create a breeze, before leaning down to check the file drawer on the right-hand side of the desk.

A man's body lay sprawled on the floor less than a yard from her feet.

For a couple of seconds Melody couldn't breathe. Then she shoved the chair back and stood up, fighting the impulse to scream as air rushed back into her lungs. She directed her flashlight toward the body, her hand shaking.

The corpse lay facedown on the fancy Persian rug, his head surrounded by a halo of bright red blood. His head was turned sideways and Melody could see enough of his features to be sure that she was looking at the mortal remains of Lawrence Springer. Even from where she was standing she could see that he was very, very dead.

Nine

Melody Beecham. Jesus Christ, the intruder was Melody Beecham! What the hell was she doing here?

Years of training kept Nick from expressing his shock by even the slightest sound or movement of his body. From his cramped hiding spot wedged between the end of the bookcase and a jutting angle of the study wall, he watched as Melody shoved the chair away from the desk and stared in paralyzed horror at Springer's body. She swallowed a couple of times, and for a moment it was clearly touch and go as to whether she'd throw up.

But she pressed her hands against her stomach and quite soon forced herself back under control. With visible reluctance she knelt beside Springer and lifted his wrist, feeling for a pulse, perhaps to reassure herself that she had no obligation to call the paramedics. Satisfied that he was as dead as he looked, she drew in a shuddering breath, brushed her hand over Springer's eyelids to close them, then jumped to her feet and sprinted for the door.

He could just let her go, or…

Nick erupted out of his hiding place and chased Melody down the kitchen corridor without consciously realizing what his plan was. Sam and Tony had worked with him often enough that he didn't need to tell them to follow. He heard their footsteps pursuing him down the hallway as he put on a final burst of speed, bringing Melody down a couple of yards before she reached the side door.

He straddled her while he tied her hands behind her back. She was panting, and her hands trembled as he tied them, but she didn't struggle. Only because she was biding her time, Nick guessed. He could feel her muscles coiling, ready to spring, and he judged she was planning to fight back the moment he released his grip.

Just to see what she was capable of, Nick stood up without signaling Sam or Tony to keep her pinned to the floor. She moved even more quickly than he'd expected, rolling onto her back and jackknifing upright in two swift moves. She must have seen at once that she was opposed by three men, all armed, but the strength of the opposition didn't stop her fighting. Her left leg swung out in a karate kick that Nick dodged easily, although he gave her credit for trying.

He didn't fight back, just waited to see her next move. With her hands tied behind her back, she was off balance after kicking, and she lurched backward, hitting the wall. With surprising skill she used the wall to balance herself and spun quickly, coming back with another kick that was more powerful than the first, since she had the wall to use as a springboard.

But Nick had seen enough. Melody had guts and some training, but her skill level was strictly amateur hour. He sidestepped the arc of her kick, and used her own weight and forward propulsion to send her crashing to the floor with a single flip of his arm.

Then he motioned to Sam and Tony, signaling that they should take charge of her.

Melody was winded by the fall, in no condition to put up any resistance as Sam and Tony hauled her to her feet and clamped her between their bodies, holding her immobile as they waited for his orders. She met his eyes with a gaze that he could see, even in this subdued light, flashed defiance. For a woman who must believe that she was surrounded by three ruthless killers, she was holding up pretty damn well. He ought to have been pleased that she was showing every quality that was desirable in a potential field agent. Instead, he felt a disquieting certainty that recruiting Melody Beecham for Unit One was potentially a huge mistake.

Still, he'd had orders that came direct from the Commander and—God knew—there was never going to be a better chance for coercion than the one that had just fallen into his lap. Talk about a target of opportunity, he thought wryly.

"Take her to the van," he said, pulling his gaze away from Melody's with more difficulty than he would have liked. He preferred his women dark, petite and pliable. Melody struck out on all three counts and yet she was like an itch deep under his skin that he constantly felt the urge to scratch. He nodded to Sam and Tony. "I'll finish up in the study and join you in ten minutes."

Sam acknowledged the order with a casual salute, and Melody finally spoke. "Working on another advertising campaign, Mr. Wolfe? This one must be a real doozy." Her voice shook a little, but only if you knew how self-assured she usually sounded.

Nick was stunned that she'd recognized him, considering that he'd been wearing a wig and colored lenses on the only occasion she'd seen him. He was also impressed with her ability to recall a name that she couldn't have had any special reason to remember, especially given the pressure she was under. Still, it wasn't part of the plan taking shape in his head to do or say anything that might offer her reassurance.

"My name isn't William Wolfe," he said.

"Well, color me amazed. I'd never have guessed."

He turned away again so that she wouldn't see the flash of reluctant amusement in his eyes. "If there's no car parked outside, find out how she got here," he said to Sam.

He returned to the study, making a final sweeping check that he and his team had left no trace of their presence for the cops to find when they let loose their forensic experts at the scene of Springer's murder. His team had been right on the brink of finishing their search of Springer's study when Tony, whose hearing was incredibly acute, had signaled the presence of an intruder. They'd had less than a minute to find somewhere to hide and to douse their powerful flashlights before Melody came into the study.

Nick's final move was to unload the film from the hidden camera, focused directly on Springer's desk and concealed within a hollowed-out volume of Robert Frost's collected poems. It was a good thing Claire, in a burst of postcoital intimacy, had told him about her husband's fetish for cameras hidden all over their homes, or Nick would never have conducted the thorough search of the study that revealed the camera's placement.

Satisfied that he'd left no clues to their presence for the cops to follow up, Nick turned the night-lighting system in the study back on and hurried to join his teammates for the return drive to Unit One headquarters.

Nick slept for three hours, took a shower and by seven-thirty was in the observation room outside the cell where he'd stashed Melody Beecham. Between the Kenneth Chung extraction in Arkansas, his various assignations with Claire Springer and last night's mission to Chappaqua, he'd had precisely nine hours of sleep in the past forty-eight hours. He felt like hell, and that was just physically. His mood was several degrees worse. He flicked on one of the monitors and stared broodingly at the image of Melody Beecham, who'd been mildly sedated for the journey back to New Jersey and was still sleeping.

Martin McShane joined him in the observation room. As a gesture of exceptional goodwill, he'd even brought Nick a cup of his own private blend of espresso. Nick sipped gratefully—the guy really knew how to make coffee—as McShane sat down in front of a monitor and watched Melody Beecham in silence for a full minute. For all his restless energy, McShane wasn't a man to speak first and think afterward.

"What made you bring her in?" he asked Nick.

"I had to make a lightning decision when she turned up at Springer's house last night."

"She saw you? Sam? Tony?"

Nick shook his head. "She saw Springer's body on the floor and immediately started to run away, so I could have let her go and she'd have been none the wiser. Instead, I decided we were never going to have a more perfect chance to coerce her into cooperating with us. So I grabbed her."

"Hmm. Precisely how will you coerce her?"

"I intend to frame her for Springer's murder."

McShane looked as close to congratulatory as he ever got. "The Commander will be pleased," he said. He didn't ask any of the obvious questions as to what in the world Melody had been doing burglarizing Lawrence Springer's study. At this point, without having interrogated Melody, Nick's answers would be speculation and a waste of both their times. "Who have you assigned as her training mentor?" he asked.

It was a moment before Nick replied. "Nobody as yet."

McShane raised a bushy eyebrow. "Why not?"

"Because I'm considering letting her go."

"Damn foolish thing to consider."

"On the contrary. I'm director of operations, and I'm responsible for the safety of the teams we send into the field. I remain convinced that she's an operational risk."

McShane's entire face wriggled in disagreement. "Letting her go now would itself be a risk."

"We sedated her as soon as we had her in the van, so she's seen nothing—"

"Except your faces," McShane said. "Not exactly a minor detail."

Especially since she'd recognized him as William Wolfe, Nick conceded silently. He lifted his shoulders, shrugging off his own doubts as much as McShane's. "Why is that important? We have plenty of established protocols to explain away anything and everything.''

''You move in the same circles she does. There's a huge risk that she'll meet you one day as Nikolai Anwar, Russian entrepreneur.''

Nick conceded the point by his silence.

''You had a choice last night and decided to take her,'' McShane said. ''Why are you changing your mind less than six hours later?''

''Because this morning I'm remembering all the reasons Melody Beecham will be difficult, if not impossible, to train.''

''Then do the training yourself,'' McShane said. ''You could train a poodle to believe it's a great Dane if you set your mind to it.''

Nick hadn't personally supervised an operative's training since he became director of operations four years ago, and Melody's relations with her colleagues within Unit One wouldn't be any easier if she became the first exception. He looked back at the monitor. Melody was just beginning to wake up.

''I'll take your suggestion under advisement,'' he said.

McShane nodded, but didn't press the issue. ''I'm curious to see how long it takes her to escape from the cell.'' He watched intently as Melody sat up and rubbed her eyes. ''What's the average time for the last ten recruits?''

''Just under three hours,'' Nick said. ''As you know, the problem isn't finding the way out. It's the need to control their claustrophobia, especially when the lights go out, combined with misdirected efforts, such as wasting time trying to make tools and weapons. Or drinking the water, which makes them too woozy to think clearly for at least a couple of hours."

"Typical recruits know they're on the first task of their training regimen, which tends to give them a certain mind-set," McShane said.

"Melody's situation is more difficult," Nick acknowledged. "She has no idea where she is or what's happening, and that will increase her panic factor. For all she knows, breaking out of the cell could be a life-threatening endeavor."

"So you think it will take her longer than three hours?" McShane asked, watching Melody, who was already prowling around the holding cell, checking methodically for a door in the seemingly smooth walls of her prison.

"No, actually I don't."

McShane glanced at his watch. "It's a few minutes before eight. A hundred bucks says she's out of there before ten."

Nick gave a tight smile. "A hundred bucks says she's out of there within the hour."

McShane cocked his head. "That good, eh?"

"That dangerous," Nick replied grimly.

Ten

If she hadn't been so completely furious with herself, Melody might have felt scared. Or at least seriously claustrophobic. If her mood had been anywhere close to normal, she would certainly have experienced more than a touch of panic on waking up and finding herself encased in what amounted to a smooth white box with no visible means of entrance or exit. As it was, fear and panic were both swept away by a flood of anger.

Her rage was directed exclusively at herself. How could she have been so rock-solid stupid? She was in this mess for two simple reasons. First because she'd neglected to follow up on her suspicion that William Wolfe was either something more or something less than a gushing fan left over from her modeling days. Dammit, she'd never even made a quick phone call to Jerrard & Colmes, the ad agency he'd claimed to work for. She hadn't bothered to check his credentials, despite alarm bells clanging at high volume with the warning that he was lying.

But more important, she was furious that she'd gone ahead with her attempted search of Lawrence Springer's study when every instinct had warned that she should back off. In all these months of pursuing Wallis Beecham, if there was one thing she'd learned it was that her instincts were better than a canary in a mine for alerting her to potential danger. And yet she'd ignored her instincts. *Stupid!*

Melody prowled around her prison, searching for a more constructive way to channel her rage than pounding the walls and yelling in frustration, which was what she felt like doing. Her captors had taken her watch, her shirt, her cap, her face mask and her cummerbund with all its useful tools. But she'd been left with her bodysuit and her ski pants, as well as her sneakers, which provided a touch of welcome familiarity in a room that felt alien in its oppressive silence and its eerie absence of decorative features.

She started jogging in place, throwing in a few jumping jacks, in part to work off steam, but more to reassure herself that she could move without pain. Aside from a couple of sore spots on her hipbone where Wolfe had brought her down in the hallway, she didn't seem to have any injuries, so she probably hadn't been handled roughly while she was unconscious. She wondered how long she'd been sleeping, and what day—or night—it was. She felt thirsty, but not hungry, and she wasn't desperate to find a bathroom, which suggested she'd been out of it for no more than a few hours. Still, it seemed a smart idea to find a way to escape before thirst, hunger or the need for a bathroom became urgent.

Escape was a great idea, but not a very promising possibility. Quite apart from what she might find lying in wait outside the room, the cell itself made for an effective fortress. Her prison was a cube, as high as it was wide and long, with fake marble walls that resembled the interior of a cheap motel bathroom, the sort made out of molded plastic to save money on tiles. But unlike a motel bathroom, the hard plastic surface continued seamlessly upward to form the ceiling. Even the floor was covered in the identical shiny substance, the white background swirled with clouds of beige and networked by spidery gold veins.

Based on her own height of five foot seven, Melody estimated that her prison was seven feet by seven by seven. Too small for exercise, other than push-ups or running in place, but not so tiny that she couldn't stretch her arms to their fullest extension without her fingertips touching the walls.

As for furniture, there was very little. When she woke up she'd been lying on a low-slung cot, with the mattress covered by a clean white sheet and a cotton blanket folded over her fully clothed body. There was no pillow, but the foam mattress was thick enough that she'd slept in reasonable comfort. Lights, not very bright and protected by mesh metal grilles, shone from three corners of the room, the fixtures attached exactly at the point where the walls flowed into the ceiling.

On the opposite side of the room from the cot a Formica table was pushed against the wall. An orange plastic chair, so battered and uncomfortable looking that it appeared as if it might have been rescued from the waiting room of the Department of Motor Vehicles, was tucked neatly under the table. A tray resting on top of the table contained a tall beaker of water and four bite-sized oatmeal raisin cookies set out on a paper plate. There was an ominous green plastic pail stuck in a corner of the room, the function of which she preferred not to contemplate.

Melody wasn't desperate enough—yet—to drink

the water, much less nibble on the cookies, either or both of which might easily be drugged, a definite possibility in view of the fact that she'd been injected with something that knocked her unconscious the moment she stepped inside Wolfe's van. Despite that, she was careful not to spill the water when she set the tray on the floor. She might remain imprisoned long enough to risk the chance of being drugged in exchange for liquid.

The water safely stowed, she turned the table and chair upside down to check how difficult it would be to unscrew the metal legs for use as a weapon or a tool. Pretty difficult, she concluded, but not impossible. The chair had one rickety leg that looked especially promising in terms of removal. Unscrewing it would be beyond her capabilities since she had no tools, but she could stand on the upturned seat and maneuver the leg back and forth until—given enough time—she might be able to tear the wobbly leg away from its metal moorings by brute force. If there was a door hidden behind the walls, she could use the chair leg as a crowbar to gouge a hole, then rip off the Formica shell.

Before she expended that much time and effort, though, she needed to know how much help a metal chair leg would provide in breaking her out of this prison. No point in wasting an hour or more acquiring a tool she then had no use for. Her first task had to be finding the door.

Using the cot as a marker to identify her starting point, Melody made her way around the walls searching for any sign, however subtle, of a concealed opening big enough for a person to squeeze through. She methodically tapped every six inches or so, listening for any change in the sound that might suggest a hollowness behind the facade. When that produced no results, she started over again, pressing at regular intervals to see if there was a spring that might magically unlock a hidden panel in the wall that was somehow invisible to the naked eye.

The activity was mindless enough that she had plenty of time to speculate about where she was and why she was being held captive. Who was William Wolfe, or whatever his name really was? And why had he taken her prisoner?

Melody had no more success answering that question than she did in finding a hidden door, but her anger gradually shifted away from herself and focused instead on Wolfe. Did he plan to kill her? He and his two cronies had presumably shot Lawrence Springer, but that didn't necessarily mean they planned to kill her, too. In fact, the evidence suggested the opposite. Wolfe could have ignored her last night. She certainly hadn't noticed him, so she'd posed no risk to his getaway from the murder scene. Or he could have shot her and gotten rid of her body simply by dumping it in the study next to Lawrence Springer's. What with her handmade custom face mask and the incriminating tools in her cummerbund, the police would have had strong reasons to suspect that she and Springer shot each other during the course of a burglary gone wrong.

Not only had Wolfe failed to seize the chance to get rid of her, he'd chosen not to murder her while she slept. Did that make it safe to conclude he'd brought her here for some other reason than a desire to kill her?

Probably, she decided. So if he wasn't planning

murder, did he have rape in mind? Melody shook her head. Rape struck her as even less likely than murder. Neither Wolfe nor the two other men had made any sexually suggestive moves toward her. Besides, if they'd been in a raping mood, wouldn't they have assaulted her right there in Springer's house? Or at least in the van as they drove to...wherever they'd driven to? Why would they wait?

On top of that, this eerie prison struck her as a bizarre puzzle she was expected to solve rather than the sort of torture chamber in which sexual psychopaths stashed their victims. If Wolfe and his cronies had constructed this creepy room as a haven where they indulged in forced sex, surely they would at least have provided a bigger bed?

But rape was supposedly about power, not sexual gratification, and there was no denying that this room was perfectly designed to inspire a sense of utter powerlessness. Melody couldn't think of anything much more intimidating than being trapped in a claustrophobic cube with no visible means of getting out. Still, unless the room had been built around her while she slept, the lack of a door had to be illusion, not reality. There must be some form of egress; otherwise her captors couldn't get in any more than she could get out.

She wished that last thought hadn't occurred to her. If her captors couldn't get in, there was no chance of being raped, but her fate would be something even worse. What if there truly was no way in or out of the room? For a few seconds panic swamped her as Melody considered the possibility that she'd been captured by madmen who had entombed her in a Formica coffin and were planning to entertain themselves by waiting for her to go insane as she died of thirst and starvation.

The only way to fight against the mind-numbing terror of that possibility was to get busy. Melody climbed onto the table to check out the ceiling. Unfortunately, it turned out to be as smooth and seamless as it appeared from the ground. Which meant that she wasn't going to find an easy escape route by removing a cleverly camouflaged section of ceiling and clambering through the ductwork to freedom.

But even if there was no ductwork in the ceiling, there must be ventilation somewhere in the room, Melody realized belatedly. Without it, she would be on the verge of passing out by now. Since she felt fine, there had to be an adequate source of fresh air. There were no grates in the floor, ceiling or walls, so the only possible source for air inflow had to be outlets tucked alongside the light fixtures and concealed behind the protective metal grilles.

Melody vaulted off the table and dragged the chair a couple of feet over to the corner so that she could check out one of the lights, eyeball to lightbulb. From close quarters she saw at once that the fixture served a double purpose. A camera lens poked through the wall next to the eight-watt lightbulb, easy to overlook behind the fancy metal grille. The lens was directed toward the table, and probably covered half the small room in its visual field.

Not allowing herself to display any reaction to her discovery—hell, she didn't plan to provide any more entertainment for Wolfe than she had to—Melody inspected the two other light fixtures. In the second corner she found an air inflow valve that was pumping significant amounts of fresh air into the room.

And in the third corner there was an air return sucking out stale air, plus another camera, this one angled toward the bed.

Melody sat down on the chair, heart pounding. Okay, so she was being watched, but that didn't necessarily mean her captors were a trio of psychopaths who got off on seeing their victims starve to death in a sealed tomb. Psychos always wanted to interact personally with their victims so that they could justify their behavior, and watching her on camera wouldn't be sufficient to feed their pathology. She was sure she'd seen a program on TV about that precise subject only a couple of weeks ago.

Besides, sexual predators followed their victims for months because planning the kidnapping and murder was an important part of how they got their kicks. Her capture, by contrast, must have been a spur-of-the-moment decision. It was reassuring to remind herself there was no way Wolfe and his sidekicks could have known she would be at Springer's house last night, so they couldn't possibly have planned to ambush her.

On the other hand Wolfe *had* followed her to the fund-raiser at the Plaza, Melody reflected. That was the first time she'd noticed him, but he could have been stalking her for weeks. Or even months.

Okay, stop scaring yourself to death, kiddo. Switch back to the power of positive thinking. Visualize doors leading out of this damn room. Visualize freedom.

That was a great idea, but hard to follow. Melody drew in a breath that was a lot shakier than she would have liked, then forced herself to think rationally.

First, assume there's a way out of this room. Sec-

ond, find it. And find it pretty damn quick before you spook yourself into a state of such terror that you're nonfunctional. That's what this room is all about—scaring you to the point that you behave irrationally. Forget scared and focus on solving the puzzle.

For a start, she could cover those damn cameras and get some privacy. Melody hung the bedsheet over one corner fixture and the blanket over the other. She immediately felt a whole lot better. Now that he couldn't spy on her, maybe Wolfe would be sufficiently annoyed to come in. Which would be great, because his entrance would not only reveal the location of the door, it would also give her a chance to tell him exactly what she thought of him. And man, would she give him an earful. The prospect of delivering a tongue-lashing to William Wolfe was so pleasurable she actually smiled.

Unfortunately, nobody came in. Instead, the lights went out, plunging the room into a blackness so profound that it felt more like the positive presence of darkness as opposed to the mere absence of light.

Melody swallowed hard. *Okay, Wolfe, so you're punishing me for covering the cameras. But that doesn't change the fact that you still can't see what I'm doing right now. Stalemate, Billy boy.*

She wished she were doing something really clever and daring instead of hurling childish insults toward a man she couldn't see. Sadly, her words were a lot braver than her stomach, which was churning with enough fervor to convince her that, stalemate or not, she was pretty damn scared. Legs shaking, she fumbled around in search of the chair, sitting down as soon as her hands reconnected with the seat. She was afraid to move the chair in case she knocked over the tumbler of water. It was beginning to seem unpleasantly likely that she would need the water, drugged or not.

The blackness pressed down on her, a physical weight smothering her face. Melody knew she wouldn't be able to endure this preternatural darkness, coupled with total silence, for very long. It was disorienting to the point that she had to grip the sides of the chair to counteract the bewildering sensation of forgetting which way was up.

The darkness got thicker. Her throat tightened, constricting to the point where breathing was impossible, and she hurriedly closed her eyes so that she wouldn't see the darkness. That was a little better, thank God. She began reciting multiplication tables, starting with twelve and ending with fourteen. Who knew that it was so difficult to work out thirteen times thirteen?

The threatening wave of claustrophobia finally receded and her throat relaxed enough for her to drag in a huge gulp of air. That in itself was reassuring. At least oxygen still seemed to be flowing freely, suggesting that her captors didn't plan to torture her physically. Everything, in fact, suggested that their goal was merely her mental disintegration.

And, hell, she wasn't going to disintegrate to please William Wolfe. She was going to keep her cool if it killed her. *Count on it, Billy boy.*

If she took the covers off the cameras, she suspected the lights would come back on, but be damned if she was going to surrender to Wolfe's coercion this fast. She'd wait him out. Eventually he'd get worried enough to come and check on her. Wouldn't he? But while she waited, she could still try to escape. For a moment Melody indulged herself with the happy fantasy of Wolfe coming into the room to check on his prisoner and discovering she was gone.

Inspired by the prospect of such blissful revenge, she pressed her fingers against her eyelids and brought a picture of the room into her mind's eye: tiny pipes next to tiny lights and tiny cameras, the entire fixture no more than four inches in diameter. Clearly no escape route there. Seamless walls and a ceiling that provided no possible place for a door to be concealed. Same smooth plastic surface on the floor.

Except that the floor wasn't quite the same as the ceiling and the walls, Melody realized. She sat up straighter, energized by the sudden insight that although the floor was as smooth and slippery as the walls and ceiling, it wasn't seamless. Now that she was seeing the room only in her mind's eye, her memory was projecting images of a thin black line where the walls joined the floor. Such a join would be logical in terms of construction, since the floor must have existed first and the preformed cube would have been set on top of it, then bolted into position on the outside.

She needed to confirm that there really was a join where the walls and floor met. Slipping off the chair, Melody lay stomach down on the floor and touched her cheek to the surface. It felt less rigid than she'd expected, and when she stretched out her hand to the place where wall and floor met, she discovered a gap into which she could insert her thumbnail. The gap, however, was no more than a sixteenth of an inch.

Not exactly an instant escape route, she thought wryly, unless you were a flea.

Sitting up cross-legged, Melody pressed her spine against the wall to keep herself oriented. When she'd put her cheek to the floor, she had felt a slight give in the surface. If the floor was covered in a sheet of linoleum carefully designed to appear identical to the rigid plastic walls and ceiling, that would explain why her captors hadn't removed her sneakers along with her cummerbund and other gear. They didn't want her walking barefoot and immediately sensing a subtle difference in texture.

The good news was that if the floor was covered by linoleum, she could surely find a way to rip it up. It might take a while, but she could do it. And once the linoleum was ripped up, Melody was betting she'd find a trapdoor set into the subfloor.

The bad news was that she couldn't check out her theory without light. She was going to have to remove the covers from the cameras and let Wolfe back into the room, at least visually. But making that much of a concession to her tormentor was a small price to pay for getting out of this damned prison, Melody decided.

She edged around the wall until she felt the blanket flap against her face. She pulled it down from the camera and waited a full thirty seconds, but no lights came back on. Gritting her teeth, refusing to consider that Wolfe might be planning to punish her with hours of light deprivation, she made her way to the second camera and pulled off the sheet.

The lights, such as they were, came on as if she'd flicked a switch. To hell with not providing her captors with entertainment. Sticking her thumbs in her ears, she poked out her tongue and waggled her fingers at the camera, a better release from tension than breaking down and sobbing tears of hysterical relief that the blackness had been banished.

Melody realized she was sick and tired of playing games with Wolfe. She wanted out of here in the worst way, not least so that she could inform Billy boy in person that he was a royal pain in the ass. Hands on hips, she surveyed the room one more time. If there was a door in the floor, the most likely place to find it would be under the cot, which rose barely nine inches from the ground, making it difficult to see what lay beneath. Impatient as much as anxious, she pulled the cot away from the wall, annoyed with herself for taking so long to do something so obvious.

She was rewarded with the sight of a shiny white, beige and gold surface that looked precisely like the floor in the rest of the room. There wasn't even a dust bunny for company. Besides, the way out couldn't be a trapdoor located anywhere around or beneath the bed, she realized belatedly. The cot sat low to the ground and rested flush against the wall. Whoever had placed her unconscious body on the cot wouldn't have been able to get out if the escape route were located beneath the bed.

Despair grabbed her again, but Melody pushed it away. Bloody hell, there *is* a door in this room, Melody told herself. Start from that premise and just find the damn thing. Her gaze roamed the room, her eyes narrowed in concentration.

The bed occupied one corner, the table and chair another. The hideous puke-green pail stood in the third corner. She'd put the tray of water and cookies in the fourth corner. Logically, if her captors had sealed the room after they left her asleep on the cot, the way out had to be in the only section of the room that had been empty when she first regained consciousness.

Melody picked up the tray of cookies and water and set it back on the table, returning the corner to its original state of emptiness. She knelt, feeling her way over the floor, searching for any difference—however small—that she could see or touch. The dim light made her task extra difficult, but she kept up her spirits by leaning back on her heels and muttering curses about Wolfe every few inches or so.

Her gaze sharpened when she finally spotted a tiny deviation in the pattern, not in the floor itself, but in the wall, close to ground level. A gold vein swirled through the splotches of being-and-white marbleized wall some seven inches above ground level. The spidery gold thread was longer than most, and it was internally bisected by a thin black line. A black line that wasn't an integral part of the pattern anywhere else in the room, Melody realized with a sensation of sheer, exhilarating triumph. The dim lighting made it extraordinarily hard to detect, but now her eye had picked it out, she could see that the black line was another seam, albeit a crooked one, and it ran for at least ten inches along the wall.

She knelt in front of the suspicious crack and resumed her earlier tactic of pressing for a hidden spring, starting in the right-hand top corner and progressing slowly downward and across. It took her barely a minute to find the spring. She heard a click and a section of the wall sprang inward, the hinged opening exactly following the seam inside the gold spider vein, leaving an opening like a piece taken out of a giant jigsaw puzzle.

Melody's mouth stretched into a silly grin. She crunched down and peered into the ten-by-seven-inch opening, feeling a bit like Alice in Wonderland when she'd eaten too much magic mushroom. Inside the opening, sitting on top of a neat square of bright green felt, there was a knife of the sort used by carpet and linoleum installers.

The gift of a knife seemed almost too easy after the difficulty of everything that had gone before. Could it be a trap? But Melody barely hesitated before reaching in and grabbing the knife. Sometimes you could be too smart, she decided.

Not wasting another moment, she made a slashing diagonal cut through the flooring. The knife, wickedly sharp, cut through the linoleum with relative ease. She made another diagonal slash to intersect with the first.

The linoleum was only loosely attached to the subfloor in this area, Melody discovered. Panting, she tugged and ripped, continuing doggedly until she could tug back the triangles made by her cuts.

A trapdoor lay beneath the linoleum. The roughly varnished wood, with a metal latch fitted into a shallow groove so that it would be undetectable by touch through the linoleum, struck Melody as the most beautiful sight she'd seen in a while.

She lifted the latch, which offered no resistance, and pulled up the trapdoor. She was only a little surprised to see a retractable ladder, already extended, leading down into a corridor. The corridor itself looked reassuringly normal, with cream-painted walls, a gray-tiled floor and several doors.

The trick had been to find that ten-inch seam in the wall, Melody thought. After that, the puzzle was essentially finished and the game was over. It was strange, considering the violence of the way she'd been brought here, that she'd never really been afraid for her life or her safety. All along, she'd been convinced she was playing a competitive game and that her opponent was Wolfe.

Melody climbed down the ladder, and as soon as she was in the corridor she saw that it branched into two, one at right angles to the other. The doors were identified only with numbers and she was debating which way to turn when the door immediately to her left opened and Wolfe came out.

He inclined his head toward her, his expression serious, with no trace of the ingratiating smiles he'd produced at the Plaza. "Congratulations, Melody, and welcome to Unit One. You just set a new record for the speed with which you found the way out of our holding cell."

"Who are you? And what is this place?"

"My name is Nikolai Anwar and this is the headquarters of Unit One. I'm here to offer you an invitation to join our organization as a field agent."

An odd shiver rippled down her spine and caused an even more peculiar tightening sensation in the pit of her stomach. Being in close proximity to this man had an effect on her that was confusing.

Not accustomed to feeling confused, Melody sent him a look that translated all her fear and all her anger into an expression of ice-cold disdain.

"First show me the way out of this place, and then you can go to hell."

Eleven

Nikolai didn't react to her insult by so much as a flicker of an eyelash. ''There's a rest room immediately to your right,'' he said. ''Just so that you don't waste your time searching, there are no cameras in there and also, I assure you, no way out except the door that leads back into this corridor. When you've freshened up, we'll talk.'' He pushed open the door he'd indicated and stood aside to give her access.

Melody was tempted to ignore him, or to repeat her suggestion that he should go to hell, but practicality won out over the luxury of being defiant. She needed the rest room, so she took the next-best option and stalked past Nikolai in haughty silence. Despite his assurances, she searched the rest room anyway, but came to the conclusion he was telling the truth on both counts; there were no concealed cameras and there was no way out other than the door she'd come in by.

The luxurious bathroom facilities made up for quite a lot of earlier deprivation. In addition to two toilet stalls, there was a big sink supplied with copious amounts of hot water and a fancy container of liquid soap. A shrink-wrapped hairbrush, toothpaste and a toothbrush still in its package were laid out invitingly on the counter. There was even a can of hair spray and a bottle of lilac-scented body lotion.

Melody recognized that she was being subjected to a version of the good cop/bad cop routine—first frighten and deprive, then provide small comforts—but by the time she'd brushed her teeth, combed her hair and soothed her face and hands with lotion, she had a new understanding of why the routine worked so well. Stiffening her resolve, she walked out of the rest room, determined not to succumb to hostage syndrome and start feeling gratitude toward Nikolai because he made her imprisonment tolerable.

When she emerged into the corridor she saw that Nikolai was no longer alone. The woman who'd been with him at the Plaza—his wife?—was standing very close to him, her head leaning against his chest, her back toward the bathroom. Melody could hear that she was crying.

The woman was so upset she seemed unaware of the door opening behind her, but Nikolai was facing the rest room, so he noticed at once. With a glance toward Melody that contained an unexpected hint of apology, he put one arm around the woman, opened a door behind him with his free hand and swiftly pulled the woman inside. It was clear to Melody that he didn't want his wife to see her.

She wasted a few seconds wondering what that little scene was all about, and then realized she'd been handed a unique opportunity to escape from Nikolai's clutches. Expecting at any moment to hear him pounding after her, she sprinted down the empty corridor until she reached the fire door at the end. She used her shoulder to push open the heavy door and burst through at a run.

A man in a black commando outfit, hefting a submachine gun large enough to blow away a convention of Las Vegas mobsters, stood facing her, gun aimed at her belly. Melody slid to a halt, sneakers screeching on the polished tile floor.

The commando nodded to her. "Mornin', ma'am." He spoke with a soft, Texas lilt to his voice.

"Er...good morning. How are you today?" Given the submachine gun, this struck Melody as an excellent moment to display her very best manners.

"I'm real fine. Appreciate it if you'd return to the corridor behind you, ma'am."

She recovered enough presence of mind to produce one of her most seductive smiles. "Actually, I'm looking for a way out of the building."

The commando did at least blink in response to the wattage of her smile, but his gun didn't waver. "Yes, ma'am. Mr. Anwar will direct you. Meanwhile, appreciate it if you'd return to the corridor behind you, ma'am."

She gritted her teeth. "I don't believe you're going to use that...that bazooka if I try to find the way out of here by myself."

The commando said nothing, which scared Melody more than if he'd insisted he would blow her away. Still, a mixture of pride and desperation prevented her from backing down and meekly returning to the corridor. Nikolai Anwar had said he wanted her to join Unit One, whatever the hell that was. Presumably she'd be no use as an employee if she was dead.

She took a tentative step forward, planning to feint to the left of the commando, then dodge around his right side. The commando wouldn't expect her to defy him, and he certainly wouldn't expect her to aim for his right side where there was less room for her to maneuver. There seemed at least a chance that she could catch him off guard and make it past him while he was still debating how to stop her without firing his weapon.

She'd barely feinted to the left, much less taken an actual step toward the right, when the commando sprang. Melody felt a painful thud in her stomach. The next thing she knew, she was on the floor and staring into the business end of the commando's submachine gun. Which definitely didn't look any more appealing on close inspection.

The commando gave her an infuriatingly polite smile. "Would you like some help gettin' up, ma'am?"

Nikolai appeared behind the commando's shoulder at that moment and stretched out his hand to Melody. "If you've finished in the bathroom, we can get started," he said, looking down at her. His expression gave no indication that he'd noticed she was sprawled on her butt, or that a damn great Neanderthal was poised over her supine body, menacing her with a gun, but she had the humiliating impression that behind their studiously blank expressions Nikolai and the commando were both laughing.

"I don't want to get started," she said, teeth gritted. "What I want is to leave this place."

Both men ignored her. Nikolai gave the commando a quick nod. "Thanks, Buddy. I'll take it from here."

"Yes, sir." The commando moved back to his original position opposite the fire door, standing with feet spread and submachine gun once again nestled in the crook of his arm.

Nikolai's hand remained helpfully outstretched toward Melody. His fingers were long and tapered, but his palms were callused, she noticed, and there was a long scar that ran from the index finger of his left hand all the way to his wrist. At some point, the back of Nikolai's hand had been sliced open with a knife.

Pity they hadn't cut out his liver while they were at it, Melody thought acidly. Ignoring Nikolai's outstretched hand, she pushed herself to her feet, smothering a moan. Damned if she was going to wince when Nikolai was watching her, even though it felt as if Bazooka Buddy had busted most of her ribs.

"You have no right to keep me here," she said, hoping she sounded authoritative, but very much afraid she sounded whiney. "I want to leave right *now*."

"Or what?" Nikolai inquired politely. "You'll call your congressman?"

She didn't answer, chiefly because she was afraid her voice might shake with frustration, and she didn't want him to make the mistake of thinking she was intimidated.

Nikolai sounded almost sympathetic when he spoke again. "I have a tight schedule today, Melody, and we have a lot to get through. You can walk to my office or I can carry you—your choice. But one way or another, my office is where we're headed."

Having Nikolai scoop her up into his arms and carry her struck Melody as only marginally less dreadful than having him pull out her fingernails one by one.

"I can walk," she snapped.

"Then let's go." Nikolai turned and strode into the corridor they'd just left, not looking to see if she followed. Since Buddy guarded the rear with his submachine gun, Melody had to concede there wasn't much risk that she was going to dash to freedom while Nikolai's back was turned.

"This is my office," he said, opening the door to the room where he'd taken his wife a few minutes earlier. The room was identified on the door only as 123. "Come in and I'll make you a cup of coffee. You must be thirsty."

There was no sign of Nikolai's sobbing wife in his office. Didn't take him long to deal with her, Melody thought testily. That figured. She could easily picture him handing the poor woman a tissue and telling her to buck up. She just bet he was one of those men who considered making love a two-minute activity, including foreplay, his big, gushing orgasm being the only part of the performance to have any real significance as far as he was concerned.

And why she was thinking about Nikolai and his orgasms she couldn't imagine.

She pulled her gaze away from his oddly compelling features and focused instead on the picture hung behind his desk. It was an interesting photograph of a sandhill crane rooting at the edge of a marsh, taken by a photographer with a highly developed sense of composition and a sensitive eye for color. She didn't want to consider the possibility that Nikolai was the photographer.

"Take a seat, why don't you?" Nikolai gestured to a chair pulled up to his desk. "It's more comfortable than it looks."

She was exhausted, Melody realized. She was also

stressed, thirsty and beginning to feel nauseated by the pain in her ribs. She needed to save her resistance for something that mattered, not waste it on a refusal to sit. She sat down in the chair, barely masking a sigh of relief as the squishy leather folded around her.

"It won't take a moment to brew the coffee," Nikolai said, crossing to a bar set up with an under-the-counter fridge, as well as a sink. He poured water into an automatic coffeemaker. "If you're hungry, I can order food to be sent up. Cereal, fruit, toast?"

Melody shook her head. "Just coffee." She almost said thank you and caught herself in time. She had no reason to express any sort of gratitude to this man. "What happened to your wife?" she asked.

"My wife?"

"The woman in the corridor just now."

"She's not my wife."

"Who is she, then, and why was she crying?"

Nikolai measured coffee into the filter basket. "She was a trainee operative for Unit One."

Was? In view of what had happened to Lawrence Springer last night, Melody found Nikolai's use of the past tense alarming. "Why isn't she a trainee anymore? What happened to her?"

"She was fired." Nikolai set the coffee to brew. "She'd just learned that she'd failed a couple of field tests, and that's why she was crying."

And she came to Nikolai for comfort? Melody would sooner have asked Saddam Hussein for a hug. "Getting fired from this place strikes me as a cause for celebrating, not crying," she said.

"In her case, you're right. She found working for Unit One more of a strain than she could comfortably handle and she'll do much better in her new assignment."

There were a dozen important questions to ask, Melody thought, but her brain was in such a state of overload that she couldn't seem to formulate any of the big ones. She settled for a small one instead. "Why didn't you want her to see me when I came out of the rest room?"

"Because she knows your real name."

"I can certainly see how that would be a problem." As always when she was unsure of herself, Melody's attitude became sardonic. "Thanks to the tabloids, there can't be more than a million or so people around the world who would recognize my name."

"It wasn't your name I wanted to protect. It was the fact that you work for Unit One. It could seriously endanger you in the future if anybody outside Unit One knows that you work for us."

"Fortunately that's not a problem," Melody said with a falsely sweet smile. "News flash, Mr. Anwar. I *don't* work for Unit One. Whatever the hell Unit One might be."

"You don't work for us yet, but you will." Nikolai took a small carton of milk out of the fridge and set it on the tray next to the mugs.

She bloody well wouldn't work for him, or his stupid organization. The arrogance of the man was made more irritating by the fact that it was so low-key. Didn't the guy ever raise his voice, even a little bit? The urge to take him down a notch or two was enough to make her skin itch. It was coming up on twelve hours since she'd had anything to drink, which made it hard to resist the aroma of freshly brewed coffee, but Melody managed it.

She rose to her feet. "Thanks so much for the job offer, Mr. Anwar, but I decline. I'm sure this is a *really* fun place to work, but between Buddy Bazooka and spending the past several hours locked in a box, I've decided to sacrifice my share of the other treats you and your colleagues have in store for me. So if you could direct me to the nearest exit, I'll be on my way. No need for an escort. I'll call a cab."

"Sit down before you fall down," Nikolai said. "I'll bring you your coffee. Do you take milk? Sugar?"

Melody reacted instinctively to the quiet note of command in Nikolai's voice, and she was actually sitting in the damn chair before she realized what she'd done. Rather than jump up, which would reveal that she hadn't meant to obey him, she leaned back, crossed one leg over the other and told him that she drank her coffee black.

He didn't express any triumph at her capitulation. His attitude—infuriatingly—suggested her compliance was so much to be expected that it wasn't worth comment. Handing her a mug of coffee, he sat down behind his desk. The overhead fluorescent light gave his straight dark hair the iridescent sheen of a raven's wing and revealed lines of fatigue around his mouth that hadn't been present when she'd seen him at the Plaza.

Good, Melody thought viciously. She hoped he was having a really bad week. If she had anything to do with it, the week ahead would be even worse.

"Let me fill you in on some of the basic facts about Unit One," he said, cradling his hands around his own coffee cup as he leaned back in his chair. Melody realized she was staring in fascination at his scar, and switched her gaze back to the photo of the sandhill crane.

"We are a covert branch of the United States government," Nick continued. "We're funded as part of the black ops budget that Congress approves as a lump sum without being given any specific details about our precise structure or mission. Unit One is a paramilitary organization, and our commander reports directly to the White House. The commander plays only a limited role in our day-to-day activities, and for most practical purposes we are controlled by Martin McShane, the director. You'll meet McShane later on this morning."

"I can hardly wait," Melody muttered.

"Mac's an interesting man," Nikolai said as if he hadn't noticed her sarcasm. "My own job title is director of operations. Among other things, I'm responsible for recruiting and training all our field agents. My counterpart, Bob Spinard, is the director of intelligence. He's in charge of our research staff, our analysts and our strategists. To oversimplify, Bob's department generates information and my department acts on it. Oh, and I shouldn't forget our mission statement. Unit One was created to enhance the security of the United States by insuring that justice is done in cases where law enforcement and the courts aren't able to act. We try to prevent criminal acts from taking place, but sometimes—more often than we would like—we can only mop up the mess afterward."

Nikolai paused for a moment in what struck Melody as a parody of the well-trained director of personnel, waiting for the potential employee to ask an intelligent question. She didn't speak, but for once she wasn't deliberately trying to thwart him. What he'd just told her sounded both incredible and frightening. Unfortunately, she couldn't come up with an alternative explanation for the events of the past few hours that sounded any less scary or more believable.

"Do you have questions at this stage?" Nikolai prompted helpfully.

"No questions, just comments." Melody decided that this was an instance where honesty was the best policy. "Even if you could convince me you're telling the truth about what this place is and what you do, and that's a huge if, I can't imagine why you would want to recruit me as one of your agents. I don't know what skills Unit One looks for in its applicants, but I'm fairly sure I don't have any of them. My education and interests all lie in the world of art. My area of expertise is eighteenth-century landscape paintings, which is about as far removed as you can get from secret missions to shine the light of justice in previously dark corners." She allowed her voice to twist with irony as she paraphrased Nikolai's words about the lofty mission of Unit One.

"Don't worry about your lack of expertise," he said. "We believe you have the necessary basic skills or you would never have been recruited. Naturally, you'll have to undergo intensive training before you're ready for assignment to the field—"

"You're missing the point, Mr. Anwar. Which is that I have absolutely no desire to be recruited, much less assigned to the field. The opposite, in fact. I'm extremely happy with my work at the Van der Meer

Gallery and I have zero desire to make a career change.'' She put her coffee mug on his desk and stood up. ''Now may I go? There are people in Manhattan who will be worried about me. I need to get back to the city from...wherever we are.''

''New Jersey. And it's true people must be worried about your absence. But the sooner we have your cooperation, the sooner we'll be able to relieve their anxieties.''

Melody leaned over the desk and spoke with exaggerated emphasis. ''Thanks for the job offer, but I... do...not...wish...to...be...recruited...into...Unit One.''

''I hear you.''

''Then what is there about that simple sentence that you don't understand, Mr. Anwar?''

''Nothing, and you should call me Nick,'' he said. ''Even though I'm your commanding officer, we prefer to keep things informal around here. Our organizational structure is pretty loose, despite the military overtones. We've found our agents function better that way, especially in the field where independent action is often vital to the success of an assignment.''

Melody abandoned sarcasm. ''You're not my commanding officer because I'm not going to work for you!'' she yelled, pounding her fist on his desk for emphasis. ''And yes, I will call my congressman if you don't let me out of here right now. And don't think the fact that you're some whoop-de-do covert ops lunatic is going to protect you. Congressman Birkoff and I happen to be pretty good friends.''

''I know you are,'' Nick said agreeably. ''The point is noted in your file. But sadly, even Joe Birkoff can't do too much to help out a constituent who's facing a murder conviction.''

Melody was seized by a premonition of impending doom. ''What are you talking about? Who is facing conviction on murder charges?''

''You are. Or you will be, if you don't cooperate.''

''That's a completely empty threat. It's crazy.''

''On the contrary. Lawrence Springer was shot last night. You were in his house at the time he died.''

Melody shivered, although she wasn't sure whether the sudden chill was caused by fear or sheer rage. ''You know damn well that Springer was dead before I walked into the study.''

''I know no such thing,'' Nick said. ''In fact, I have conclusive proof that you killed Springer.''

''You can't have proof of something that never happened. We both know that you killed Lawrence Springer. You and your two sidekicks.''

He glanced at her with undisguised mockery. ''Did you see me kill him?''

''No, of course not—''

''Then what makes you believe we killed him? I'm an agent of the United States government, and so are Sam and Tony. You surely can't believe that we would murder a fine, upstanding citizen like Lawrence Springer?''

Melody did a silent double take. Now that he mentioned it, government complicity in Springer's death did seem unlikely. Even a covert government organization would surely never authorize its employees to murder a citizen in cold blood? But Nick or one of his partners must have shot Springer. So had he lied about being a government agent? And if he had, where did that leave her?

In the swamp, totally surrounded by alligators, Melody concluded grimly. "I've no idea whether or not you had authorization to kill Lawrence Springer. But you must have shot him, because there was nobody else around."

"On the contrary. *You* were around," Nick said.

"Two can play at this game, Mr. Anwar. It's your word against mine, and I'm willing to bet my word will play better with the police. I have no reason to murder Lawrence Springer."

"Try telling that to a jury when they've seen this." As he spoke, Nick pressed a button on his desk and Melody heard a mechanical whirring sound behind her. She glanced over her shoulder and saw that a white viewing screen had dropped from a slot in the ceiling.

"I have some video footage to show you." The mildness of Nick's voice struck Melody as distinctly ominous. "What you are about to see is the security tape taken from a camera concealed inside a book in Lawrence Springer's study. You'll note the date and time stamp among other things. Here we go."

Melody stared at the screen, heart thumping against her sore ribs. She watched as a narrow beam of light came on, revealing a slender, masked figure who crossed into camera range and sat behind the desk. She recognized Lawrence Springer's desk, in the study of his Chappaqua home. The date scrolled across the bottom: Saturday, September 27. Time: 2:23 a.m.

She was watching herself go into Springer's study last night, Melody realized. Appalled, she saw herself reach up and take off her mask, shaking out her hair and fanning her face to get cool. If she'd set out to provide the camera with a superb view of her features she couldn't have done a better job. The focus was perfect, and the light from her high-powered flashlight did an excellent job of providing illumination.

Melody watched herself lean down behind the desk, disappearing briefly from sight. She'd been checking the file drawers, Melody remembered, which was the point at which she'd first noticed Lawrence Springer's dead body.

Compromising as the tape was, what worried her even more than its mere existence was the fact that she hadn't double-checked Esperanza's statement that there were no internal security cameras. How could she have been so careless, when she prided herself on the meticulous care with which she conducted her investigations? Well, she'd blown it big time on this occasion and Nick Anwar was, unfortunately, correct. If this tape ever made it into the hands of the police she would certainly have a lot of explaining to do, and she had nobody to blame except herself.

But worse was to come. The film kept rolling, and events on screen soon diverged dramatically from events as Melody knew they'd unfolded. A man walked across the screen, his back to the camera. He soon passed out of camera range, so that the images on screen remained pictures of Melody. The time scrolling across the bottom of the viewing screen indicated that the man had crossed into camera range only seconds after Melody was seen taking off her mask and bending down behind the desk.

A man's voice spoke, harsh with anger. "How did you get inside the house? What the hell are you doing here?"

Melody recognized Lawrence Springer's voice, even though she knew he'd never said any such thing to her, since he was already dead by the time she entered the study.

"You wouldn't take my phone calls, so what choice did I have?" Melody watched her lips move and heard herself ask the question. The synchronization was perfect and the voice so convincingly hers that anyone who knew her would have sworn in court that she was the woman speaking. The effect was eerie enough to give her chills.

"It's over between us," Springer said. "Can't you understand that, for Christ's sake? I'm not divorcing Claire."

"I'm pregnant," the screen Melody said. "Don't you care that the baby is yours?"

"No, I don't care," Lawrence Springer's voice said. "In fact, I don't give a damn."

"How can you say that about your own child—"

"Don't be a sentimental fool. It's not a child, it's a cluster of cells. You can't be more than a few weeks pregnant. Get rid of the damn thing. I'm not having my marriage destroyed over a couple of nights of hot sex." The man moved briefly into camera range, confirming that it was, indeed, Lawrence Springer.

"How can you do this to me?" the screen Melody asked. Hypnotized, Melody watched her screen image rise to her feet and step out from behind the desk.

"Easily." Springer gave a short laugh. "You're a good lay, but you're not that good. Besides, I like being married to Claire. She appreciates the fact that she would have no life if not for me and she's always willing to express her gratitude. You're too damned famous—too independent—to make a really good mistress."

"I'm not going to have an abortion, Larry, so get used to the idea of becoming a father. I've never had anyone to love me, and I want this baby."

"For Christ's sake, you sound like some pathetic teenager from the inner city. Get a life—"

"That's what I'm planning to do. Get a life, for me and my child. I'll sue you for support, Larry. I don't care about the publicity. I've lived with notoriety and media attention all my life."

"Don't threaten me, because I'll threaten right back. Get rid of the fucking baby."

"I won't. And you can't make me."

Even though she knew the scene had never happened, even though she knew that the words apparently coming from her mouth were utterly alien to her character, Melody couldn't turn away from the screen. She watched, paralyzed by a mixture of fascination and disbelief, as Lawrence Springer lunged toward her. Sounds of a scuffle ensued, although the two people fighting were almost off camera and only an arm or a leg occasionally appeared in the region of the empty desk. Finally there was the sound of a gunshot and a muffled feminine scream. The next thing the camera showed clearly was Melody kneeling alongside Lawrence Springer's dead body, her expression panic-stricken as she used her fingers to close his eyes.

She'd actually done that, Melody remembered, except that she'd been wearing latex gloves, and the woman in the video had bare hands. Finally the Melody clone in the video ran toward the door of the study and the screen faded to black.

For a moment the only sound in the room was the mechanical whir of the screen retracting into the ceiling. Torn between admiration for the technical wizardry and horror at how the wizardry had been used, Melody had trouble finding her voice.

"What do you think of our handiwork?" Nick asked when the screen had disappeared. "It's impressive, don't you think? Bob Spinard keeps a team of video specialists on hand and they do fabulous work. The wonders of the digital revolution and all that."

From her point of view, the video wasn't so much impressive as terrifying. "You've produced an interesting work of fiction," Melody said, struggling not to show how frightened she was. "But the police will know it's a fake."

Nick spoke softly. "I can promise you that neither the police nor any experts your defense lawyers call in will be able to prove that the tape is a fake."

"Then any competent defense lawyer will be able to demonstrate how easy it is to produce a fake just like this."

"Not unless they have access to Bob Spinard's team," Nick said. "Besides, the video is only part of the evidence the police will find. There's lots more. The face mask you took off got left in Springer's study. There are a couple of your hairs attached to it. With that tape as their guide, you can bet they'll get a court order to run a comparative DNA test between you and the hairs. That's a good piece of scientific evidence for the jury to dig its teeth into. And Claire will testify that she suspected all along that Springer was having an affair with you—"

''You're very confident about what Claire will and won't do.''

''Yes,'' Nick said. ''I know Claire quite well.''

Melody experienced a burst of star-spangled enlightenment. ''My God! You're the man Claire Springer was having an affair with!''

Nick said nothing, but his silence was eloquent.

''I'm not pregnant, and I've never been pregnant,'' Melody said, fighting back. ''I can get a doctor to prove that. That's a massive problem for your so-called evidence. Why would I kill Springer if there's no baby?''

Nick shrugged. ''That's easy. You lied about the baby to test Springer's feelings for you. You were furious that he rejected you despite believing you were carrying his child. The fact that you've never been pregnant doesn't make much difference to the credibility of the tape. If you combine the DNA evidence with the tape, plus the fact that you won't be able to give yourself an alibi proving you were elsewhere, you're in big trouble.''

''But you're never going to give the tape to the police,'' Melody said, struck by sudden inspiration and hoping like hell she was right. ''Of course you're not. You're trying to use the tape to coerce me into working for Unit One. You hope I'll be so scared that I'll just fall into line, no questions asked. But I'm calling your bluff. Go ahead. Do your worst. I refuse to join Unit One.''

''Then, reluctantly, I'll be forced to send the tape to the homicide detectives working the Springer case.''

Melody shrugged, gaining confidence as she saw

how to evade the trap Nick had set. "And how would that help you achieve your goal?"

"You'd be arrested within hours—"

"Probably. But the object of the exercise isn't to get me convicted of a murder I didn't commit. You're trying to coerce me into joining Unit One. What use am I to you if I'm behind bars for the rest of my life?"

"None," Nick acknowledged. "Fortunately, Unit One has several ingenious methods it can utilize to spring you from the criminal justice system at various points along the way. Trust me, there is no defense lawyer who can get you off from the case we'll help the D.A. to build. And when your lifetime prison sentence is handed down, I'm guessing you'll be so thrilled to see me walking through your cell door that you'll accept any terms and conditions that I care to offer, just so long as I get you out of there."

"You've miscalculated," Melody said, her voice as soft as his. "I still refuse to join Unit One. So send the tape to the D.A.'s office. I don't give a rat's ass. Now, show me the way out of here. I'm really tired of listening to you."

"You're too smart to test me on this, Melody."

"Oh, please. Not that tired line. You sound like the headmistress at one of my boarding schools when she knew her threats of some dire punishment were having no effect at all." She stood up. "I want to leave now."

"Do you want me to say out loud what we both already know? Okay, I will. You're not leaving. There is no way out of Unit One for you without my permission."

Melody's stomach swooped in renewed fear.

''Maybe you can keep me imprisoned here, but you can't make me work for you. That requires cooperation on my part.''

''True, but you'll cooperate eventually.''

''That's your hope, Nick, and you stick with it. I know otherwise.''

''So far, I've only shown you the stick, but you haven't heard about the carrot. Instead of refusing blindly to cooperate, why not listen to what it is that I'm offering you?''

''I've seen exactly what you have to offer me. You've given me the chance to claw my way out of a windowless box, spiced up with the chance to slaughter respectable businessmen like Lawrence Springer. Thank you, but I'll stick with my stubborn refusal to join in the fun and games.''

For the first time, Nick appeared impatient. ''Lawrence Springer wasn't respectable and I suspect you know that already. Otherwise what were you doing breaking in to his house last night?''

She was too tired to come up with an answer that didn't reveal more than she wanted Nick to know. When he saw that she was temporarily silenced, he got up, walked around the desk and dragged up a chair so that he was sitting only inches away from her. At this close proximity, his presence was overwhelming and her heart began to pound.

''I can offer you your heart's desire,'' he said softly.

Melody laughed without mirth. ''I very much doubt it.''

His dark brown eyes narrowed with the intensity of his gaze and he spoke just two words. ''Wallis Beecham.''

For a moment it felt as if her heart stopped beating. But somehow, she had no idea how, she managed not to leap off the chair and demand to know precisely what he meant.

"Wallis Beecham is merely the man who married my mother and isn't my father," she said with a credible pretense of casualness. "I'm not sure what you hope to achieve by mentioning his name in that mysterious way."

"Then I'll make it crystal clear," Nick said. "I'm offering you Wallis Beecham, publicly disgraced and his assets stripped away from him, the Bonita Project destroyed before it effectively gets off the ground. Does that make the prospect of joining Unit One any more palatable to you?"

Nick knew about the Bonita Project. Melody was tempted to beg him to reveal everything he knew, but she resisted the temptation. She understood intuitively that letting Nick know just how much she wanted to bring down Wallis Beecham would be a mistake. There was already a power struggle going on between the two of them. If he ever found out how much she was willing to sacrifice in the cause of exposing Wallis Beecham to the world, then the balance of power would tip decisively in Nick's favor. And she absolutely didn't want to feel powerless vis-à-vis Nikolai Anwar.

She also knew that mixing in a lot of truth with a few lies was the best way to keep her real motivations hidden. If Unit One could give her Wallis Beecham, then she was willing to join them, no more questions asked. But she wasn't about to let Nick know that he'd found the key that wound her up and set her in motion.

"Wallis Beecham deliberately sabotaged my plans to open an art gallery in London," she said. "He also blackened my reputation in financial circles so that I couldn't raise a loan to finance any art-related business venture. Obviously I have no great affection for the man. However, my life has moved on very successfully since that bleak period and I can assure you that revenge against Wallis Beecham ranks low on my current agenda."

Nick smiled, the first smile she'd seen him produce since their encounter at the Plaza hotel. "Good try, Melody. But if exposing Wallis Beecham ranks low on your current list of things to do, how come you broke in to Lawrence Springer's house last night? What other reason could have caused you to risk imprisonment and a criminal conviction for burglary if not the hope of finding out more about his connections to the Bonita Project?"

Twelve

Nick caught the flash of surprise in Melody's eyes, even though she dropped her gaze almost instantly. Her reaction suggested his guess was correct and that she'd broken in to Lawrence Springer's home in search of information about the Bonita Project. Still, for a person with no formal training, she was amazingly good at guarding her feelings. Poor Bree should have hung around to take notes, he thought wryly.

Frustrating as it was to his plans, Nick couldn't help admiring the way Melody had called his bluff in regard to the "evidence" Bob Spinard's team had spliced together in a mix of genuine film and digital genius. Her failure to be intimidated provided a demonstration of why technology could so often be beaten by a smart human. Instead of being overwhelmed by the damning nature of the so-called evidence, Melody had penetrated straight to the heart of the matter and seen that Nick would undermine his own purposes if he had her arrested for Springer's murder.

Score one for Melody.

Since his threats were empty, he was left with no other lever as a recruitment tool beyond Melody's own desire to bring Wallis Beecham down. Nick hoped like hell that her yearning to expose her onetime father's criminality was as obsessive as he judged it to be, because that was the only way she might decide to throw in her lot with Unit One.

The most enticing lure he could offer was evidence that Unit One knew more about the Bonita Project than she did. Unfortunately, for security reasons he couldn't reveal very much until he was sure she was fully committed—a frustrating vicious circle. He knew that she had already ferreted out the existence of the Bonita research lab in Arkansas, because she'd paid a visit there after they had the place under surveillance. He also knew that she'd been thwarted in her efforts to determine what was going on there, since the shell operation the Bonita partnership had established provided pretty effective cover.

Nick took a rapid decision to tell her the truth about Kenneth Chung's research, and then fill her in on the details of Lawrence Springer's plans to murder Kenneth Chung, as well as the promised payoff from the cartel of Saudi Arabian oil princes. Melody would find all the information intriguing, and yet he would need to reveal nothing about the true nature of the Bonita Project—and so give her nothing to betray if she couldn't be successfully recruited.

Melody listened without interruption until he got to the point where he described setting up a meeting with Lawrence Springer at the Chappaqua mansion for Friday night, supposedly for the purpose of getting paid off for the Kenneth Chung assassination. He explained that instead of going to the meeting alone, as Springer anticipated, he'd taken one of his most experienced extraction teams with him. The extraction was intended to be the culmination of several weeks of intensive work that had carefully baited th trap for Lawrence Springer.

Melody finally interjected a question, her voic thick with distaste. ‘‘Is that what you call your ex cution squads?’’ she asked. ‘‘*Extraction* teams? Do the euphemism make you feel better about wh you're doing?’’

‘‘It isn't a euphemism,’’ he said. ‘‘Extraction tea means just what it says. A team that takes a pers out of one situation and transfers him or her to different location. We don't have execution squa working at Unit One. The closest we come to suc a thing is a crew of technical experts that speciali in cleaning up after a death. They're called in those very rare occasions when we're aware of a ki ing and we don't want law enforcement authoriti to know what's happened because it would jeopa dize an ongoing mission.’’

Melody made no effort to hide her skepticism. ‘‘ view of what I saw last night, not to mention yo pal Buddy standing on guard in the main entran hall with a submachine gun for company, you'll u derstand why I'm finding it a little hard to belie that nobody in Unit One ever kills anybody. Becau if Buddy's just posing for decoration, you need change your designer.’’

‘‘I didn't say Unit One operatives never kill. I sa we don't have execution squads. We're authorized kill in self-defense, just as cops are. But every tin a death occurs during the course of a mission, we through the same type of review process as a poli officer would. The only difference is that our revie process is secret. You can argue that because of th secrecy we're able to hide our screwups from the public—"

"Yes, I would argue that."

"And you'd be right, of course. Still, bottom line, we have rules we follow and we try never to hide our screwups from ourselves, even though outsiders may not hear about them. We're an agency of the U.S. government, not a goon squad, and we're required to stay within certain guidelines even if we have tacit permission to stretch the law a lot of the time."

"You sound like the personification of sweet reason, but your team didn't *extract* Lawrence Springer," Melody said. "You killed him. I saw his body."

"Precisely. You saw his body. You didn't see us killing him."

"Because you'd already killed him by the time I arrived at the house!"

Nick shook his head. "Why would we kill Springer? We needed him alive and feeling vulnerable enough to answer our questions about the Bonita partnership. Questions he sure as hell can't answer now he's dead. My team is frustrated as hell that Springer is dead. We've been working for six weeks to set him up. The reason I hired myself out as Lawrence Springer's assassin wasn't just so that we could remove Chung to a place of safety—we could have picked him up at any time without the need for such an elaborate setup. We needed Lawrence Springer to go through with hiring me and paying me off in order to provide Unit One with an effective blackmail weapon to utilize against him."

Melody quirked an eyebrow. "You seem very fond of blackmail in this place—"

"Because it usually works," Nick said shortly. "We deal mostly with bad guys, and they tend to have a lot of blackmail pressure points." He didn't add that most of his victims weren't as smart as she was, but that would have been the truth.

"My team was in Chappaqua on Friday night to bring Springer to a secure location for questioning, and for no other reason," he said. "We found him dead when we arrived at the house, which was about twenty minutes before you."

"So why were you still there when I arrived, if your intended quarry was dead?"

"We stayed behind to search his study. Since we no longer had Springer alive to question directly, I was looking for exactly the same thing I suspect you went for, namely information. And if it makes you feel any better about your abortive mission, we didn't find much that shed light on the activities of the Bonita partners. Wherever the partnership keeps its records, it isn't in Springer's study."

"Did you check the wall safe behind the Alfred Munnings painting? I'm betting there was one."

"You'd be right. And yes, we cracked it. It was full of cash and jewelry, which we left, just as Springer's killer had done."

Melody looked at him long and hard, as if assessing the likelihood that he was telling the truth. Apparently she was satisfied enough to ask a question in a tone of voice that finally sounded puzzled rather than accusatory. "If you and your team didn't kill Lawrence Springer, then who did? Good grief, how many intruders were wandering around his house last night?''

''Damn good question. We're working hard on finding answers. However, the house was empty when we arrived, except for Springer. We checked.''

She frowned, and he sensed a further shift in her mood from hostility to interest.

''So Springer's killer had left already when you and your team arrived?''

''Yes, unfortunately.''

''What about the tape from the hidden camera? The real one, not the one you doctored. Doesn't that show the murderer?''

''I wish. But the security camera was turned off for the crucial time period, then turned on again.''

''That's interesting in itself. How many people can possibly be aware of those internal security cameras? I don't believe the housekeeper knows, for example, which would suggest there's a very limited pool of suspects.''

''You're right that it's a limited pool. Claire Springer told me that only she and Lawrence knew of the precise placement of the cameras. Not even the security company had been informed of the locations.''

''Well, if you're correct, that reduces the suspects to a pool of one. Since Lawrence is dead, doesn't that mean Claire must be the killer?''

Nick realized he was revealing far more than he'd intended, but Melody's growing interest made the trade-off worthwhile.

''The fact that the murderer knew to turn off the security camera would make Claire the most likely suspect, except for one problem. We happen to know she was in her room at the Carlisle when Springer died."

"How do you know she was there?" Melody asked. "Just because she was registered at the hotel doesn't mean she slept all night in her room. Maybe she sneaked out for a few hours—"

"Not possible." Nick gave Melody another piece of the truth. "I planted a tracking device on Claire the last time we were together. We're quite certain she didn't leave the Carlisle until after breakfast this morning."

Melody's eyes widened. "How do you plant a tracking device on somebody so that they don't notice they've been tagged, for heaven's sake?"

"In this instance, I was able to position it subdermally," he said.

"And Claire didn't *notice* that you were injecting a microchip under her skin?"

Nick spoke with a careful lack of emphasis. "I waited until she was asleep and then used local anesthesia to place it just above her shoulder blade."

Melody didn't say anything, but for once her reaction was visible on her face, presumably because she wanted him to know exactly what she thought of him. Which clearly wasn't much.

Nick was surprised to hear himself offering a defense of his actions. Not a defense of planting the tracking device, but of the seduction that had made the implantation possible. "I didn't seduce Claire away from a loving relationship," he said tightly. "I simply made myself available when she was already out looking for a sexual partner."

"Of course I understand." Melody smoothed her expression into one of sophisticated mockery. "Besides, it's all in the noble cause of keeping America safe for democracy, right Nick? Which has to be one of the better excuses I've heard recently for getting it off with a cute piece of ass."

Incredibly, Nick found himself swallowing a laugh. There was something so incongruous about Melody coming out with American slang in a prissy upper-class British accent. He decided to get her off the subject of Claire, which was making him more uncomfortable than he'd ever have imagined, by revealing the real cause for worry concerning Springer's death.

"Since we know Claire didn't kill her husband in a fit of marital jealousy, we're left with the mystery of who did do the deed," he said. "And the biggest concern from our point of view has to be that Wallis Beecham is behind the death."

"Why is that a concern?" Melody asked. "Thieves and murderers make for unreliable business partners. Why do we care if Beecham offed his former buddy Larry? That's one less bad guy for the world to worry about. Chalk up a victory for democracy, motherhood and apple pie."

She'd said *we,* Nick noted. Another sign that offering her information about the Bonita partnership had been a good way to draw her into the Unit One fold. "It depends on the reason Beecham gave the order for Springer to be killed. We don't care if it's because he and his partner had a disagreement about offshore oil drilling rights in Florida, or shipments of gold bullion to Iran, or some other slightly sleazy but legal business venture they're pursuing together. We do care if Wallis Beecham ordered Springer killed because of Kenneth Chung's disappearance."

Melody's brow furrowed. "Okay, I see that would be a problem, since Unit One has gone to a lot of trouble to insure that everyone will believe Chung is dead. But there's no suggestion of a link between Chung's disappearance and Springer's murder, is there? Other than the coincidence of the timing?"

Nick shrugged. "I have an incurably suspicious mind, and I don't like coincidences. Wallis Beecham assigned Springer the task of eliminating Kenneth Chung on behalf of the Bonita partnership. Springer screwed up by hiring me to do the deed. We were about to bring Springer in for questioning. There was a fair chance we would succeed in extracting a great deal of lethally damaging information about the Bonita Project from Lawrence Springer. If I were Wallis Beecham and I had any clue about what was really going on, I'd sure as hell have ordered Springer's death."

Melody's frown intensified. "But there's no way for Wallis Beecham to know that Kenneth Chung is alive, much less that he's in your custody. The media reported Chung's disappearance as a tragic murder, probably the sad result of a carjacking. You said there was even a body, found in a field near the interstate highway and identified as his."

"Yes to all that."

"Then I repeat my question. How could Wallis Beecham know that Chung is still alive? As far as the entire world outside Unit One is concerned, he's dead. Even Springer believed he was dead."

"Yes."

Nick didn't elaborate, and Melody needed a few seconds to work out the implications of her own logic. "My God! If Beecham knows Kenneth Chung is alive and in your custody, then somebody in Unit One has told him so. Is that what you're worried about?''

''Bingo,'' he said softly. ''Give the lady our grand prize.''

Her eyes widened. ''You really think there's a traitor inside Unit One?''

''It's never happened before in the twenty-seven-year history of the unit,'' Nick said grimly. ''We're a close-knit group. We have to be, since the nature of our work complicates our ability to make friends outside the unit. Naturally, we're careful about the people we recruit. But we've had problems making headway in our investigation of the Bonita partnership, and Springer's death confirms my opinion that the problems might be more than happenstance.''

This time Melody took longer to make the leap to the next step. ''If there's somebody inside Unit One who's reporting to Wallis Beecham, then Beecham will soon know that I've been recruited.''

''You'll meet only a limited selection of personnel while you're in training. But eventually, yes, if there's a mole inside Unit One, you'll meet him. Or her. And then, presumably, Wallis Beecham will know, too.''

Melody leaned back in her chair, expelling her breath in a sigh that sounded almost relieved. ''Now I understand why you're so keen to recruit me,'' she said. ''You want me for bait. You're going to set me up to trap Wallis Beecham, aren't you?''

''Are you willing to be used as bait?'' Nick asked.

He saw the subtle clues that indicated her struggle. Which, he realized, wasn't over whether to agree to his proposition. It was a struggle to conceal her eagerness to accept. Melody wasn't about to let him know that by offering her the chance to bring down Beecham, he'd scored a hit on her deepest emotions.

After a few seconds she flicked her hair away from her face, the gesture a little less casual than normal. "I've been offered more boring assignments," she said.

He allowed her to believe he'd been deceived about her degree of eagerness. "I'll take that as a yes?"

"If you like."

It was Nick's turn to hide his satisfaction. He'd given away a lot more information than he'd originally planned, but every scrap of revelation had been worth it. In retrospect, he couldn't understand why he'd wasted time on a blackmail project instinct had warned him was doomed.

More to downplay the importance of what had just been agreed than for any other reason, Nick didn't end the interview right then and there. He filled Melody in on some unimportant details of Lawrence Springer's activities on behalf of the Bonita Project, using their conversation as a means of clarifying in his own mind exactly how much Melody had managed to find out for herself and confirming that she'd originally been set on the trail of the partnership by documents she'd found when clearing up Lady Rosalind's personal effects.

She'd done surprisingly well, Nick decided, considering that she'd been working alone, with no technical resources to tap into. She didn't have a clue about the true goal of the project, but Lady Roz's cryptic notations had eventually led her to the conclusion that Walter Beecham was working with four other men: Lawrence Springer, of course, and Senator Lewis Cranford, along with Victor Heston, scion of one of the oldest and most powerful banking families in the country, and former vice president Johnston Yates.

One ramification of the plot that Melody had apparently never considered—even though it ought to have leaped out at her—was the possibility that her mother's death had been the result of murder rather than suicide or an accident. This was a strange omission on her part, given all the media speculation following Lady Roz's disappearance. It was especially strange in view of the fact that Lady Roz had died on board Johnston Yates's yacht. Melody had uncovered the fact that Yates was a member of the Bonita partnership several months ago and yet she still seemed to consider her mother's death an unfortunate accident rather than the elimination of a woman who'd learned enough to be dangerous.

Nick wondered if Melody's blind spot had developed *because* of all the media speculation following her mother's death. She'd probably dealt with so many lies about herself in various media outlets that she now had a knee-jerk distrust of everything the tabloids wrote. As she'd been a victim of some of their wilder flights of fancy, it would be easy for her not to notice how often their more bizarre stories turned out to be true. Whatever the reason for the blind spot, Nick resolved not to raise any questions about Lady Roz's death at this point. If he ever needed a spur to jolt Melody into action, the suggestion that her mother had been murdered might be exactly what he needed.

It was past noon by the time Nick was satisfied

he'd done all he could to forge a secure commitment from Melody toward Unit One. He knew she must be close to exhaustion after the stress of the past twelve hours, especially since she'd had less than four hours' sleep, but she had never once shown her fatigue. She'd kept her emotions under tight control, too. If she was reluctant to allow Nick to see how badly she wanted revenge against Wallis Beecham, she was even more fiercely determined to drop no hint as to the tangled web of hurt and betrayal that lay behind her need for revenge.

Nick didn't attempt to probe. He doubted if Melody herself understood all the psychological underpinnings of her desire to destroy the man who had once been her father, and he sympathized with her wish to avoid digging into the emotional tar pit of her feelings toward her parents. Nick had several unexplored tar pits of his own, and he firmly believed that adults who wanted to retain their mental health would be smart to avoid contemplating the roots of their hang-ups. Accept them and move on was his motto. Life was too short to waste time poking at the past like a dental hygienist probing teeth in search of cavities.

His purpose with Melody achieved, Nick rose to his feet. "It's past lunchtime, and I'm starving. Are you hungry?"

"I'm starving, too," Melody said.

"Good. Come and meet Martin McShane, our director. He's expecting to see us in his private dining room right about now."

Thirteen

Nick awarded Melody bonus points for keeping her jaw from dropping when she was introduced to the director, although her eyes did glaze slightly in shock. Mac was never a man to go for the understated look, and today he'd togged himself out as if he'd been sent along by central casting to audition for a role in *Austin Powers III.* His sparse gray hair was spiked into a vaguely punk style that revealed patches of pink scalp and he wore a Hawaiian shirt, together with his favorite cowboy boots, teamed with immaculately pressed khaki dress pants and a belt with a Mickey Mouse buckle. Fortunately, he chose not to demonstrate that the buckle squeaked if you pressed the mouse's nose, which might well have sent Melody over the top.

Mac shook Melody's hand. "Glad to have you on board. You're going to enjoy working with us."

Melody responded with neutral courtesy, although Nick would have given good odds that she was wondering just what sort of a paramilitary organization would select this man for its director. She was probably calculating just how soon she could extract every drop of information Unit One had about Wallis Beecham and then run like hell from their clutches.

"I've ordered chicken salad and fresh fruit for

lunch,'' Mac said. ''Boring, but I didn't think you'd be in the mood for quail's eggs or stuffed snails. Been a rough night for you.''

''Quail's eggs taste just like regular eggs as far as I can tell,'' Melody said. ''And I'm never in the mood for stuffed snails.''

Mac shot her a warm smile. ''Smart woman. So let's sit down and get on with it.'' He led the way to a small table covered in a starched white cloth and already laid with three place settings. ''Nick, have you told her how we take care of training?''

''No, I didn't get that far.''

''I'll explain.'' Mac offered Melody a basket of warm rolls. ''Here's the deal. Basic training lasts eight weeks. Takes that long to get the recruit in shape—''

''I'm already in shape.''

''No, you only think you are,'' Mac said. ''Iced tea?''

''No, thank you. I prefer water.'' Melody's knuckles turned white where she gripped the butter knife.

Nick smothered a grin. Mac had better watch it, or he'd look down and find a butter knife sticking between his ribs.

''Fitness is only part of basic training,'' Mac said, ignoring the white knuckles although he'd undoubtedly seen them. The guy might have the dress sense of a drag queen on PCP, but he had the observational skills of an eagle. ''You also need weapons training, and lots of instruction in how to play a part when you're on assignment. Although Nick says you do that all the time anyway.'' Mac gave her a bland smile.

Melody smiled back. Sweetly. ''I certainly do, Mr.

Director. Why, right now I'm managing to act as though I'm not lunching with two men who seem to have just been released from the psych ward at Bellevue. Believe me, it's an Oscar-winning performance."

Mac laughed. "Quick under pressure. That's good. Here's the story we've come up with to explain your absence. You've had a car accident. You're in a hospital in New Jersey, somewhere out by the shore. Intensive care. Not expected to survive. No visitors. In a few days you'll recover enough for visitors. We'll arrange a show for Jasper Fowles. Get you tucked into bed with a few bandages and IV drips. Nick, you can set up the hospital?"

He nodded.

"Why do we need to explain my absence?" Melody asked. "Why can't I just hand in my notice to Jas..." Her voice died away and she stared unhappily at her chicken salad. Clearly she had just grasped how difficult it would be to convince Jasper that she'd decided, overnight, that she no longer wanted to work for him. "I guess I'm not allowed to tell Jasper the truth?"

"You're not allowed to tell anyone the truth," Nick said crisply. "First rule of basic training. Never, under any circumstances, reveal the existence of Unit One. To be sure that new recruits understand how important that rule is, they live on the premises. Unless you're accompanied by a senior operative, you won't be allowed to leave this facility during basic training."

"In other words, I'm a prisoner."

"Yes, but this is a real nice place to be imprisoned,'' Mac said cheerfully. ''Food's good. Uniform's comfortable—''

''Uniform? I have to wear a uniform?'' Melody gave up on her salad and pushed the plate away. ''You've got to be kidding!''

''I never joke about Unit One,'' Mac said.

Nick saw Melody sneak a glance at the director's purple-and-pink Hawaiian shirt, a joke in itself. Presumably she was assessing what sort of uniform the owner of such a shirt might order for his underlings.

''We're a paramilitary organization,'' Mac said, blithely ignoring her glance. ''Uniforms help create the right mind-set. But you'll not be unhappy. You'll have your own room with cable TV. The library has all the latest bestsellers as well as the classics. CDs and DVDs, too. Why would you want to leave?''

''Because I have a life of my own?''

''Not anymore,'' Mac said. ''You're a trainee agent with Unit One. For the next eight weeks your life is ours.''

Fourteen

Melody fell onto the bed in her small room, too tired to turn back the covers. Which was probably a good thing, since she was also too tired to take off her sneakers. If she'd had even a drop of spare energy, she would have spent some time asking herself if anything, even defeating Wallis Beecham, was worth the six days of hell she'd already put herself through, not to mention the seven weeks and one day still remaining.

However, she didn't have the capacity, since she'd just run five miles in the rain, with Bazooka Buddy sprinting along behind to prevent her slowing down. She simply lay on the bed, her mind a formless cloud except for its ability to register the exquisite ache and pain of her muscles. Nick's training regimen required her to complete the course in thirty-seven minutes. She'd turned in a time of thirty-four minutes and fifteen seconds. Unfortunately, she might not live long enough to enjoy her triumph.

How the heck many muscles were there in the human body anyway? She had no idea, but several thousand of hers were currently conspiring to demonstrate that Martin McShane had been correct, and that she hadn't been anywhere near as fit as she'd imagined when she started the Unit One torture course, laughably known by the code name of basic training. The only muscles in her body that didn't ache were the ones that had already given up and died after six days of nonstop abuse.

From somewhere, God knew where, she summoned the energy needed to roll onto her stomach, her favored sleeping position. It felt as if no more than a couple of minutes had passed when she felt a hand shaking her shoulder. "Hey, Melody, wake up."

"Go 'way. I'm dead."

"Time to get up, Melody. This is your second warning."

She recognized Nick's voice. Dimly, even in sleep, she remembered that disobeying orders had unpleasant consequences, usually involving groups of sadistic men standing around watching her do push-ups. She pulled her weary body upright, set her feet on the ground and opened her eyes. Did eyeballs have muscles? If so, hers were aching.

Nick wasn't standing over her. Instead, she saw that he was kneeling by the side of her bed. He chose not to speak and she didn't have strength to spare for constructing intelligible sentences, so they just looked at each other for a long, silent moment. Her stomach gave an odd little jump when she finally pulled her gaze away.

"I'm sorry I haven't been able to catch up with you for the last few days," Nick said. "I've been getting daily reports from your trainers, though. How are you doing, Melody? It's been rough, I bet."

His voice was husky, almost tender. In the shadowy glow of the night-light she thought she saw a hint of desire in his dark eyes. That must surely be a trick of the dim lighting, or perhaps an illusion created by her sleep-heavy eyes.

A quiver of sensation rippled down her spine, although whether she was responding to the tenderness in his voice or the desire that might be in his eyes she wasn't sure. "I'm not as fit as I thought I was," she admitted, too exhausted to pretend. "But I guess I'll survive."

"Sam says you're doing well with the training program. Very well. He told me you turned in a great time on the run this evening. Buddy had to sprint to keep up with you."

Sam, ex-marine drill sergeant, was the man charged with getting her fit. Tony was responsible for teaching her unarmed combat. Dave gave her weapons instruction. Buddy was on hand for general backup. All four could have given the priests of the Spanish Inquisition tutorials on how to torment the human body.

For a woman who planned to escape from the clutches of Unit One the moment she'd sucked them dry of information about Wallis Beecham, Melody was surprised by the pleasure she felt hearing Nick's praise. The training for Unit One recruits was so intense it was impossible to avoid a feeling of accomplishment each time she reached the end of another day, although she remained determined not to fall into the trap of finding herself emotionally committed to Unit One. Despite what Nick might think, she wasn't a genuine recruit. She simply planned to accomplish her mission of bringing down Wallis Beecham and then she would be out of here.

"It's easy to do well on the training program," she said. "I have good teachers." That made two reasonably civil remarks in a row she'd addressed to Nick, which had to be a record, she thought wryly.

"You're right, they're the best," Nick agreed, his voice still warm. "Did you know David and Sam are both ex-military commandos?"

"I knew about Sam. I guessed David might be, although he doesn't talk much about his past."

"They have some fascinating stories about the wars in Afghanistan and Iraq to tell when you get to know them better. David's cheated death so many times he could make a coven of cats jealous."

"I'll look forward to hearing their stories sometime." Melody closed her eyes, so tired that she was drifting off to sleep where she sat.

Nick joined her on the bed, putting his arm around her shoulders to keep her upright. "Hang in there for a minute or two longer, Melody. I have a scheduling message for you."

"I'm awake." It was more or less true.

"I came to let you know that we've finalized preparations with that hospital out by the New Jersey shore. We have a room assigned for you tomorrow, and I get to play doctor when Jasper Fowles comes to visit you. He's been calling there three and four times a day. He's very relieved that you're out of intensive care and he's looking forward to seeing you. Now that you're supposedly recuperated, we've made arrangements so that he can phone the hospital and the call will automatically be rerouted here so you can talk to him. Remember not to sound too energetic."

"Thank you. I know Jasper must have been worried sick." If she hadn't been so sleepy perhaps she would have remembered more clearly that the source of Jasper's worry was Unit One—they'd kidnapped her, then lied about her state of health. As it was, she felt a rush of gratitude toward Nick. In addition to which, the idea of spending several hours lolling around in a hospital bed sounded as close to bliss as she was likely to get in the next several weeks. She might get as much as four hours of extra sleep. The prospect was enough to send a little shiver of ecstasy chasing down her spine.

"What time do we have to leave here for the hospital?" she asked.

"Three-thirty. You can sleep for two hours more."

She reached out to reset her alarm clock, knocking it off the nightstand she was so clumsy with fatigue.

Nick caught the clock and set it for 3:00 a.m., then placed it so that it would face her as she slept.

"Thanks," she said, yawning.

He touched her lightly on the cheek, then quickly dropped his hand, as if the gesture had been against his better judgment. "I'll leave you to get some rest, Melody. You look exhausted. Totally wiped, in fact."

"Just what every woman wants to hear." She had no idea what psychic hole that remark had popped out of, since she never cared about how she looked and was indifferent to compliments about her appearance. Her modeling career had left her feeling detached from ownership of her own body, although she appreciated the social acceptance that came from the genetic accident of regular facial features and a lithe body.

Confused by her own comment, she dropped her gaze, in part because she was experiencing a disastrous longing to have Nick touch her again and she wanted the sensation to stop. When she'd woken up, she would have sworn she was barely this side of comatose. She was still light-headed with fatigue, but her body was suddenly tingling with sexual awareness.

"Even though you're tired, you're still very beautiful," Nick said.

Having observed Lady Roz in action for years, Melody knew just what beauty could achieve—and how much more it couldn't. But she still felt a shiver of response to Nick's words, and that was as unexpected as everything else that had happened in the past five minutes.

Nick held her gaze for a moment, then reached for the zipper of her jacket. "This is damp, you know. You shouldn't sleep in it."

He unzipped the jacket and helped her to shrug out of it, his hands running down her arms as he pulled off the sleeves. Melody knew she must be imagining the hint of a caress she'd felt in his touch. Nikolai Anwar caressing her? There was an idea that didn't compute. She tossed the hooded jacket over the bedpost, but when she turned back she found Nick's gaze fixed on her again and this time there was no mistaking the desire in his eyes.

"I was running," she said, a slight tremor in her voice. Then she remembered that they'd already discussed the run. She cleared her throat. "It was raining."

"I know your schedule. I designed the training program."

"And ordered up the rain?"

"Of course. Especially for you. A reminder of England."

"A bunch of bluebells would have been nicer. Or some Cornish cream."

"Next time." Nick gave a tiny smile that melted something deep inside her. "You should probably take off your sweatpants. They look damp, too."

"I guess they are."

"I'll leave you, then. I remember how exhausting basic training can be. Good night, Melody. Sleep well." Still looking deep into her eyes, he took her hand and raised it to his mouth, brushing his lips lightly across her knuckles.

His mouth barely touched her skin, but an electric charge jolted Melody's body, racing through her veins and raising her body heat. It was so long since she'd experienced honest-to-God sexual need that it took her a moment to recognize what she'd just felt, even though she had been aware of the undercurrent of physical attraction in her relationship with Nick right from the start. Even when he'd been playing the role of William Wolfe, there had been an elemental awareness simmering beneath her irritation at his fawning compliments.

In normal circumstances she would never have surrendered to the stirrings of desire, however enticing. She preferred relationships where she was in control and her emotional investment was minimized. Nick was high risk on both counts. She didn't imagine for a second that he would allow his sexual partners to call the shots, nor was she sure that sex with him would be emotionally safe.

But she was still in a dreamy place between sleep and wakefulness and her defenses were at their lowest ebb. She reached up to put her hands on his shoulders, wanting the physical contact, and she didn't protest when Nick gently pushed her back against the pillows, then followed her down. The bed in her assigned room was twin-size and there wasn't much room for two people, so Nick lay very close to her. She'd noticed the hard, muscled fitness of his body even at the Plaza, when he'd been playing the role of stoop-shouldered William Wolfe. Lying this intimately entwined with her, his body felt like a piece of sculpted marble, except warmer and a lot more exciting.

"I grew up in Maine," he said, massaging her aching shoulders in a rhythm that managed to be both soothing and erotic at the same time. "Isn't that where you spent the summers with Wallis Beecham when you were growing up?"

"Yes," she said. She sighed with drowsy pleasure as Nick unlocked the kink in a muscle that had seemed permanently twisted. "Wallis has a vacation home right on the beach near Frenchman's Cove and I spent half a dozen summers there when I was a teenager. Where was your home?"

"About sixty miles from Frenchman's Cove. But we lived farther inland, in a small town in Piscataquis County, called Corston. Do you know it?"

She shook her head. "Not even the name."

"It's a small place, so I'm not surprised. There wasn't much entertainment, so I spent a lot of time hanging with my friends, trying *very* hard to be cool."

She smiled. "Same for me in Frenchman's Cove. Luckily I didn't have much adult supervision. Wallis flew in for the occasional weekend, but mostly it was just me and the housekeepers."

Nick stopped massaging. He rested his chin on his

hand so that he was gazing down at her while his other hand drifted away from her shoulders and began to stroke her thigh with unmistakable eroticism. Melody wasn't too sleepy, or too willfully blind, to realize she was being seduced. Rather expertly seduced, in fact. She debated calling a halt, and decided there was still lots of time for that. Because what he was doing felt…wonderful.

"You must often have been lonely," Nick murmured, his hand trailing up her body again, and this time coming to rest tantalizingly close to her breasts. "Especially since the States was almost a foreign country for you."

"Not all that foreign. I lived in Chicago until I was four, and I traveled back here every year after that. Besides, there was a terrific family living next door in Frenchman's Cove. They had two sons who were in high school, and their place was always crammed with teenagers—"

"Hanging out, trying to be cool, of course."

"What else? The boys were a year older and a year younger than me and we had a great time together. They taught me to sail, and to fish." She smiled at a sudden memory. "And to kiss."

"Both of them?" Nick asked, sounding startled.

"One at a time in different summers." She laughed, experiencing a rare flicker of nostalgia. "The younger one was definitely a better kisser."

"Lucky boys," Nick said softly. His hand cupped her breast and he leaned toward her. For a moment she was sure he was going to kiss her. Instead, he brushed a strand of loose hair out of her eyes, tucking it behind her ear, the gesture far more gentle than she would have expected from him. His thumb stroked back and forth over her nipple, his touch somehow more erotic through her cotton athletic shirt than it would have been on naked skin.

''Did your stepmother and stepbrother stay in Maine for the summer?'' he asked. ''How did you get on with them?''

''They were almost never there. Sondra likes beaches to be tropical. And Chris... Well, Chris never enjoyed being in a town where people didn't care a hoot that his daddy was a multimillionaire.''

''Let me take a wild guess here. You don't much like Chris Beecham.'' Nick gave another of his too-rare smiles, and Melody felt desire wash over her in a warm, intoxicating wave. Instead of answering with words, she linked her hands behind Nick's head and pulled him down, her mouth already opening in anticipation of his kiss.

For an exciting moment she felt his lips pressed firmly against hers, his tongue reaching deep. The hardness of his erection pressing against her belly was deeply pleasurable and she arched toward him, tiredness momentarily subsumed in a rush of desire.

The kiss had barely begun, the pressure of his erection had barely registered, when Nick pulled himself away from her. Disoriented, Melody didn't move when he swung his feet down onto the floor and stood up, running his hand through his cropped hair.

''Training lesson number thirteen,'' he said coolly. ''Far more secrets are given up in the bedroom than in the torture chamber.''

It was a second before Melody grasped what had happened. Then rage flashed at white heat, consuming her. ''You son of a bitch! You set me up!''

"This is a good time for me to remind you that I'm your commanding officer."

"You can go to hell, *sir.*" She tumbled helter-skelter out of the bed, the mists of sleep finally banished from her brain even though her legs still had a problem holding her steady. "You deliberately came and woke me up when you knew I would be exhausted. You took advantage—"

"Of course I took advantage," Nick said curtly. "As an interrogator looking for information, that's my job. I persuaded you to lower your defenses by telling you a lie—I've never set foot in Maine—and then I asked you a string of personal questions you would never have answered if I'd asked them in a different setting. I wanted to catch you off guard, with your defenses down, and I did. You're lucky I chose not to ask you anything you would regret having answered."

"What about you, Nick? Were you caught off guard, too? Because you sure as hell were aroused."

"And your point is?" He shrugged. "I'm a healthy male. You're a beautiful and desirable woman. Physical arousal while seducing you meant nothing except that I was doing my job."

"No problem whoring for the cause, Nick?"

"None whatsoever. Remember Claire?"

She should have known by now that he never reacted to her insults, simply turned them back against her. Melody swung away, not willing to let him see not only that he had breached her defenses, but that she still didn't have them back in place.

"Let's cut to the chase, since I'd like to get to sleep," she said, speaking without looking at him. "Was your message about going to the hospital tomorrow a ruse or has a meeting with Jasper really been set up?''

''The message is for real. I'll expect to meet you in front of the elevators at three-thirty.''

''I'll be there.'' Melody got back into bed, rolling to face the wall. She refused to acknowledge his presence even to the extent of asking him to go.

She heard Nick open the door, and willed him to leave, but he lingered a moment longer in the doorway. She sensed his hesitation before he spoke. ''Tenderness. Kindness. That's how I got to you, Melody. Your shell is tough, but inside you're vulnerable. Learn how to defend yourself better or Wallis Beecham will chew you up and spit you out in tiny pieces when we send you up against him.''

''I'll keep your advice in mind.'' He didn't have to worry; she was a very quick study. She already knew how to defend herself against Wallis Beecham, and she would never again make the mistake of allowing Nikolai Anwar anywhere within a thousand miles of her heart.

Fifteen

The climbing wall was forty-five feet high and ran the entire thirty-foot length of the narrow storage area in which it had been built. A projection mimicking a rocky overhang was located about two-thirds of the way up, looming over the storage corridor and cutting off a clear view of what horrors might lurk in the final fifteen feet of the climb. The corridor lighting was somewhere between gloomy and dim, and the temperature hovered at forty brisk degrees Fahrenheit, either to protect the materials being stored or to mimic typical mountain-climbing conditions. But it wasn't the chilly atmosphere that had Melody shivering. After one terrified glance upward, she ducked her head and concentrated on tying her shoes, as if perfectly matched laces would somehow make her fear of the wall go away.

"You growin' roots out of your ass?" Sam inquired. "If not, you might want to think about climbin' the wall."

Not for the first time, Melody wished she had a different personality and that she could simply throw herself at Sam's size-thirteen feet and beg for mercy. After six weeks of training, Sam had become a friend, and she was sure he'd be sympathetic. Unfortunately, about the only thing that scared her more than climbing the stupid wall was the prospect of admitting to a man she'd grown to admire that she was terrified of heights and couldn't do it.

She drew in a deep breath, dipped her hands into the box of resin and stepped up to the wall. "I'm ready."

Sam clipped the safety line to her harness. "This isn't a timed test. The aim is accuracy and correct utilization of your upper body strength. You fail if the safety line deploys. It's electronically monitored, set to buzz if you make a major error. Most climbin' is done with a partner and ropes, of course, but in our situation we don't always have pitons and cable when we need 'em, so we train for what we're likely to encounter. You have to find a way up the wall without employing the usual aids. Okay?"

"Peachy keen," she said gloomily.

"I'll be right ahead of you the first time, showing the easiest route up. Not that there's any danger, with you wearing a line an' all."

The first time. Holy Jesus, Sam was going to make her climb this…this stalagmite more than once. Unless she died of fright the first time around, which was a distinct possibility.

"All you have to do is follow me. Watch and remember."

Sam gave a light spring and grabbed a steel handhold some seven feet from the floor. He swung by one arm for ten seconds or so before reaching up to another hold about a foot higher. His feet quickly found a niche, enabling him to reach higher with his arms. He progressed until his feet were about ten feet above the ground before turning around to hang one-armed and one-footed so that he could observe Melody.

"Your turn," he said cheerfully, no more concerned than if he'd been lolling in an armchair. "Remember, follow my route—it's the easiest way up. On a commercial wall the handholds would be color coded to indicate various degrees of difficulty. We don't have that here, of course."

Of course they didn't. Why make life simpler for the unfortunate Unit One recruits when they could add an extra layer of torment? Nick's sadistic fingerprints were all over this exercise, just like the rest of the training program, although he'd been away for the past two weeks on some mission that nobody, of course, had explained to her. Not that she cared. The longer he stayed away, the better.

Melody drew in a deep breath and prepared to tackle the torture of the day, but she was so nervous that when she ran and jumped her hand slipped off the steel hold. The only reason her monitoring line didn't activate was that she hadn't left the ground.

"Your arthritis playin' up? Jesus, Melody, what's with you this mornin'? Get your ass in gear, girl."

She made another run and missed again, her arm muscles turned to water by sheer reluctance to take the first step that would in short order have her hanging in space.

"Hey, what's the matter?" Sam demanded. "Melody, what's going on? You broke your arm or somethin'?"

The mere fact that he wasn't cussing her out indicated that he knew there was a serious problem. Okay, enough was enough. She needed to tell Sam the truth. How difficult could it be to admit that she had a serious phobia about heights? She'd volunteer to do a million push-ups instead, but she wasn't going to crawl up the face of a mock cliff that struck her at this moment as only slightly less intimidating than Mount Everest in a blizzard. As for that overhang… How would you get past it without hanging upside down like a tree sloth? She closed her eyes at the mere thought, quite sure she must be turning green given the quantity of bile churning in her stomach.

Since Melody's eyes were closed she didn't see Nick come in, but the hair on the back of her neck stood up even before she heard his voice speaking behind her. So he was finally back from…wherever. Not that she gave a damn, one way or the other.

"Morning, Sam. I had a free half hour, so I came to get in some wall time. It was a long flight home and I need to work out some kinks."

Sam gave Nick a casual salute. "Mornin', boss. Good to have you back. We're only usin' the right-hand route, so you've plenty of room to play."

"Great. So, Melody, how's it going? Looking forward to your first climb?"

"Sure. I can hardly wait."

Nick gave her a smile that, as usual, contained only mockery. Which had to be the reason for the instant clenching of her stomach muscles. He looked tired, lean and predatory. Also infuriatingly sexy, if you happened to be one of those crazy women who liked to climb into bed with men who left you emotionally devastated.

"Don't let me keep you," he said. "I know how exhilarating this climb is the first time around. Go ahead, Melody. I'll watch you for a while."

Exhilarating? Dammit, he was taunting her. He knew how scared she was and had come to observe her humiliation. But how could he know, when almost nobody in the world had any idea about her phobia? And if he didn't know, why was she getting such strong subliminal vibes from his direction?

There was no way in the universe that she was going to throw herself on Sam's mercy with Nikolai Anwar there to witness her pathetic weakness. She'd wanted to know what it would take to persuade her to climb the damn wall, and she'd just found out. It took Nikolai Anwar.

Without bothering to acknowledge Nick's presence, she ran and caught the steel hold. This time her grip was firm and she managed to support herself in a one-armed swing exactly as she'd seen Sam do. Fueled by determination that Nick wouldn't be treated to the sight of her screwing up, she rotated her body to face the wall, her left hand reaching up for the next handhold as her foot found a supporting niche.

She couldn't look down, or it would be all over. Fortunately, that precluded the possibility of knowing whether or not Nick was still watching. The burning sensation in the middle of her back suggested that he was. In addition to being unable to look down, she couldn't bring herself to look more than a couple of inches upward, so she climbed doggedly, numb with fear, staring at the patch of wall in front of her nose until the top of her head bumped up against Sam's feet.

"Good," he said. The praise was unusual, but she was too upset to register it more than peripherally.

"Watch where I go," he ordered. "These next few holds are complicated."

She'd trained herself to have a near-photographic memory for the precise details of a work of art, so she ought to be capable of remembering the placement of a few handholds on a climbing wall. But her mind wasn't blank with panic when she looked at a painting, whereas right now a ball of cotton had more functioning neurons than her brain. Melody fixed her gaze on Sam's hands and willed herself to register the pattern of his advance up the wall, even though it meant tilting her head to watch his progress.

Once she had the pattern assimilated, she followed Sam, stubborn and desperate. After about five feet she lost the mental pattern and froze, unable to do anything except cling to the wall. Only sheer obstinacy prevented her succumbing to the dizziness that threatened to send her flying into the abyss.

With her face pressed against the rough gray concrete, blind with stress, she gradually registered the sounds of somebody climbing to her left. Forcing her lids apart, she saw Nick speeding up the wall at an inhumanly fast pace. And he was probably taking a route designed to be three times as difficult as any other, she thought acidly, panic dissolving. Good grief, he'd already reached the overhang and was now traversing it by some method that had to be a near relation to Spider-Man's sticky fingers, since there seemed no other means of support keeping him from dropping straight to the ground. Paralyzed, she couldn't tear her gaze away from his progress along the overhang.

After a couple of tense minutes—tense for her, at least, even if not for Nick—he hauled himself onto the top of the ledge and sat there, peering down at her.

"Is there a problem?" he asked. "Why aren't you climbing, Melody?"

She couldn't answer him, because if she spoke she was seriously likely to throw up. She gritted her teeth, and by some miracle managed to recapture her mental image of Sam's route up the next few feet of wall. Grimly determined, she crawled upward, handhold by painful handhold, until the top of her head once again bumped into Sam's shoes.

"So far so good," Sam said cheerfully, as if they didn't both know that her climb had been a clunky scrabble, and that she'd avoided deploying her safety line more by good fortune than by any smidgen of skill. "You're almost two-thirds of the way up the wall already."

Only two-thirds of the way up? Melody would have said something rude if she'd had any breath to spare from her renewed panic attack. She absolutely had not needed a reminder that she was now hanging thirty feet in the air without a safety net. She was a human being, not a monkey, which meant she belonged on the ground, since *her* ancestors had made their way down from the trees about five million years ago. In contrast to Nick's ancestors who, judging from his activities right now, must have been swinging through the jungle mere decades earlier—

"Look to your right," Sam ordered, cutting through her increasingly hysterical thoughts. "There's a route to the top that avoids the overhang. That's the way we're going to take today."

From this height she could see that in the direction he pointed the overhang curved in and then out again, so that for a space of about eighteen inches the ledge was no more than a narrow projection that could be climbed over without the need to utilize any special techniques. The catch was that she would have to move horizontally for at least eight feet to reach the gap, and the necessary handholds for sideways movement were pathetically few and far between. Plus she'd be hanging thirty feet above the ground the entire time she edged sideways, with only her arms and shoulders for support, since she failed the test if the safety line deployed.

"Watch me. Concentrate." Sam stretched out and grasped a hold over to his right. His arm reach was at least six inches longer than hers, Melody calculated, and even he had needed to stretch. To grasp that same hold, she would need first to climb into the position Sam had just vacated, and then to swing out and lean significantly far over to her right side. She might even need to balance with only one foot lodged in a niche and the other one waving in space. It was a move that she could have made at ground level with almost no difficulty. At this height it was ridiculous to expect her to do something so crazy. Her entire body had already frozen in rejection of the mere thought. And why not? Her body seemed to grasp the concept of self-preservation.

Her stomach, the only part of her capable of motion, swooped threateningly. To make matters worse, she could feel Nick's gaze fixed on her with uncomfortable intensity. Well, at least that meant she had no choice other than to move. Be damned if she would upchuck with him watching.

Melody drew in a couple of fortifying breaths, and with painstaking slowness climbed into the position

Sam had just left. Then she turned her head toward the left, once again resting her cheek against the surface of the wall. Even though turning in this direction meant that she was looking straight at Nick, she needed to give herself a moment's respite from staring at the huge gap separating her fingers from their next designated handhold.

Nick, she discovered, was moving toward her, his arm-over-arm motion casually rhythmical as if he were swinging on a piece of playground equipment instead of hanging, without a safety line, from a projection thirty feet up in the air. Rationally, Melody recognized that what he was doing needed upper body strength rather than any special skill. Emotionally, she couldn't imagine how he avoided plummeting to the ground in stark terror.

He arrived at her side, hauled himself up onto the ledge once again and leaned over to speak to her. "You really need to pass this test," he said conversationally. "I want you to accompany me on a field mission tomorrow. To do that, you need to have graduated from basic training."

"You want me to go on a real field mission?" Melody was startled enough to tilt her head back far enough to meet Nick's eyes.

He nodded. "That's the plan."

"But I have almost two more weeks of training still to go."

"Actually, you don't. I'd never tell you this if you weren't about to puke your guts all over the wall and ruin your record, but you've completed the standard training course ahead of schedule. Your unarmed combat skills are still pretty minimal, but your marksmanship scores were phenomenal right from the start.''

''They were?''

''Yep. I guess we can attribute that to all the chasing after foxes you did on your granddaddy's estates when you were a kid.''

''My grandfather doesn't shoot foxes,'' Melody said. She sounded stiff because she was still in acute danger of puking.

Nick actually grinned. ''You're right. I forgot. You Brits don't do anything barbaric like shooting foxes. You leave your hounds the treat of tearing them to pieces. So what did you shoot at to perfect your aim? Easter bunnies?''

''Clay pigeons,'' she said dryly. ''My grandfather was one of the coaches for the British biathlon team, and he used to let me practice target shooting with them.''

''Interesting. But back to the problem of the wall. In case you haven't noticed, Sam is already at the top and he's starting to get one of his ferocious scowls, which scare the shit out of me, even if they don't worry you.''

Even one of Sam's ferocious scowls couldn't compete for terror with the prospect of launching herself sideways along the wall. ''Sam said this wasn't a timed test,'' she said weakly.

''True. Still, we prefer recruits not to make the project into an overnighter.''

Melody didn't answer. She couldn't because she was too busy eyeing the handhold to her right that, she would swear, had moved at least a couple of inches farther away since her last fearful glance.

Nick spoke with quiet authority. ''Release your

right hand from its death grip on its current hold. Do it now. That's right. Your feet and your left hand are giving you more than adequate support. Let your right arm relax at your side until you recover your sense of balance. Okay?''

''No,'' she mumbled.

''Yes, it's okay and so are you. Now lean back from the wall and make a small arc with your right arm and leg, so that you can grab the handhold on your inward swing. There's a niche for your foot, too, as you complete the arc. You'll find it easily.''

''How about I just take a quick bobsled run to the moon?'' But Melody swung out as Nick had suggested and grabbed the handhold that had previously seemed impossibly distant. Her right foot scrabbled for a moment, then her toes found the accommodating niche, enabling her to move her left hand and foot. She hung on, panting with relief—and dread of the next move.

Nick shifted along the overhang to her new position. ''You're doing great. Right now it's looking pretty good for your field mission tomorrow. The idea is for you to attend a housewarming at the redecorated Manhattan penthouse apartment of Johnston Yates and his wife, Cynthia.''

''How will I get an invitation? I barely know them beyond the fact that they were at my mother's funeral.''

''Jasper Fowles received a much-coveted invitation, so if you'll just haul your butt up this wall and complete the test, you can be briefed this afternoon, then go home tonight and attend the party tomorrow as Jasper's guest.''

''I can?'' The prospect of going home was so glo-

rious that for a moment Melody actually forgot sh
was hanging on to a concrete wall by her fingernail
What would it be like to sleep in her own queen-siz
bed in Jasper's elegant penthouse, with no aları
clock to wake her up for a 5:00 a.m. run through th
chill mists of November in New Jersey? A littl
shiver of ecstasy coursed down her spine at th
thought of sleeping in.

"How do you know Jasper received an invita
tion?" she asked.

"I know because I saw the guest list."

"How did you manage that?"

"Brilliant and highly dangerous detective worl
How else?"

"You bribed someone?"

Nick actually grinned for the second time. "Oucl
In fact, no bribe was needed. It was even easier tha
that. The security guards have a complete guest li
so that they know who to let in and who to keep ou
Bob Spinard accessed the security company's con
puter and—voilá, there was Jasper's name. Wonde
ful things, computers."

It wasn't difficult to work out that parties throw
by former vice presidents didn't happen every da
especially ones to which she could secure a guarai
teed entry. "You obviously need me at this party
you and Mac wouldn't dream of springing me earl
from basic training," Melody said.

"Of course we need you," he agreed. "I just sai
as much. And your point is?"

"Why can't we bag the wall? The test can't b
that important, relatively speaking."

He looked at her for a long, silent moment. "

that what you want?'' he asked finally, his voice neutral.

Of course it was what she wanted. Why did he even bother to ask such a ridiculous question? Melody closed her eyes. ''No,'' she muttered, her stomach performing a cancan of mingled fear and disbelief at what she was saying. ''I want to get to the top.''

''Okay. So let's do it. If you'd just pry your eyes open, you'd see that you need to reach out a mere eighteen inches or so to find your next handhold.'' His voice fell fractionally. ''Go for it, Melody. You've come this far. The rest isn't hard.''

He was right. The next two moves were easy, especially with Nick climbing near by. ''Precisely what am I supposed to do tomorrow night once I get to the Yateses' party?'' she asked, pausing to eye the last remaining chasm separating her from the narrow passage through the overhang. ''Presumably you're not springing me from basic training just so that I can enjoy Cynthia Yates's hors d'oeuvres.''

He shook his head. ''You have to get to the top of this wall before I give you any more details.''

''Nick, I'm not three years old. You can't bribe me out of my phobic fear of heights by doling out snippets of information as if they were candy.''

''Why not? Seems to have worked so far.''

Melody only noticed that she'd admitted to having a phobia when it was too late. Nick, she was relieved to see, took her admission in stride, neither gloating nor offering sympathy, which would have been worse.

''You have one more handhold to reach for before the ledge, and this one's a little tough,'' he said.

She winced. ‘‘Define *a little tough.*’’

‘‘This is the place where two-thirds of first-timer end up dangling from the end of their lifeline.’’

Fear washed over her in a giant wave. ‘‘Nick, can't—’’ She swallowed, cutting off the admission

‘‘Sure you can. You'll do fine,’’ he said.

‘‘I have a phobia about heights,’’ she yelled. ‘‘ will not do fine.’’

‘‘Sure you will.’’ Nick was infuriatingly casu about her earth-shattering admission of inadequacy ‘‘Fortunately, your pride is even more supersize than your phobia. You're too stiff-necked to live wit the knowledge that one-third of all candidates climb ing this wall did a better job of it than you.’’

Melody recognized that she was being manipu lated, but Nick's ploy worked because he was ex ploiting a simple truth. Between them, Wallis Bee cham and her mother had left her with an indelibl need to prove to herself that she could beat the odd that she could achieve, that she was worth somethin Achievement was the way she convinced herself th she was all grown up and no longer a captive of th painful emotions generated in a small child by pa ents who routinely abandoned her to the upscale ne glect of nannies and boarding schools.

Nick rolled off the ledge and grabbed a couple o handholds seemingly at random, nevertheless endin up shoulder-to-shoulder with her on the wall. ‘‘Th only way you can bridge the gap at this point is b moving downward about six inches.’’

‘‘I can't look down.’’ She heard the shake in he voice and despised herself for it.

‘‘Then don't think of it as looking down. Think o it as looking sideways at a forty-five-degree angle.

There was laughter in Nick's voice and Melody scowled at him. Dammit, if he could swing like a gorilla, she could at least scuttle like a...like a cockroach. Fueled by impatience with her own lack of courage, she slid her gaze along the wall and found the necessary handhold. Then she focused on the hold and simply allowed her body to make the same natural movement toward it that she would have employed at ground level.

The move worked. "I did it!" She turned to Nick, so flushed with triumph that she forgot how important it was to keep him at an emotional distance.

"You sure did." He grinned back at her, for once no trace of mockery visible anywhere.

"Hate to rain on your parade," Sam called down. "But there is the minor problem of the remaining fifteen feet to the top."

Melody managed to peer up through the narrow opening in the overhang, and Sam waved to her. "Good climbin', girl. Now you've only got the easy part left to do. Piece o' cake from here on up. You get no more help from Nick or me."

He was exaggerating, but the fifteen feet of wall ahead of her was peppered with handholds and visibly easier than the sections she'd already conquered. Melody started to climb fast. The sooner she reached the top, the sooner she could get off this damn wall. She was helped by the fact that the ledge cut off her view of the corridor floor, creating the comparatively reassuring illusion that she was only a few feet away from solid ground.

Her concentration was intense, but she was aware that part of what made the final few feet of the climb easier was the knowledge that Nick followed right behind her. She reached the top, panting and triumphant. And determined never to set foot on the wall ever again. Not in this lifetime, for sure, and preferably not in her next several reincarnations.

Sam was generous with his praise when she reached the top. Nick, by contrast, didn't congratulate her on overcoming her fear of heights, or on her successful completion of the basic training course. Instead he pulled on a pair of thin black leather gloves and gave a test tug to the cord wound over his shoulder and around his waist.

"Okay, we're done with climbing. Now for the fun part," he said.

Before she had time to protest, he clamped his arm around her waist, locked her legs around his hips and pushed off into space, rappelling down the wall at high speed, his feet barely touching the sides of the wall.

"Hey, recruits are supposed to rappel down by themselves!" Sam shouted from his perch.

"Who said?" Nick yelled back.

"Heard it from the hotshot director of training, just the other day."

"Yeah, but you can't pay any attention to that guy," Nick said cheerfully. "He's always blowing smoke out of his ass." He turned to Melody, more relaxed than she'd ever seen him. "Come on. I'm officially declaring you a graduate of Unit One's basic training program. Let's get out of here before Sam sends you back up the wall. I want to brief you on tomorrow's mission."

Sixteen

It was difficult to deceive somebody who knew you as well as Jasper knew her, Melody thought, wrinkling her nose at her reflection in the bedroom mirror. Last night she had returned to Manhattan after supposedly undergoing weeks of intensive residential rehab at an orthopedic clinic connected to Johns Hopkins. Unfortunately, at least from the point of view of her cover story, Unit One's brutal training regimen apparently suited her, and she looked visibly healthy even though she'd used all her makeup skills in an attempt to appear pale and tired.

Yesterday had been bad enough, but tonight she was having even more problems with her appearance. The prospect of what lay ahead at the Yates party excited her. Not because it was her first mission for Unit One and she wanted to do well. Of course not. She was excited because tonight's party led one step closer to exposing Wallis Beecham, and her face kept flushing a healthy pink however much powder she slathered on. Any more layers of makeup and she wasn't going to look like a convalescent—she was going to look like a kid who'd dipped her face in the flour jar.

Disguising her body posed even more of a problem than toning down the color in her cheeks. She'd ransacked her closet to find an outfit that hid the betraying new muscles in her arms and thighs, but anything that provided adequate concealment also looked depressingly dowdy after weeks of Unit One's drab cotton uniforms. She finally selected a long-sleeved, rust-colored velvet suit with black satin trim that she'd bought last fall for reasons that now entirely escaped her. Thank goodness it was drizzling rain, which provided some justification for turning up at the party covered from neck to knee. Melody grimaced as she fastened the top button of the jacket. She looked like a politician's wife anxious to avoid offending potential voters.

Jasper knew too much about women's fashion not to notice that her choice of outfit was on the odd side. Still, better an off-key cocktail suit than having to face probing questions about her flashy new crop of muscles. Melody added the burnished gold lapel pin that concealed a voice transmitter and fingered the tiny wireless microphone behind her ear one last time to reassure herself that it was still firmly stuck to her skin. It was. Grabbing her evening purse, she shoved a lipstick inside and went to find Jasper before the insanity of throwing in her lot with Unit One became overwhelming enough to send her on the first available flight back to England.

Jasper was waiting for her in the living room, the vertical metallic blinds on the picture windows drawn back to reveal the spectacular nighttime view over Central Park. He popped the cork on a split of champagne as she came into the room, and held a glass out to her, smiling. "It's really good to have you home, sweetie. And looking smashing, too. I've missed you."

"Nowhere near as much as I've missed you." *Looking smashing?* Well, that was a surprise. Jasper usually had pitch-perfect taste. Melody took the champagne and kissed him before taking her first sip. "Oh my, that's good."

"You're not still taking painkillers, then? I should have asked."

"No, I've been off pain medication for the last three weeks. But there was no alcohol in the rehab center, of course. No soda, either." She managed to say *rehab center* without stuttering, although she hated to lie to Jasper.

"Not even soda? So what delights did they have available for you to drink?"

For a moment Melody's mind blanked, as if the question were truly important and her reply mattered. "Most of the staff at the center were fanatic devotees of carrot juice," she said after a noticeable pause. "They tried hard to convert me. Without success, I might add. You can imagine how good this champagne tastes by comparison."

"Carrot juice?" Jasper gave an exaggerated shudder. "Take heart, sweetie. I promise nothing so horridly healthy will ever come into this household while I'm alive to protect you."

She grinned. "I knew I could count on you to advance the cause of sin."

"Always." Jasper wandered off to the kitchen and came back with a dish of his favorite marinated Greek black olives. "You're looking really well," he said, offering her the dish. "You're lucky you didn't get any severe cuts on your face. I saw your car before they finally junked it and I have to say, sweetie, that I expected to find you minced into small pieces when I came to the hospital that first time. At the very least, I expected you to need loads of plastic surgery."

"I was fortunate paramedics arrived on the scene so fast. The doctors told me that made a big difference to my recovery. My ankle was badly messed up, but it could have been a whole lot worse." The pitch of her voice was subtly off, Melody realized, making her remarks sound like the lies they were.

Fortunately—surprisingly—Jasper didn't seem to notice anything wrong. He asked several more questions about the rehab center and her doctors. Melody had been well briefed and she didn't have any problem with the factual content of her answers, but their conversation brought home to her that lying to Jasper on a daily basis was going to prove difficult on many levels. It wasn't that she'd previously confided every detail of her life to him. She'd never told him about her quest to bring down Wallis Beecham, for example. Still, in the past she'd been guilty only of lies of omission, whereas now her entire life had become a giant illusion, designed expressly to hide her true purpose. That sort of wholesale deception didn't matter where her dealings with strangers were concerned, but it mattered a lot with Jasper.

"Poor you. It sounds as if your rehab was gruesome," he said, responding to her fictitious account of tiring hours spent in physical therapy. "But you seem to have survived relatively unscathed. Although I do sense something different about you...."

"I have metal rods in my right ankle?" Melody suggested lightly, and immediately wondered if people with newly inserted artificial joints could wear the sort of high-heeled evening sandals she had on.

Jasper winced. ''Sweetie, if you *must* talk about the barbaric details of your rehabilitation, I'll try to overcome my loathing of blood and gore and listen to your war stories—''

''I'll spare your delicate sensibilities.'' She gave his arm an affectionate squeeze, relieved to have an excuse not to utter any more lies. ''In fact, I've wasted altogether too much time recently worrying about the accident. It's time to move the conversation on to more interesting subjects. Like getting back to work tomorrow. I can't even imagine what my desk must look like.''

''Not to put too fine a point on it—buried.''

''After the past few weeks, with other people organizing every minute of my day, clearing up the accumulated mess actually sounds like a welcome challenge.''

''You don't want to rush things,'' Jasper cautioned. ''I'd be thrilled to see you back on the job, of course, but only if you're sure you're ready.''

''I'm absolutely sure,'' Melody said. Her assignment from Unit One was to pick up the threads of her old life as quickly as possible, an instruction that meshed perfectly with her own wishes.

''Thank God,'' Jasper said with a sigh of sheer relief. ''Ellen is a good person, and she's worked hard to fill in for you. Unfortunately, she has about half your knowledge and a tenth of your artistic judgment.''

''You do flattery so well, Jasper.''

''Yes, I do. But in this case it's not flattery, it's the truth.''

It was odd that after only six weeks away, her life at the art gallery seemed faintly unreal, whereas the steel-and-concrete bunkers of Unit One felt like home. Not anxious to consider the ramifications of that particular insight, Melody walked over to the window to inspect the view of the park and streetlights shimmering in the rain. After weeks of living below ground except for occasional cross-country runs, even the gaunt-fingered shadows of the bare tree branches were a beautiful sight.

"It's terrific to be home," she said, seized by a momentary sensation of well-being. "Everything looks better than wonderful."

"Indeed." Jasper's voice was very dry. "I've always been a devotee of November drizzle and muddy sidewalks myself."

Melody laughed. "It must be your company that's adding a sparkle to the dreary weather." She swung around, holding out her glass for more champagne. "Tell me about the party we're going to tonight. Did Johnston Yates buy something from the gallery? Is that why you're invited?"

"He did buy a drawing, an especially lovely sketch of a Spanish dancer by John Singer Sargent, but that's not why he invited me to the party. Johnny and I go way back. In fact, it was Yates who first introduced your mother to me."

"More than eighteen years ago?" Melody asked, startled. "You've known Yates that long?"

Jasper nodded. "Longer. I met him just before he became vice president. God, I can't believe I'm that old." He smoothed his hair and sucked in his stomach, which was still impressively flat, and peered into the mirror behind the bar, apparently to reassure himself that the few signs of middle age that had dared to establish themselves on his person remained well concealed.

"I never realized that Yates and my mother had been acquainted for so long," Melody said. "For some reason, I was under the impression that Mother had only just met the Yateses when they invited her to join them on his yacht."

"Oh, no. How did you get that impression? Roz met them at a White House reception for the British foreign secretary when Yates was vice president. At least I think that's how they met. It's been a while, but I seem to remember hearing some story from Roz about the foreign secretary spilling Scotch on her dress and Cynthia personally escorting her to find a maid who could clean her up."

"That sounds typically Roz," Melody said, feeling a flash of rueful nostalgia. Her mother had been so dazzling that well into her forties men were forever spilling their drinks as they stared, mesmerized, into her eyes.

"Mmm, it does, doesn't it? God, I miss her elegance." Jasper's attention was still focused on his own reflection in the mirror and he squinted around a bottle of his favorite Belvedere vodka for a better view of his profile. "When Roz and Wallis were married they created a real splash on the social scene both here and in D.C., although in those days there were still people around who cared about quaint old customs like social exclusivity, and Wallis would never have made the A list on his own merits."

"Because he was a self-made man?" Melody asked.

"Good heavens, no, not because of that. We Americans admire people who've pulled themselves up by their bootstraps—you should know that. It's the Brits who prefer their social elite to have done absolutely nothing worth rewarding for as many generations as possible."

Melody laughed. "So what was the problem, then?"

Jasper turned away from the mirror after making a final adjustment to his black tie. "Manhattan society rejected Wallis Beecham because he was a phony and a bore. He's still full of bullshit, of course, but in those days he wasn't quite rich and powerful enough to conceal the odor. He's gotten a whole lot better at that over the years."

Jasper had never talked like this about her parents before, and Melody found his insights fascinating. "How did Roz manage to create such a social splash if Wallis couldn't make the A list of invitations? A lout for a husband is usually the kiss of death."

"Maybe in general, but Wallis was irrelevant to their social life. Your mother, as the stunningly beautiful daughter of a British earl, was guaranteed invitations to all the best parties regardless of her partner. Wallis tagged along, making business and political deals as he trailed in her wake. I think that's part of what kept them married for as long as they were—the doors Roz could open for Wallis. And speaking of parties and opening doors, we're going to be way beyond fashionably late for the Yateses' if we don't leave now."

Despite the rain, Jasper managed to do his usual trick of standing in the street, lifting his hand and seemingly generating a taxicab by Harry Potter alchemy. "How do you do that?" Melody laughed.

"God, Jasper, I'd forgotten how much I love going out with you."

"Sweetie, I've lived in Manhattan for all of my fifty-six...ahem, for more years than I care to remember. I've acquired the necessary survival skills for life in the city, in the same way a man in the Brazilian jungle learns how to avoid stepping on a cobra."

"I don't believe there are cobras in the Brazilian jungle, Jasper. I think cobras come from Asia."

"I see that rehab hasn't cured you of your infuriating tendency to quibble," he said waspishly.

Melody laughed again, leaning back against the torn leather of the seat. "I do so love you, Jasper. Are you absolutely sure that you aren't my father? I wish you were, you know."

As soon as she'd spoken, the cab filled with silence, suffocating in its intensity.

It was several moments before Jasper spoke. "No, I'm not your father," he said finally. "Your mother and I never slept together, Melody."

"I'm sorry, Jasper." She could feel herself blush. "I should never have said anything—"

"Why are you apologizing?" He put his hand over hers, the gesture both intimate and comforting. "There's absolutely nothing to apologize for. I wish you were my daughter, too. But you were already ten years old when I met you for the first time."

"I knew that. Of course I did. I can even remember our first meeting."

"I fed you vast quantities of chocolate, I seem to recall. Anything to keep you quiet, since I had zero experience dealing with children."

"At least they were the finest imported Belgian truffles," she reminded him.

"I'm lucky you didn't regurgitate everything over my favorite Persian rug. It would have been no more than I deserved." Jasper turned to her, his expression hard to read in the alternating dark and glow of the passing streetlights. "Have you been worrying about who your father is ever since your mum died? Is that where your question suddenly sprang from?"

"Not consciously." Melody gave a shrug that felt awkward rather than casual. "Life at the rehab center apparently gave me too much time for pondering life's mysteries. Although you would have thought that with all those sadistic physical therapists working me over for the past few weeks I'd have been too busy to ask myself pointless existential questions."

"It isn't pointless to want to know who your father is. Far from it."

"It's pointless when there's almost no chance of discovering the truth."

Jasper hesitated for a moment. "Why are you so sure there isn't much chance?"

"Where would I start looking for him?" Melody asked. "Roz was married at the time she got pregnant with me, so she had every incentive to conceal the truth. She successfully passed me off as Wallis Beecham's child from the day I was born until the day she died, and—God knows—Wallis isn't an easy man to deceive. If even he never doubted I was his daughter, you can be pretty sure that there wasn't a whisper circulating anywhere that my mother was having an affair."

"I don't agree," Jasper said, shaking his head.

"Spouses are notorious for being the last to know when their partner is being unfaithful. Just because Wallis was blissfully ignorant, that doesn't mean everyone else in their social circle was equally unaware. Remember, Roz was the insider and Wallis the outsider, even though he was the American."

"Roz may have been the ultimate insider, but there's still a limit to the loyalty she would have been able to command. Does it seem likely an entire group of people would keep a secret about adultery for thirty years?"

"Well, no..."

"Exactly. For once in her life, I think my mother was amazingly discreet. And nobody knew about the affair."

"You have a point," Jasper conceded. "But at least one other person knew."

"Her lover, you mean?"

"Her lover," Jasper agreed quietly. "Your father."

"Who is apparently not at all anxious to acknowledge the fact that I exist." Melody realized there was a faint wobble in her voice and she hurried on. "Whoever he is, he must suspect the truth about our relationship—"

"It's possible he hasn't heard about the outrageous tag end to your mother's will and so is reluctant to step forward for fear of causing trouble between you and Wallis."

Melody made a disparaging sound. "Unless he's returned to his alien starship, he must have heard. All the tabloids reported that DNA evidence confirms that Wallis isn't my father."

"Well, sweetie, I can't understand why, but not

everyone shares my addiction to the inside pages of the *National Enquirer*. It's possible, you know, that your father prefers the *Times* or even, God forbid, the tight asses over at the *Wall Street Journal*."

"But Wallis made sure everyone got the word. He even managed to insert a couple of paternity disclaimers into articles in the *Washington Post* and *Business Week*."

Jasper digested her comments for a moment, his silence an acknowledgment of their accuracy. "Perhaps your biological father is dead," he suggested finally.

"He might be dead," Melody agreed with a sigh. "Which would probably mean there's no hope of tracing him, ever. Or else he's alive, but just doesn't want to acknowledge his affair with my mother, not even to me."

"He was probably married at the time you were conceived. That's more than likely. Otherwise why were he and Roz both so discreet about the affair? If your father isn't dead, maybe he's still married to the same woman. In which case it might be difficult for him to fess up. Maybe his wife has all the money, and he can't risk offending her."

"But his wife never needs to know," Melody protested. "My father only needs to acknowledge the truth to me. It isn't as if I'm planning to broadcast the details on *The Jerry Springer Show*."

"But your father has no way of knowing what a private sort of person you are," Jasper pointed out. "Given the way pictures and stories about you constantly appear in the tabloids, he might conclude you can't keep a secret."

"I guess so." Melody repressed another sigh, but Jasper picked up on it anyway.

"You *are* worrying about this, however much you try to pretend otherwise. After Roz died, I had the impression that you didn't much care about her bombshell, except to feel relief that Wallis Beecham wasn't your father. Apparently I was wrong?"

Melody stared out of the cab window at a man heading home from the park with six dogs on leashes. "No, you weren't wrong. Not at the time. Immediately after the funeral I was so angry with my mother for the way she'd chosen to break the news that I didn't have much space or energy for wondering who my biological father actually was. Now most of the anger has dissipated, and I'm...curious."

"If you want my help, I might be able to give you some leads," Jasper said. "Your mother didn't tell me everything, of course, but she confided more in me than in most of her other friends. I know the names of a lot of the men she had affairs with, including several from the years before we met."

"Knowing her, she probably took care not to mention my father's name to you."

"You might be right about that," Jasper conceded. "She was talented at revealing a great many trivial secrets in order to hide a single big one."

Jasper's observation was spot on, Melody reflected. It had been from her mother that she'd learned the trick of telling reporters most of what they wanted to hear in order to protect the few aspects of her life she was really anxious to keep private. But Roz hadn't hidden her true self only from the media; she'd presented the same carefully crafted facade to everyone, including her most intimate circle of friends and family. It was only in the wake of her mother's death that Melody realized just how little she knew about "Lady Roz," despite the fact that her mother had been among the most photographed, most gossiped-about women in the world. If somebody had asked Melody to name the three most important events in her mother's life, she wouldn't have been able to do so. Ditto for the three people Roz cared most about. Had it been Roz's parents? A lover? Her daughter?

"You're looking sad," Jasper commented.

Melody smiled, albeit a bit wanly. "I was regretting that my mother and I never managed to get close enough to each other to have a really honest conversation."

Jasper rolled his eyes. "Sweetie, trust me on this. That isn't a cause for sorrow. It's the mark of a well-adjusted adult to look back on life confident in the knowledge that your parents know absolutely nothing about the inner you, and vice versa. The fact that I have no clue about what makes my mother tick is one of the few things for which I thank the Big Hominid in the Sky on a daily basis."

She laughed, as Jasper had intended, and their conversation turned back to trivialities until they arrived at the Yateses' town house in the East Sixties. The building dated from 1923, and Cynthia Yates had inherited it from her grandparents shortly after her husband became vice president. Cynthia was a talented homemaker and had exquisite taste in home furnishings. However, she spent little time in New York, preferring her native state of Georgia, and in the early nineties the house had been vandalized by a decorator whose taste ran to Louis XVI rococo, cross-fertilized by Las Vegas glitter. The ornate French antiques and gilded crystal candelabras had now been sold at auction and, under Cynthia's personal supervision, the interior of the house had been restored to its eighty-year-old art deco splendor, with the added comfort of appliances and plumbing that worked with the efficiency of the twenty-first century.

Melody and Jasper negotiated their way through the thronged main reception room toward the dining room at the back of the house. The entire rear of the house was built around a paved courtyard, artfully lit, with a centerpiece of a tall fountain that splashed water into a series of carved stone bowls. Huge verdigris urns held potted spruce and pine trees, providing an attractive oasis of living greenery even though winter nipped at Manhattan's heels.

At first Jasper kept Melody company as they circulated, greeting friends and clients. Then Jasper, a devoted fan of musical theater, glimpsed Ethan Hyrak, the newest and brightest star glittering on Broadway, and immediately took off in hot pursuit.

Melody, whose own brushes with notoriety made her hesitant about cornering celebrities, didn't follow Jasper. Instead, she joined Sir Anthony Reith-Cooper, the British ambassador to the United Nations, and an old friend of her grandfather's. Together they strolled the length of the buffet table, which was laden with gourmet delicacies, admiring the imaginative floral arrangements that Cynthia designed herself and for which she was justly famous. The food was also spectacular, and Melody and the ambassador were debating the relative merits of the exquisite ginger-spiced prawns and the buttery tuna tartar when she became aware of Nick's voice speaking in her mike.

She'd spent many hours training with her ear mike. From the beginning she'd found it easy to keep her face expressionless when David and Tony deliberately tried to provoke her by making outrageous comments about her physical attributes, or telling each other off-color jokes. She'd found it much more difficult to acquire the knack of continuing a coherent conversation despite hearing a different dialogue in her ear. Her respect for TV newscasters had increased exponentially during the training exercises. Finally, after a great deal of practice, she'd learned how to achieve the difficult trick of splitting her concentration, monitoring the dialogue in her ear mike just enough to know when she needed to react to an instruction without stopping her conversation in midsentence or moving around the room with the dazed look of a zombie.

During their briefing session yesterday, Nick had explained that he would be attending the party in the guise of a prominent Russian banker, a man who claimed the ability to cut deals and smooth the path for American industrialists wanting to do business in the former Soviet Union. She and Nick weren't supposed to know each other, and she didn't anticipate speaking to him, except in an emergency. In fact, Melody suspected she was wearing a mike tonight more as a training device for more complicated missions that would happen in the future rather than because Nick needed to be in constant communication with her on this particular occasion.

Despite having been warned about the role Nick was to play, it was a shock to hear him speaking

Russian. Given his name, his fluency shouldn't have been entirely surprising, but she was caught off guard by the reminder of how one-dimensional her acquaintance with Nick actually was. Had he grown up in the Soviet Union and immigrated to the States as a teenager, after the communist regime collapsed? she wondered. Or had he learned the language from grandparents who'd escaped during the upheavals of World War II? Whenever he'd arrived in the States, he spoke American so that it sounded like his native tongue. Which, of course, didn't necessarily mean that it was.

It occurred to Melody, not for the first time, that although she and Nick had spent multiple hours together during her training, he'd told her nothing about himself or his past except that he'd never set foot in the state of Maine. And that disclaimer was as likely to be as false as his conflicting claim to have grown up there. The bottom line was that she knew nothing about Nick beyond the simple facts of how he looked and where he was employed. His personal life, his past and his aspirations were all totally unknown to her. He could be married and the father of quintuplets for all she knew.

Melody looked away as he passed by, but not before she managed to observe that he was engrossed in conversation with a short, heavyset man. The heavyset man nodded and smiled to the British ambassador, but didn't stop.

''My Russian counterpart at the UN,'' Sir Anthony explained to Melody. ''He's a pretty decent fellow and we get on rather well. He often chooses to be entirely honest when it would be much more convenient for him to lie.''

"Do you know the man who was with him?" Melody asked as Nick's voice abruptly ceased, presumably because he'd cut off his mike. Her own mike had no such cutoff mechanism, leaving her conversations open to constant monitoring. For her protection, she'd been told. To make sure she didn't screw up, Melody had concluded.

The ambassador shot her a teasing glance over his glasses. "So you noticed Nikolai Anwar, did you? I hear he's a devil of a lad with the ladies. I can introduce you, if you like."

"Heavens, no. I wasn't angling for an introduction."

"I'm sure you weren't, but you might want to change your mind. One of the junior diplomats in my mission tells me he's a fabulous man to date."

"Thanks, but I'm currently in one of my periods where I've sworn off men." Melody managed to sound languidly amused rather than flustered, which was how she felt. It had never occurred to her that the ambassador would recognize Nick, much less identify him by his correct name. "I just thought I'd seen him around before and wondered who he was."

"You may well have seen him before," Sir Anthony said. "He visits New York every couple of months or so, and he gets invited everywhere. I seem to recall that he even maintains an apartment somewhere in Manhattan. And my informant tells me that he throws a great party."

"What line of work is he in, do you know?"

"International wheeling and dealing would be the best way to describe it. He's been very successful in negotiating deals in Russia for various big American companies, and a couple of British firms, too. All very high-level stuff, and strictly aboveboard these days, although the rumor around the UN corridors is that he got his start by selling off stolen Soviet missiles to Iraq—part of the mysterious stockpile of weapons of mass destruction that nobody seems able to account for."

Melody allowed her astonishment to show. "If that's true, given the feelings of this administration toward Iraq, I'm surprised he hasn't been locked up on suspicion of being a terrorist."

"One might think he would risk such a fate."

"Yes, one would. So why doesn't he?"

The ambassador's gaze became openly cynical. "Nikolai Anwar is much too useful to this administration to be locked up. And on that distinctly undiplomatic note, I'd better go and redeem myself by shaking hands with the Speaker of the House and listen to him lecture me about the failure of my government to single-handedly change the European Union's agricultural trade policy."

"That seems an excessive penance for a very small sin."

"But a penance I can't escape." The ambassador gave an exaggerated sigh. "My dear Melody, heed the advice of an elderly man who became wise far too late in life. If you ever think of joining the diplomatic service, take a crash course on the world's agricultural trading agreements and you will instantly decide to change your choice of career for something much pleasanter and more rational. Such as shoveling elephant manure at the circus."

She laughed, and the ambassador gave her a mock salute before wending his way across the room, leaving Melody free to wonder how in the world Nick had managed to maintain his role as a Russian financier over a period of months, and probably years. She wondered if his frequent absences during her training course had been caused by a need for him to be in Russia, or perhaps meeting with his clients in the States. Presumably, if blue-chip American and British corporations used his services, he did actually have to achieve some successes for them, not just keep his impersonation going by sleight of hand and generous use of smoke and mirrors.

Melody was grateful that her familiarity with the ritual of formal cocktail parties enabled her to maintain the facade of a polite guest while simultaneously mulling over these new insights into the organization and methods of Unit One. It seemed logical to conclude that she and Nick weren't the only two operatives who led double lives, which might explain why she'd not been introduced to any of the other field agents during her training and why she'd been given so few details about operational methods. She'd met more than a dozen of the analysts and technicians who worked for Bob Spinard, but she hadn't met any of the people who worked in the field, other than the men responsible for her training. If many—some? most?—operatives retained their true identities, she could see why she would have to prove her loyalty and efficiency before she was trusted with introductions.

Melody glanced around the crowded reception room, wondering if anybody else here was part of Unit One's organization. It was a mind-blowing possibility, but she couldn't dwell on it, because it was time to begin her mission and she needed to focus. More excited than she cared to admit, and a lot more nervous, she smiled and chatted as she made her way toward the confrontation with Johnston Yates. She'd been instructed to time her conversation with the former vice president as closely as possible to nine o'clock, and she'd been keeping him in her sights for the past fifteen minutes. At two minutes before nine she arrived at the entrance to the library, where she'd seen Yates retreat with a small group of friends. Among the group she recognized the mayor of New York, as well as the managing editor of the *New York Times* and Jodi Dencher, president of the Helix Corporation, a business leader who appeared on everyone's list of the ten most powerful women in America.

This party would have been right up Roz's ally, Melody reflected, feeling a stab of regret that her mother would never again charm her way through one of New York's or London's most splendid parties. Nick's voice spoke into her mike before she could drown in melancholy. ''Detach Yates from the group before you confront him. Do it now. The timing is tight.''

Melody had been so absorbed in the task confronting her that she was startled by Nick's order, which, because of the mike, sounded as if it had been spoken mere inches behind her. She only just managed to prevent herself turning around to look for him.

''Acknowledged,'' she murmured, moving her lips as little as possible.

Given the fact that she barely knew Johnston Yates, there was no way to be subtle, or even polite, in fulfilling Nick's orders. Drawing in a deep breath, Melody walked up to the foursome in the library and waited for their conversation to die away, which it did pretty quickly when confronted by her uninvited presence in their midst.

"May I help you in some way?" Johnston Yates asked, his courtesy a silent reproof of her bad manners.

"I'm very sorry to intrude, Mr. Vice President." Melody gave him a smile that she hoped hovered somewhere between shy and apologetic. She knew from past encounters that although it was twenty-eight years since Yates had held office, he still liked to be addressed by his former title. "I wonder if I could have a moment of your time? In private?"

Yates was a handsome man with silver hair and strong, lean features, and he was known for his Southern charm. But he could be intimidating when he chose, and this was clearly one of those times. He tilted his head so that he could more effectively look down his nose at her.

"As you can see, I am somewhat busy at the moment." His voice was cold enough to flash freeze upstart guests.

Melody held on to her smile. "It's about my mother, Mr. Vice President. I had almost no chance to speak with you after her memorial service in Malmesbury last year—"

"My dear child, of course!" Yates's haughty expression dissolved into one of warm recognition. "I'm so sorry. How could I not have recognized you? You'll have to forgive an elderly man with failing eyesight who has somehow managed to misplace no less than three pairs of glasses today. You're Melody Beecham, of course. Lady Rosalind's daughter."

"Yes, and I need just a couple of minutes of your

time, if I could, Mr. Vice President. I won't keep you any longer than that, I promise.''

Yates turned to the trio of other guests. ''If you would excuse us for just a moment? I'll be right back.'' He flashed a teasing smile toward the president of Helix. ''And Jodi, my dear friend, please be merciful to my other guests. Don't eviscerate His Honor while I'm gone.''

''Don't worry, Johnston. The mayor is safe unless he insists on claiming that raising taxes on commuters is sound fiscal policy.'' Jodi Dencher laughed to soften the definite sting in her words.

Johnston Yates put his hand beneath Melody's elbow and guided her toward a book-lined alcove where they were secluded from the ebb and flow of the party. ''How may I help you, Melody? As you know from the phone conversation we had right after your mother's tragic death, Cynthia and I were absolutely devastated that something so terrible could happen on board our yacht. Really, we're both still in shock, so I can only begin to imagine how dreadful it must be for you.''

''The official reports made it clear that you and your crew had no responsibility for what happened, sir. I loved my mother, and I miss her a lot, but that doesn't blind me to the fact that she had a reckless streak in her personality. Sadly, her decision to go up on deck during a powerful storm proved one risk too many.''

Melody had offered variations of the same reply many times before to many different people. She answered Johnston Yates almost by rote and then was caught off guard by the wave of sadness that crashed over her. She'd often wondered in the weeks following her mother's death what Roz had been doing up on deck, alone, in the middle of the night, while a tropical storm raged. Somehow her thoughts had never moved forward from the question to provide an adequate answer. Belatedly, Melody realized that the chances of her mother taking a solitary stroll on deck unless lured there by some compelling force were almost nil. While it was true that Roz had been reckless, her recklessness had always been emotional, never physical. So what on earth had her mother been doing on deck in the middle of the night? Not just admiring the sight of heaving waves, that was for sure. Few things would have been less appealing to Roz's fastidious nature.

It was suddenly crystal clear that she'd clung to the belief that Roz's death was accidental because it had been too painful to contemplate the most likely alternative, which was that her mother had committed suicide. But Melody finally acknowledged that she'd wasted the past eighteen months tiptoeing around a bogeyman that didn't exist. Roz was a survivor, who would never in a million years have chosen to die by throwing herself into the stormy waters of the Atlantic Ocean. But if her mother hadn't committed suicide, and if her death wasn't accidental, then only one shocking option remained: Roz must have been murdered.

The likelihood that her mother had been murdered didn't produce the sort of emotional earthquake Melody would have anticipated, which suggested that at some profound level she'd accepted the possibility long ago. However, it was impossible to pursue this new train of thought at the same time as she monitored her ear mike for further instructions and kept track of her conversation with Johnston Yates. The important thing now was not to screw up her mission.

Yates offered further condolences on the loss of her mother, his face taking on the solemn expression of a funeral director about to sell his most expensive casket. "I'm deeply relieved to hear you say that you harbor no hard feelings, Melody," he murmured. "For my part, I can assure you that your mother enjoyed every minute of her birthday, and that her last few hours on earth were happy ones. We all had a most peaceful and harmonious few hours together on board. I believe I mentioned to you when we were at your grandfather's that Cynthia and the ship's cook got together and prepared several of your mother's favorite dishes for dinner. Roz was very appreciative."

"Yes, you did mention that, sir, and I'm glad my mother's last few hours were so pleasant." Melody took pride in her ability to sound polite when she felt anything but. If Yates expected her to believe that Roz enjoyed turning fifty, then he was clueless about Roz's personality and had misread all the signals of misery she'd undoubtedly been giving off. Or he seriously underestimated Melody's intelligence. Or he was lying. Or all of the above. As for peace and harmony reigning on board, it seemed unlikely. Why would Yates make such a point of it, unless the opposite were the case? Given that Roz ended up dead, probably not by accident, at least one person on board must have been pissed off to the point of murderous rage. Logic suggested that the birthday celebrations had been preceded by some heavy-duty quarrels and arguments.

It was eerie to realize that she might be talking to

her mother's killer, but Melody managed to bury that possibility for future consideration as she concentrated on the task at hand. "In a roundabout way, it's my mother's death that I would like to talk to you about, sir. I don't want to keep you too long from your friends and guests, so I'll get straight to the point, if I may. I'm sure you must know that my mother's will contained an announcement to the effect that Wallis Beecham is not my biological father."

"Er…yes. I had heard, of course. I confess I was shocked that Lady Rosalind chose to deliver the news in such a very public fashion. It must have been difficult for you to lose the only father you'd ever known hard on the heels of losing your mother."

"I'm sure my mother never anticipated dying when she was so young, relatively speaking. It's likely she even assumed Wallis would be dead." Melody automatically made the excuse for Roz, although it couldn't withstand scrutiny. The relish with which her mother had written the final clause of her will suggested that she had hoped Wallis would be alive to suffer the humiliation of being publicly identified as a cuckolded husband.

"I'm sure she expected me to be a middle-aged woman before I learned the truth," Melody added.

"That's true," Yates said, nodding his agreement. "Still, her method of delivering the news can't have been helpful to either you or Wallis."

"No, it wasn't, I must admit. And in a way, that's why I need your help. I've gradually been going through my mother's papers in the months since her death and there are some documents I've found recently that are a little disturbing."

"What sort of documents?" Yates asked, his voice sharpening.

"The contents are such that I'm uncomfortable revealing the details to anyone other than Wallis Beecham," Melody said. She kept her voice bland, aware that her very blandness would add a weight of threat to her words if Yates were as deeply involved in the Bonita Project as Roz had indicated in the few scribbled notes that had originally set Melody on the trail of her ex-father and his coconspirators.

She looked up at Yates, her gaze limpid. "I really feel it's important for me to talk with Wallis as soon as possible."

"Then I would urge you to do just that," Yates said crisply.

Melody had the odd impression that he was relieved at the direction their conversation had taken—almost as if he'd been expecting her to say something else. Whether or not that impression was correct, she certainly had to give him points for not losing his cool.

Yates met her wide-eyed innocence with an urbane stare of his own. "I confess, Melody, that I'm not at all sure why you felt the need to share this information with me?"

"For very practical reasons," Melody replied. "The problem is that Wallis won't speak to me. He cut me off the moment he realized I wasn't his biological daughter. I've tried to reach him at his various offices, but his assistants refuse to put me through. I would be very grateful if you would tell Wallis that we've had this discussion, and that you believe it's important for him to take my calls."

A flush of bright color spread along Johnston

Yates's cheekbones, and he abandoned distant courtesy in favor of more genuine irritation. "My dear girl, I can't possibly interfere in such a delicate family matter. Whether or not I feel that Wallis is behaving wisely, in the last resort his relationship with you is none of my business."

"My mother died while she was a guest on your yacht, Mr. Yates. Her death set in motion a chain of events that resulted in the fact that Wallis Beecham won't speak to me. I have found...items...in my mother's personal effects that make it imperative for me to speak to Wallis. I know you're one of his closest business associates—"

"Hardly so, my dear. We're the barest of acquaintances."

"Nevertheless, he will certainly take a phone call from you. You are, after all, a former vice president of the United States. And if you would mention to Wallis that I need to speak with him about the Bonita Project, I'm quite sure you'll discover that you have a hundred percent of his attention."

Yates betrayed his knowledge of the Bonita Project by no more than a flicker deep in his gray eyes, but Melody was watching closely and she saw the tiny gleam of awareness even though it was doused almost instantly.

"What project did you say that was?" he queried, sounding distracted.

His first mistake, Melody thought. Yates shouldn't have pretended vagueness about the Bonita Project, since he'd sounded extremely sharp about everything else.

"The Bonita Project," she repeated. She gazed up

at him, the picture of naiveté. "Perhaps you've heard of it?"

"No, nothing." Yates managed to sound no more than mildly curious, although Melody detected new tension in the line of his mouth. "Will Wallis know what you're talking about? From the way you're speaking, I assume you believe he's likely to be familiar with this project?"

"Oh, yes," Melody said. "You can count on it, Mr. Vice President. Wallis is well-informed about the Bonita Project and he'll be anxious to take my calls once he knows that I have *all* my mother's papers concerning the topic." Melody gave a honeyed smile, as if they didn't both know that she was challenging Wallis Beecham to take her calls or face unpleasant consequences.

A muscle in Yates's jaw twitched once at her emphasis on the word *all,* but aside from that small betraying sign, he remained impassive. He nodded stiffly, his avuncular and slightly patronizing manner vanishing now that it served no purpose.

"I promise nothing except that I will pass on your message to Wallis," he said.

"Thank you so much, Mr. Vice President." Sweet to the end, she was aware there was nothing in her conversation that could possibly be construed as a threat, even though Johnston Yates undoubtedly knew that it was.

She held out a business card. "My cell phone is the best way for Wallis to reach me. The number is on my card."

Johnston Yates took the card, but didn't return her smile. "Good night, Melody." He nodded curtly, tucked the card into his vest pocket and walked away from her without looking back.

Seventeen

Ellen Peyton burst into Melody's office at the gallery. "There's the most gorgeous man waiting in the main showroom. Tall, dark and brooding, with devastating bedroom eyes. Makes me hot just to look at him. He's asking for you."

Melody put down the stack of files she'd been trying to clear from her desk and blew upward in a vain attempt to get rid of the hair flopping onto her forehead. She wasn't impressed by her assistant's announcement. Ellen was suffering through a state of self-imposed sexual deprivation and quite ordinary-looking men could send her into orbit these days.

"Sorry, Ellen, but I'm way too busy to waste time on a man, even if he is tall, dark and brooding."

Her assistant shook her head, oversize earrings jangling. "Trust me, no woman in her right mind is too busy for this guy. Not even you. He gave me goose bumps." She extended her arms in proof.

"Then go get him. Give your goose bumps a workout." Melody gestured to her desk, buried under the debris of six weeks' mail, catalogs and memos. "Unless he looks likely to spend at least a hundred thousand bucks, I have no interest."

"He's wearing washed-out jeans, no socks, an Armani jacket, and his Patek Philippe watch definitely didn't come from a suitcase on the corner of Broadway and Forty-second. I'd say he's a poster boy for the customer most likely to drop at least a hundred thousand. Besides, I'm no dummy. I already tried to persuade him I was the woman he wanted. Unfortunately, he insists he needs to speak with you."

"What's his name?"

"Er...he didn't say." Ellen blushed crimson, and Melody realized her assistant had been so captivated by the customer's hunky appearance that she'd forgotten to ask. It figured. Ellen wanted to get married, so she'd sworn off sexy alpha males in favor of solid reliable men who, according to her theory, were more likely to have marriage and kids on their minds. So far, her theory hadn't produced anyone she wanted to marry, but it had left her seriously sex starved and intermittently loopy.

Muttering mild curses under her breath, Melody grabbed her tailored gray wool jacket from the back of the chair and shrugged into it as she walked along the corridor leading from her office into the main showroom. She recognized Nick the second he came into sight, long before he turned around at the sound of her approach into the main gallery.

Her heart gave an annoying lurch as he smiled at her, so she met his gaze with a faint scowl. Dammit, she was worse than Ellen. She hadn't felt sexually attracted to a man in almost three years, so why did her body react with this constant and infuriating tug of desire toward Nikolai Anwar? Didn't her hormones have even a grain of sense inside their throbbing little cells? If she held a contest for the man least likely to make her happy in or out of bed, Nick would be a strong contender for the grand prize. And that was assuming he was single, by no means a safe assumption given her total lack of knowledge about his personal life.

Fastening the final button on her jacket, she adjusted her grouchy expression to one of professional courtesy. "I'm Melody Beecham. You were asking to see me? How may I help you?"

Nick flashed another devastating smile, his eyes still locked with hers. She tried to ignore Ellen's gaze boring into her back when he took her hand, carrying it to his lips and pressing a kiss into her palm. The gesture sent sparks shooting down Melody's spine. Behind her, she heard Ellen let out a sigh.

"How can you help me?" Nick folded her fingers over the spot where he'd kissed her. "First, my dearest one, you can stop pretending that we do not know each other *very* well. Second, you can have lunch with me and prevent my passionate Russian heart from cracking in two."

He spoke with just the slightest foreign accent, so that instead of sounding ridiculous, his declaration sounded soulfully Slavic and romantic. Melody reminded herself that—burning bedroom eyes notwithstanding—this was the same man who'd reduced her to a puddle of sexual yearning and then informed her that more secrets were betrayed in bed than in the torture chamber. So the least she could do was make him work a little harder for the debriefing meeting that this show of passion was most likely all about. During her modeling career she'd resisted seduction by some of the world's most famous sex symbols. With a track record like that, surely she could armor herself against Nikolai Anwar.

She disengaged her hand and gave him a peppy

smile. ''Sorry, Nick. Thanks for the invitation, but I'm too busy today for lunch dates. As you know, I've been out of the office for six weeks and right now I barely have time for a carton of yogurt at my desk—''

He cut across her excuses. ''You are still mad at me. You have every right, and I'm sorry. It's new for me to have these intense feelings and I'm still learning how to handle them. You, too, I think? We are both people who like to be in control of our passions, not the other way around.''

She blinked, disconcerted by the way his corny role as torrid Russian lover had suddenly taken on an element of truth. Nick took advantage of her silence and moved closer, taking both her hands and drawing them to his chest. ''Have lunch with me, Melody, and I'll buy some insanely expensive painting from your gallery to hang in my bedroom. Then I will be reminded of you even when you aren't there.''

''Bribery, Nick?'' Melody understood that Nick's patter was designed for Ellen's benefit, but her heart was still beating way too fast and her question sounded embarrassingly breathy.

Nick shrugged, the gesture subtly foreign in contrast to his usual casual American body language. ''Why not? Whatever works. The sale of a painting and your favorite beluga caviar in exchange for a little of your time and...attention. That is an excellent bargain, no?''

Melody's eyes widened. ''You're offering me beluga caviar for lunch? The real, honest-to-God stuff from Russia?''

''But of course from Russia.'' He looked affronted

that she could even suspect otherwise. "I remember you told me it has been a favorite of yours since childhood."

Melody *really* hoped Nick was making a serious offer. "Okay, so much for my high moral principles. For beluga caviar I'm prepared to be a bought woman."

"I'm glad I knew exactly how to corrupt you." His eyes gleamed with amusement, sending another annoying shiver racing down her spine.

Melody didn't bother to waste time wondering how Nick knew that she'd loved caviar ever since childhood. She'd acquired a taste for it when she was still a little girl, since Roz was never well prepared for school vacations and would invariably run out of child-friendly food. That was on those occasions when Roz even remembered that Melody was coming home. Until she was thirteen and took over the grocery shopping, Melody had assumed that cans of tuna and jars of caviar were basically interchangeable food items, except that Roz was a lot more likely to have the caviar in stock. By the time she discovered the astonishing price differential, she was already hooked.

Nick bowed to Ellen, who was watching him with the besotted expression she usually reserved for Hollywood's most glittering celebrities.

"Thank you for your help," Nick said to her as he put his arm around Melody's waist and propelled her toward the glass doors of the showroom. "We'll see you later this afternoon, I hope? Perhaps you would be so kind as to tell Melody's boss that she is going to be very busy for the next couple of hours selling me a piece of art that I don't need." He flashed another of his ravaging smiles. ''I expect I will require a great deal of expert persuading.''

His damn smiles ruffled her hormones even though she knew they were fake. Melody didn't wait to hear Ellen's awestruck answer. She marched outside and found a limo waiting at the curb, with David sitting behind the wheel, placidly ignoring the honking horns of irate drivers squeezing past him. He sprang out and held open the car door for Melody and she greeted him with relief, glad to duck into the spacious rear, out of sight of Ellen's wide-eyed stare. When Nick decided to play the role of millionaire Russian lover, he certainly did it in style.

''The apartment, please, Dave,'' Nick said as soon as they were all inside the limo.

''Yes, sir.'' Looking like the perfect chauffeur, David pressed a button and the smoked-glass dividing panel glided upward, leaving Melody and Nick isolated in the rear of a limo that suddenly didn't seem very spacious after all.

Melody cleared her throat, annoyed with herself for feeling vulnerable. That ridiculous banter in the gallery showroom had actually left her aroused, and if Nick touched her now they were alone… She shook her head, impatient with the trend of her own thoughts. If Nick made a move she would, of course, realize that it was a ploy on his part and rebuff him.

''I hope you were serious about the caviar,'' she said, determinedly matter-of-fact. ''Nothing else could have tempted me away from my desk right now.''

''Of course I was serious. I'm half Slav and half Welsh, which makes me genetically incapable of being anything less.'' He grinned, belying his own words. "Except when I'm drunk, and then I become tragic or pathetic depending on your point of view."

She started to smile, then quickly looked away. She wasn't sure what role Nick happened to be playing at the moment, but she wasn't crazy enough to believe that he was allowing her to see the real man. And she refused to be captivated by a chimera, even if he was accustomed to adoring women tumbling into his arms, not to mention his bed, at the flick of a brooding Slavic eyebrow.

"I was surprised to hear you speaking Russian last night," she said, attempting to return the conversation to a topic that was more securely related to their working relationship. "How did you learn to speak it so fluently?"

"My mother was from Russia. I grew up in a bilingual home."

"But your father wasn't Russian?"

Nick shook his head. "He was American. Anwar is actually a Welsh name, although most people in the States hear Nikolai and assume Anwar is also Russian."

"I did, even though I'm from Britain," Melody admitted. "Was your father born in Wales?"

"No, he was born in Maryland, in Bethesda Naval Hospital, to be precise. My American grandmother, Molly McDonald, was a nurse sent overseas to Britain during World War II. My grandfather's plane was shot down over the English Channel in October of '43 and he was floating in the sea for more than an hour until he was picked up by a patrol boat. He almost died of pneumonia, since penicillin was in short supply back then, but he became one of my grandmother's patients and she managed to keep him alive. By sheer willpower, I think, since she was the most stubborn woman I ever met. My grandfather always claimed she nagged him back to life. They fell in love while he convalesced, despite the nagging. They got married as soon as he could stand upright for ten minutes, and eventually settled in Maryland, which was her home state."

"Were they happy together, do you think, once the intensity of the way they met wore off?"

"Blissfully, as far as I could see. They were pillars of their community. They loved their kids and spent huge amounts of time together turning their yard into an English flower garden. My father was the middle son in a family of three boys. He was an engineer. One of my uncles became a lawyer, the other's a pediatrician."

"What an interesting story," Melody said. She waited a beat. "Is any of it true?"

"All of it, as it happens."

The story about his grandparents' courtship sounded believable, but then his story about growing up in Maine had sounded believable, too, so Melody didn't count on it. "Do you have any brothers and sisters?" she asked, since Nick appeared to be in what was for him a confiding mood. She really wanted to ask if he was married, but that question was too revealing of her own interests.

"No, not anymore." Nick was silent for a moment, and she expected him to change the subject. "I had a little sister," he said finally. "She was five years younger than me. She died in the same car crash that killed my parents."

Nick's voice was flat, his face expressionless, but for once Melody had no doubt that he was telling the truth. She didn't make the mistake of assuming that Nick's lack of outward emotion meant that he didn't care about his sister's death. On the contrary, she knew that his reluctance to display his feelings was caused by the fear of being overwhelmed by grief. She often utilized the same method for concealing hurts too deep to risk exposing to the light of casual conversation.

"I'm so sorry," she said. She kept her own voice polite, carefully skirting the danger zone of too much compassion. She was pretty sure Nick could handle only modest doses of sympathy. "I didn't mean to revive painful memories for you."

"My sister's name was Gwynnyth," he said, still avoiding her gaze. "It's related to an old Welsh name that means morning star, and it suited her perfectly. She was only fourteen when she died, but she burned brightly for the years she was alive."

Which meant that Nick must have been nineteen when the car accident wiped out his family. Definitely too young to be left to fend for himself.

"Gwynnyth is a lovely name," Melody said softly. Confiding the truth about his sister was the first token of genuine friendship that Nick had extended toward her, and she was surprised at how much she valued it.

Nick straightened, visibly reclothing himself in the armor of their professional relationship. "Your conversation with Johnston Yates went well last night," he said.

"I thought so." Melody was more than willing to change the subject and take them both out of the danger zone of too much intimacy. "I'm sure Yates is worried enough about my comments that he'll at least call Wallis Beecham promptly."

"You're right. Yates is worried. In fact, he's already placed a call to Beecham. He sounded as hot under the collar as I've ever heard him."

Melody tipped her head to the side so that she could see Nick better. "How do you know that Yates has called Wallis?"

"I bugged the phone in Yates's town house last night. While you were talking with Yates, I slipped into his study. He has a private phone line there that he uses for almost all of his business conversations. That's why the timing of your encounter with him was so crucial. I needed to have everything coordinated with Bob Spinard's people, who were working on the line outside the house. Anyway, we succeeded in getting an intercept installed, so Unit One can now monitor the calls Yates makes from that phone."

"That's really good news." Melody was impressed that Nick had managed to bug the phone despite the mobs of guests wandering around the house. "So what did Wallis say when Yates called him this morning?"

"Nothing. Beecham wasn't at home—or at any rate he didn't pick up the phone. Yates left a frantic message requesting an immediate callback. We're optimistic that they'll be in touch with each other soon."

"Maybe Wallis has returned the call since you were last in contact with headquarters," Melody suggested.

"Could be, although I checked just before I came into the gallery." Nick pulled out a PalmPilot from inside his jacket and flipped open the leather case, checking the screen. ‘‘Nope, nothing so far. I’ve asked to be notified as soon as Beecham places a call to Yates.’’

‘‘And once the two of them have spoken, Wallis should call me soon afterward.’’

‘‘Let’s hope,’’ Nick agreed. ‘‘But in the meantime we need to write a script for exactly what you’re going to say when Wallis does get in touch with you.’’

‘‘Is that why you came to the gallery? So you can brief me on what to say when Wallis calls me?’’

‘‘In part.’’ Nick leaned forward to speak to David. ‘‘There are also a couple of other issues we need to discuss.’’

They had reached an apartment building on East Sixty-ninth, between Third and Lexington. Dave maneuvered the limo behind a truck delivering laundry, and parked so tightly in front of the canopied entrance that the limo wheels grazed the curb.

Nick asked Dave to return in two hours to pick them up. ‘‘Unit One owns an apartment in this building,’’ he said, helping Melody out of the limo. ‘‘When I’m not at headquarters, I live here. The apartment’s automatically swept for bugs every twenty-four hours, so it’s a safe place for us to talk.’’

The apartment was on the eleventh floor, one level below the penthouse, a typical two-bedroom, two-bathroom unit from the early sixties, with a view of nothing much except a similar building across the street. Despite its modest size, because of its prime location Melody knew that the apartment would cost a small fortune to buy or rent. It made a very suitable Manhattan pied-à-terre for a wealthy Russian financier whose main home was supposedly in Moscow.

Nick gave her a brief tour. The living room, furnished for entertaining with expensive antique reproductions, was larger than Melody would have expected, at least thirty feet by twenty-five, with a dining nook that opened directly off the kitchen. The second bedroom had been converted to a pleasant book-filled library/office with a lovely oak plank floor, and the bathrooms and kitchen had been updated with lots of gleaming stainless steel fixtures, along with counters converted from sixties Formica to more upscale granite. But the master bedroom decor was definitely over the top, suggesting a designer who believed that oversize furniture, bulging phallic lamps and aggressively puffed comforters were a good way for a lusty bachelor to convince potential bedmates that he possessed an equally generous endowment in more personal areas.

"The apartment is very attractive," Melody said, deciding not to comment on the bedroom. She wasn't sure she could handle joking about phallic symbols with Nick. She leaned against the arch that led into the kitchen while Nick took the promised caviar from the fridge, along with a carton of sour cream and a lemon that he proceeded to slice with swift efficiency. "The study is the only room that looks as if you might have chosen the furniture yourself, though."

"You're right. I was intimidated by the decorator." He grinned. "Early on in the process, when he announced that he was painting the bedroom walls a shade of yellow that would remind me of the sunny warmth of an Italian villa tucked into a Tuscan hillside, I wimped out. As far as I could see, he meant he was painting the walls the color of the mustard people squirt on hot dogs. I lacked the courage to share that insight with him."

Melody laughed. "Poor man. You must have been a nightmare to work with."

"On the contrary. I was the perfect client. Once we'd agreed on the office, he was given a budget and left to get on with it. Isn't that a designer's fantasy?"

"Maybe, although the artwork looks as if he'd given up in despair by the time he reached the point of choosing wall hangings. You really do need to upgrade it."

Nick glanced up from dropping bread into the toaster, sending her a teasing grin. "You don't like my naked island ladies, huh?"

"They suck. And that's my highly professional assessment, of course."

"Let's hope the accountants at Unit One agree. Otherwise I guess I'm going to be out the cost of a fancy lithograph from the Van der Meer Gallery."

"I'm willing to certify to the moneymen that you need something better than a really bad Gauguin rip-off hanging above your bed if you're going to be convincing in your role as a successful Russian Mr. Fixit."

Nick laughed. "Good luck. Ever tried explaining the nuances of art to a government accountant?"

"Rarely. Only when I experience an upsurge of masochism. The rest of the time I try hard to avoid having conversations with government accountants on any subject whatsoever."

"Smart woman." Nick handed her two linen place mats and matching napkins. "Put those on the table, would you? What would you like to drink with the caviar?"

"Iced Stolichnaya," she said promptly. "But since it's lunchtime and we're working, I guess I'll make do with water." And she'd really be a smart woman if she reminded herself at frequent intervals that they were together right now strictly because of the job, not because Nick enjoyed her company.

"Sparkling water okay?" he asked.

She nodded and Nick took bottled water from the fridge, then carried out the rack of hot toast, together with the caviar and its accompaniments. For a few minutes while they ate Melody managed to think of nothing beyond the moment, and how much she was enjoying the caviar.

"That was wonderful," she said, leaning back in her chair. To give the designer credit, it was very comfortable. "Thank you, Nick. Any time you want to bribe me into having lunch with you, beluga caviar is guaranteed to do the trick."

He didn't return her smile as he pushed his empty plate toward the center of the table. "Unfortunately, the rest of our agenda isn't likely to please you as much as the caviar. You didn't ask why I made such a point of coming to the gallery to pick you up when I could just as easily have phoned and asked you to meet me here."

That was because when Nick was around, her brain function tended to be less than snappy. She'd assumed that he was putting her through another test, to see how she would react to a come-on from him that—unfortunately—he knew made her uncomfortable. In retrospect, she realized that Nick would never have wasted his time on something so trivial. If he didn't believe she was capable of handling the minor curveballs he'd tossed at her in the gallery, she'd have been booted from Unit One weeks ago.

Melody took a final sip of water. "No, I didn't ask. I assumed you wanted us to go somewhere private so that you could critique my performance last night."

"There's nothing to critique. You did well. Very well."

His compliment pleased her more than it should have. Much as she wanted to maintain an emotional distance from Unit One, she could feel herself sliding closer and closer into genuine cooperation. There was something seductive about the knowledge that you were part of a secret group, privy to important information that outsiders didn't share.

"Then why did you want to see me?" she asked.

"I made a mistake in setting up the arrangements for last night," he said. "I shouldn't have let Jasper Fowles take you to the party. I should have acted as your escort and made a big show of being hot for you. News of our affair would have been featured in every gossip column in the city by now."

Thank God he'd screwed up in his planning, Melody reflected. She was fairly sure that she wouldn't be able to feign desire for Nick without edging dangerously close to feeling the real thing—and maybe not only desire, but the scary four-letter word she had spent her adult life determined to avoid.

"Why would you want to persuade people that we're an item?" she asked. She didn't quite manage to hold on to her usual cool, but at least her voice didn't crack in midquestion.

"Chiefly for your protection," Nick said.

"My protection?" He had to be joking if he believed that feigning attraction to him was a way to make her feel protected. Exposed, vulnerable and frightened half to death would be more like it. She'd survived being ignored by both of her parents while she was growing up chiefly because her grandparents and cousins took up the slack and made her feel wanted. But love had been in scarce supply in her life and it wasn't an emotion she treated casually. She'd decided when she was trundled off to boarding school right after her tenth birthday that she'd never make the idiotic mistake of falling in love with a man who had the power to break her heart.

"If we're having a passionate affair, then I have an excuse to be near you twenty-four hours a day," Nick explained, cutting across memories she didn't often allow to surface.

"True, but twenty-four-hour protection sounds like serious overkill." Not to mention fatally hazardous to her psychological health.

"It's far from overkill. You do realize that as soon as you delivered your message to Johnston Yates last night, you were setting yourself up as a target for Wallis Beecham."

"Of course. That was the whole point of the mission. We discussed this at the original briefing with Mac and Bob Spinard. Wallis can't afford to ignore the possibility that I know enough about the Bonita Project to cause him trouble, so once he gets the message from Yates, he'll come after me. I'll insist on a face-to-face meeting with him, and Unit One will provide the technology that will enable me to record what he says. Hopefully, we'll get enough to incriminate him and the rest of the partners. Don't worry, Nick, I understand my role in this and I'm not going to screw up."

"The problem is not that you might screw up. The problem is that Unit One has put you in significant danger. Consequently, it's my responsibility to see that you get around-the-clock protection."

"You're overstating the danger, surely. As far as Wallis knows, Kenneth Chung is dead and the Bonita Project has been a wonderful success. Beecham and his partners are three hundred million dollars richer, not exactly chump change by anyone's standards. With Lawrence Springer dead, Wallis only has to share the money with Victor Heston, Johnston Yates and Senator Cranford. That's seventy-five million tax-free dollars each, enough to keep anyone happy. Wallis might be furious that I'm popping up making annoying blackmail demands, but he isn't going to send a hit man to eliminate me. He'll offer to pay me off—"

"What in the world makes you believe that?"

Melody blinked. "Well...because anything else would be an overreaction. Because it's much easier to pay me off—"

"Because a payoff is how Beecham chose to deal with Kenneth Chung?" Nick leaned forward, his expression grim. "Because a payoff is how he dealt with Lawrence Springer? Because a payoff is how he dealt with your mother?"

Melody stared at Nick in silence, her attention caught more by the reference to her mother than by his warning about her own safety. So Unit One believed that Roz had been murdered. Odd that she'd considered such a possibility for the first time only last night, and now here it was being raised again.

"Do *you* think my mother was murdered?" she asked, her voice husky.

"Do you?"

"Dammit, Nick, give me a straight answer. Does Unit One believe that Wallis Beecham arranged to have my mother killed?"

Nick was silent for a moment, then spoke crisply. "Yes, on balance, it seems more likely than not that Lady Rosalind was murdered. With no body, and apparently no witnesses, it's hard to be sure. Unfortunately, when Lady Rosalind died, Unit One was unaware of the existence of the Bonita Project, and we certainly had no idea of the identities of the high-powered people who were involved in the partnership. Two months ago, when we finally launched our full-scale investigation, we realized that three of the Bonita partners were on board the yacht when Lady Rosalind died—"

"Springer, Yates and Senator Cranford."

"Yes. That's a suspicious circumstance in itself, worthy of checking into. We reviewed the police reports, talked to the Mexican officials and concluded that there was both motive and plenty of opportunity for any one of them to have killed your mother."

"On the other hand, nobody could have predicted that such a perfect opportunity for murder would arise," Melody pointed out. "Nobody knew when they set sail that there would be a violent storm on the night of my mother's birthday. It wasn't forecast until after they were at sea."

"True. So the killer got lucky with the weather. But a yacht in the middle of the ocean presents plenty of opportunities for a fatal accident even without a storm."

Melody pushed her chair away from the table, carried her plate into the kitchen and put it in the sink, the loss of her mother suddenly painfully vivid once again.

Nick followed her, putting his plate on top of hers and running water over them. "I've let you take the discussion away from the main subject," he said. "We need to get back to the issue of your safety."

"I consider the fact that my mother might have been murdered pretty central to the case against Wallis Beecham."

"It is," Nick acknowledged. "But from a safety standpoint, it doesn't matter whether your mother's death was murder or a tragic accident. We already know that Beecham and Springer have both proved themselves willing to commit murder in order to achieve their goals, and we have to assume that Beecham would be willing to kill again. Presumably the other partners, too."

An image of Johnston Yates looking down his patrician nose at her the previous night flashed into Melody's head. From what little she knew of him, she wasn't at all sure that she liked the guy, but it was hard to visualize him as an accomplice to murder. "Don't you think Johnston Yates might kick up a stink if I turned up dead in the near future?"

Nick shrugged. "Possibly, but by that point you would already be dead, which makes his protests somewhat irrelevant, wouldn't you say? And don't be deceived by Yates's patrician appearance, or his past stint as vice president. There's no reason to assume Yates and the other members of the partnership are any less willing to kill than Springer and Beecham. The Saudis required the death of Kenneth

Chung before they were willing to make their payoff, and the partners must have known that."

"You can't be sure of that."

"No, I can't. But I'm not willing to stake your life on a slender chance that Beecham and Springer weren't entirely honest with their coconspirators. Given the level of ruthlessness the Bonita partners have already demonstrated, we must assume that you will be targeted for elimination." He looked at her sharply. "Why are you fighting such an obvious conclusion, Melody? Dammit, you understood the score from the day you joined Unit One. You told me flat out that we wanted to recruit you chiefly because you made such perfect bait."

Nick was correct, and it was crazy to continue protesting. "Okay, I'm at risk," she conceded. "I still don't understand why it's necessary to pretend that you and I are involved in a passionate affair." She managed to sound mildly irritated at the prospect of having him hanging around, rather than totally panicked. "Why not just pretend I've hired a bodyguard?"

"Because too many people know me in my other role, as the guy businesspeople need to contact in order to grease the wheels of Russian commerce. I can't suddenly become a professional bodyguard. I've spent ten years building my credentials. I can't afford to blow them over something that could so easily be avoided."

"Then Unit One could send in Sam or Tony or Dave to act as my bodyguards. Why wouldn't that work?"

"In part because Sam, Dave and Tony know nothing about the details of the Bonita Project—"

"How can they know nothing?" she protested. "They're part of your personal team. Sam and Tony were with you at Lawrence Springer's house!"

He sent her a quizzical glance. "Come on, Melody. Every spy movie you've ever seen points out that covert organizations operate on a need-to-know basis. That means Sam and Tony knew Unit One's mission was to extract Lawrence Springer for questioning, nothing more."

"They also know that you found Springer dead and that you kidnapped me," she reminded him.

Nick frowned. "That's true. And in view of the fact that we suspect there's a traitor inside Unit One reporting back to Wallis Beecham, I wish they didn't know that we recruited you, much less how and where. Anyone other than me acting as your bodyguard increases the risk to you exponentially."

Melody was incredulous. "You surely can't suspect Sam or Tony of being in the pay of Wallis Beecham? Or Dave?"

"I suspect everyone," he said curtly.

"Including me?" She tossed off the question almost idly.

"I've considered the possibility, yes."

Melody could feel her mouth drop open. "Aside from the fact that Wallis quite possibly ordered the murder of my mother, Lawrence Springer was killed before you forced me to join Unit One. For heaven's sake, Nick! I couldn't have betrayed Unit One's plans to extract Springer for questioning, because I didn't know the damned organization existed."

"That might be true. Or there's the possibility that you were brilliantly inserted at precisely the point in the operation when there was most chance that you would never be suspected of treachery if we recruited you."

She drew in a sharp breath, not bothering to make the useless gesture of protesting her innocence, or her loyalty to Unit One. The fact that she was here with Nick meant he'd decided that, on balance, she was unlikely to have been sent by Wallis Beecham to penetrate the organization.

For a moment she actually felt sorry for Nick. "How can you operate in an environment where you don't trust *anybody?* Doesn't it drive you crazy?"

"Now and again." His voice was once again tightly controlled. "In fact, for what it's worth, I don't seriously suspect you of being planted by Wallis Beecham."

"Why not? Given that you suspect everyone."

"You won't like my answer."

"Tell me anyway."

"I don't believe you're in Beecham's pay for the simple reason that you hate him."

"That's an exaggeration—"

He cut her off. "You work really hard to hide the fact that you were devastated by Beecham's rejection of you after your mother died. But despite the fact that you tried to disguise your motives, I'm aware that you agreed to join Unit One because you're aching for revenge. You plan to bring him down and then leave."

So much for keeping her deepest feelings private. Melody walked out of the kitchen, needing breathing room. The risk of falling in love was frightening enough, but nothing in the world scared her more than having people see feelings she wanted to keep hidden. By comparison, scaling the forty-five feet of climbing wall had been a doddle.

Nick followed her into the living room. Thank heaven he stopped when there was still a safe eighteen inches of space between them. "There's an added bonus to having the two of us pretend we're in love," he said.

Sure there was. In between wondering just how much he was learning about her most private hopes and dreams, she could wait, nerve ends tingling, for him to deliver a fake kiss or two. Or if she really wanted to be humiliated, she could have sex with him and discover what it was like to be expertly seduced by a man whose feelings were totally disengaged from the process. A neat role reversal from her usual behavior. God was apparently indulging Her sense of humor.

"What's that?" she asked wearily.

"Johnston Yates has used my professional services, although our business dealings happen to have been strictly legitimate. But Senator Cranford and Wallis Beecham are also acquainted with me, and their dealings were more problematic. They sold their shares in a Russian oil consortium and hired me over a year ago to find a way to transfer their profits out of Russia straight into their bank accounts in Switzerland, thus avoiding all U.S. taxes. Senator Cranford could lose his reelection bid if the details of the deal became public, and even Wallis Beecham's notorious armor plating is going to feel a bit scorched if he learns that you and I have become lovers."

Just as she'd been forced to concede that her conversation with Johnston Yates put her life at risk, Melody was compelled to acknowledge that rumors of an intimate relationship between her and Nick would be an excellent way to pile extra pressure on Beecham and his partners. Ever since her mother's funeral, her major goal in life had been to bring down Wallis Beecham. It was crazy to back off from that goal simply because she felt threatened by Nick's sexuality. Sex, after all, was only sex, which had never been all that earth-shattering a component of her life. And it wasn't as if she and Nick were actually going to become lovers. They were simply going to fake it. How threatening could that be?

Better not to answer that question. Melody forced herself to meet Nick's gaze. "I guess I have to agree with your analysis," she said, shrugging. "Everything you say is so logical, I'm only surprised that you screwed up in planning last night's mission."

For a split second she had the impression that Nick was disconcerted. But before either of them could say anything more, his PalmPilot beeped. Relief flickered in his eyes at the interruption, and he quickly checked the device.

"Wallis Beecham just called Yates," he said, reading the text message on the screen. "I'm going to headquarters to listen to the tape."

"You've no idea what Wallis said?"

"No." Nick pushed back his cuff and glanced at his watch. "Dave should be waiting for us already. I'll drop you back at the gallery and then pick you up there this evening. I'll take you to dinner and we can get a head start on creating the impression that we're lovers."

Oh, boy. Just how she wanted to spend the night. "That sounds delightful," Melody said gloomily.

Eighteen

Mac, wearing a neon emerald-green turtleneck that made him look like a leprechaun minus the bells, greeted Nick's arrival in his office by waving a tape recorder in one hand and the inevitable mug of coffee in the other.

"You look more tight-assed than usual, if that's possible," Mac announced. "What the hell's been gnawing at your shorts since you got back from St. Petersburg?"

"Nothing." If you ignored the fact that he was about to spend the next several days not taking Melody Beecham to bed, his life was perking along just fine. True, he had about as much chance of ignoring his desire to bed Melody Beecham as Monica Lewinsky had of winning the League of Women Voters' Good Citizen Award, but why get hung up on facts? He'd been obsessing about Melody ever since the night he delivered his warning about seduction as the best route to uncovering secrets. Hell, he'd been obsessing about her ever since he first saw her, but with a little self-discipline he'd soon have her out of his system. Or, if he wanted to make his life totally miserable, he could seduce her. All in the line of duty, of course, and not because he got a goddamn ache in his gut every time she half smiled at him.

Mac took a slurp of coffee. "The recording's not going to improve your mood."

"My mood's just swell. Peachy keen, in fact."

"Yeah, I can see that. How was Melody when you left her?"

"Would you play the damn tape?" Nick shot a look at the director that would have withered a lesser man. Mac merely wriggled his eyebrows. Fortunately, he made no further comments about Melody. Instead, he depressed the start button of the tape player.

"Okay, here goes. As you'll hear, Johnston Yates is clearly rattled but Wallis Beecham sounds as cool as a polar bear at a fishing hole."

The recorded conversation began with Johnston Yates saying hello.

Beecham responded. "Johnston? Glad I reached you. It's Wallis Beecham. How are you doing?"

"Fine, thank you—"

"Sorry not to have returned your call yesterday. It's been hectic as all get-out around here."

"I'm relieved to hear from you, Wallis. I had a somewhat disturbing conversation with your… um…with Melody yesterday."

"So you mentioned in your message. What's the problem?"

"She asked me to pass on an urgent message to you. That may seem a little strange, but she gave me to understand that you won't take any phone calls from her." Johnston paused, but there was no response from the other end so he plowed on. "She asked me to let you know that she's been trying to reach you for some time, but she claims her calls are being turned back by your various assistants. She says it's important for you to talk to her."

"I expect she does." Wallis Beecham made an impatient clicking sound. "Like her mother, Melody has a problem with exaggeration and overdramatization. If she has something important to say to me—and I can't imagine what that might be—tell her she can write me a letter. Thanks for passing on her request, Johnston. Goodb—"

"Wallis, don't hang up! Look, I understand that you might have some problems surrounding the issue of Melody's paternity—"

"You do?" Wallis gave a hard laugh. "Rosalind was sleeping with half the male population of Manhattan, and then passed off her bastard as my child for twenty-eight years. You bet your sweet ass I have problems surrounding the issue of Melody's paternity."

Johnston Yates drew in an audible breath. "Believe me, I'm not attempting to intrude into your personal life." His voice sounded thin with distaste for Beecham's crude language. "This is strictly a business call or I wouldn't have agreed to be in touch with you. Melody informed me that she'd discovered among Roz's papers documents that relate to the Bonita Project. She implied that it was urgent for her to talk with you about them."

Wallis betrayed not a trace of reaction to his partner's mention of the Bonita Project. "I repeat—she can write me a letter."

"You might be wiser to call her. Actually, Wallis, I got the strong impression that Melody was threatening you. Her implied threat, which she was clever enough not to spell out, was that you need to phone her soon, or you will face some very unpleasant consequences. Naturally, I have no idea what those consequences might be, or why she feels that mentioning the Bonita Project is a way to catch your attention.''

''Well, I surely do appreciate you calling me, Johnston, but I can't get my bowels in an uproar over every scheming bitch who decides to come after my money.'' Wallis managed to sound his usual unruffled and folksy self, despite his vulgar turn of phrase.

''Melody is not a...ahem.'' Johnson broke off and tried again. ''Melody was raised in your family, as your own daughter, until a couple of years ago, Wallis. Surely it's not too much to take a phone call from her?''

''You know, Johnston, as I get on in years, I realize the old country proverbs have a lot of wisdom in them. Here's a real good one from my father. You can dress up a pig in a silk dress, but it's still a pig, and soon the silk dress is going to stink of pig shit. And here's another. The apple never falls far from the tree. I guess we're seeing here how true that is in Melody's case. She may have spent some of her childhood in my homes, but she learned nothing from me. She's taken one hundred percent after her grasping whore of a mother.'' For a moment Beecham's voice was laced with venom, but he soon recovered his equilibrium. ''Fortunately, her mother's in no position to cause any more trouble and Melody herself is nothing to do with me.''

''Biologically speaking that may be true, but I believe she could make things very unpleasant for you—''

''Trust me on this, Johnston. I watched Melody

grow up, and the only way to deal with her threats is to ignore her."

"I question your judgment on this. And I am personally involved in this matter. I'll remind you that I'm one of the partners in the Bonita Project."

Wallis didn't miss a beat. "I don't see any way that your interests are going to be advanced by having me discuss our private business affairs with Melody."

"Then you need to look more closely at what's at stake—"

"Why would either one of us care if Melody wants to discuss the funding that you and I and our fellow partners have chosen to provide for the development of an effective vaccine for chickens?" Wallis Beecham's words were silky smooth.

There was a noticeable pause before Johnston replied and when he spoke, his voice was unexpectedly firm, echoing with the confidence of a man who had once been only a heartbeat away from the presidency of the world's most powerful nation. "I don't share your assessment of the potential for damage that we're looking at here, Wallis. I'm sorry that Rosalind committed adultery during your marriage to her, and I'm sorry that Melody isn't your daughter. However, I feel compelled to point out that Rosalind always struck me as an intelligent woman, and her daughter strikes me as equally intelligent and a great deal more self-disciplined to boot. A dangerous combination if she chooses to turn it against you. The development of a vaccine to prevent the spread of avian flu in flocks of chickens is a worthy investment, but I don't believe either you or I would care to have the details of the project splashed across the front page of our nation's newspapers. I recommend that you reconsider your present arrogant attitude and place a call to Melody Beecham. Pretty damn quick."

The tape ended with the click of the phone being disconnected.

Nick looked across at his boss, surprised. "So Yates got in the last word. I wouldn't have expected that."

Mac nodded. "Me, neither. Called Beecham arrogant, too. Doesn't mean Wallis Beecham is going to follow Johnston's orders. He likes to tell other people what to do, not be given instructions."

"That's true as a general rule, but the Bonita Project is important enough for even Beecham to swallow his pride. Let me hear the tape one more time, may I?"

"Of course." Mac rewound the tape, then pressed the play button.

Nick listened again to the recording. "Wallis isn't anywhere near as unconcerned as he's trying to appear," he said when it reached the end for the second time. "He's a man who's normally a master at changing his speech patterns to fit in with the expectations of his audience—"

"I thought he was famous for being the prototype of the country bumpkin made good. Never makes an effort to hide his origins."

Nick made a gesture of denial. "His good ole country boy manners aren't a result of honest pride in where he comes from. They're a carefully calculated ploy that he used when he was starting out to hide his education and high IQ. Anything to give him an edge in business deals. Now the act has become an ingrained habit. After so many years, he rarely moves too far out of character, regardless of where he is and who he's talking to. But I've noticed that he moderates his use of language to fit the profile of the people he's with. If he's talking to a group of construction workers, for example, he cusses with the best of 'em. If he's with a group of social conservatives, he has a quote from the Bible for every occasion. When he's with his inner circle of business associates, he gets right to the point, even if he tosses in the occasional country-boy witticism just to remind them who they're dealing with."

"Isn't that what he did in this conversation with Yates? Kept to the point, but threw in a few old proverbs to prove he's an honest country boy at heart."

"Not quite. Every time the discussion turned to Lady Roz, he lost control. Johnston Yates is the ultimate American aristocrat, and Wallis knows that. He's even a bit intimidated by it, in my opinion. If he'd been fully in control, he'd never have offended Yates by referring to Roz as a scheming bitch, and his anecdote about the pig was definitely pushing the limits as far as Yates is concerned. Remember, Yates and his wife knew Roz for years and presumably enjoyed her company, at least to a certain extent. I doubt if Yates appreciated being told that he and Cynthia had been close friends with a whore. Or a pig dressed up in silk. He's notorious for being somewhat protective of his wife."

"Good point." Mac offered Nick a cup of coffee by way of reward for his insight. "What's your conclusion, then? Is Beecham rattled enough to take the bait?"

"I don't believe he can ignore it."

"Sure hope you're right on that. So outline your precise plan of action for me."

Nick hesitated for a moment. "My plans are still fluid right now. In fact, they depend on you."

"Why?" Mac pulled the handle on his espresso machine and steam hissed, intensifying the coffee aroma that always permeated his office. "Because you're waiting to find out what my security review has turned up about the possibility of a leak from within the department?"

Nick nodded. "Yes. Obviously if we have a leak inside the department, that has a huge impact on my plans. I'm having a hard time believing that somebody in Unit One has sold us out to Wallis Beecham. On the other hand, I'm having an even more difficult time believing it was simple bad luck that caused Lawrence Springer to be murdered minutes before we were scheduled to bring him in for questioning."

"Springer's death was a damn shame." Mac looked regretful. "He was enough in Beecham's confidence that we'd know the location of the clinic and be closing it down by now if we'd been able to question him."

Nick agreed completely with the director's assessment. The death of Lawrence Springer had ruined a brilliantly designed operation, even if he said it himself. Unfortunately, none of the other three partners served equally well as pressure points against Beecham. Heston was strictly the money man, moving funds through various untraceable overseas accounts in order to feed the monstrous start-up costs of the project. Cranford was the point man for keeping unfriendly legislation to a minimum, and Yates was on board to provide a veneer of respectability when the project went public. Nick was confident none of them had been provided with complete information by Beecham, especially concerning the less savory details of the project. It was even possible that they had never been informed as to how Beecham planned to raise the quarter billion dollars required to bring the Bonita Project to fruition.

Nick realized he was pacing the room, and stopped. "I need to know what you found out during your review, Mac. As you can imagine, I'll be thrilled if you can convince me I'm being way too suspicious and that the timing of Springer's death was sheer coincidence."

"You're not being too suspicious," Mac said flatly. He handed Nick a cup of coffee and began the soothing process of making another one for himself. "It's taken me a while to get the complete picture, but I'm there now. Given the need to keep what I was doing secret, I couldn't go the easy route and ask Bob Spinard to run a computer analysis of the operations we've conducted so far in connection with the Bonita Project. I had to do my analysis the old-fashioned way, which is why it's taken me so long."

"And having run the analysis, you've decided there's definitely a leak?"

"Yes, I have."

Nick let out a quick, sharp breath. "Who?" he demanded.

"I'm getting to that. As you pointed out to me some time ago, the only mission in connection with the Bonita Project that's gone completely as it should is the extraction of Kenneth Chung from the research lab in Arkansas."

"Yes, and I've tried to assess what was different

about the way that operation was set up, and I can't come up with a damned thing,'' Nick said.

''There were no differences major enough to attract attention at the time,'' Mac said. ''But in retrospect... Remember how stretched we were for personnel at that point? You didn't get to name an extraction team until a couple of hours before the plane was scheduled to take off for Arkansas.''

''That's true, but I briefed Sam and Tony before we took off, and the pilots knew where we were going. They had to know our destination in order to file a flight plan. Nothing different there from the operation a few days later to bring Springer in for questioning. Except we didn't need the plane, of course. I used Sam and Tony again, so the setup was very similar. However, the outcomes were polar opposites.'' He shot Mac a questioning glance. ''You surely don't suspect one of the pilots? Lou and Jose have both been with us for years. Besides, it would be difficult as hell for them to get reliable intel on a steady basis.''

''No, I don't suspect Lou or Jose.'' Mac grimaced as if his coffee tasted bad. ''Your first choice as a team for extraction operations is usually Dave and Tony. But, like I said before, we were tight on personnel, so you couldn't take Dave on the Chung mission.''

''Right. Dave was working the Glasser case in California, so I substituted Sam.'' Nick could almost feel the color drain from his cheeks. ''Jesus, Mac! You're not suggesting that there's anything significant about the fact that Sam came with me instead of Dave? Are you suggesting somebody on *my* team is fucking us over?''

Mac stirred sugar into his coffee, a sure sign of stress. ‘‘Dave didn’t come with you on the Lawrence Springer operation either, even though the Glasser case was wound up by then. He was back from California, and he’s your first choice on any extraction mission.’’

‘‘You know why he didn’t come—it’s in my notes.’’ Nick paced the office, feeling a strong urge to hit something. ‘‘There’s no mystery, Mac. Dave was injured at the last minute.’’

‘‘But you actually got as far as briefing him, didn’t you?’’

‘‘I briefed him four hours before we left for Chappaqua,’’ Nick said. His mouth was suddenly bone-dry and he needed to take another swallow of coffee before he could breathe. Speaking was impossible.

‘‘You did indeed brief Dave,’’ Mac said, his voice drained of every drop of warmth. ‘‘Which means he knew exactly what you planned to do and when you planned to do it.’’

Nick found his voice. ‘‘Dave only knew the bare minimum—that we planned to bring Springer in for questioning. Naturally I didn’t inform him that Lawrence Springer was a partner of Wallis Beecham’s, or that the extraction was part of our investigation of the Bonita Project.’’

‘‘No, you didn’t. But if Dave is working for Wallis Beecham, he already knows that, doesn’t he?’’

Nick looked at Mac, wondering if his own expression was as bleak as the director’s. ‘‘Precisely what are you saying, Mac? Spell it out for me.’’

‘‘Okay, here it is. Right before you were scheduled to leave for Chappaqua, Dave tore the muscle in the rotator cuff of his shoulder in a dumb accident that he ought to have been able to avoid in his sleep, let alone right before an important mission."

"The injury was real. One of our own doctors checked him out. He was in a lot of pain."

"I know. In view of the doctor's report, you ordered him to stay home. Then you took Sam with you to Chappaqua in his place. Dave not only knew exactly what your plans were in regard to Springer, but the fact that you'd ordered him home provided him with ample opportunity to call Wallis Beecham and inform him of what was about to happen. It would have been easy for him to get instructions from Beecham on how to deal with the situation."

"You think Dave made his way to Chappaqua and killed Lawrence Springer," Nick said, his voice edged with ice.

"I believe he did precisely that," Mac agreed. "An injured shoulder wouldn't pose much of an obstacle to Dave if he was determined. He's accomplished feats for us that are a hell of a lot more demanding than driving to Chappaqua and shooting a man when he has a torn rotator cuff."

Nick had considered Dave a friend for a dozen years, ever since Dave joined Unit One, recruited directly from the army's Special Forces. Nick had already been two years with Unit One at that point, but he remained hotheaded and only marginally effective, seething with resentment at the loss of his family, and furious at having been tricked into following in his dead father's professional footsteps. Dave, ten years his senior, a combat veteran with successful missions in a dozen of the world's most dangerous trouble spots, had shown him how much more could be achieved with cool rationality than with hot passion. Dave had taught him fly-fishing. Dave had taught him to shoot to kill with the first bullet, and had saved his life on at least two occasions. It was beyond painful to contemplate the possibility that Dave had also sold him out.

"Right now this is all conjecture on your part," Nick said, needing to make the protest even though he didn't believe it.

"Not really." Mac tossed the dregs of his coffee into the bar sink, the gesture jerky with frustration. "I'm sorry, Nick. I know Dave is a good friend of yours, but I've checked up, down and sideways, and for every problem you've encountered in running the Bonita investigation, the answer points straight to Dave."

Nick's frustration exploded. "Goddammit, if you're right, what's his reason for selling out? I won't believe that Dave has been bought off by Wallis Beecham. He doesn't give a damn about money."

"Of course he hasn't been bought off with money. You know what the Bonita Project is all about. He's been bought off with promises that he can participate once the clinic is up and running."

"Oh, Jesus." Enlightenment dawned, leaving Nick sick to his stomach. "He wants to bring back his wife. He thinks Beecham can do that for him."

"Either his wife, or maybe the baby his wife was pregnant with when she died."

Nick was torn between rage and compassion on Dave's behalf. God knew, he understood what it was like to grieve. Losing Gwynnyth had in some ways hurt even more than losing his parents, because his sister's life had been cut off before any of its promise could be fulfilled. At least his mother and father had lived long enough to reach adulthood. They'd fallen passionately in love, raised children and followed careers, even if those careers had gotten them assassinated in the end. Because of losing Gwynnyth, Nick understood the temptation of fantasizing about what it would be like to bring back the people you loved. He would give almost anything to have a fresh chance to show his kid sister that, beneath all his sullen teenage behavior, he'd always loved her as she deserved to be loved.

But he would only give *almost* anything. At rock bottom, Nick understood that cloning Gwynnyth was never going to reproduce his sister, nor would it repair the gaps in their relationship that he now so bitterly regretted. Most clearly of all, he understood that the ethical and medical issues connected to the subject of cloning were much too complex to leave in the untethered hands of a ruthless profiteer like Wallis Beecham.

If Dave had sold out to the opposition, it must mean that he knew the real purpose behind the Bonita Project. Murdering Kenneth Chung and making over a quarter-billion-bucks in profit had never been Wallis Beecham's ultimate goal. The purpose of the harmless-sounding Bonita Project had always been to establish a state-of-the-art clinic for the benefit of the few millionaires able to afford the astronomical costs of healing their psychic wounds with an illegally cloned baby. The hundreds of millions of dollars Beecham had raised from the Saudis was his way of obtaining untraceable funds to pay the start-up costs of recruiting top-notch scientists and paying poor but healthy women to become surrogate mothers. Most of all, he needed megabucks to build a research lab and medical facility in some remote location, away from the scrutiny of governments, university ethics boards and hospital peer review committees.

One of Beecham's chief reasons for needing to be free of supervision was the fact that if human cloning results followed the pattern of animal cloning, there were going to be thirty or so deformed fetuses to be disposed of for every reasonably healthy baby that reached the point of successful delivery. However determined Wallis Beecham was to bring his project to successful completion, Nick was twice as determined to stop him. Which meant that he couldn't waste valuable time stopping to lament over Dave's treachery.

"What do you suggest we do about Dave?" he asked Mac. The only way he was going to cope with his friend's betrayal was to take practical steps to thwart it.

"Do you think there's any chance Dave knows the location of the clinic? Because if so, we should question him. Press him to give up the location."

Nick shook his head. "It's doubtful he knows. There are clear risks for Beecham in sharing that information, and no benefits as far as I can see."

"That was my conclusion. And, of course, the moment we question Dave, we give away the fact that he's been made."

Nick stared at the blank wall, seeing himself with Dave on the banks of a stream in Idaho, a six-pack chilling in a cooler and a box of fishing tackle between the two of them. He drew in a sharp breath, banishing the debilitating image. "My recommendation is that we leave Dave in place and make sure that he carries back as much disinformation as possible to Wallis Beecham.''

''Agreed. We're at too advanced a stage in our investigation to expose him now.''

''Obviously Dave has already told Wallis Beecham everything he knows,'' Nick said. ''From here on out, we simply have to make sure he doesn't know anything useful.''

Mac rubbed his forehead, pinching the bridge of his nose as if to relieve the buildup of tension. The gesture betrayed a degree of stress that Nick could never before remember observing in his boss.

''Should we bring Victor Heston in for questioning?'' Mac asked. His uncertainty was another signal that Dave's betrayal had left him feeling raw. ''You could organize a standard extraction operation. Obviously you'd have to make sure that Dave was kept completely out of the loop. We don't want to put Heston at risk of meeting the same fate as Lawrence Springer.''

''We could certainly bring Heston in for questioning,'' Nick said. ''Trouble is, where does that get us? The reason we targeted Lawrence Springer in the first place is because the other partners seem to be remarkably clueless about the big picture.''

Mac shook his head in disagreement. ''Heston knows about the money,'' he said. ''In an investigation, it's always a damn good idea to follow the money trail.''

''But not in this investigation,'' Nick said. ''Heston is one of the smartest financial minds in the country. Bob Spinard and I have gone over every scrap of data Unit One has managed to accumulate on him and we've checked every financial transaction that might have been made in connection with the Bonita Project. After weeks of excruciatingly detailed analysis, Bob's opinion is that Heston has committed no indictable offense."

"Jesus, Nick, Heston is squirreling away hundreds of millions of dollars in offshore accounts—"

"Yes, Heston's moving a lot of money around on Beecham's behalf, but it's all money raised overseas, from foreign sources, and the funds have never touched any corporation or entity subject to U.S. jurisdiction. I concur with Bob on this. Not only would we have a hell of a time persuading Heston to give up what he knows, but even if we succeed in breaking him, it probably wouldn't lead us where we want to go. Beecham managed to recruit big-name, high-profile people like Heston, Cranford and Yates because he could promise them that the Bonita partnership wasn't going to break U.S. law."

Mac snorted. "Lawrence Springer knew otherwise."

"Yes," Nick agreed. "Springer knew where all the Bonita Project bodies are buried. He was also our best chance of acquiring hard evidence that Beecham ordered Kenneth Chung's murder." He gave a mirthless smile. "That, of course, is precisely why Springer is dead."

Mac walked over to his espresso machine and set the coffee-bean grinder whirring noisily, but his heart clearly wasn't in it. "Then we're forced back to plan B. Using Melody Beecham," he said.

Nick had spent the past six weeks trying to come up with an alternative plan C, and he'd failed. "From Wallis Beecham's point of view, she's the most threatening of our available weapons," he said. "If we try to use Heston or Cranford or Yates, we're at a disadvantage going in. Beecham knows more about them than we do. With Melody, the situation is reversed."

"In view of Dave's treachery, we have to assume Beecham is aware of the fact that Melody has been recruited by Unit One," Mac said.

"And also that I'm the director of operations," Nick agreed.

"How is that going to affect Beecham's response to Melody's threats? Give me your best guess."

"It means he'll take the threats more seriously," Nick said. "Beecham has every reason to believe that Lady Roz left some incriminating papers behind and that Melody has found them."

"Which happens to be true as well as believable," Mac commented dryly.

"Yes, and on top of all that, we have to assume Dave has given Beecham a pretty complete account of the facilities and resources that Unit One has at its disposal. It's a safe bet that Beecham will feel compelled to come after her."

"To kill her," Mac said.

"To kill her," Nick agreed grimly. He drew in a deep breath, but his heart still beat in double time. "One other factor—we have to consider the possibility that Beecham will use Dave to get to her."

Mac actually pushed the freshly ground coffee away, as if the smell sickened him. "You'd better be damned sure they don't succeed."

"I'm working on it." Funny to think that only a couple of months ago he'd been opposed to recruiting Melody to Unit One because he wasn't sure he would ever be able to count on her loyalty. Her loyalty wasn't what worried him anymore. What worried him now was how the hell he could keep her safe. Unit One had stuck her out in the middle of a battlefield with a damn great targeting circle painted around her heart. Standing in front of her to take the bullet wasn't going to be enough. Beecham would just keep shooting until Melody went down.

"So back to my original question," Mac said. "What are your plans in regard to the Bonita Project?"

"Keep Melody alive. Neutralize Dave until we can send him to the brig. Make sure Beecham dies." Sure, he could do it. And in his spare time he could organize world peace and eliminate hunger.

Mac gave him a wintry smile. "I approve in principle. Now, could you fill me in on a few of the details, please?"

Nineteen

Nick deliberately chose to use Dave as his chauffeur when he drove into the city to pick up Melody. He'd taken on a lot of difficult roles over the past twelve years, but pretending he still considered Dave a good friend was proving among the most difficult, and he needed practice in a situation where he was likely to encounter minimal outside risks and pressures.

By the time they arrived at the Van der Meer Gallery, he felt exhausted by the deception. Fortunately, Nikolai-the-seductive-Russian-charmer was a role he could play by rote, and he greeted Ellen with his standard Nikolai smile, its effectiveness boosted by the half dozen yellow roses he'd bought for her en route to the gallery.

"Melody's in Jasper's office," Ellen said, beaming with pleasure as she thanked him yet again for the flowers. "I'll let her know you're here— Oh, no need. Here she comes."

Nick had arrived at the gallery well prepared to deal with Melody. He had a charmingly risqué routine worked out for their encounter, designed to amuse her and to impress any of her colleagues who happened to be in the vicinity. Unfortunately, at the sight of her, the lines of clever patter vanished.

She stopped a couple of feet away from him, not smiling, not speaking, but not turning away, either. He reached for her hands, holding on too tight and for longer than he'd intended. He wasn't sure whether he held her hands because Nikolai would certainly have done so, or because Nick needed the human contact. He hoped like hell it was the former.

"Can you leave now?" he asked. "Right away?" His words came out flat and earnest. All wrong for Nikolai, who would have lowered his voice to a husky whisper and then ridden roughshod over Melody's protests, if she made any. If he'd delivered his lines according to his prepared script, Melody would have found herself entranced into the limo almost before she knew what was happening, although no real emotion would have been traded between the two of them. As it was, the air around them was thick with… God knew what. Better not to overanalyze exactly what was going on with him right now, Nick decided.

Melody didn't answer him for a moment. Instead, she looked at him with an expression he couldn't read in her startling blue eyes. If he hadn't known it was impossible, he would have sworn that she sensed the sadness of Dave's betrayal churning inside him.

"Yes, I can leave," she said finally. "I'll get my coat."

She came back less than a minute later, her bright scarlet coat defying the winter gloom, a long black scarf framing her face and highlighting the gold strands in her hair.

"You look…tired." She gave him one of the not-quite smiles that always ripped his insides in two.

"Just a little, maybe."

"We don't have to go out tonight." She kept her voice low, taking care not to be overheard, making him believe that the offer was meant just for him—for Nick—and had nothing to do with the parts they were playing. "We could stay home. Watch a movie. Order in Chinese."

It sounded more wonderful than he wanted to admit, so he deliberately broke the beguiling sensation of intimacy. From somewhere he dredged up a jaunty Nikolai grin. "Agree to Thai instead of Chinese, and you have a deal."

She didn't respond to his smile, just gave him one of those scary glances that hovered dangerously close to sympathy. After a moment of silence she agreed soberly that she would be fine with Thai food.

Nick was careful not to give her the chance to ask any difficult questions while Dave drove them to the apartment, but once they were inside Melody confronted him, brushing aside his offer of a drink with an impatient gesture, tossing her coat and the jacket of her suit over the back of the nearest chair. "Something's happened since lunchtime. What's bothering you, Nick?"

Various suitable lies sprang to mind, instantly available after years of subterfuge and prevarication. They all died somewhere between his brain and his vocal cords. He had no idea how or why Melody was able to see through his facade when most people found it impenetrable, but the bottom line was that he felt bruised by Dave's betrayal, and she had recognized his battered state. He'd been debating what story to concoct about Dave that would reveal nothing about his partner's betrayal while still insuring that she was armored against an attack from him.

Suddenly he realized that far and away the best solution was to dispense with lies and tell Melody the simple truth.

It was unheard of for him to trust a new recruit with such a major secret. On the other hand, it was equally unheard of for him to allow a new recruit to become the prime target in a major investigation. He decided that Melody deserved to know exactly what she was up against.

"You're right, I had some bad news today." Nick started to explain about Mac's internal security review, and the bitter conclusion the two of them had reached about Dave's loyalty, or lack thereof. He realized halfway through that he was revealing way too much about his own sense of loss and betrayal.

He cut back abruptly, retreating into a bare-bones account of exactly how Dave had been seduced into cooperating with Beecham, and outlining the Bonita partnership's plans to build a clinic and research facility for human cloning in some unknown location: a fourth world country, or on a previously uninhabited tropical island, or in a remote region such as Patagonia at the tip of South America. For all that the world was supposedly such a small place, there were still an amazing number of locations where it was possible to conceal construction from the probing lens of a spy satellite. As for hiding from human inspection, that was even easier than hiding from a satellite. With a few bribes to the officials of whatever impoverished town happened to be closest to the building site, Wallis Beecham could buy discretion. With the provision of electricity or clean water to local villagers, he could buy not only gratitude but also undying loyalty and total secrecy.

Melody listened to him with such intense concentration that Nick could detect no sign of movement. Even her breathing was invisible. When he finished his explanation, she sprang up from the sofa, exploding into motion. She walked into the kitchen and returned with a can of soda in one hand and a bottle of beer in the other, the cap already flipped. She handed Nick the beer and he took an immediate grateful gulp.

"You don't seem as surprised as I would have expected," he said.

Melody reflected for a moment. "At one level, I'm totally blown away. At another level, it makes perfect sense to me. Having known Wallis Beecham for years, I'd say that his dominant characteristic is a lust for power. What better way for him to feed his ego than to acquire the ability to create human beings designed to fit his own specifications?" Her mouth turned down. "How much do you bet the first baby scheduled for birth is going to be a Wallis Beecham clone?"

"A few million bucks," Nick said dryly. "It would be an easy way to make my fortune if anybody would take the bet. And I agree with you about Beecham's motivations. The Bonita Project is about power, ego and fame, not science."

In his judgment, Beecham's ambition bordered on the pathological. In the global environment of the twenty-first century, national fame was no longer enough for Beecham. He wanted his name to inspire awe on a worldwide basis. The Raelians, who asserted that earthlings had been cloned by beings from outer space, had managed to garner headlines on five continents simply by announcing that they'd cloned a baby. All that media attention had been generated even though almost nobody believed the Raelians were telling the truth.

Beecham, by contrast, was going to deliver the real thing: a state-of-the-art clinic, staffed by qualified scientists, with clients pulled from the aristocracy of the world, and the birth of genuinely cloned babies on a regular basis. The clinic and its master creator would be lightning rods for international fame and fortune. Wallis Beecham would be hailed as a savior or a monster, depending on who was doing the hailing. Either way, he would be front and center of world attention.

Nick also suspected that Johnston Yates's recruitment to the Bonita partnership was for a darker purpose than merely to provide a dignified PR front when news of the first cloned baby broke in the world's media. Wallis would never attempt to run for U.S. president himself. He was smart enough to realize he would be unelectable with all the baggage resulting from his role as founder of the clinic. But Johnston Yates might be electable. After all, Yates had not only been vice president, he'd been the front-runner for the Republican party presidential nomination until he was forced to withdraw because of Cynthia's life-and-death battle against uterine cancer.

With enough of Beecham's money available to buy clever ads, and brilliant spin doctors to downplay any unsavory connections to the Bonita Project, Yates could be presented as a highly attractive candidate. Beecham would then have the best of all possible worlds: freedom to continue expanding his commercial empire, and a puppet dancing to his tune in the White House. The man supposed to hold the most powerful office in the world would in reality have strings attached to every part of his body.

"Let me make sure I have this straight." Melody kicked off her shoes and sat on the sofa with her feet tucked under her.

Nick found the implicit intimacy of her gesture erotic in the extreme. Or perhaps it was just Melody whom he found erotic, and he would have been equally aroused if she'd sat upright on the sofa with her hands folded primly in her lap.

She nursed her soda rather than drinking it. "Leaving aside the whole issue of the legality of Wallis's plans to start cloning human babies—which is a huge issue to leave aside—I don't understand why Unit One has a problem going out right now and getting a warrant for Wallis Beecham's arrest."

"There are no grounds for a judge to issue a warrant."

"Oh, please!" Melody shot off the sofa, impelled by frustration, then forced herself to sit down again. "Unit One already knows that Wallis Beecham plotted with Lawrence Springer to murder Kenneth Chung in exchange for a three-hundred-million-dollar payoff from a consortium of Saudi princes. In fact, you personally have firsthand proof of what would have happened to Mr. Chung if Unit One hadn't intervened. After all, *you* were the guy hired to commit the murder. Unit One also has solid reasons to suspect that Dave conspired with Wallis to murder Lawrence Springer, and you could surely extract a confession from Dave if you need even more proof."

"True, but that's not enough—"

She interrupted him again. It was as if having remained so still and quiet while he explained about the cloning project, her protests were now boiling over. "Good grief, what does Wallis Beecham have to do before he can be brought to justice? Stand in the middle of Times Square and aim an AK-47 at passing tourists?"

"Just about," Nick said wryly. "We're not talking about some hapless Joe Schmoe here. We're talking about one of the most powerful industrialists in the country, with a private army of lawyers at his beck and call."

Melody radiated frustration. "That may be. He's also the murderer who ordered the death of Kenneth Chung and Lawrence Springer! Why is he above the law?"

"He isn't above the law, he's simply clever." It was a mark of how passionately Melody loathed Wallis Beecham that she wasn't seeing the giant flaw in her analysis. "I wish you were right that we already have him nailed," Nick said. "Unfortunately, there's not a shred of proof that Wallis Beecham ordered the murder of either Chung or Springer."

"What more proof do you need? He hired you to kill Kenneth Chung, dammit!"

"No, he absolutely didn't. I was hired by Lawrence Springer, and Beecham's name was never mentioned between the two of us." Nick gave a rueful grimace. "What's more, Unit One has tapes of every conversation I ever had with Springer just to ram the point home. Can you imagine what Beecham's super high-powered lawyers would make of my claim that Wallis Beecham is really the person who paid me to murder Kenneth Chung? Roadkill surrounded by hungry vultures would be a pretty sight in comparison to my carcass by the time Beecham's lawyers finished with me.''

Melody conceded defeat, albeit with evident reluctance. ''Okay, I suppose you have a point. Unit One has proof that bad things have happened in connection with the Bonita Project, but not that Wallis caused the bad things. So if you can't go after Wallis directly, back to my earlier question about Dave. Can't you persuade him to see reason and turn state's evidence against Wallis?''

''Eventually we can. Mac has a two-person team working on building a legal case against Dave as we speak. The fact is, though, it's not in our best interests to let Dave know he's been identified as working for Beecham. Right now he's more useful to us neutralized but still in place.''

''Because you need to know where the Bonita clinic is before you make a final move on Wallis?'' Melody queried.

''Partly that. We need to know where the clinic is located so that we can run like hell to get the place closed down before the first cloned baby is born. Because once that particular genie wriggles out of the bottle, there won't be a way on God's green earth to squeeze it back in again.''

Nick tossed down the last of his beer in a single long gulp. A more civilized alternative than crashing his fist into the wall, which was what he really wanted to do. ''The real kicker is that I don't suppose Dave knows much more about the details of Beecham's plans than we do, so what's the point of questioning him? What's more, even when Dave has been squeezed dry, I can almost guarantee there will be no hard evidence that leads from him back to Wallis Beecham.''

''How can that possibly be?'' Melody's question expressed all the frustration Nick was feeling. ''How could Wallis recruit Dave, order him to murder Lawrence Springer and still leave no trail?''

Nick scowled at his empty beer bottle as if expecting it to provide answers. ''By working on the simple principle of never telling anyone more than the absolute minimum they need to know,'' he said. ''Nowadays we tend to assume that criminals need to be as brilliant as Hannibal Lecter to succeed. That's a fallacy. Except in the movies, brilliance and criminality don't sit well together in terms of evading capture. A criminal who's too clever ends up wanting to score points not only against law enforcement in general, but also personally against the people who are trying to bring him to justice. As it happens, that's a surefire way to get yourself captured.''

''I thought we'd just agreed that Wallis Beecham has one of the world's larger egos.''

''True, but he doesn't seem to have any twisted need to go *mano-a-mano* against his opponents. He may have the odd psychological quirk, and he's eaten up by ambition, but he's basically sane. That means he keeps his eye on the prize and doesn't get distracted by a Lecter-like compulsion to carve up his victims and eat them with fava beans. Instead, he has an amazing degree of cunning, coupled with a strong sense of self-preservation. He's managed to run rings around Victor Heston, Senator Cranford and Johnston Yates, three of the most sophisticated brains in this country. If Beecham can outwit that trio, I'm damn sure he's managed to protect himself against

Dave, who is basically a guy who reacts to situations using his physical skills rather than his mental abilities."

"I wish you weren't right, but I suspect you are." Melody pummeled one of the sofa cushions into a fresh shape and propped it beneath her elbow, clearly feeling as out of sorts as Nick himself. "You mentioned that Beecham most likely recruited Dave by promising to clone his wife or maybe his baby. What happened to them?"

Nick grimaced at the unpleasant memory. "Jackie died seven years ago in her eighth month of pregnancy. She had elevated blood pressure and developed preeclampsia while Dave was away on a mission for Unit One. She was alone in their apartment and, for whatever reason, she kept putting off calling her doctor. By the time she did call, it was too late. She died with full-blown toxemia of the pregnancy en route to the hospital. The doctors in the E.R. tried to deliver the baby posthumously, but he didn't survive, either."

"Oh, my God." Melody's cheeks lost color.

"Yeah, that about sums it up. Dave has always blamed himself for not being home when Jackie and the baby needed him, although it's not clear that she was having symptoms that either one of them would have recognized as dangerous. So she might not have been saved anyway, even if Dave had spent the afternoon sitting right next to her. Still, I'm hoping there will be more compassionate ways to extract a confession from Dave than to exploit his grief over the loss of his family."

Melody expressed heartfelt agreement. Nick got up and headed for the kitchen and another beer. "Are you sure you don't want to switch from soda to a glass of wine?'' he asked. ''Or how about some of that iced Stolichnaya you were talking about at lunchtime?''

''I'm working.'' Melody followed him into the kitchen and leaned against the counter as he rooted in the fridge in search of another beer. ''Alcohol is against the rules.''

He was too on edge to pay attention to the subtle hint of teasing in her voice. He turned around, slamming the fridge door. He wanted to yell at her that of course she wasn't working. That of course the rules about not drinking on duty didn't apply. Not here. Not with him. That he was talking to her as a *friend,* goddammit.

Fortunately, he had just enough self-control left to prevent himself doing something so disastrous. Even more fortunately, he knew an excellent way to destroy the seductive illusion of camaraderie weaving itself around them before he did something truly idiotic. Like kissing her. Or taking her to bed and making love until the ache in his head and his heart both went away.

''I have something to show you,'' he said abruptly. ''It's in my office. Will you come?''

With her uncanny ability to pick up on his mood, Nick could feel her tension increasing as she watched him key in the combination to open the wall safe hidden behind one of his favorite photos. The shot was of an indigo bunting perched on the branch of a maple tree in full leaf. The picture had been taken in early summer, on a rare vacation trip to the Adirondacks. It had been right around mating season, and the iridescent feathers of the male bird glowed with a blue that appeared too intense to exist outside a fairy tale.

Melody's eyes were a similar blue, he mused. Equally startling and equally captivating. The safe door swung open before he could slide deeper into that perilous train of thought.

Nick reached inside and took out a thick black leather notebook. He heard a gasp from Melody. She had recognized the notebook immediately, of course, which was what he'd anticipated. What he'd wanted.

"Where did you get that?" she demanded. "It's my mother's."

As a mood breaker, the notebook was 100 percent effective. Melody was looking at him with all the affection a newly hatched turtle might demonstrate toward a hungry crocodile.

"I know it's your mother's." Nick forced himself to meet her gaze, his features schooled to reveal nothing of his thoughts. "I arranged for it to be removed from your safety deposit box several weeks ago, shortly after you joined Unit One."

She met his gaze, and the eyes he'd been rhapsodizing about only moments earlier were now colder and bleaker than the Arctic tundra in January. "I'd say *how dare you,* except it seems foolish to waste my valuable time."

Nick could have attempted some sort of defense. He could have reminded her of all that was at stake. Of how little reason Unit One had to trust her. Of how much information about her mother's dealings with Wallis Beecham she'd held back, with no way for him to judge whether the information she'd withheld was important or trivial. Instead he moved straight to the point of the exercise.

''You never told us that your mother made her living by blackmail,'' he said, flipping through the notebook. ''By the time she died, it looks as if she'd developed quite a lucrative trade in squalid secrets.''

He heard the tiniest quiver of indrawn breath from Melody, but her voice was both cool and steady. ''Yes,'' she said. ''That notebook makes my mother's blackmail activities quite clear.''

''Did you know about the true source of your mother's income before she died?''

''No.''

Melody was smart enough not to expand on her answer. Nick had to admire her self-control. Now that he'd put her on guard, he could see the protective barrier around her emotions hardening by the second.

''How do you think Lady Roz managed to persuade Wallis Beecham to pay up for so many years?'' he asked. ''Your mother was still receiving regular payments long after the court-ordered child support for you had ended.''

''Wallis believed he was my father. Perhaps Roz appealed to his better nature on my behalf.''

''That's not one of your better lies, Melody.'' Nick wouldn't allow himself to feel sympathy for the way she tried to put a positive spin on her mother's actions. ''We both know Wallis Beecham gave you no money after you were eighteen, either directly or through your mother. You were already a world-famous model by the time you left school, entirely self-supporting financially, and you didn't go on to college until several years later. Your father cut you off without a penny on the day court-ordered child support ended.''

She looked bored, one of her favorite defenses. "He didn't approve of my career. He wanted me to attend college in the States and then to come and work for him."

Which probably went a long way toward explaining why she'd gone to university in England and Italy, Nick reflected wryly. "Your mother's records are haphazard to say the least, but by my calculations, Lady Roz was accumulating somewhere close to a hundred thousand dollars a year just from Wallis Beecham. This was a decade and more before he started the Bonita Project, and we both agree he isn't the generous sort. How did your mother persuade him to hand over such sizable chunks of change?"

"That's a rhetorical question, I assume?" Melody's voice was uninflected, her face blank of expression. "I'm sure you've read the charts at the front of the notebook."

"Yes, I have. As far as I can tell, Lady Roz seems to have achieved her goals with a combination of threats and rewards, the rewards being sexual favors. Long after the divorce, your mother continued to have sex with Wallis Beecham on a fairly regular basis. Is that what you concluded from studying her notes?"

"My mother's comments tend to be cryptic, so your guess is as good as mine."

"I already know my guess. Give me yours."

Melody shrugged. "That the two of them had sex fairly regularly. The idea of cheating on wife number two with wife number one would have had great appeal for Wallis, I imagine. Much more intriguing than plain old adultery."

"And would it have appealed to your mother?"

Nick asked. "Do you think Lady Roz was jealous enough of Sondra to enjoy the idea that she was exacting some sort of sexual revenge?"

"No," Melody said. "My mother had no desire to resume her marriage to Wallis Beecham, and she didn't care enough about Sondra to be interested in revenge of any sort."

That sounded eminently believable, Nick reflected. Roz had just wanted Beecham's money and was prepared to do whatever was needed to get it. As a fleeting aside, it occurred to him that, given Wallis Beecham's lifelong insistence on receiving value for money, Roz must have been truly spectacular in bed.

"The illicit sex was presumably the sweetener in the pot," he said. "Beecham didn't hand over a hundred thousand bucks a year just because he enjoyed the thrill of sexual dalliance with his ex-wife a few times a year. Lady Roz must have had some really potent goodies to threaten him with in order for Beecham to keep paying her off."

"I expect she did," Melody said. "But I don't know precisely what. Wallis undoubtedly has dozens of tawdry secrets, and although a hundred thousand dollars is a lot of money by most people's standards, for Wallis it's no more than a line item in the petty cash account."

"How do you think Lady Roz kept tabs on Beecham?" Nick asked. "Ferreting out truly damaging secrets would seem a daunting task for a woman like your mother."

"Like my mother?" Melody's eyes flashed fire. "What sort of a woman do you think my mother was, Nick?"

He couldn't bring himself to tell her the truth, so

he fudged it. ''A woman working without professional investigative help, and having no particular financial or commercial training.''

''But let's not forget her amazing sexual talents,'' Melody said with icy sarcasm, not in the least deceived by his attempted fudge. ''Being a crackerjack in bed sure makes up for a lot in a dumb woman, doesn't it, Nick?''

Since there was no acceptable answer to that, he sent Melody a look that was all cool professional interrogation, even though he could barely keep his hands off her. He not only ached to make love to her, he also wanted to comfort her, he realized. To take her in his arms and tell her that she could stop worrying, because she was nothing like the dreadful Lady Roz, except for the good fortune of winning the genetic lottery and being every bit as beautiful as her mother.

It wasn't his desire to have sex with Melody that worried Nick. It was the urge to offer comfort that scared the hell out of him. So naturally he protected himself by asking another brutal question. ''Did you help your mother in her blackmail attempts?''

''By dispensing my sexual favors or by ferreting out nasty secrets?'' she asked with lethal sweetness.

''Either. Both.''

''In fact, neither. I've already told you that until my mother died, I knew nothing about the way she generated her income. While she was alive, I merely paid her bills and handled her bank accounts *after* the money had come into her possession.''

''And yet, acting without any help, your mother managed to put the squeeze on Beecham for the best part of a quarter century. We agreed only a few minutes ago that three of the smartest men in the country are basically in Beecham's control, but Roz managed to outmaneuver him. How did she do it?''

''More easily than you imagine, I expect. My mother belonged to a generation and a social class where women who were both smart and beautiful quickly learned to emphasize their beauty and downplay their intelligence. Contrary to your belief, Roz was a very bright woman who chose to pretend otherwise. I'll give you an example of how she outwitted Wallis without him even being aware until it was all over. It wasn't until after my mother's funeral that Wallis learned how Roz had tricked him into giving the blood sample she needed for a paternity test. The solicitor's message made it pretty clear that my mother manipulated Wallis into cutting his thumb on a broken brandy snifter and then, under the pretense of tending to the wound, she collected the blood sample she wanted. Wallis never had the smallest clue what had happened to him until my mother chose to let him know.''

''I can barely imagine how furious Beecham must have been,'' Nick said with perfect truth.

Melody nodded. ''He was seething with fury. I think what upset him so much was the fact that he'd always assumed he was exploiting my mother with their sexual encounters. Wallis relishes unequal relationships, and he probably harbored the fantasy that she was still in love with him despite the divorce, whereas he was just using her for meaningless casual sex. The fact that she'd taken his blood without his consent made it plain that Roz wasn't being exploited at all. On the contrary, she was using *him.*''

''In the end, though, you would have to say she

failed and Beecham won. His payments to your mother stopped a year before she died."

"So it seems." Melody turned away, her brief moment of shared insights coming to an abrupt end.

Nick refused to let her off the hook. "Why did Beecham's payments finally stop after so many years, do you think?"

"Because the secrets got too old to be threatening, perhaps? Because my mother didn't manage to generate enough solid information about the Bonita Project to use her knowledge as a blackmail tool?"

"Either one is possible, of course, but I believe something quite different happened," Nick said. "When we first debriefed you at Unit One, you told us that Lady Rosalind's papers about the Bonita Project hadn't been stored in either of her known safety deposit boxes—"

"Which seems another example of my mother's extreme good sense," Melody interrupted acidly. "I expect she was afraid Wallis would make the same sort of illegal search of her private papers that you made of mine."

Nick chose discretion over valor and ignored that piece of highly accurate analysis. "You told us you were sent a key by Nathaniel Sherwin, Lady Rosalind's solicitor, immediately after the funeral. The key led you to a safety deposit box in a bank where Lady Rosalind had no other accounts. In fact, for extra secrecy, she'd rented the box under an assumed name. You found a letter from your mother in that box, along with her research notes on the Bonita Project. Nathaniel Sherwin didn't tell you about the key at the memorial service because he'd been instructed not to reveal its existence to anyone except you.''

''That's all true. It's another example of how smart my mother was at evading retribution from Wallis Beecham, wouldn't you say? If she hadn't taken those additional precautions, Wallis might have found her research notes on the Bonita Project. And if he'd also found her letter advising me to go get him, I'm betting I'd be in the cemetery right now, providing an all-you-can-eat dinner buffet for the maggots.''

Nick was very afraid she might be right, which was why he needed to find out what it was that she'd been holding back from Unit One. He had to make sure there wasn't a single scrap more of relevant information that she could provide.

''But none of this is new information for you,'' Melody said. ''As you very well know, I gave Unit One all my mother's notes about the Bonita Project, such as they were. I even handed over her personal letter to me, so why the sudden urge to interrogate me?''

''Because you didn't tell me about her notebook,'' he snapped. ''Because I'm wondering what the hell else you're holding back.''

''Nothing,'' she said, looking straight at him with every appearance of complete candor. ''I didn't tell you about my mother's notebook because there's nothing in there that's relevant to Unit One's investigation of the Bonita partnership. The conversation we're having right now is proof of that. We've spent the past half hour talking about my mother's blackmailing activities. We've barely mentioned the Bonita Project.''

"But we're not finished yet," Nick said. He flipped the pages over and held the book up by its cover. "Look closely and you'll see that several pages have been torn out of the back of the notebook. Except for those financial charts at the beginning of the book, your mother wrote her notes in chronological order, so those missing pages must have contained information from the final year of her life. That's the exact period when she was working so hard to dig up dirt about the Bonita partnership. What do you think those missing pages said?"

Melody shook her head. "I've wondered about that myself. Unfortunately, we'll never know. My mother must have torn out those pages before the notebook came into my possession."

The pitch of Melody's voice was innocence personified, the expression on her face exactly what Nick would have expected, given the intrusive nature of his questioning. He was, however, 100 percent sure that she was lying. The missing notebook pages had been torn out by Melody herself. She'd probably destroyed them as too dangerous, or too hurtful, to keep. Either way, he needed to know what they said.

"Why would your mother have destroyed the final few pages of her journal, do you think? After all, she wanted you to read the rest of it. What could there have been in those final few pages that was too intimate, or too dangerous, for you to see?"

Melody looked at him steadily. "I'm sure there was nothing dangerous in those missing pages. I expect my mother destroyed them because the information they contained was very personal and had absolutely nothing to do with the Bonita Project."

She was tacitly admitting that she'd read the

pages, but he had to be sure that she wasn't miscalculating, and that the pages really were irrelevant to Unit One's investigation—and to her own safety.

"Tell me what your mother wrote on those missing pages," he pleaded, his voice low. "I promise you if the information has nothing to do with the Bonita Project then I won't repeat it to anyone, ever."

That made her laugh. She gave him no other answer.

When she laughed, she looked defiant, beautiful and breathtakingly vulnerable. Nick finally lost it. He grabbed her arm, pulling her close. "Talk to me, goddammit! We're not playing a stupid game! It's your life that's at stake here!"

She looked down at his hand gripping her arm. "Let go of me." Her voice for the first time was unsteady.

"I can't." There was perhaps one last moment when he could have broken away, but it vanished before he fully recognized the turning point. Desire and frustration poured over him in a giant, disordered wave, mingled with a deep-rooted need to shatter Melody's formidable barriers and be rewarded with a glimpse of the passion he knew was hidden deep inside.

He bent to kiss her, his mouth covering hers with an urgency that left no room for elegance or finesse. Her lips were warm and impossibly soft. Claire Springer had told him once that he was the best kisser of any lover she'd ever had and, heaven knew, Claire's comparison pool was large. Right now, though, Nick couldn't for the life of him have summoned up any of the techniques that apparently made him so expert. The minute Melody's lips parted, he was lost, totally out of control at the touch of her tongue against his and the feel of her soft breasts pressing against the hard wall of his chest.

If there was one thing Nick never did when he made love, it was to lose control. Especially not over a simple kiss, for God's sake. For a few seconds he let the unfamiliar tornado of sensations whirl around him. Then, with an effort that broke sweat all the way down his spine, he dropped his hands to his sides and tore his mouth away from Melody's. Some emotion balled tightly in his chest, almost choking him, but he took care not to identify it. If he walked away now, maybe he could still convince himself that he was capable of remaining night and day in Melody's company without blowing his operational capability.

He might as well have saved himself the trouble of pretending. Melody simply reached up, linked her hands behind his neck and pulled him down to kiss her again. Nick's sigh of relief—or maybe it was regret—came out as a groan of longing and he knew damn well he wasn't going anywhere in the near future except to his bed.

He picked her up and she wrapped her legs around him, pulling open the buttons of his shirt as he carried her into his bedroom. Melody's mouth was still locked with his, and the incredible silkiness of her hair fell forward against his cheek. He could feel the strands catching against the stubble of his twelve-hour beard, and for a moment that small intimacy seemed like one of the most erotic things he'd ever experienced.

She was still on top of him when he sank down

with her onto the bed. He took off her sweater and then her bra, tossing them over his shoulder, where they were instantly lost in the billowing, down-filled puffs of his ridiculous comforter. Melody didn't seem to care, or even to notice.

Nick kissed her breasts, his breath hot on her nipples, and she reached for the buckle of his belt, tugging at his zipper. He scrabbled to pull down her slacks and the black thong she wore underneath at the same time as he kicked off his jeans. They were both panting by the time they'd finished, but not from the exertion. He rolled over so that she was underneath him, her legs opening and her hips arching to take him inside.

Nick experienced a single moment of lucidity before he plunged into her. He realized that less than five minutes had elapsed since the moment of their first kiss and that neither of them had spoken a single word. He thought that if he had an idea in hell of what to say, he might at least try to break their silence. As it was, anything he genuinely wanted to tell her was too dangerous, and he found that the usual lies wouldn't make their way past his vocal cords.

Melody made a low, urgent sound deep in her throat and her legs tightened restlessly around him.

Nick, Unit One's stud supreme, champion provider of high-quality female orgasms, managed to last another thirty seconds before it was all over.

He lay collapsed on top of her for another few seconds, then carefully moved to the side of the bed. He folded his hands behind his head and stared up at the invisible ceiling, grateful for the darkness. In his obscene haste to bed Melody he'd neglected to switch on any of the lights. Now he was grateful for the omission. Perhaps he could make love to her again. More slowly this time. He could surely to God manage slow the second time around.

He realized Melody was getting up from the bed. She spoke before he could get his brain and voice to function together. "My mother was having an affair with Christopher Beecham," she said.

What the hell was she talking about? For a second or two, Nick couldn't place who Christopher Beecham was.

He heard her walking away from the bed, saw the shadowy outline of her body heading toward the bathroom. "Wait!" He pushed himself into a sitting position on the side of the bed.

She turned around. "That's what was in the missing pages of the notebook," she said. "My mother was having an affair with Christopher Beecham. Wallis came in and found them together. I guess he didn't like the idea of his ex-wife screwing his son. That's when his payments to her stopped."

She walked into the bathroom and closed the door. He heard the click of the lock and started to curse, long and hard. It didn't make him feel any better.

Twenty

Ellen tapped on the door to Melody's office. She wore the smitten look that had by now become familiar whenever Nick was in the vicinity. "Sorry to interrupt you both, but Nikolai Anwar has just arrived to pick up Melody."

Melody put down the pencil she was holding, lining it up neatly with the edge of her blotter. At least she could keep her desk tidy, even if the rest of her life was spiraling out of control. "Thanks, Ellen. Tell him I'll be there in a couple of minutes, would you?" Amazingly, she managed to sound like a regular person instead of a panic-stricken jellyfish, which was how she really felt.

Ellen dashed off, presumably to enjoy five minutes of Nick's company all to herself. Jasper watched her hasty departure, then turned back to Melody. He gave her one of his half amused, half paternal looks, his left eyebrow quirking. "That's the third time in two days that Nikolai Anwar has turned up at the gallery to escort you somewhere."

"Er…yes." Melody-the-jellyfish decided to prove to herself that she possessed at least a slither of spinal cord. She gestured to the small suitcase standing in the corner of her office. Might as well get her announcement over with. "I…um…went home and packed an overnight bag at lunchtime. Don't wait up for me, Jasper. Not that you ever do, of course. I just meant that tonight I'm…well, I might not… I probably won't be coming home. Maybe not for a couple of days. Nights.'' She stumbled into mortified silence before she could make an even bigger fool of herself than she already had.

Jasper quirked his other eyebrow. ''My, my, my. So we finally have a man who can reduce my very own ice princess to incoherence. That's a turnup for the record books. Nikolai was at the Yateses' party, wasn't he? I didn't realize the two of you had even met.''

''Oh, yes. We've known each other for quite a while. In between his business trips to Russia and my accident and everything, you know.''

''No, I had no idea. Nikolai Anwar certainly has an interesting reputation. But isn't he just a little…farouche…for you, sweetie?''

Of course he was too wild for her. Nick was too everything for her, and after the debacle of last night it was humiliating to realize that her heart was pounding and her pulse racing at the mere prospect of seeing him again.

Melody ignored her thumping heart and gave a carefree laugh that sounded only a little forced. ''Jasper, darling, Nick and I are going out to dinner, that's all. We're not shopping for picket fences.''

''Dinner. Hmm.'' Jasper directed a single, pointed glance at the suitcase, then gave her hand a quick squeeze. ''Enjoy your night, sweetie.'' He left her office before she could come up with a suitable response. Enjoy her night? Perhaps there was no suitable response to that other than a hollow laugh.

Dave was playing chauffeur again, and Melody actually felt a small spurt of gratitude toward Nick for that decision. Dave's presence gave them both a welcome excuse during the drive not to say anything about any subject that mattered. Like sex. Or last night. Or tonight. Or why Nick only had to sit in the far corner of the limo and look at her with smoldering brown eyes and her nipples started to tingle.

Unfortunately, there was no reason for Dave to come with them into Nick's apartment and once there, Melody's problems immediately intensified. Where was she supposed to put her suitcase? she wondered. Where was she going to sleep? Last night Nick had taken a pillow and blanket onto one of the living-room sofas. Was it her turn to take the sofa tonight? Were they actually going to discuss their sleeping arrangements and risk trampling deep into each other's emotional no-go zones? The zones they both worked so hard to keep off-limits. Her stomach churned at the prospect.

Bloody hell, this teenage-style angst was ridiculous. But ridiculous or not, Melody realized she was far too cowardly to introduce any topic that might lead the conversation back to last night and the two of them in bed. Where she had practically consumed Nick alive, she'd been so embarrassingly eager.

Which brought her full circle to the problem of her suitcase. Giving up on decision making, Melody dropped the darn thing where she stood, then pushed it up against the living-room wall. Nick displayed no interest in her maneuver. But then, why would he? Unlike her, he wasn't demonstrating advanced symptoms of insanity. Presumably his nipples weren't tingling, either.

"I've already ordered dinner from the deli on the corner," he said. "I hope that's okay with you?"

"That's fine," Melody replied, so determinedly polite that she'd probably have agreed to eat sheep's eyeballs. "But I thought you wanted us to eat out? Be seen at restaurants, and so on."

"It seems a bit late in the game for that, don't you think? Since we're expecting—hoping—that Beecham will phone at any minute, it seemed wiser to stay home. He might call when the waiter is standing right by the table, or when an acquaintance has stopped by to say hello. It would be awkward for you to respond to Beecham in those circumstances, especially since you have a tight script to follow."

"I suppose you have a point." Of course, being alone with Nick in his apartment wasn't exactly a walk in the park. Melody removed her cell phone from her purse and put it on the table, praying that Wallis would call right now this moment, so that this excruciating wait would be over.

Wallis, with his unfailing capacity to be disagreeable, didn't oblige.

"About last night," Nick said, and stopped.

"Don't give it another thought." Melody adjusted her mouth into a bright smile. "I always feel sex is rather self-explanatory, don't you?" She hoped—she really hoped—that her voice didn't shake as she tossed off that little piece of nonsense. A fraction too late she realized that her reply said more about her own obsessions than Nick's question. He might not have been referring to their sexual encounter at all.

Thank God, it appeared that he had been. "Never apologize, never explain?" he asked.

"Something along those lines." Her voice was so damned airy, her words practically blew away.

"I used to think that," he said. "But last night doesn't seem very self-explanatory to me. The opposite, in fact."

"We wanted each other. We had sex. I see nothing complicated about that."

"You're right. The sex and the wanting were easy. It was afterward that it got complicated."

"Only if we let it."

He looked straight at her then, and she felt her cheeks grow hot under the force of his gaze. "So answer me this, Melody, since you find the situation so damn simple. Do we want each other again? Now? Tonight?"

She realized that she'd walked herself right into a corner from which there was no elegant escape. Not without revealing far more than she wanted to about a whole heap of subjects she preferred to keep strictly private. Worse, she wasn't even sure she knew the true answer to his question, so it was hard to invent an appropriate lie. Her body, with its twitching hormones and vibrating pheromones, was quite sure her answer should be yes. She wanted Nick again. Preferably right this second, or maybe in five minutes if they decided to hold off for the fun of letting the anticipation build. The rest of her, the rational part that knew how to keep her heart safe and her emotions protected, was equally sure her answer should be no.

At this precise moment, given her pathetically confused state, the only two things she knew with complete certainty were that if she had been even a little smart, she would never have had sex with Nick in the first place. And unless she was totally self-destructive, she would never have sex with him again.

Melody opted for emotional safety. No surprise there. She'd been opting for emotional safety ever since she was old enough to make a conscious choice. "This doesn't seem a very good moment for either one of us to start a physical relationship."

"It's already started."

"Then we should end it," she snapped.

"You're absolutely right. Last night was a mistake—"

"Exactly. I'm glad you see it that way." Melody let out the breath she'd been holding. Nick's agreement was unflattering in its promptness, but she was sure she would feel relieved some time very soon.

"Well, I'm glad that's all settled." She found her smile and flashed it again, although it felt frayed from insincerity and overuse. "I'm now officially declaring myself off duty, if that's okay with you. How about a glass of wine before the deli delivers our dinner?"

She started to walk past Nick en route to the kitchen. He held out his arm, preventing her passage. "Last night was a mistake," he said. "But tonight we can do it right."

Melody opened her mouth to disagree. He kissed her before she could speak, a hot, tongue-in-the-throat kiss that sent her stupid hormones into an immediate and ecstatic dance. She murmured half-hearted protests against Nick's mouth even as she pressed into him, her hands reaching up to tangle in his hair despite her clear decision that they should do no such thing.

Desire flooded her, battling both with panic and a tiny voice of cool reason that told her to quit right now, while she was still in marginal possession of her senses. Reason lost the battle. Her desire grew stronger the more she tried to repress it, like a bright yellow dandelion flowering defiantly in the middle of a manicured lawn.

She was soon woozy from the effect of his kisses, drunk from the exuberance of her own need. Nick lifted his head, still holding her close. ''Do you really want me to stop?''

''Yes.'' She looked away from him and her voice fell as she admitted the truth. ''No.''

''I'm glad.'' His mouth was only a breath away from hers. ''I'm very glad.''

He kissed her again, his hands linked low behind her, holding her crushed against the muscled plane of his body. Melody felt a raw ache of longing, a rush of sexual need that shocked her with its intensity, despite her experiences with him last night. The physical sensations Nick was arousing seemed even stronger than yesterday, perhaps because she could no longer conceal from herself the emotional component of the desire ripping through her.

She didn't understand why Nick so easily breached all her defenses and made her respond—not just to his actions, but to *him.* She'd had sex before, with lovers as handsome and accomplished in their own ways as Nick. She'd even tried to turn the sex into genuine lovemaking on a couple of occasions, but this was the first time she'd ever truly yielded a part of herself. The section of her brain that normally remained on permanent guard duty, monitoring her actions to make sure she didn't open herself to the risk of emotional damage, had somehow switched itself off. But instead of feeling vulnerable, she was flooded with a sense of well-being, able for the first time in her life to fully enjoy the rich, dark sensations of desire.

Nick caressed her everywhere, and where he touched, heat shimmered on her skin. Pleasure started at each point of contact, then sank deep inside, where it was magically transformed back from pleasure into a need that pushed her into giving more and more of herself. She found herself tumbling headlong toward a place she'd never been before. For a moment the sentinel in her brain switched on again, shrieking out a clarion call of alarm, but Nick soothed her sudden trembling with kisses. Kisses that merely incited more trembling, except this time the quivering of her body had nothing at all to do with fear.

Last night everything about their coming together had been quick, hard and urgent. Tonight everything was slow, silky and tender. Last night there had been no words. Tonight Nick told her often how beautiful she was and how much he wanted her. She told him that she wanted him, too, not worrying for once about whether and if and how he could misinterpret what she said. And since her sentinel had gone off duty, nobody warned her that what she felt for Nick might be something a lot more dangerous than mere wanting. That what she felt might be something that she had sworn never to feel for any man she didn't completely and totally trust.

They waited until they were in the bedroom to take off each other's clothes. The slowness and the tenderness began to vanish as each successive item of clothing landed on the floor. At the end, when they were finally naked, there was no slowness left. The air surrounding them had become heavy and too thick to breathe. Blood pounded in Melody's ears, a roaring, deafening accompaniment to the pulsing drumbeat of her approaching climax. Nick's touch no longer warmed her. Instead, it scorched. His kisses no longer satisfied. Instead, they drove her to fist her hands in the sheets and arch her hips off the bed, rocking in a primal, inviting rhythm.

Nick spoke her name once as he entered her, that was all. No more reminders that she was beautiful or that he wanted her. Just her name, whispered softly against her mouth. Melody felt as if all the emotions of the universe had fused into one exquisite point of need deep inside her. With a shuddering gasp she surrendered to her own need, and the world shattered around her.

The darkness was a comforting blanket, wrapping her emotions inside its folds where they could be safely hidden. Melody floated in the warm darkness, drowsy and replete, not yet ready to consider what had just happened between her and Nick even though her head still lay in the crook of his arm. A low buzz punctuated her cocoon, but she ignored it, as she might a bee too far away to sting.

Beside her, Nick suddenly jackknifed upright. "Jesus, that must be Beecham!" He tumbled out of bed at a run.

Beecham? Oh, my God, *Wallis!* Melody grabbed the sheet, wrapping it around her as she ran into the living room. She seized her cell phone—only Yates and Beecham had the number—and flipped it open, drawing in a steadying breath as she scrambled for focus.

"Hello."

"This is Wallis Beecham."

"Why hello, Daddy." She gave her greeting a touch of mocking emphasis.

Wallis was silent for a moment, and she could sense his anger. But he was too crafty to be provoked by such a relatively low-key gibe. "Johnston Yates called the other day," Wallis said. "He told me you've been trying to get in touch with me."

"Why yes, I have, but you're a hard man to reach."

"Why do you need to speak to me?"

"It's about my mother's papers. It's taken me just the longest time to sort through all her affairs, but the other day I was reading some old airmail letters I found.... Well, you can imagine how old they are because most of them were from the days when people still actually wrote letters instead of picking up the phone or sending an e-mail—"

"You have sixty seconds to say something interesting enough to hold my attention."

Melody's voice changed from imitation Southern belle to crisp New York businessperson. "In amongst all the trivia from the eighties, I found a letter to Mother from Christopher."

"Nice try, Melody, but there's nothing you can tell me about your mother and my son that I don't already know."

"Are you sure of that?" She deliberately paused for a moment. "This letter from Christopher is dated shortly before my mother died. It happens to be about the Bonita partnership."

Wallis didn't respond for a full thirty seconds. From the tension vibrating into the silence, Melody could only assume that he'd picked up on her not-so-subtle hint that Christopher—his spoiled and pampered son—had been passing confidential information to Roz about the Bonita Project.

When Wallis finally did answer, he made no reference to Christopher or her mother. "Speaking of the Bonita partnership, Yates told me that you had some concerns about the project that you wanted to discuss with me," he said brusquely.

"Did he? Yes, I believe I may have mentioned that to him."

Wallis waited for her to expand her answer, but when she said nothing more, he must have realized that he'd lost the psychological battle. Unless she volunteered more information, he had no way to decide whether Christopher had merely been marginally indiscreet about the Bonita Project or whether something much worse had happened, such as a deliberate betrayal by his son.

Wallis was a smart enough businessman to know when it was time to cut his losses.

"I'm flying to New York tonight," he said. "I plan to spend the weekend at my penthouse on Fifth Avenue. I'm willing to spare you thirty minutes of my time tomorrow. Come alone, with the letter, at twelve noon. You've been to the apartment before. Do you remember the address?"

"Yes, I remember the address, and I agree to come alone," Melody said. "But I should warn you that I plan to tell my friends exactly where I'm going and when they can expect me to return. It wouldn't be wise to have me killed, Wallis."

By way of answer, he hung up the phone.

Twenty-One

At three minutes before noon Melody gave her name to the doorman who guarded the lobby of the aggressively expensive building on Fifth Avenue where Wallis Beecham maintained his New York residence. The doorman checked the list on his clipboard, found that she was already cleared for admission and pointed her to the elevators after informing her that today's code for accessing the penthouse was 213.

The fact that her name was on the doorman's list made her upcoming meeting with Wallis seem reassuringly risk free, despite the fact that Nick had spent the past six hours alternately double-checking their plans and delivering one dire warning after another. Unit One's techies had loaded her with so many gadgets that she was practically a walking microchip. Bob Spinard's team at headquarters would be tracking her every move, and listening in to every word she said. An armed rescue team waited with Nick in the coffee bar at the corner of the block. Although, as Melody had pointed out to anyone who cared to listen, even if Wallis was positively itching to kill her, the one day when she was known to be visiting him hardly seemed a smart moment to choose for carrying out the murder.

All in all, fear for her own safety was low on Melody's list of worries. She was much more concerned that Unit One's efforts to connect Wallis directly to the murder of Lawrence Springer and the attempted murder of Kenneth Chung would come to nothing. Given that the Bonita partnership couldn't be prosecuted under U.S. law for their plans to develop an offshore clinic for cloning babies, conspiracy to commit murder might well be the only charge that could be leveled against Wallis, and she was praying she could make Unit One's plan work.

When she'd joined Unit One, she'd been dubious about the idea of a covert government agency, basically unsupervised, zipping around the country taking the law into its own hands, kidnapping people, coercing confessions and heaven knew what else. It was amazing how her perspective had changed over the past two months. Right now she considered that the world would be a significantly better place if Unit One had the authorization to send in a team armed with Uzis and simply blow Wallis away.

The elevator stopped in a private lobby that opened directly into Wallis's penthouse. As the doors slid open, Melody could see Christopher Beecham leaning against one of the marble columns that marked the entrance to the living room. For the past twenty-four hours Wallis had been under constant surveillance by a Unit One team, and she'd already been warned that Christopher had flown in last night from Chicago with his father. Despite the advance warning, and despite the fact that Christopher's presence was likely to make her task easier, she still experienced a shiver of discomfort at finding him there.

Melody didn't allow any sign of that discomfort

to creep into her voice. ''Hello, Christopher.'' He mostly took after his mother in looks, but he was short like his father, and her eyes were on a level with his. She met his gaze head-on, just so that he wouldn't make the mistake of thinking she was intimidated. ''I'm here for a meeting with your father.''

''I know you are.'' Christopher looked her over, his familiar lascivious expression tinged with resentment. Melody discovered to her enormous relief that he'd lost most of his power to disconcert her. Now that she knew he wasn't her half brother, his lust struck her as annoying rather than disgusting. Even the picture of Roz in bed with him—a man almost thirty years her junior, and the son of her ex-husband—wasn't as mortifying as it might have been. She'd had a while to become accustomed to those particular mental images, and she'd learned how to handle them.

''Follow me,'' Christopher said. ''My father's in the library.''

The library was lit by recessed lighting set into the ceiling and hidden inside pewter-trimmed wall sconces, making the windowless, oak-paneled room brighter than the gloomy November day outside. The library still didn't contain a single work of fiction, Melody noticed, and no more than half a dozen leather-bound reference books graced the bookcases, but the shelves provided a useful space for Wallis to display his golf trophies and his various civic awards for service to humanity. His framed and signed photographs taken with presidents, kings and even the occasional Hollywood celebrity shared the shelves with the trophies and were highlighted by overhead spotlights to make sure visitors got the message: Wallis Beecham was a man who won, in life and on the putting green.

"Hello, Wallis." Melody came to a halt on the far side of his oversize desk.

Wallis took off his glasses and closed the file he'd been reading. He made no direct acknowledgment of her presence. "Search her," he said to Christopher.

Melody made no protest. She stretched her arms and moved away from the desk, pretending to give Christopher more room to conduct his search. Unobtrusively she flexed her muscles, making sure she was ready to move.

Christopher found her gun almost at once and removed it from her waist holster, setting it on his father's desk. Wallis unlocked the clip of bullets and tossed them into a drawer while Christopher ran his hands over Melody's body a couple more times. Christopher didn't attempt to conduct the search impersonally and his attitude alternated between unnecessarily rough and unpleasantly dissolute as he squeezed her breasts and forced his hand between her thighs, groping.

"Is she wired?" Wallis asked his son.

"Not that I can detect so far."

"Use the wand," Wallis ordered.

Christopher walked over to the bookshelves and pulled open one of the drawers built at its base. He removed a device from the drawer that looked similar to the wands used by airport security personnel and came back to stand behind Melody. He waved the wand over her right shoulder and it immediately beeped.

Wallis looked up, his gaze narrowing. ''Take off your jacket,'' he said to Melody.

Silently she complied. Beneath her suit jacket she wore a cherry-red cashmere shell with a turtleneck but no sleeves. Christopher slipped his fingers under the shoulder seam of the sweater and pressed the tips of his fingers over her skin until he found the microchip that had caused the wand to beep.

It was obvious to Melody that he'd been warned what to look for. Dave had presumably alerted Wallis Beecham to the fact that all Unit One field operatives had tracking chips implanted on the outside of their right shoulder blades. Fortunately, Dave's betrayal had been anticipated and prepared for.

''She's wired,'' Christopher confirmed to his father. ''It's a subdermal implant.''

Melody finally spoke. ''It's a tracking device, that's all,'' she said. ''A simple safety precaution. My friends want to be sure they always know where I am.''

Beecham looked past her, exactly as if she hadn't spoken. ''Take out the implant,'' he ordered his son.

''Yes, sir.'' Not bothering to disguise his pleasure, Christopher returned to the same drawer that had held the wand, and removed a small leather case. He opened it, revealing a surgical suction instrument, which he held up so that Melody could see it. He walked back toward her. ''This is going to hurt,'' he said, smiling. ''I'm *so* sorry.''

''I assure you the chip in my shoulder isn't a recording device,'' Melody said with no particular emphasis. ''I would prefer to leave it right where it is.''

Christopher laughed. ''I'll just bet you would.'' He glanced toward his father, who nodded curtly.

"Take it out," Wallis repeated, sounding impatient.

Melody waited until Christopher was in midstep, leaning toward her and slightly off balance. She swung her right leg backward, hooking her foot around his leg. At the same time she rammed her elbow into his gut, using the full force of her weight. His own forward movement would probably have sent him sprawling anyway, but she used her hip to toss him onto his back. He hit the floor with a satisfyingly heavy thud. She straddled him, her thumbs pressing down on his jugular. When she was sure he wasn't able to move, she drew her right hand back and delivered a punishing uppercut to the precise spot on his jaw that Tony had taught her did most damage. Christopher's mouth snapped shut, then dropped open again as he sank into unconsciousness.

Melody stood up, straightened her cashmere sweater and put her jacket back on. She gestured to Christopher's inert body. "Where would you like me to put him?" she asked Wallis with mocking courtesy. "Don't worry. He should come around in a few minutes."

"Leave him where he is." Wallis finally stood up, a subtle concession that they were now dealing with each other as equals. He glared at her. "You'd never have been able to take Christopher out if he'd been prepared."

"Perhaps not. But then, one of Christopher's problems is that he's so seldom prepared when it really counts."

"You always were jealous of him."

She didn't even bother to reply to that.

Wallis looked at her with an expression close to

loathing. "Are you wired to record this conversation? It'll do you no good, you know, even if you are."

"Then it doesn't matter whether I'm wired or not, does it?"

Wallis made a small sound of frustration, quickly cut off. "Did you bring the letter?"

"Of course." She reached into her jacket pocket and handed Wallis the folded letter. "Here you are."

He put his glasses back on and read the three lines of message. "This says nothing of any importance. You're wasting my time, trying to create a breach between me and my son." Wallis flung the letter onto his desk.

He was exactly right about what she was trying to do, and Melody hoped like hell she would succeed. Two and a half years ago, when Wallis had found out about Roz's affair with his son, Christopher had been very much out of favor. But in the period since Roz's death he had gradually been drawn back into his father's good graces. In the past three months all the signs indicated that Christopher's rehabilitation had been accelerated. Wallis had apparently forgiven his errant son for past transgressions and Christopher was being groomed as the official heir to the Beecham empire. The only outstanding question was how much confidential information had been passed from father to son along with the PR grooming. Melody—and Unit One—hoped it was a lot.

"I'm surprised you don't grasp the importance of the letter," Melody said, her voice cool. "It clearly states that Christopher has found the answers to the questions my mother asked, and the information is attached."

"And so?" Wallis held up the single sheet of paper, waving it in her face. "There is no attachment. Your mother could have been asking Chris to find out the price of tea in China...."

Melody permitted herself a small smile. "Naturally, I also have the attachment." She patted her other jacket pocket. "It's right here."

"Give it to me."

She ignored his extended hand. "First we need to discuss why I should be so obliging. We're negotiating a deal here, Wallis. I haven't come to share information with you out of gratitude for my wonderful childhood memories."

"Give me the attachment, and stop trying to fuck with me. You'll lose. You should have recognized by now that when you go up against me, you always lose. Just recollect what happened with your plans to open an art gallery in London if you need a reminder of what I can do without even leaving my desk."

Melody allowed herself to be sidetracked, just for a moment. "You never did intend to let the financing for my gallery go through, did you, Wallis? You always planned to cancel the lease and cut the funds off at the last moment. You intended to leave me with nowhere to turn. Unfortunately for you, Jasper Fowles was able to provide me with the job of my dreams."

"If you enjoy working with that fading faggot, you're more hopeless than I realized." Wallis's mouth turned down in disgust. "You should have come to work for me years ago, when I told you to."

"The fact that I never spent a day in your employment is one decision I've never regretted. Not for a nanosecond."

He brushed his hands together in a dismissive gesture. "Enough of this pointless discussion. Just give me the damned attachment. You have no bargaining power where I'm concerned. Accept that and be done." Wallis stepped out from behind his desk and began to stride toward her.

Melody grabbed her gun from his desk and backed up, using her right hand to aim it directly at him, her left hand reaching behind her. "I think my bargaining position just improved a whole lot. You probably remember that I'm a crack shot."

Wallis laughed scornfully. "Waving that gun isn't going to do you a lick of good. Didn't you see me take out the bullets?"

"You seem to suffer from a touch of Christopher's problem, Daddy dearest. You really should stop underestimating me." Melody found the fresh clip of bullets she'd been reaching for and shoved the clip into her gun just as Wallis made a furious lunge toward her.

"Your son should have spent less time feeling me up and done a better job of searching me. He took the gun, but not the extra bullets. No, don't move any closer, Wallis. Not unless you want to give me an excuse to use this. In which case, to borrow a great phrase—go ahead, make my day."

Wallis went back to his desk and sat down, trying to look as if that was what he'd planned to do all along. "What do you want from me, Melody? Money? That's what it always comes down to in the end, I guess."

"I have no interest in your money, Wallis, hard as that may be for you to believe. What I want right at this moment is for you to acknowledge that the son you spoiled rotten has betrayed you—"

"If you're referring to the fact that Chris slept with your mother, that was more than two years ago. Ancient history. Besides, I can't get too upset about the fact that my son and I shared the same whore. It happens."

Melody let the insult wash over her and slide away into oblivion. "I'm not talking about sex, Wallis. I'm talking about the fact that Christopher was conspiring with my mother to blackmail you. That's what the documents I've brought with me plainly show. Christopher didn't just sleep with your mistress, who also happened to be your ex-wife. He planned to bleed you for all the cash he could get."

Dark, angry color suffused Wallis's cheeks and he turned abruptly away. Confirmation, if Melody had needed it, that she'd been correct in her assessment that Wallis had been deeply angered—even hurt—by Christopher's affair with Roz, however much he tried to pretend otherwise. If she could persuade Wallis to accept that Christopher hadn't just slept with Roz but had also conspired with her to blackmail him, Melody hoped his rage would be powerful enough to leave Christopher isolated, and once again bereft of funds.

When she'd first discovered her mother's collection of documents about the Bonita Project and realized that Christopher Beecham had been Roz's prime source of information concerning the partnership, Melody had wondered how in the world her mother had persuaded Christopher to help her. Sex, even the most fabulous sex, surely couldn't be the answer. So if not for sex, why had Christopher been willing to ignore his own long-term best interests and plot with Roz against his own father?

After scouring her mother's cryptic notes for clues, Melody had pieced together the story. Wallis had been so furious when he discovered his son in bed with Roz that he'd punished both of them the only way he knew how: financially. Within hours he'd not only cut off all payments to Roz, he'd also cut off his son's allowance.

Wallis's revenge hadn't ended there. Christopher had just graduated from college, but instead of being allowed to spend a year touring the world at his father's expense, he'd been ordered to go to work for the family's road-building company in Chicago—the original source of the Beecham family fortune, and not a business likely to appeal to Christopher's inflated sense of his own dignity.

Wallis had made it crystal clear that his son's only hope of regaining favor was to keep his nose well and truly to the grindstone. Christopher, who had previously assumed that physical exercise was something that occurred only inside an air-conditioned health club, had actually spent two months shoveling hot tar onto interstate highways before he'd been promoted to a junior clerical job.

Her mother's notes made it clear that Christopher had been given almost no time off for play, and his salary had been a mere pittance, even when he was finally assigned to the desk job. Worst of all, he had to endure his father's constant displeasure. And Melody knew from personal experience that Wallis's displeasure was no easy burden to bear.

Christopher had reacted with predictable resentment to finding his luxurious lifestyle precipitously whisked away. Sondra hadn't been sympathetic to her son, which wasn't surprising, given her lifelong loathing of Roz. Besides, even if she could have forgiven him for sleeping with Mrs. Beecham Number One, Sondra had no money of her own, and she couldn't replace her son's missing income without openly defying Wallis—something she would never do.

Christopher, therefore, had secretly continued his high-risk affair with Roz. He was already suffering from a genuine sexual infatuation for her, and his poverty was a powerful extra incentive to find a successful blackmail weapon they could use. The two of them had agreed that Roz would extort as much money as she could from Wallis without revealing Christopher's role in the deal. The spoils would then be shared equally between the two of them. Roz, in effect, had become Christopher's best hope of a meal ticket—or at least a dessert ticket—in unexpectedly hard times.

Wallis turned around again, his display of emotion under complete control. "Fortunately, your mother died before she was able to inflict permanent damage on my son."

His comment was deliberately cruel, but Melody wouldn't let the hurt take hold. "It was because of Christopher that you arranged to have Roz murdered," she said. "It wasn't just because she was trying to blackmail you, was it? My mother had been blackmailing you for years, in a halfhearted sort of way, and you didn't really care. You had her killed because you were furious with her for sleeping with your son and driving a wedge between the two of you."

Wallis's fingers drummed a tattoo against the edge of his desk. "I don't expect you'll believe me, but I had nothing to do with Roz's death. Personally, I believe she committed suicide."

Melody had anticipated that Wallis would deny any involvement in her mother's murder. After all, he had to suspect their conversation was being taped, so he would inevitably take care to say nothing incriminating. What she hadn't anticipated was her sudden shocked belief that he might be speaking the truth. For just a moment his voice had resonated with unexpected sincerity. She looked at him intently, but of course there was no way to decide whether or not he had lied. If it suited his purposes for some reason, Wallis would be honest. If it didn't suit his purpose, he would lie.

Christopher moaned, breaking Melody's train of thought. He stirred, but didn't attempt to get up. Wallis looked at his son's huddled body with a disgust that bordered on contempt.

"Show me the attachment to the letter," he said to Melody. "I want to see the proof, in writing, that Christopher did what you claim."

Her reluctance to show Wallis the attachment had been feigned, of course. In truth, she badly wanted him to see exactly what his son had done. Silently Melody reached into her jacket pocket and handed over the three incriminating pages.

Wallis took a long time to read them, his face expressionless as he studied their densely packed exploration of questionable business dealings between himself and Lawrence Springer. The final section listed the names of the five partners in the Bonita Project, concluding with the information that a research lab in Arkansas had already been established in connection with the project. It was these three pages of information, in fact, that had formed the basis of Melody's own attempts to investigate the Bonita Project.

Wallis cast a single furious glance at his son as Christopher staggered to his feet. His hands clenched into fists, then relaxed. Wallis was too clever to allow himself to act in the heat of anger.

"Go and clean yourself up," he ordered his son, his voice rough with suppressed rage. "Then stay in your room until I come for you."

Christopher pressed his hand to his swelling jaw, wincing at the touch. "What lies has Melody been telling you about me?" he asked thickly. "Why are you angry with me? She's the one causing all the trouble—"

"I don't give instructions twice," Wallis said. He turned to Melody as Christopher slunk from the room. "You've made your point," he said. "Now tell me what's in it for you."

"Help from you in finding out who my father is," Melody said promptly. She hoped that her request would not only seem a credible motive for having shown Wallis her mother's papers, but would also create enough of a diversion that Wallis wouldn't reflect later and realize her true purpose had been to provoke precisely the confrontation with Christopher that seemed imminent.

The look Wallis directed at her was genuinely incredulous. "You expect me to reward you for what you just did here today?"

"Of course. Knowledge is power. You surely wouldn't have preferred to continue in the belief that

Christopher could be trusted? Now that you know the truth, you can act accordingly."

He shrugged. "I can't help you. I don't have any clue who your father is. Nor do I have any interest in finding out."

"Don't lie, Wallis. Not to me. It's a waste of time for both of us. I know you too well. Within hours of learning I wasn't your daughter, you set out to discover who my father really was. Or is. First because he cuckolded you. Then because he committed the unpardonable sin of scamming you and getting away with it for twenty-eight years. There's no way on God's green earth that you'd allow my biological father to go undetected. You've either found him already or you intend to keep searching until you do find him. And then you'll hand out the retribution you believe he deserves. I know that with as much certainty as I know you're already planning exactly how you'll punish Christopher for betraying you."

"You're right, you know me well." A gleam of something that might have been admiration flickered briefly in Wallis's eyes. "I'll amend my statement. I may or may not know who your father was. Or is. However, I have no intention of helping you to do anything, least of all find your father. You're a lousy negotiator. You've already given me the letter and the attachment. I have nothing to gain by revealing confidential information to you. Sorry, Melody. You lose."

He knows, Melody thought, reacting to the subnote of gleeful satisfaction threading through Wallis's words. *Dear God, he knows who my father is.*

She recognized that there wasn't a chance in hell of persuading Wallis to part with what he knew, so she didn't prolong the interview by attempting the impossible. If Wallis could uncover her father's identity, she could do it, too. No need to humiliate herself by begging for information Wallis would never give her.

She drew in a couple of calming breaths to be sure that her voice wouldn't betray any lingering trace of emotion. "You've never understood the single most important rule about negotiating, Wallis. Sometimes you can lose by winning."

Wallis finally smiled. "But not this time," he said. "This time I just plain won."

Twenty-Two

"Come in, Nick. Melody, you handled Wallis Beecham very well." Mac waved the two of them into his office. This afternoon he wore a gray business suit, a starched white shirt and a soberly striped navy blue tie. Melody was so disconcerted by the sudden switch to conservatism in the director's wardrobe that she almost spilled the mug of coffee he handed her.

"Debrief," Mac said, sitting down in his chair and bouncing a couple of times to get comfortable. "Time's a-wasting and the Commander is getting anxious. Anything more we need to know before I give the final authorization for the Christopher Beecham extraction, Melody? Anything that wouldn't be apparent to us in listening to the tape of your meeting?"

"We're assuming the thumps we heard were you giving Christopher a practical demonstration of Tony's theories about unarmed combat," Nick said, flashing a grin.

Melody returned his smile. "Then you're assuming correctly. I have to admit that particular part of the meeting was deeply satisfying." Ninety minutes had passed since she'd left Wallis's penthouse, and

Melody was beginning to feel a spurt of optimism that Unit One's plans might actually work.

"Wallis was sufficiently disconcerted at the sight of his son out for the count that he didn't bother to continue checking to see if I was wired for sound," she added. "That was good in one way, but all Bob Spinard's hard work hiding the mike wasn't put to a real test."

"Don't worry. There will be plenty of other occasions to test that," Nick said dryly.

"Beecham didn't check for a mike because he didn't care." Mac scowled. "He assumed he was being recorded and behaved accordingly. He came across on the tape as a thoroughly unpleasant man, but he gave us nothing we could toss to the feds to help them build a legal case against him. Not that we really expected him to walk into that particular trap, of course. Anyway, back to my earlier question. What else do we need to know about your meeting with him, Melody?"

"Nothing much. Most of what happened is self-explanatory. A couple of minor points. Wallis is not only furious with his son, he's also hurt. That's good news for us, because I don't suppose Wallis often experiences hurt feelings, and it's likely to intensify his negative reaction. I believe he could go a lot further than simply cutting off Christopher's financial support. I think he might decide to banish him permanently."

"Drastic," Mac commented.

"Yes, but at a certain point Wallis is surely bound to ask himself if he can't trust Christopher, why keep him around? It isn't as if he has a brilliant intellect or outstanding people skills."

''Especially since Beecham anticipates having a clone of himself to raise some time very soon,'' Nick interjected. ''From Beecham's perspective, why try to rehabilitate somebody who's betrayed him twice when he has this perfect duplicate of himself ready to pop out of a rented womb any month now?''

Mac's snub nose wrinkled in distaste. ''Hope you're correct, Nick. Hope Christopher gets cut off at the knees. Hope Beecham is busy right now telling Christopher never to darken his doors again. That will sure make it easier to pressure Christopher into making a deal with us. Okay, anything else, Melody?''

''Just one more thing,'' she said. ''In my opinion, Christopher is not only afraid of Wallis, he also deeply resents his father's power. If we handle Christopher properly—more carrot than stick—I think he might not only be willing to cooperate with us to bring Wallis down, he might actually be eager.''

It was only when Melody finished speaking that she realized she'd said *we* and *us*. What really scared her, though, was the fact that even in retrospect the pronouns didn't seem out of place. Unit One was a seductive employer in more ways than one, she reflected ruefully.

''I agree with Melody's assessment,'' Nick said. ''Bribery and the promise of reward fit better with Christopher's psychological profile than threats. Unfortunately, however good a job we do of questioning him, there's still the problem of how much useful information he has. He may be more than willing to play, but if he doesn't have a bat, or a mitt, or even a ball, the game isn't going to get very far.''

Mac tugged at his lower lip, his shoulders hunched

and his expression gloomy. "If Beecham has the sense he was born with, he hasn't told Christopher anything more confidential than the fact that the White House is located in Washington, D.C."

"I'm more optimistic than you two," Melody said. "I believe Christopher could be a point of real vulnerability for Wallis. As far back as I can remember, he's always excused Christopher's faults and exaggerated his achievements. Then there's the fact that Wallis has nobody in the entire world he really trusts. Can anybody, even an egoist like Wallis, bear to feel completely alone all the time? I don't think it's unrealistic to assume that he succumbed to a touch of normal human weakness and chose to confide in his son."

"Well, no point in sitting around speculating," Mac said. "Either Christopher knows enough to be helpful or he doesn't. We'll find out when we have him here, under our control. Right now we need action, and fast. The Commander's called me three times today already. Nick, what's the status of your plans for the extraction?"

"My team is ready to go," Nick said. "We'll move as soon as Wallis has had enough time to rip Christopher to shreds. In the meantime, we're continuing comprehensive surveillance on both Beecham men, just to be sure that Christopher doesn't dash off somewhere in a panic."

"Who's on the surveillance team?"

"Simon is currently assigned to watch Wallis, and Buddy is covering Christopher. So far, neither father nor son has stirred from the apartment. Bob Spinard will buzz me if there's any action that I need to hear about."

"Simon and Buddy are reporting to Spinard's team in the usual way?" Mac asked. "Is that wise?"

"Because of Dave, you mean?" Nick said.

"Yes." Mac tugged at his tie, leaving the knot skewed under his ear and the point of his shirt collar sticking up. Melody was almost relieved to see that he hadn't undergone a complete sartorial transformation.

"We have to assume that Dave has penetrated a significant number of Unit One systems," Mac said. "He's had ten years of operational experience with us and freedom to roam almost the entire organizational structure for the last three of those years. He's not a tech wizard like Bob, but he's no slouch, either. He could easily be monitoring communications between the surveillance team and Central Control. In fact, we should assume he is."

"I took that possibility into account in giving Simon and Buddy their orders," Nick said. "In the end I decided not to break with standard protocol. Dave most likely knew about Beecham's meeting with Melody. And if Dave knew about the meeting, he also knows we were watching the building the whole time Melody was inside. If the surveillance teams had suddenly gone dark and ceased all communications, or changed their reporting system, Dave would wonder why."

"Good point," Mac conceded. "But we have to be damned sure there's no trace of the fact that we're targeting Christopher Beecham for extraction anywhere on our central system."

Nick nodded. "As you and I discussed at length yesterday morning, Mac, the extraction plans are totally shielded from Dave's scrutiny. I've set up the mission outside normal protocols, so whatever systems Dave may have penetrated, he won't be able to access the mission profile. I briefed the extraction team off-premises last night. Their tracking chips have been removed, so nobody can keep tabs on their whereabouts. Including us, of course, but not Dave, either. Whatever problems the team may run into during the extraction, they won't be checking in with me for instructions. The entire operation will be black, in fact."

"How about the launch order for the mission?" Mac asked.

"The command will come directly from me via cell phone, utilizing an authorization code only the team knows."

Mac grunted his approval. "It's time for us to shut Dave down," he said, striding around the room, hands shoved deep into his jacket pockets. For somebody whose chubby cheeks and button nose were as close to cherubic as human faces ever get, he managed to look extremely grim. "Now that Melody's completed her assignment, it doesn't matter as much if Beecham realizes Dave has been identified as his informant inside Unit One. We need to get Dave locked up where he can't cause us any more trouble."

"Do you want me to give the order to have him arrested?" Nick asked, his voice flat.

Mac was silent for a moment. "Where is Dave right now?" he asked finally.

"Somewhere in the building for sure. Bob has him monitored full-time, with orders to buzz me if he attempts to leave headquarters." Nick checked his PalmPilot. "In fact, he's still in his cubicle. I gave him a desk assignment this morning. I told him we needed to initiate an urgent search of Senator Cranford's offices in Washington and asked him to find us a way in."

"Mission impossible," Mac said. "The Senate building is bristling with security since 9/11."

"Yeah, that was the idea behind the assignment. Searching for an entry route that would avoid all those guards and checkpoints seemed a good way to keep Dave safely occupied for a couple of days at least."

Mac muttered something inaudible, then fell silent for a moment, staring gloomily at his beloved espresso machine. Melody realized that Dave's betrayal of Unit One had hit him so hard that he didn't even have the spirit to make himself a cup of coffee.

He finally swung around, tugging at the knot of his tie again. "Goddamn stupid thing," he said, pulling it off and flinging it onto the nearest chair. It missed and landed on the floor. He stared at it for a couple of seconds, then looked up at Nick.

"Take Dave out of play right now," he said. "It's over. We're done. Make the call to security. The red phone is scrambled and isn't connected to the central communication system. Use it. Order his arrest."

Nick gave a nod. "Yes, sir." He picked up the receiver on the red phone and punched a series of numbers into the base. He had to wait no more than a couple of seconds for his call to be answered.

"This is Nikolai Anwar," he said. "Agent Dave Ramsdell is currently working in his office cubicle, number 14 in D zone. Send a two-man armed security detail to pick him up. Then take him to a level-one holding room. Maximum security to be in effect.

Post a guard outside the door pending Agent Ramsdell's transfer to a military prison.''

He waited for a moment while the person at the other end asked a question. ''My authorization code for today is alpha seven delta. You can confirm that with the director of security. I'm currently in Director McShane's office. Report here in person as soon as you've carried out my orders. Don't use any of the internal communications systems. Report only to me or to the director.'' Nick hung up the phone.

''How long before they get back to us?'' Mac asked, pacing. ''Fifteen minutes?''

''That sounds about right.''

''Okay.'' Mac walked over to his espresso machine, but still couldn't work up the enthusiasm to actually brew a cup of coffee. ''Fill me in on the basics of the Beecham extraction while we're waiting. Who have you assigned to the team?''

''Tony, Sam and Charlene. We acquired architectural plans to all Beecham's homes and offices two months ago, at the start of our investigation, and the team spent two hours this morning familiarizing themselves with the layout of the penthouse. They're waiting in the vicinity of the apartment building right now. As I said, they're ready to go in as soon as I give the order.''

''Tony and Sam are obvious choices,'' Mac said. ''Lots of experience. Self-starters. Problem solvers. But why Charlene? She's still a bit wet behind the ears.''

''She's far and away the best climber we have in Unit One. Amazing upper body strength for a woman and exceptionally agile. She's also tiny, and the mission profile calls for her to gain access to the kitchen through an air-conditioning duct before letting in the other two team members through a balcony window."

"Hmm. No full-time staff for us to worry about?"

"No. Maid service is sent in each morning when Beecham's in residence. They're gone by eleven."

"I assume you and your team have the problems of removing Christopher all worked out? No chance Wallis will alert the police?"

"None," Nick said. "Sam has been assigned to take care of Wallis. Tony and Charlene will handle Christopher. Charlene's combat skills are nowhere near as good as her climbing and she might not be able to take Christopher alone. Tony obviously compensates for any weakness there."

Mac took off his jacket, stared at it blankly for a moment, then tossed it onto the chair. It promptly slid to the floor, next to his tie. "Send in your team, Nick. Wallis has had plenty of time to do his worst in terms of threatening Christopher. No point in waiting any longer."

Nick inclined his head. "I'll give the order now."

Mac flexed his shoulders, unbuttoning his shirt collar as Nick removed his cell phone from the belt clip at his waist. If the guy got too much more stressed, he'd soon be down to his jockey shorts, Melody reflected wryly.

Nick took out his cell phone and silently keyed in a series of numbers. He was still tapping in a text message when there was a knock at the office door.

Melody glanced at her watch as Mac crossed the room to open the door. It was barely ten minutes since Nick had issued the command to arrest Dave.

Could the security team have completed their assignment already?

When Mac opened the door, Melody could see two young security guards, carrying M-4 assault rifles, standing in the corridor. They both saluted—with more formality than was usual in Unit One, she noticed at once.

The shorter of the guards stepped forward. "Sir, I'm sorry, but we weren't able to carry out Mr. Anwar's orders."

Mac displayed no reaction, which Melody found more alarming than if he'd demonstrated his usual hyperactivity. "Step into my office," he said mildly. "Shut the door behind you. Wait until the director of operations has finished his phone call before you give us your report."

Nick keyed in a final command on his cell phone and shut it down. He spoke quietly to Mac. "The extraction mission has been launched as you instructed," he said, then stepped forward to greet the guards. They both saluted again.

"What happened?" Nick acknowledged their salute with an authority that looked both comfortable and natural. "Why couldn't you take Agent Ramsdell into custody?"

"He wasn't at his desk, sir." The shorter guard was apparently the spokesman. "We proceeded to zone D, cubicle 14, as ordered. There was nobody seated at the desk. We asked two clerical staff working in the area if they had seen Agent Ramsdell recently, or if they knew where he might be. Both clerks agreed that Agent Ramsdell had left the office area at lunchtime and hadn't returned since. We contacted Central Control and asked for a location check on Agent Ramsdell. The report came back immediately that he was seated at his desk, cubicle 14, in zone D. Except he wasn't, of course. That's why we'd asked for the check. So we looked around his cubicle and we found this. It's a tracking chip."

The guard held out a silver-colored disk, smaller and thinner than an aspirin. "We asked Central Command to identify the tracking chip, and they confirmed it was Agent Ramsdell's. That's why you all believed he was at his desk when he wasn't. The chip was attached to a coiled spring, and the spring moved whenever somebody walked by. That made it seem as if a person was maybe wriggling in his chair, or something. Security believes he must have left the building." The guard ended his report, looking justifiably proud of his powers of deduction.

Mac and Nick exchanged a single swift glance. Then Nick let rip with a couple of obscenities, before switching to Russian and delivering what sounded to Melody like an explosion of powerful expletives.

"Thank you," Mac said to the security guards. "Your report was very thorough."

"Dave knew," Nick said as soon as the door closed behind the guards. "Goddammit, he knew he'd been made. I should have arrested him earlier, as soon as your investigation fingered him."

"Maybe, maybe not," Mac said. "We had valid reasons for leaving him in place."

Nick paced the office, tension radiating from his body. "Bad enough that Dave ran. But it really sticks in my craw that he fooled us with the twenty-first-century equivalent of a straw dummy stuffed in the bed. Jesus, why didn't I double-check that he was really where the computer said he was?"

"Because you were doing other important things. Because we rely on computers to provide accurate information. Don't let him mess with your mind, Nick. Stay focused. Dave isn't your problem anymore, he's mine. Your task is to bring in Christopher Beecham and make sure our questioning of him produces the results we need."

Mac hung his tie back around his neck and picked up his jacket, thrusting his arms into the sleeves, visibly gearing himself up for battle. "I'm about to call an emergency meeting with the head of security. The two of us will confer with Bob Spinard and we'll activate an emergency firewall around Central Control. We will have a secure communication and data processing system up and running within the hour. Something that Dave won't be able to breach. In the meantime, avoid using Central Control for any communication you don't want Dave to access."

Nick nodded his agreement and started to walk out of the office. Melody stood up. "Is there anything I can do to help?" she asked.

Both men looked at her with slightly startled expressions, as if they'd forgotten she was still in the room. "Stay at headquarters overnight," Nick said promptly. "That way, I'll have one less person to worry about."

Melody agreed willingly. The truth was, she had no desire to leave headquarters at this point, when the success of Unit One's pursuit of Wallis Beecham teetered on a knife-edge. "If you need me to provide any insights or background information when you're interrogating Christopher, just let me know, Nick. In the meantime, I'm going to the gym for a while."

* * *

Sam arrived in the gym just as Melody ended a workout that left her sweat-drenched and tired enough to realize that she was already a couple of notches down from the peak of fitness that she'd attained at the climax of her training. She made a mental note to run harder, longer and faster each morning, and used the towel slung around her neck to wipe away the sweat dripping into her eyes.

"What happened?" she asked Sam. "Did you manage to get Christopher? What about Wallis?"

He stared down at her from six feet three inches of perfectly toned muscles. "Man, I'm seein' one seriously out-of-shape lady in front of me."

"Don't do this to me, Sam, not now. Did you get Christopher or not?"

He scratched his head. "I could have sworn there was a rule right there in the basic training manual that said somethin' about not discussing missions and not sharing information except on a need-to-know basis."

Melody knew that Sam's allegiance to Unit One was absolute, and that he took the rules and regulations with a degree of seriousness that often surprised her, especially when contrasted with her own more casual attitude toward authority. Having grown up in a boarding school where breaking some of the more ridiculous rules was a badge of honor among students, she tended to view most regulations with a healthy degree of skepticism.

"Please, Sam, just this once, don't quote the damn training manual at me, okay? I'm the one who set Christopher up for the extraction. Don't I have any right to know if you guys succeeded in bringing him in?"

The answer to that was undoubtedly no, but for whatever reason, Sam decided to take pity on her. "The mission was a success. Christopher's in a holding cell right now, being questioned. Wallis didn't even know we were in his apartment. I guess that's one of the disadvantages of having a seven-thousand-square-foot penthouse." He actually smiled at her.

"Hey, that's terrific. Fabulous." Melody realized she was beaming from ear to ear. "When I've showered, want to come with me to the cafeteria for a celebratory dinner? My treat."

Meals at headquarters were provided free. Sam rolled his eyes. "Man, there's an offer I can't afford to refuse. Hurry up and shower or I might change my mind."

The cafeteria was crowded, but they managed to find an empty table in a quiet corner and carried their trays of food over. Melody tried to keep her thoughts focused on their conversation, as opposed to what Nick might be persuading Christopher to reveal right now this minute. She thought she was doing a pretty good job of holding up her end of their conversation until Sam leaned back in his chair and said, "Okay, I give up."

She looked at him, puzzled. "On what?"

"Havin' a coherent discussion with you about *X-Men.*"

"Is that what we were talking about?" Melody heard her own question and winced. "Oh jeez, I'm sorry, Sam. I guess I'm a little obsessed right now."

"That's obvious. Who are you obsessing about? Christopher Beecham or Nikolai Anwar?"

"Christopher, of course."

She'd replied too quickly and too vehemently,

Melody realized, even though she'd answered honestly. At least up to a point. Her fixation with Nick had become a permanent landmark on her mental horizon, whereas her need to know what was happening with Christopher was a more immediate obsession.

Sam's response was oblique. "A couple of times today I thought Nick might lose it while you were in Beecham's apartment."

"You did?" Melody was astonished. Nick's calm during operations was legendary within Unit One. "What was wrong with him?"

"You. The mission. He didn't say anythin', of course. Kept his usual poker face. But he was wound so tight you could have sent him into orbit with a single push."

Melody experienced a moment of intense frustration. She wished Nick would have more confidence in her abilities and not constantly anticipate that she would screw up. "There was no reason for him to be worried. It wasn't a difficult mission, given all the background I have on Wallis. Besides, Nick had coached me over and over again on precisely what I had to do and say."

Sam looked amused. "Nick wasn't worried that you'd screw up. He was worried something might happen to you."

"Oh." Melody felt her cheeks grow hot. "Well, that wasn't at all likely, you know."

"I do know. In fact, everyone knew it except Nick." Sam pushed his dinner plate aside and leaned forward across the table. "And since we're on the subject of Nick, you mind tellin' me what your intentions are toward him?"

She stared at him, wide-eyed with dismay. First Jasper, now Sam had noticed her infatuation with Nick. Unit One was supposed to train its field operatives in the art of deception, but she seemed to be getting worse and worse at hiding her feelings instead of better and better. ''I don't have any intentions,'' she said.

''Figures.'' Sam leaned away from her and proceeded to eat his ice cream in silence.

She would have been smart to let the conversation drop right there, while Sam was giving her the chance. Naturally—when had she ever done anything smart in regard to Nick?—she couldn't leave well enough alone.

''Why does it figure that I don't have any...intentions...toward Nick?''

Sam's gaze narrowed speculatively. ''You have the reputation of bein' a bit of a ball breaker, if you'll pardon my French. Nick doesn't need that sort of a complication in his life.''

That surprised a laugh out of her, even though there wasn't much humor in it. The possibility that anybody could believe Nick needed protection from her couldn't provoke any reaction other than wild mirth.

Sam set down his spoon. ''Mind sharin' the joke?''

She'd gone too far to retreat into silence now. She shrugged. ''The idea of Nick needing protection from me is crazy enough to be funny.''

''Why? You think just because he's real good at unarmed combat that he doesn't have any vulnerabilities?''

"I have to admit that *Nick* and *vulnerable* aren't two words that leap together in my mind."

"More fool you. I figured you for smarter than that."

Melody gritted her teeth. "Okay, Sam, I always was lousy at riddles. Would you take pity on a dim-witted Brit and try telling me in simple language what's on your mind?"

Sam stirred sugar into his coffee, clearly debating what to say next. "Has Nick told you anything about his family?" he asked finally.

"A little. He told me his parents and his sister were all three killed in a car crash when he was nineteen."

"Did he tell you they were murdered by the KGB?"

She gulped. "No. Why in the world would the KGB want to kill Nick's family?"

"His mother, Svetlana Gromov, was once a KGB agent. His father was the CIA agent responsible for persuading Svetlana to defect to the United States. His parents had both been targeted for assassination for years, but they were living under assumed names, with false documentation, and the Soviets couldn't find them. The KGB finally tracked them down to their home in suburban Philadelphia in 1989. They rigged the ignition in the family car and Nick's sister was just unlucky enough to be with her parents when the bomb went off. The kicker to the story is that the entire Soviet system collapsed a few weeks later. The Berlin Wall was torn down, the KGB ceased functioning, Russian citizens poured into the streets demanding democracy. If Nick's family could have survived another couple of months, they would all have been safe.''

It was a moment before Melody could speak. ''Nick must have had a hard time wondering why he was the only one to escape with his life.''

''If you can understand that much about him, then you ought to be able to see that he doesn't need to fall in love with a woman who has a habit of rippin' out a man's heart and then sendin' it back to him tied up in fancy ribbon.''

''You should know better than to believe everything you read in the tabloids, Sam.''

''Yeah, but when you hear about a trail of broken hearts a couple of miles long, you get to wonderin'.''

''Most of the broken hearts you've heard about exist only in the imagination of paparazzi looking for hot copy.''

''But one or two were for real, I'm guessin'.''

''Never intentionally on my part.''

''Broken is broken, however it happens.'' Sam held her gaze. ''Nick is my friend,'' he said. ''In my line of work, you don't have too many of those. He's already torn damn near to pieces by what Dave's done. This wouldn't be a good moment for you to take him out to play and then forget to bring him home again.''

The chances of her forgetting Nick any time soon seemed somewhere between slim and none. But it was impossible for Melody to admit that to Sam, despite the fact that she very much wanted his friendship. ''There's nothing serious going on between Nick and me,'' she said. ''Don't worry, Sam.''

He just looked at her until she dropped her gaze. Then he picked up his spoon and went back to eating his ice cream, his silence an eloquent reproof of her cowardice.

Twenty-Three

Melody woke to the sound of soft knocking. Rubbing her eyes, she sat up in bed and saw a security guard standing in the doorway of her sleeping cubicle. He was rapping on the wall, since the cubicle had no door. Her old room as a resident trainee had been the height of luxury in comparison to this Spartan space.

Voice low, he apologized for waking her. "Sorry to disturb you at this hour, ma'am. The director of operations has asked me to escort you to one of the interrogation rooms. He needs your assistance as soon as possible."

Nick had sent for her. Melody came immediately to full alert, feeling a little flattered that Nick needed her. Okay, feeling a lot flattered that he needed her.

"I'll be right with you," she said to the guard. She glanced at her watch. A few minutes before two. She wasn't surprised to be summoned at this hour, since standard interrogation techniques worked on the principle of sleep deprivation, combined with unrelenting psychological pressure. The fact that Nick was still questioning Christopher was a positive sign, she hoped. It suggested Christopher had information that merited working hard to extract.

"I'll wait outside while you get dressed," the

guard said, stepping around the privacy curtain. Tactfully he drew the curtain closed behind him.

Energized by the prospect of making a contribution to Nick's interrogation of Christopher, however minor, Melody took only a couple of minutes to throw on her clothes and pull her hair out of her eyes into a ponytail.

"I'm ready," she said, opening the curtain. Like the guard, she kept her voice low in deference to the people still trying to sleep in the nearby cubicles.

"Thank you, ma'am. If you could follow me." The guard set off down the corridor, feet padding almost without sound on the carpeting until they reached the double doors of a fire exit leading to a stairwell.

"We have to walk down two flights," he said, holding the heavy door open for her. "They're having problems with the elevators tonight. Something to do with needing to reprogram them in response to a security breach."

Probably the aftermath of something Dave had done, Melody thought, feeling a spurt of anger. Much as she sympathized with the tragic loss of Dave's wife and unborn baby, she found his defection from Unit One unforgivable. The fact that his betrayal had been precipitated by Wallis Beecham added a sharp edge to her anger.

It was cold in the stairwell, and she wrapped her arms around herself, glad when the guard picked up the pace so that they were almost running down the stairs. "This way, ma'am," the guard said as they reached another exit. "Watch how you tread. There's a step right behind this door."

Melody followed him into a corridor that was low,

narrow, cold and even more dimly lit than the stairwell. She shivered, only in part because of the cold. She'd always assumed that Unit One interrogations took place in clean, brightly lit rooms, with the subjects pressured more by sterile efficiency and psychological cunning than by brute force. She really hoped she wasn't about to discover that interrogations took place in dank dungeons, with resident rats for company.

The guard stopped. "Here we are." They had reached yet another door, this one heavily barred and padlocked. A glowing sign warned that opening the door would cause an alarm to sound.

"It'll take a moment to deactivate the alarm." The guard flashed her a cheerful smile, his teeth very white against his black skin. He lifted the flap on a small control panel set into the wall to the right of the door and keyed in a command. The tubular red light surrounding the door blinked out, and the warning sign lost its illumination.

The guard unlocked the padlock and raised the steel bar. Despite his obvious strength, the door was so heavy he needed to use his shoulder to open it. Unit One was taking no chances that Christopher would escape, Melody thought wryly, following the guard through the door.

Darkness and bitter cold immediately surrounded her. Freezing rain fell, soaking her. She shook raindrops out of her eyes. What had happened? Why were they outside?

In the split second before her confusion changed to understanding, the guard sprang, unleashing a blow that knocked her to the ground. She tried to fight back, but her opponent wasn't a flabby blowhard like Christopher Beecham. This man was not only strong, he was also a superb fighter. Within humiliatingly few seconds, Melody was pinned flat on her back, held so that she couldn't move without breaking her arm.

The guard straddled her, slapping surgical tape across her mouth and slipping a corded noose around her neck. Releasing her just enough to roll her over on the wet concrete, he cuffed her hands behind her back.

"Get up," he said as soon as the cuffs were latched.

To hell with him. On principle, Melody didn't move, not even to turn her gaze away from him. The guard shrugged, then slowly stood up, keeping hold of one end of the garrotte. Fortunately, her body reacted to save her life before her mind had time to weigh the comparative merits of continuing her defiance or meekly submitting. Her body chose obedience. She stood up along with the guard and avoided choking to death.

"I'm going to walk to my car," the guard said. He tugged on the garrotte, tightening it enough to hurt, but not enough to strangle her. "I recommend you keep up with me. Otherwise you'll die."

He spoke with a hint of Texan drawl, but his voice suddenly sounded eerily familiar. Heart pounding, Melody stared through the obscuring rain, scrutinizing the guard's dark skin and black, close-cropped hair as she stumbled along beside him. It couldn't be, she thought. This man was African-American. Dave was white, with light brown hair. She had Dave on the brain, that was all.

The kidnapper's car was apparently parked at

some distance from the point where they'd exited the Unit One building, which was probably why he hadn't knocked her unconscious. Even though he appeared superbly fit, carrying her this far would have been a brutally demanding chore. As it was, he set a punishing pace across deserted warehouse yards, avoiding streets where they might encounter people and squeezing through chain-link fences that had been cut, presumably in anticipation of their arrival. As they ran, the rain blew into her face and the freezing night air sucked the heat out of her body, plastering her inadequate clothing to her ice-cold skin with every gust of wind.

Melody was so completely chilled that she was actually grateful when her captor bundled her into the rear of the getaway car, following her inside. Another man was seated behind the wheel of the Subaru and he had the engine running, putting paid to any lingering hope of escape, but at least the heat was blasting full force and the noose around her neck was no longer threatening to choke her if she slowed down even for a second.

Her captor gave the order to drive south. The driver didn't speak or acknowledge the command, but he instantly set the car in motion.

There was a certain advantage to her situation, Melody thought bleakly, wriggling her toes in an effort to warm them. She was outnumbered, handcuffed, had her mouth taped shut and was attached to her captor by an extremely efficient noose, so she really didn't need to waste her time or energy wondering how she could escape. The simple answer was that she couldn't. Since there was nothing more useful to do, she allowed herself to appreciate the warmth seeping into her, although her clothes were so wet that she still couldn't stop shuddering, or prevent her teeth from chattering.

Her captor gave her less than a minute of respite before he unbuttoned her jacket and shoved it down from her shoulders. There was nothing remotely sexual about his action, and Melody knew at once what he was looking for. He moved his fingertips quickly and impersonally around the outer edge of her right shoulder blade until he found Unit One's tracking chip.

His next action set Melody's stomach into instant-churn mode. He took a slim flashlight and a Swiss army knife from the belt at his waist, using his thumb to flick open one of the knife blades. With none of the sadistic enjoyment Christopher had shown yesterday, her captor put the flashlight between his teeth, directed the beam to her shoulder blade, then silently and expertly excised the chip from beneath her skin. He wadded a tissue over the wound, covering it with a piece of the same surgical tape he'd used on her mouth. Through a haze of pain, Melody watched him crack the car window and toss the chip into the street. Where Unit One would track it to a useless dead end.

"You can turn back to our final destination now," her captor told the driver.

The driver braked, did a U-turn, drove for two blocks in the direction they'd just come from, and then made a right turn to the east. Melody shrugged her shoulders back into her damp jacket and stared at the falling rain, terrified that some trace of hope would creep into her determinedly blank expression. Whoever or whatever her kidnapper might be, he was clearly familiar with Unit One practices. That was evident from the confidence with which he had led her through headquarters, quite apart from his knowledge of precisely where to look for the tracking chip. But his assumption that he knew exactly what to expect from her might yet be her salvation. He believed that with the chip gone, Unit One no longer had any way to trace her.

He was wrong. She was certainly grateful now that Nick had been so paranoid about her meeting with Wallis Beecham, Melody thought.

Her kidnapper seemed to feel no urge to talk as they drove through nearly empty streets. Pity it was only in the movies that villains always felt compelled to boast about their twisted genius before killing their victims. On the positive side, her captor obviously hadn't been given instructions to kill her, or she would be dead by now. Not only did he carry an assault rifle, he had shown every indication of being more than capable of killing her with his bare hands. Since she was still alive, somebody powerful must want her that way. She hoped that was a good thing and that she wasn't about to face the sort of torture that would make her long for death.

It would be a really smart move to stop thinking about the possibility of being tortured, Melody concluded. She sneaked a glance at her captor, who was sitting disconcertingly still and relaxed beside her. He sensed her interest at once and held her gaze for a few seconds before turning to look out the car window.

She couldn't shake the feeling that she was looking at Dave Ramsdell, despite the fact that his features were unfamiliar. She had an idea that the reason he was saying so little wasn't only that he felt no compelling urge to boast, but also that he didn't want her to recognize his voice.

Could thin-featured, ruddy-cheeked Dave really have transformed himself into an African-American? Skin dye wouldn't be enough to do the trick. He would need a contoured mask to explain the altered shape of his features, and surely it would have to be customized by an expert to fit perfectly around his eyes? But she supposed the transformation was possible in theory. If she looked closely she might be able to detect subtle signs that the skin was artificial, or his face shaped with molded latex, although the dim lighting inside the car was far from ideal for that sort of inspection.

In the end, Melody decided not to risk staring at her captor with too much intensity. He would surely notice that she was studying him and, on balance, she suspected it would be to her advantage not to let him know that she had questions about his identity.

Her battered pride was soothed somewhat by the possibility that she had been tricked by one of Unit One's most expert field operatives, a man with years of experience in the art of deception. It was also comforting to think that she had been pinned to the ground so fast because she'd been fighting against an acknowledged master of unarmed combat. Still, she'd been a humiliatingly easy mark, happily co-operating in her own kidnapping. That would teach her to get uppity, Melody reflected ruefully. She'd allowed her minor success with Christopher and Wallis Beecham to give her an inflated sense of her own competence. She'd damn near skipped down the stairs behind her kidnapper, she'd been so willing to follow him. The fact that she'd been pinned to the ground with his hand on her carotid artery less than a minute after leaving the protection of headquarters provided a grim reality check on her true ability to defend herself.

If she survived this kidnapping, she'd do whatever it took to become a more effective field agent, Melody promised herself. She'd work on her strength training; she'd spend all her weekends being thrown to the mat by Sam and Buddy and Tony. She would even submit to the special torment of having Nick analyze her inadequacies, but she was going to make damn sure nobody could ever take her this easily again.

Given the impossibility of escape, it didn't make much difference to her behavior right this minute whether her kidnapper was Dave or somebody else, but his identity did make a difference to the possible reasons for her kidnapping. If she'd been kidnapped by Dave, she could surely assume that Wallis Beecham was behind tonight's events.

The moment that idea entered Melody's head, she wondered why it had taken so long to get there. Of course this kidnapping had been orchestrated by Wallis Beecham. Who else? The only remaining question was why.

Because Wallis needed a hostage from Unit One to trade for Christopher.

The sudden realization carried such force that a small sound escaped from her throat before she could prevent it. Fortunately, since her mouth was taped, she managed to pretend that she was coughing, and in need of air.

"Don't panic," the kidnapper said. "Breathe slowly. Relax."

Melody leaned back against the leather seat and obediently drew in a couple of deep breaths, although there wasn't much point in pretending to be resigned to her fate. If her captor was Dave, he knew how she'd been trained and he wouldn't believe in her docility. And since her kidnapping only made sense in the context of Unit One's acquisition of Christopher Beecham, she could just about guarantee that the man sitting next to her was indeed Dave Ramsdell.

She had no practical hope of fooling an operative with his years of experience into behaving carelessly. However subdued she managed to appear, Dave would be aware that she was on tenterhooks, looking for any opening that would offer a chance of escape. Ironically, he was the one who'd trained her in methods of escape, and how to survive captivity. Any tricks she knew, he knew, too. Worse, her knowledge was merely theoretical, whereas Dave had years of practical experience, having invented several of the most effective tactics during his daring combat missions in Bosnia and Afghanistan.

They had just exited the Holland Tunnel and were speeding north through New York's financial district, turning onto Second Avenue. Melody finally had an idea where they were headed. Until 9/11, the corporate offices for one of Wallis's subsidiary companies had been located in the World Trade Center. After the disaster, Wallis had reaped a lot of positive PR by purchasing a run-down building in the vicinity of Stuyvesant Square and announcing that he would renovate it as a way to help jump-start the shattered economy of lower Manhattan. From the direction the driver was taking, it seemed the renovated building, now known as Beecham House, would be their destination.

The car slowed as they approached East Fourteenth Street, confirming her guess. Melody wondered if she was about to find herself face-to-face with Wallis for the second time in fifteen hours. It was unlikely, she concluded. Wallis wasn't in the habit of getting too close to any of his dirty deeds and Dave was more than competent to handle whatever it was Wallis had planned for her. Unit One trained their field agents well, and Dave had been a star product of the system. He clearly hadn't lost any of his skills since defecting to the opposition.

Even at three in the morning, the city streets in this neighborhood close to New York University were anything but deserted. They passed a delivery truck on the corner of the block, as well as a couple of pedestrians who were hurrying toward the subway station. Despite the tantalizing nearness of other people, Melody knew she had little hope of attracting their attention. Dave wouldn't have brought her here if he expected to encounter major problems transferring her from the car to the building.

The driver halted the car only long enough for Dave to open the rear door and drag Melody onto the sidewalk. Then the Subaru was in motion again, disappearing around the corner of the block without arousing so much as a blink of interest from anyone. Unable to scream because of the tape covering her mouth, Melody couldn't even put up a physical struggle, since Dave had tightened the noose to the point that she was gagging. If she moved too sharply, she was afraid she would lose consciousness.

Still holding firmly on to the noose, Dave wrapped

one arm tightly around her waist and used the other to pull her head down onto his shoulder as if he were a lover sheltering her from the rain. They were across the sidewalk and under the covered portico of Beecham House within seconds. There the combination of ornamental overhang and sheeting rain effectively shielded them from the view of any passersby.

Even newly renovated, Beecham House was too small and not sufficiently high-rent to warrant twenty-four-hour security guards. An aluminum box affixed to the building's brick facade protected the keypad that controlled the alarm system. Dave tapped in the deactivation code and a green light blinked, indicating success. Then he swiped his key card through the lock, and one of the plate-glass doors audibly clicked open. He pushed Melody into the lobby, the high-tech security vanquished in approximately forty seconds.

This wasn't an area of high-rises and, to fit in with its neighbors, Beecham House had only seven floors. An elevator carried them swiftly to the top floor, without sight or sound of any possible rescuers. The transfer from vehicle to building had been so simple, Melody realized, that Dave hadn't needed to speak a single word since advising her not to panic.

He propelled her past a series of darkened offices to a small and windowless storage room located at the very end of the corridor. The storeroom had a floor covered in linoleum that still smelled new, and contained no furnishings other than empty metal shelving. There were overhead fluorescent light fixtures, but Dave turned on only a dim security lamp in one corner of the room. Another sign that he didn't want her examining his features and skin color too closely?

With impersonal efficiency Dave padlocked Melody's cuffed hands to one of the steel pillars that supported the shelves. The position of her arms, immobile behind her back, was merely uncomfortable rather than painful, but she couldn't sit or move more than a few inches to either side, which meant that her muscles would soon start to cramp, especially since her clothes were still damp enough to cling. Melody suspected that within a couple of hours, what was now discomfort would be edging closer and closer to real pain.

Dave left the storeroom, still without speaking. When he returned, only minutes later, he brought Wallis Beecham with him, confounding all Melody's expectations. Why had Wallis risked associating himself with her kidnapping? she wondered. It seemed almost incredibly careless of him.

Wallis looked her over, personally checking to make sure that her handcuffs were securely attached to the shelving unit. His expression bordered on gloating as he assessed the full discomfort of her situation. "Not quite so full of yourself now, are you?" he said. "You didn't put up a very good show once you were matched against somebody halfway competent, did you?"

Melody wished she could point out that he'd just implied he and Christopher were less than halfway competent, but the tape across her mouth made speech impossible.

"I'm tired of Unit One's antics," Wallis said. "When Lewis Cranford first warned me about a covert government agency that enforced justice against citizens who managed to evade criminal prosecution, I was amused. The idea of secret agents running around the country pretending to fight for truth, justice and the American way would be frightening if it wasn't so funny. However, the joke is wearing thin. It's time for Unit One to be shut down."

Melody thought such an ambition was a bit megalomaniacal, even for Wallis.

He turned to Dave. "Make the phone call," he said.

With a nod, Dave took a cell phone from one of his pockets and dialed. His call was answered almost immediately. He spoke with the same Texan drawl that he'd been using ever since he woke Melody over an hour ago, but it wasn't his accent that shocked her into a state of near paralysis.

"Mr. Fowles, I'm calling you on behalf of Mr. Wallis Beecham," Dave said. "Time is short, so don't interrupt. I've been reliably informed that your home lacks the specialized equipment needed to trace my call. However, as an extra precaution, I will be disconnecting shortly. You can expect a second phone call from me sometime soon. Here is our message in a nutshell. Mr. Beecham believes Unit One is operating far outside the parameters established when Congress first appropriated funding for your agency. The kidnapping of his son, Christopher, is an egregious example of the way in which Unit One has overstepped its bounds. He intends to bring the excesses of Unit One to the attention of the appropriate Senate funding committee.

"In a moment I will be calling you with instructions as to where you should deliver Christopher Beecham in order to return him to the freedom he is entitled to enjoy as a United States citizen. I remind you that Christopher has not even been indicted, much less convicted of committing any crime. His kidnapping by your organization, and his retention against his will at your headquarters, is entirely illegal.''

Dave closed the flap of the cell phone, ending the call. It immediately began to ring. Dave ignored it.

''I thought you said Fowles couldn't trace the call,'' Wallis said, looking anxious.

''He can't trace the physical location that we're calling from,'' Dave explained. ''But he can call this number just by pressing the callback button on his own phone.''

The phone continued to ring. Dave continued to ignore it. Finally, after a full two minutes, the ringing stopped. Dave displayed no reaction, but Wallis visibly relaxed.

Melody closed her eyes, the only way she could even begin to disguise the stupefaction she felt at what she'd just heard. Dave had not only called *Jasper Fowles* to make his threats, he'd spoken as if Jasper held a position of significant authority within Unit One.

She felt the touch of Wallis Beecham's beefy fingers beneath her chin, and smelled the lingering odor of the Cuban cigars he smoked each night after dinner. When she tried to turn away, he jerked her head back around to face him. Reluctantly she opened her eyes and forced herself to meet his gaze. He looked at her searchingly, appearing a little disappointed that Dave's phone call to Jasper Fowles hadn't produced more of a reaction from her. Astonishingly, it seemed that she was managing to screen the shock from her expression. Or perhaps the shock was so extreme that she had passed beyond the ability to register any emotion at all and Wallis was misinterpreting her blankness for lack of interest.

"You didn't know that your precious Jasper Fowles was the commander of Unit One, did you?" Wallis demanded, but there was a hint of uncertainty threading through his question, as if he was afraid she might have known after all and spoiled his bombshell.

The commander? Jasper was actually *the Commander?* Bloody hell, of course she hadn't known. Hadn't entertained the faintest suspicion, in fact. Until a few seconds ago, Jasper would have been about number thirty-two million on her list of likely candidates for the position. In fact, she was still having a hard time believing it, despite the evidence of Dave's phone call.

But for all her incredulity, there was a tiny part of her that acknowledged the plausibility of what she'd just heard. In a strange and complex way, it was both completely impossible and oddly credible that Jasper was the Commander. No wonder Unit One had been so anxious to recruit her, she thought bitterly. Every confidence she'd ever shared with Jasper was probably now an entry line in her personnel file at headquarters. Misery washed over her as she contemplated the magnitude of Jasper's betrayal. However, she certainly wasn't about to add to Wallis's triumph by permitting him to witness her devastation. She fought to keep her eyes wide, clear and empty of any emotion.

Wallis flashed a taunting smile. "Makes you wonder if Jasper gave you that job in his art gallery out of the goodness of his heart, or because he always planned to sell you out to his cronies at Unit One, doesn't it?''

Yes, that was exactly what she was wondering. Was there never going to be anybody in her life whose love she could trust to be unconditional? Or even offered to her with only small strings attached? An image of Nick, softly whispering her name as they made love, came into her mind. She hardened her heart. God alone knew what Nick's motives were in starting an affair with her. She certainly didn't. She didn't understand anyone's motives anymore. From here on out, as far as Nick was concerned, she would just enjoy the great sex while it lasted and forget about those aching, treacherous feelings that had begun to insinuate themselves into her soul.

Melody twisted her head to the side, escaping Wallis's probing fingers. She gave no other sign that she'd even heard his question, much less that it bothered her. Defying Wallis was old and familiar ground to her, especially easy to accomplish since the tape on her mouth prevented the need to shape her defiance into words.

''What Melody knows is irrelevant to our plans,'' Dave said. He held up the phone. ''I'm going to call Fowles again with the rest of your message, Wallis.''

Dave's second call was answered just as promptly as the first. He spoke crisply, his voice professionally brisk rather than triumphant. ''Mr. Fowles, you have undoubtedly been informed that Melody Beecham is missing from her sleeping cubicle at Unit One headquarters. I'm sure you would like to see her safely and quickly returned. To that end, you will personally arrange for Christopher Beecham to be brought to the southwest corner of the intersection of Broadway and Houston. You will make sure that Christopher is there no later than one hour from now, which will be 4:30 a.m. When Mr. Beecham's representatives inform me that Christopher has been restored to his family's care, I will arrange for Melody to be released.''

Dave waited, listening to something being said at the other end of the phone. ''There is no negotiating of terms, Mr. Fowles. First you deliver Christopher to us, and then we release Melody. She's our guarantee of your cooperation. It's Unit One that has broken the law, not Mr. Beecham. *We* need protection from *your* lawlessness.''

David listened to another comment. ''No, sir,'' he responded. ''That's not correct. Wallis Beecham, in fact, has no direct knowledge of these negotiations and he certainly wasn't aware that Melody had been taken from Unit One headquarters. That was strictly my idea. Knowing how much affection you feel for Melody, I was quite sure you wouldn't want anything to happen to her. I hope her absence will persuade you to see this situation from Mr. Beecham's point of view. Christopher is his son. Melody is as dear to you as a daughter. I'm sure everyone wants the same happy outcome—Christopher returned to his family and Melody returned safely to hers. That said, you have no cause of action against Mr. Beecham. Melody is an operative in your agency. Christopher is an innocent civilian. Two very different situations.''

Dave listened once again. ''Yes, Mr. Fowles. Wallis Beecham intends to go to the intersection of Broadway and Houston to welcome home his son. There is one other matter before we end this call.

Your funding is approved by a special Senate finance committee that has for many years been chaired by Senator Howard Shore of Massachusetts. Last night Senator Shore resigned from that committee because of...family circumstances. His place will be taken by Senator Lewis Cranford of Kentucky, who has never been a fan of Unit One, or its mission. If Mr. Beecham informs the new chairman that Christopher was kidnapped by your organization, I can almost guarantee there will be no funds for Unit One in next year's black ops budget. Your agency's continued existence is in peril, Mr. Fowles. I advise you to cooperate by returning Christopher to us as quickly as possible."

Dave cut off the call again before Jasper could respond.

"Well done," Wallis said, clapping Dave on the back. "Damn, you're good. In fact, you're better at this than my lawyers."

Dave accepted the compliment with a brief nod. "I'm leaving now to supervise the arrangements for Christopher's return," he said. "We don't want any mishaps there."

"And I'll come with you as agreed," Wallis said, and something about his manner triggered those few alarm bells in Melody's system that hadn't been bludgeoned into uselessness by the shock of learning about Jasper.

Wallis avoided her gaze, confirming her suspicions. "Goodbye, Melody. Your release will be taken care of as soon as Christopher has been restored to us. By the way, don't expect some office worker to come rushing to your rescue while we're gone. The first tenants aren't scheduled to move into this building for another month."

Dave and Wallis left the room, locking the door behind them.

They planned to kill her, Melody realized, although the insight wasn't very startling. She was being left alive only until Christopher was returned to their custody. Wallis had needed a hostage to add strength to his bargaining power vis-à-vis Jasper and Unit One, but they didn't need that hostage alive once Christopher was back in the family fold. On the contrary, they needed her dead. She was a dangerous witness, since she could give the lie to Dave's claim that Wallis knew nothing about this kidnapping.

Melody gave several hard tugs on her handcuffs just to confirm her gloomy conviction that there was no way for her to escape unless somebody helped her. The tugs achieved nothing except to make the padlock rattle. The rattle was loud enough that it might have been useful in attracting attention if there had been anybody in the corridor to hear it.

This would be a *really* good time for a rescue team from Unit One to put in an appearance. Unit One presumably knew where she was, since a second chip had been implanted in her thigh immediately prior to her meeting yesterday with Wallis. She could only hope that when Mac and Bob Spinard had installed their strong new firewall to protect the Central Control computer system from Dave's tampering, the signal from her chip hadn't somehow been lost.

She'd liked this escape-from-a-locked-room game a lot better when she'd played it at the start of her training, Melody thought ruefully. At least the idea of the Unit One test was to escape. Here the idea was to make sure that she didn't.

The storage room wasn't as featureless as Unit One's test room, but even here there wasn't much to look at. Bare walls, bare shelves, a ventilation grille above her head. The closest thing she could identify as a tool that might aid in her escape was a protruding screw sticking out from the steel support post just an inch or so below the level of her mouth. She'd unintentionally caught her hair on it several times already. By bending her knees slightly, she discovered she could hook the screw into a tiny gap between her skin and one end of the surgical tape stuck over her mouth.

Removing the tape wasn't going to move her any closer to freedom, but at least it was a small gesture of defiance against her captors. Melody worked the screw as deep into the gap as she could. Then she drew in a deep breath and quickly jerked her head away from the post. The tape ripped away from her mouth, sticking to the screw.

She was absurdly pleased with her tiny success. "Hey, I did it," she said, liking the sound of her own voice, even if it croaked a bit.

"Good move," Nick's voice said from over her head. "But what do you plan to do for an encore?"

Melody looked up and saw Nick's face peering down at her from the air-conditioning vent. Her heart, supposedly hardened, gave a giant leap. But only because he was here to rescue her. Not for any other reason.

Hell, why not admit that she was thrilled to see him? Her sore mouth stretched into a huge grin. "What took you so long?" she asked.

Twenty-Four

Nick removed the grille from the air-conditioning duct and dropped onto the top shelf, before swinging down to the floor. He landed right next to Melody and immediately leaned toward her. He tilted her head back, his eyes locking with hers. His gaze tender, he pushed a strand of still-damp hair off her face and tucked it behind her ear. Then he noticed the noose, and his mouth tightened into a grim line.

"Did Wallis give you these bruises on your neck?" he asked, working to loosen the knot.

She shook her head. "Dave did."

"Was it Dave who took you from headquarters?"

"I think so. He dressed himself in the uniform of a security guard and disguised himself with a mask. He pretended he was African-American, but I'm almost certain it was really Dave."

"Dave is good at disguises," Nick said, lifting the noose over her head. He tossed it onto the linoleum without making any other comment. Then he slowly traced his forefinger over the sore skin around her mouth, his eyes dark with anger.

"I've brought gifts," he said after a moment.

"Nice ones, I hope." There was a definite wobble in her voice. Now that Nick was standing right beside her, Melody was beginning to feel some of the fear that she'd previously forced herself to keep at bay.

Nick heard the wobble, of course. He squeezed her arm reassuringly, then touched her very lightly on the cheek. Thank heavens he didn't say anything sympathetic or she'd have burst into tears.

Instead of offering sympathy, he extracted a bunch of keys from the pouch in his commando-style belt and dangled it in front of her, smiling. "Is this a prime-quality gift, or what?"

She returned his smile. "Depends what they open."

"Handcuffs," he said. "And let's hope one of them works, because I don't have a blowtorch to cut you loose."

He reached around her and began fitting various keys into the handcuffs. At the fourth try, Melody heard a click. She felt him opening the cuffs, and suddenly her hands were blessedly free to move and wriggle.

"Well, the good news is that one of my keys worked," he said, drawing her hands forward and gently massaging her wrists.

Melody assumed it was reaction to the stress of the past couple of hours that had her weak at the knees, not reaction to Nick's touch. "I'm almost afraid to ask. What's the bad news?"

"That it's been close to twenty-four hours since the last time we made love." He lowered his head and kissed her softly, taking care not to put pressure on her tender mouth. Melody told herself that all she felt was simple sexual desire and tried hard to believe the lie.

Nick ended the kiss before her lie became transparently ridiculous. "Actually, there's some more bad news. This room was designed as a secure storage area and the door is reinforced with a steel core. There's no way for me to break open the lock. You're going to have to get out the same way I came in—through the heating ducts."

"In comparison to the alternatives, that seems like a small problem," Melody said. "It's a new building, so I'm assuming there shouldn't be too many gross spiders and cobwebs?"

"Not a one that I noticed," Nick said cheerfully. "There's not even much dust. Okay, let's get this show on the road. Are you ready to go?"

She nodded. "Raring, in fact."

Nick stepped onto one of the shelves about two feet above the ground and quickly climbed to the top. "Need a hand?" he asked Melody, leaning down. "You might have more difficulty than you anticipate, since you've been handcuffed for a couple of hours."

"Thanks, but I can manage." It was such a relief to be free of the cuffs, the gag and the noose—not to mention Wallis and Dave—that she felt damn near ready to tackle the slopes of Mount Everest, let alone a mere set of storage shelves and a heating duct.

"The ducts branch off in a couple of places," Nick said when she was sitting next to him. He strapped a circular flashlight to the back of his wrist and scrunched down, ready to slide into the narrow opening. "I'll go first to be sure we head in the right direction."

The crawl through the ducts was longer and harder than Melody would have liked. However, it was approximately one zillion times better than remaining welded to a metal post in Wallis's storage room, waiting for him to decide precisely how he was going to off her.

They emerged through another air-conditioning grille into the center of a room that had partitions already erected to form office cubicles, but with pieces of desks and chairs still sitting unassembled in shipping crates.

"What next?" Melody asked, wiping grime off her hands onto the seat of her pants. "I'm half expecting you to come up with some reason why we need to rappel down the side of the building with only one rope between us."

"We could do that if you like, but since it's raining, I figured we might as well ride the elevator."

She laughed and Nick caught her face between his hands, kissing her again with tantalizing swiftness. "We have to go somewhere I can do that properly," he said, putting his arm around her. Tired as she was, Melody thought that sounded like a pretty great idea.

They walked together toward the elevators, his arm still around her waist. In a moment, when they were riding back to headquarters, she would have to ask him what was happening with Christopher, Melody thought. But right now she was tired, bruised and content not to question anything with too much intensity.

The elevator doors opened as they arrived in front of them, and Dave stepped out, assault rifle slung casually over his shoulder.

"It's Dave," Melody said, afraid Nick wouldn't recognize him because of his disguise.

Nick gave no sign that he'd heard her. He and Dave stared at each other without either one of them moving a muscle. Then they both launched into an attack at what looked like precisely the same moment, Dave reaching across his body to pull his rifle into firing position, and Nick kicking upward to prevent the move.

If she hadn't cared so much about the outcome, and if the fighting hadn't been so brutal, Melody would have been awed by the dazzling display of unarmed combat that the two of them put on. Dave didn't want to abandon the potential advantage of having a gun, and Nick was equally determined that the assault rifle was never going to be fired. It soon became clear that, impressive as Dave's skills were, he was losing the fight. Nick finally kicked the rifle out of Dave's grasp, and Melody edged toward them, grabbed the weapon, then hustled fifteen feet back down the corridor so that the gun couldn't become a prize to be regained.

She stood with the rifle trained on Dave, and she knew she would use it as a last resort. She was almost relieved, though, that the men were fighting in too close quarters for her to risk firing unless Nick went down. Despite everything that had happened in the past couple of days, she discovered that she wasn't quite ready to take Dave out in a hail of bullets.

Nick ended the fight with a triple move, delivering a punishing kick to the region of Dave's kidneys, followed by an uppercut to his chin and a downward thrust on the back of his neck. Dave fell to his knees, then toppled forward onto his face.

Nick staggered backward for a couple of steps, then collapsed against the wall, his eyes closing. Melody realized that he was exhausted. His fight with Dave might have looked elegant, but Nick had been fighting for his life—for both their lives.

"Did he break any of your bones?" Melody asked softly.

"No. But I need to call headquarters and get medical help for him." Nick unzipped a jacket pocket and took out a phone. "I'll tell them to have a paramedic on standby at headquarters."

Melody looked at the man sprawled on the floor. "You think it really is Dave?"

"Yes." Nick's expression was momentarily somber. "We've fought alongside each other often enough for me to be sure."

There was nothing Melody could say that would make Dave's betrayal less painful, so she resorted to the strictly practical. "I'll get something to tie him up," she said, heading back toward the office they'd just left.

She returned with several lengths of plastic twine salvaged from around one of the packing crates and found Nick kneeling beside Dave, patting him down and systematically removing anything that could be used as a weapon. Melody handed Nick some twine to tie Dave's hands and kept the rest to tie up his feet. She took care not to cut off Dave's circulation, but still made damn sure that he was too hobbled to be capable of launching another attack the moment he regained consciousness.

"You were right—he's wearing a mask," Nick said just as she secured the final knot. "Look."

Melody watched as Nick peeled black latex skin from Dave's neck, almost as if he were removing a Band-Aid. Slipping the blade of his pocketknife into the gap he'd created, Nick slowly tugged the knife upward. The mask split open, revealing the white skin beneath. Propelled by a rush of sudden anger, Melody leaned over and ripped the sides of the mask apart.

Dave's eyes flickered open and his familiar features stared up at her. He didn't speak and neither did Melody. He twisted his head so that he could locate Nick.

"I'm sorry," he said. His eyes closed again, although Melody didn't think he was unconscious anymore.

Nick busied himself stashing Dave's collection of weapons into various pouches and pockets in his clothing. Melody didn't attempt to speak or to help him, except to pick up the assault rifle and hand it to him.

"Thanks." He slung it over his shoulder. "I have transportation waiting for us," he said. "If you'll help me get Dave into the elevator, I'll call to let the driver know he should come right now."

Their transportation turned out to be a panel truck with the logo of the Energy Cooperative of New York on the side. Dave was fully conscious and not pretending otherwise by the time they loaded him into the front passenger seat, but he was in no shape to cause trouble, although the driver helped Nick lash him to the seat just to be extra safe.

They were emerging on the New Jersey side of the Holland Tunnel and Melody was dozing with her head on Nick's shoulder when his cell phone buzzed. He answered the call, making few comments as he listened, but he was smiling when he hung up.

Melody yawned. "Good news?"

"The best. Wallis Beecham has been arrested. The

New York police have him in custody right now, but he's going to be charged tomorrow by the federal government with two counts of conspiracy to commit murder.''

''That's amazingly wonderful news.'' Relief washed over Melody in a giant wave. ''Can we...can they make the charges stick?''

''Yes, almost certainly, thanks to Christopher,'' Nick said.

''So he did know enough to be useful?''

''Not only does he know enough to be very useful, he apparently has a strong sense of self-preservation. He decided early yesterday evening that telling us everything he knew was about the only way he had left to protect his sorry ass. In fact, he was so afraid of what Wallis would do to him that he flat-out refused to be returned to his father. It was pretty funny watching Christopher beg Unit One to keep him in custody.''

''For once he's using some sense,'' Melody said. ''I agree completely with the strategy. He's a lot safer with Unit One than with Daddy. I'm quite sure the only reason Wallis wanted Christopher back was to kill him.''

Nick looked interested. ''Do you think that was really Wallis's intention? To kill his own son?''

''Yes, despite what I said the other day about the special place Christopher holds in his father's affections. Nobody is important enough to Wallis to be forgiven twice. Christopher had become a threat, and Wallis eliminates threats. He planned to kill me, too, of course. I expect he'd already arranged a nice little car ride off a cliff for the two of us.''

''I'm glad he didn't succeed. You were a pain in

the ass during training, but you've turned out to be quite a good field operative. Callow, but with a lot of potential."

"I'm overwhelmed by your praise. Sir." In fact, she was just that, despite the ironic tone of her reply.

Nick looked at her, his expression unreadable in the darkness of the truck's interior, and spoke into her ear. "Will you come back to my apartment tonight, Melody? Will you spend the night with me?"

"Because we're running a scam?" she whispered back. "Because Unit One thinks I still need protection? Because Nikolai Anwar needs to be seen in the company of Melody Beecham for some reason?"

"Because I want you there," he said. "Because I want like hell to make love to you."

She looked at him, unsmiling, her heart aching with the emotion she wasn't brave enough to name. "Yes," she said. "I'll come."

Epilogue

Two weeks later

Nick's cell phone buzzed shortly after dawn. He eased out of bed, hoping to avoid waking Melody by taking the call in the living room. It was from one of his business associates in St. Petersburg who needed on-the-spot help in fighting his way through the complex and corrupt Russian banking system.

Nick promised to catch a flight back to Russia within thirty-six hours, but for once there was no adrenaline rush as he hung up the phone and contemplated all that had to be done before he could get away. He went to the kitchen for a glass of juice, mentally assessing which markers he would call in, which markers he would pay out and where he might need to beg for a favor or two in order to grease the wheels of a financial system that was barely functional. Keeping his ever-expanding network of legal and illegal contacts inside Russia healthy was a full-time job in itself, but Nick was aware of a sudden impatience with the unrelenting demands on his time and his energy.

He wanted to stay home with Melody, he realized. And that thought was even more scary than the potential risks he might encounter while negotiating a new deal with the Russian Mafia.

Meanwhile, the Bonita investigation was winding down, the cleanup operations being parceled out to other government agencies. Wallis Beecham himself continued to maintain total silence about his involvement in the Bonita partnership. Asked about the cloning project, his deal with the Middle Eastern oilmen, the attempted assassination of Kenneth Chung and the murder of Lawrence Springer, his response was a blank stare. His silence wasn't achieving much, however. Yesterday a federal judge had stunned Beecham's retinue of lawyers by declaring that their client was a flight risk and denying him bail. Incredibly, it seemed that Wallis Beecham was going to await trial behind bars.

Christopher, determined to avoid the same fate, was talking as fast as he could wrap his tongue around the words of accusation. He told them that the Bonita clinic hadn't been built on a tropical island, or in the wilds of Patagonia, or even in the lawless rain-forest areas of the Amazon River basin as Unit One had anticipated. Instead, Wallis had bought a small cruise ship, which had then been converted and equipped as a floating, state-of-the-art research lab. The ship was sailing under the Liberian flag, and was in theory untouchable by U.S. law, since it had never put into a U.S. port and Wallis had been smart enough to buy all the scientific equipment from companies in Europe.

Fortunately, the prosecuting attorneys had managed to convince a judge that enough evidence existed of Wallis Beecham's involvement in the murder of Lawrence Springer and the attempted murder of

Kenneth Chung that search warrants had been issued for his various homes and offices. The mere threat of what might be discovered among Beecham's papers had been enough to scare Senator Cranford, Johnston Yates and Victor Heston into limited cooperation with the authorities. All three seemed genuinely appalled by the idea that Wallis Beecham and Lawrence Springer had conspired to murder Kenneth Chung. All three appeared shocked and horrified that Beecham had been charged with hiring an assassin to murder Lawrence Springer. And all three were adamant that they had no idea the end goal of the Bonita partnership had been to produce cloned human babies.

Senator Cranford, more vulnerable than his former partners since he had to persuade voters to reelect him, was disassociating himself from Wallis Beecham as fast and as furiously as he could. For the first couple of days after the story broke, Victor Heston and Johnston Yates simply refused to comment on their participation. But when the media conducted interviews with three young Bangladeshi women who'd been hired as surrogate mothers, they broke their silence. Using an expensive PR firm, the two of them issued statements insisting they had believed the object of the partnership was to raise overseas funds in order to support stem cell research. Their motives, they maintained, had been as much humanitarian as financial. Humanitarian because—like most other Americans—they disagreed with the federal government's partial ban on stem cell research. Insofar as their motives had been selfish, it was only because both of them had relatives suffering from diseases likely to be among the first to benefit from advances in stem cell technology. The financial benefits had been less important, they insisted, since the start-up and development costs were so enormous that it would take years to see a return on their investment.

Nick would have had less trouble believing in Heston and Yates as great philanthropists if their start-up capital had been provided out of their own pockets, as opposed to courtesy of the supposed death of Kenneth Chung. Still, he supposed Unit One could be said to have achieved its objectives, since Wallis Beecham was behind bars and the Bonita partnership wasn't going to be producing a cloned baby any time soon.

Nick put his juice glass into the sink and went back to the bedroom. Melody had woken after all. She was sitting up in bed, knees bent, the covers drawn up to her chin, her hair tumbling around her shoulders.

She was so beautiful, it hurt him to look at her. "I'm sorry," Nick said. "I hoped the call wouldn't wake you."

"Don't worry about it. Do you have to go in to headquarters?"

He sat down next to her on the bed. "Worse, I have to fly to St. Petersburg."

"Now? This morning?"

"Tonight."

She wrapped her arms more tightly around her knees. "I hope you have a safe trip."

She didn't say that she would miss him, Nick noticed. She didn't nag him to hurry back. The perfect goddamn mistress.

He cradled her cheek with his hand, his fingers

tangling in her hair, substituting the gratification of touching her for all the things he couldn't allow himself to tell her. "I wish I didn't have to go," he said, and his voice was husky with the difficulty of admitting even that much of what he was feeling.

She looked at him for a long, silent moment, her incredible eyes seeming more mysterious than usual in the darkness of the bedroom. "I wish you didn't have to go, too."

She got up as soon as she'd spoken, found her robe at the foot of the bed and put it on, tying the belt tightly around her waist. The body language spoke volumes.

"I'm moving out of Jasper's apartment this weekend," she said.

"Where are you moving to?" he asked, astonished at how badly he wanted to suggest that she should move in with him. It was impossible, of course, since this apartment belonged to Nikolai Anwar, and Nikolai couldn't afford to have a live-in lover.

"I've found a small apartment on East Thirty-first," Melody said. She smiled a little. "It's tiny, and it has all the charm of an ice cube, but I can afford the rent, which is the main thing."

"What does Jasper think about the move?" As if he didn't know.

She turned away, heading toward the bathroom. "I haven't told him yet. I'll do that at the gallery today."

Nick wasn't surprised that Melody planned to move. Nor was he surprised that she hadn't yet told Jasper about her plans. Jasper didn't confide in him, of course, or even in Mac, but it was obvious to anyone who'd seen them together that Melody felt deeply and bitterly betrayed by Jasper's deception.

"He couldn't tell you the truth, Melody."

Anger narrowed her gaze. "Maybe not. But he didn't have to set me up for recruitment by Unit One, either."

"He didn't. Not in the way you're imagining, anyway."

"So you've said before."

"Then believe me."

Her entire body stilled. "I wish I could. But we both know you'll lie to me again the very next time it's necessary."

There was no credible way to deny the truth of her statement. As had happened far too often over the past couple of weeks, Nick sublimated everything he couldn't express verbally into physical action. He intercepted Melody on the way into the bathroom, tilting her face upward and kissing her. He'd intended nothing more than a kiss, a silent apology for too many important things left unspoken. But somehow the kiss deepened and grew as it so often did between the two of them. Before he understood how it had happened, they were back in bed, making love.

Afterward she rolled away from him, lying on the edge of the bed for a minute before sitting up. She spoke to him without turning around. "How long will you be in Russia?"

He had no idea. The correct answer was *For as long as it takes.* "I'll be back by Christmas Eve," he said.

She finally turned around to look at him. She even smiled. "I'm glad," she said. "I'll be waiting."

Turn the page for an exciting preview
of

FULL PURSUIT

by Jasmine Cresswell

Available November 2004
from MIRA Books

Prologue

The home of Judge George Lawson
Greenwich, Connecticut

It took Melody Beecham less than ten seconds to jimmy the lock on Judge Lawson's study door and slip inside the book-lined room. Not quite a record, but satisfyingly close to her personal best. After six months of field experience with Unit One, she was getting pretty damn good at this breaking-and-entering stuff, even if she said so herself. Home invasion, wiretapping and computer hacking weren't exactly the skills she'd expected to develop into a career when she graduated from the University of Florence with an honors degree in fine arts, but she had to admit that carrying out missions for Unit One had a certain seductive appeal. Sometimes—often enough to be worrisome—she forgot that she was still working under duress and not because she was committed to their goals. Relocking the study door behind her, Melody tucked the electronic pick down the cleavage of her black cocktail dress and switched on the microlight she wore disguised as a jeweled wristwatch. She directed the narrow beam around the room, checking for anything that didn't conform to the information she'd been given during her briefing. Everything looked exactly as she'd anticipated.

"I'm in," she murmured into her mike, crossing to the desk, the sound of her footsteps swallowed by the thick Persian rug. "No surprises. The judge's laptop is on the desk. I'm ready to start the download."

Nikolai Anwar responded. "The judge is talking to the governor's wife and the PR crew is still with them. They're taking photos. Lots and lots of photos." Nick's voice sounded clearly in her ear mike, even though he was at the other end of the house, on the ground floor, where the party to celebrate Judge Lawson's nomination to the Supreme Court of Connecticut was in full swing. "Go for it, Melody. I estimate you have at least fifteen minutes."

Fifteen minutes was more than she needed. Still, Melody's heart was racing as she opened the laptop and waited for the operating system to load. Since Judge Lawson was in the midst of a PR binge, the chances of him walking in on her were slim to none, but there was always an adrenaline rush at this crucial stage of a mission. She drew in a long slow breath, imposing calm. She knew from experience that an adrenaline high could spiral out of control with dangerous swiftness.

The moment the judge's computer was functional, Melody began to download the contents of his hard drive using a high-speed device developed by Unit One's own technical division. Unit One had accumulated significant intelligence to the effect that Judge Lawson's verdicts could be bought, despite his golden reputation for integrity. His recent appointment to the state supreme court was widely popular and Unit One needed rock-solid evidence before approaching the FBI with their accusations. The fact that Judge Lawson's verdicts were almost never overturned on appeal made it extra difficult to suggest that those judgments were often bought and paid for. A wiretap, in operation for the past two weeks, had suggested that concrete proof of his corruption would be obtained if Unit One could get hold of the contents of his hard drive. Hence tonight's mission.

The laptop buzzed and whirred its way through the download. The screen flashed Melody a message that one more minute was required to complete the transfer of information. She barely had time to sigh in relief before Nick spoke again.

"Senator Lewis Cranford is coming upstairs. Judge Lawson just gave him a key, and he's coming directly to the study." Nick delivered the bad news with the sort of calm that warned Melody this was a major crisis. During an operation Nick sounded more tightly controlled the more serious the threat.

"Abort the mission, Melody. Get out of the study."

"Get out how?" She saw that only twenty seconds remained on the download and left the computer humming its way through the last vital moments. "If Senator Cranford's in the hallway, he's blocking the only possible exit."

"Go out the window. You need to climb out onto the ledge, Melody. I'll be waiting to let you into the next-door room." If possible, Nick's voice became cooler, quieter and even more calm, a sure sign to Melody that full-blown hysterics were probably in order.

He wanted her to climb out onto a window ledge? Being caught by the senator was a significantly preferable alternative to crawling out onto a narrow slab of concrete, thirty or more feet above ground level. She had many skills useful to an undercover agent, but making like Spider-Man on the side of a building was definitely not one of them.

"Melody, get out of there." Nick's voice was flat with urgency. "You're not just compromising yourself. You're compromising the entire mission."

"I'm going now." It seemed that the habit of obedience died hard. The computer burped to a halt. Melody ejected the supercapacity disk, clicked the mouse to shut down the laptop and banged the lid closed. She ran to the window and pushed it up.

Holy God. The ledge couldn't be more than six inches wide, and it was drizzling with rain, which meant that it was too narrow and slippery to support a cat, let alone a human being wearing a skimpy satin cocktail dress and evening sandals with two-inch heels.

"Jesus, Nick, if I wanted to commit suicide I could think of lots more enjoyable ways than climbing out onto this damn ledge."

"Get out, Melody, and that's an order."

The sound of footsteps approaching down the hallway finally jolted her courage—or her fear—to the point where she could obey Nick's instructions. Stepping behind the drapes, Melody drew them tightly closed behind her. Then she swung around and sat backward on the window sill, pulling herself out until she could tuck her feet underneath her body, rest them on the outer ledge and push herself upright. Once vertical, she stretched her arms wide and clung to the ornamental shutters, her body pressed flat against the upper half of the window. Rain splattered on her head and naked shoulders, but as long as she had the minor comfort of solid surface against a major portion of her body, she didn't give a damn about getting wet. There was no need to remind herself not to look down, since she was incapable of movement.

She'd escaped just in time, Melody realized as she heard the sounds of a key turning in the lock, followed by footsteps moving around the judge's study and a dim glow of light seeping out into the darkness. Since she could see the lights Senator Cranford had switched on, she wondered if the silhouette of her body might be visible to him through the thickly lined drapes. Fortunately, she was already so terrified that the prospect of being discovered on the ledge added barely a quiver to the overall level of her fear.

Nick's voice spoke into her ear mike. "Melody, don't answer me, because the senator might hear your voice."

Since her vocal cords were paralyzed along with the rest of her, there was no danger that she might disobey Nick's order. No doubt he was about to announce their escape plan. She sure as hell hoped he had a magic carpet handy. Otherwise, she was going to be stuck here for the rest of her life, because she had no intention of ever making any movement that involved turning her head, lifting either of her feet, or releasing her death grip on the window shutters.

"I'm actually up above you," Nick said. "But I'm climbing down as we speak."

Climbing? He was seriously expecting her removal from this ledge to involve climbing up or down or along the brick facade of the judge's house? Hah! The man had a truly amazing sense of humor.

"So here's the plan," Nick said, his voice soft and

faintly amused in her ear. "Remember when you were kidnapped by Wallis Beecham and he had you locked inside of his office building in Lower Manhattan? Remember how you expected me to have organized an escape route that involved rappelling down the side of the building, in the rain, with one thin safety line between the two of us? Well, that's exactly what we have to do this time. And, honey, please don't make any more spluttering noises. You have to be really, really quiet or Senator Cranford is going to hear us, and since he's determined to shut down Unit One, you know how many problems that would cause."

Melody heard a slight scrabbling noise above her head, no more than a squirrel might cause. A moment later she felt Nick's arms around her waist, and his body pressed reassuringly against her back, the steel clips of the rappelling cord comfortingly hard between them.

Feet braced against the wall, his weight supported by the line, Nick reached up and silently pried her hands from the window shutters, then wrapped them around the line just above his. His torso and legs formed a cradle in which she could simply sit and leave him to do all the work of climbing down, but Melody's panic was sufficiently alleviated by his presence that her training kicked back in and she was able to look up. She saw where the line was anchored around the chimney stack and calculated how she would have to cooperate in order to get safely down to the ground.

"We're lucky it's raining," Nick said as soon as they were on the ground. "Otherwise we might have had an audience."

Melody was more than willing to be appreciative of the rain, or any other natural phenomenon that indicated she was still alive, with both feet firmly on the ground. She turned her back to the wall and pushed her soaking-wet hair out of her eyes. "Thank you," she said.

Nick gave her a smile. Not one of his patented, curl-your-toes sexy smiles that he dished out to 90 percent of the women who crossed his path. This was one of his slow, sweet smiles that Melody sometimes hoped might be reserved only for her.

"You're very welcome," he said. "I'll have to see if I can't strand you on the top of a few more buildings. It's the only time you ever cling to me as if I'm your last best hope of heaven."

If only he knew how often she would like to cling to him, Melody reflected ruefully. If it weren't for the fact that she still retained some pathetic remnants of pride, combined with a primitive urge toward self-preservation, she would probably spend hours at a stretch curled up in his arms. If Nikolai Anwar ever realized just how far in love she'd fallen with him over the past six months, she suspected there would be smoke billowing from his heels as he dashed for the nearest escape route from their relationship.

"Take your rewards where you can," she murmured, kissing him with a casual passion that contained no hint of the deeper emotions seething inside her. He kissed her back, his passion as fierce as hers, his emotions just as difficult to gauge.

There was no way to remove the anchor from the chimney stack without climbing back on the roof, so Nick quickly cut the line and concealed the harness and steel hooks under his cummerbund. "There's no point in going back to the party, even if we weren't soaking wet,'' Nick said. ''Let's go find the car.''

Melody was more than happy to leave. She patted the front of her dress, where the disk and the lock pick were rubbing uncomfortably. ''At least we got what we came for.''

''You managed to finish the download?'' Nick looked cheered. ''That's great news.''

When they reached the sweeping circular driveway at the front of the house, the parking valet made no comment on the fact that they were both soaking wet. Fortunately, since it was May and the night was warm, Melody's lack of jacket or a wrap didn't appear too suspicious. The valet returned with Nick's Mercedes sports coupe, showing no sign that he would remember either one of them five minutes after their car rolled out of the driveway.

Melody leaned back against the soft leather of the passenger seat, yawning. Reaction to the adrenaline rush of the mission, and the panic of being perched on the window ledge, was leaving her sleepy. Nick handed her his cell phone. ''Call headquarters, will you? Let Mac know that we're coming in and that we have the disk.''

Melody pressed the speed-dial button that connected her with Martin McShane, the director of Unit One. ''Hi, Mac,'' she said blithely when the director answered. ''Nick and I are on our way back to New Jersey. The mission was successful, and we'll see you in about ninety minutes.''

''Congratulations. I need to speak to Nick.''

Mac was always abrupt, but this was carrying curtness unusually far, even for him. Melody offered the phone to Nick, her sleepiness dispelled by a twinge of apprehension. "Mac needs to speak with you."

Nick took the phone. "Yes, Mac." He listened, his face hardening into an expression of such granite neutrality that even Melody couldn't imagine what he was hearing, except that it wasn't likely to be good news.

"We'll discuss options as soon as I get back," he said to Mac and hung up the phone, for once almost as curt as his boss.

"What is it?" Melody asked. "Nick, what's happened?"

He kept his gaze fixed on the road. "David Ramsdell has escaped from custody."

Melody felt her stomach heave. Dave had betrayed his colleagues in Unit One so badly that the idea of him roaming free was sickening. "Oh, no. How in the world did that happen? The military were warned that he was an extreme flight risk."

Nick shrugged. "They're full of excuses, but the bottom line is that Dave's one of the best. Unit One trained him, remember? Apparently he was being escorted back to military prison by a couple of young enlisted men. He'd just attended a judicial hearing regarding his case and he was shackled, which must have given the soldiers a false sense of security. He overcame the two guards, stole their Jeep and was last seen heading toward the interstate in Kansas. The Jeep's already been found, abandoned at a rest stop thirty miles down the road. Presumably he hitched a ride out on a truck, headed who knows where. I think we can safely assume that regular law enforcement officials aren't going to have much hope of catching him."

Melody doubted if Unit One would have a much better chance of finding Dave than the rest of the law enforcement community. Dave was a master of disguise, an ex army special ops officer and a twelve-year veteran of Unit One. He had all the skills necessary to hide in plain sight, so he wouldn't even need to go underground to evade capture. Dave knew exactly how Unit One agents functioned and could take all the necessary steps to protect himself from capture. Melody felt a frisson of fear shiver down her spine and realized that she was reacting with a lot more than intellectual frustration to the news Dave Ramsdell was on the loose.

With the disconcerting ability Nick had to read what she was feeling, he reached out and rested his hand briefly on her knee. "Dave isn't going to risk coming anywhere near you or anyone else in Unit One," he said quietly. "Don't worry, Melody. He's way too smart to risk his freedom for the sake of revenge."

She hoped very much that Nick was right.

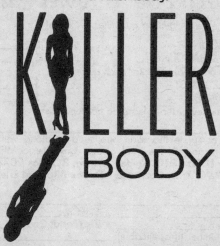